# IMMINENT DANGER

# THE BLOODLINE REVELATIONS

## ΑΩ
### MISSION: 1

# IMMINENT
# DANGER

## Ryan J Alls

Copyright © 2013 by Ryan J Alls

Book Cover design by Ryan J Alls

Printed in the United States of America

First Printing, 2013

Alls, Ryan J

Imminent Danger/by Ryan J Alls

THE BEGINNING OF A LEGEND: A young man joins the Academy in order to learn how to master his abilities, which were passed down through an ancient bloodline.

ISBN-13: 978-0-9893454-0-8 (Hardcover)

ISBN-13: 978-0-9893454-1-5 (Trade Paperback)

ISBN-13: 978-0-9893454-2-2 (E-Book)

*This book is dedicated to my mom, for all of the heart-to-hearts. To my sister, for all of the loving advice. And also to the young readers, who are finding themselves in this world.*

# PROLOGUE

The winds blew swift and violent, as if in response to the treachery that had unfolded. The night sky was set aflame with an unforgiving force that took with it the memories and lives of the souls that once lived there. Neutralizing Agents ran in and out of the many burning homes around Cur, as he made his way through the familiar lifeless bodies that littered the ground around him with crimson childhood memories.

A stranger appeared between two burning homes that had collapsed into one another. Lord Egon's leather black robe and long black hair were nearly invisible in the night's dark air. His pale face and emerald eyes pierced the veil of darkness that covered the village. Cur felt the temperature drop slightly, when the Lord took his place at Cur's side.

"No sign of it Master," said an Agent. His head was bowed and his arm sat firmly across his chest.

"No sign? As in not here? Rather curious, wouldn't you say so my young friend," said Lord Egon turning to Cur. Cur could feel the suspicion in the Lord's voice, and wondered if his fate would soon resemble that of the bodies that lay around him.

"Then he must have taken it with him—if your men were not thorough enough to eliminate everyone as ordered," said Cur glaring at the Agent. The Agent's expression turned hostile, signaling that he had deciphered every bit of the insult and doubt that Cur threw at him.

"I assure you Master that," started the Agent before falling silent to Lord Egon's lone finger.

"Assure? Assure me what? That your incompetence has cost you your life, or that our new ally's deceit has cost him his?" The Agent's eyes instantly met Cur's. He housed the same fear in his heart; however, Cur knew that he had a lot more on the line than any of the Agents there.

"We found him Master!" said a voice behind them. Cur joined Lord Egon as he and the Agent turned their attention towards two other Agents that carried a limp body by its arms. The face of the person they were carrying was hidden, but Cur already knew his identity. "He refuses to tell us its whereabouts."

The flames atop the surrounding houses that continued to burn, was the only movement amidst the night, when Lord Egon closed the distance between him and the prisoner. "Show me his face."

A hand grabbed a fist-full of the prisoner's short dark hair before revealing his identity. His chiseled jaw and dark eyes gave no hints as to any thoughts. Cur quickly joined Lord Egon.

"Hmm my tongue ravages my mouth and my palms moisten at the fear I see in your eyes," said Lord Egon. His emerald gaze seemed to bore into the prisoner, while the prisoner's gaze sat fixated on Cur, causing him to look away. "Give me what I want—and I will spare your life."

*Why did you come back?*

"I'm not afraid of you," said the prisoner glaring at Lord Egon. The corner of his lips curled into a snarl that told Cur he would pounce at his first opportunity. "You think you're so bad and scary, but you would not last thirty seconds in a one-on-one fight with me." Lord Egon's slap not only silenced the prisoner, but filled the air with a *crack* that was proof of its power.

"How do you want to kill this one Master? Dismemberment again?" asked one of the Agent's holding the prisoner.

Lord Egon did not answer as quickly as Cur had expected. Instead he gazed deeply into the prisoner's eyes. Soon tears fell from the prisoner's eyes causing a smile to smudge across Lord Egon's face. "No, I have another idea."

Cur's heart began to beat rapidly when the Lord's eyes fell on him. He could feel anxiety washing over him, but remained stern and emotionless underneath Egon's gaze.

"He is one of *your* people. Make him give me what I want—or end him," said Lord Egon to Cur. Cur's eyes immediately found the prisoner as he approached him.

"Please—don't do this," said the prisoner. He struggled under his captive's grip, but to no avail.

"Tell us where you hid it, or take your last breath," said Cur. He knew the prisoner would not answer. The question was a gimmick, entertainment for the eyes that thirsted for the blood of their captive.

"Kill him," said Lord Egon. The prisoner looked from Egon to Cur as the unbearable winds blew the prisoner's dark hair across his face. Cur's hands rose flat and sharp.

"No! Please! We're family..." The tears turned into endless streams on their way down the prisoner's face. His pleading was heartfelt and filled with sorrow. His jaw shivered while his eyes begged.

"I have no family." Cur felt the implosion of the prisoner's heart after his attack. A sinister laugh pierced the night and covered the sky with its bone-chilling power.

"Well done," said Lord Egon unclasping his hands from behind his back. "I was beginning to think that both of you would be dirt décor tonight. But it seems as though you kept up your end of the bargain. What do they call you?"

The prisoner fell, relinquishing all signs of life. A burden had been lifted, and took with it the anxiety that had once overwhelmed Cur.

"Fox. My name is Fox."

ΑΩ

# SCREAMS IN THE NIGHT

The clouds were thick and the moon was full, when a cold wind passed through the streets. While men, women and children began to submit to their pending dreams, a nightmare was brewing at the gates. As Bishop took one last look out his balcony window, over the white-stone homes of his people, worry began to creep over him. The night was calm and quiet as it should be, but to Bishop, the night was eerily too quiet. A veil of uncertainty and nefarious signs shrouded the normal cloudbank that enveloped Kismet. Just as he began to scold himself for worrying in vain, a scream erupted from the Western Hold.

"Somebody help me!"

Bishop screamed for the Agents of his inner circle, before taking his robe, and heading for the front door of the castle. The night's cold brisk air passed over his face making him shiver, when he opened the door. He closed his eyes and scanned the area for the woman's presence. He instantly took off in the direction his legs were taking him, just as another familiar scream arose.

"Someone please, please help me!"

Bishop turned passed the Market District and passed the fountain of the Three Brothers, gaining more and more speed as the street turned downhill. Just as Bishop thought he would never find her, a shadow greeted him at the turn of the next corner. There lying in the middle of the street—on the cold cobblestones—was a figure holding someone. Grateful that someone had reached the woman in time; Bishop began to approach them. However, the closer he got to them, the more he smelled something—an odor. A very strong odor that he might have smelled upon exiting his castle, if panic had not dominated him. It was the smell of death. Bishop approached the figures, noticing that the one holding the woman was a man.

"Is she okay?"

No reply.

"Son I know you must be frightened, but it's me, Bishop. I can help her if she's hurt, but you have to tell me what happened."

Just as Bishop took another step, he felt water beneath his feet. He instantly cast a spell to neutralize the darkness. A purple glow surrounded him as he took in the crimson puddle that surrounded his footsteps. Just as he looked up, the man's head whipped around letting loose a canine snarl. Bishop jumped back readying himself.

"Step away from her!"

The man continued to snarl while he rose to his feet, dropping the lifeless body of the woman. Bishop scolded himself when the two of them locked eyes. Why had he not guessed sooner: the cuts, the smell, and the decomposition. This was no longer a man. Just as all the pieces of the puzzle came together, the man lunged at Bishop. Just before he got too close, Bishop was able to see the flesh between his teeth, the absence of lips, and the hollow eye socket—festering with maggots and gore. A locket shined cautiously around his neck.

"Whoever your family is, I beg for their forgiveness, and yours," said Bishop.

The quiet night air was soon replaced with the sound of an ocean, as streets flooded from every end. The water rushed towards the creature, ensnaring him in an unforgiving force, which imprisoned him in an arctic tundra of ice. Just as Bishop's feet touched the ground, four Agents came from nearly every direction.

"My Lord, are you okay?"

Bishop looked upon the limp and lifeless body of the woman, feeling the fury begin to boil inside.

"No. I am not okay."

"You Magi! Tend to his wounds at once," ordered the Combat Specialist.

"There's no need for that," replied Bishop. "Physically I am fine, however, can you explain to me why no one was on watch in this part of the city. While you're at it, you can also begin writing your condolences to the family of this poor girl!"

The creature's head whipped back up with hunger and rage, snapping violently at Bishop. Bishop snatched the locket off of the creature's neck, and walked back towards the direction of the castle. Just before rounding the corner away from his men, he met their gaze.

"By the way, I would express caution when handling her body. She has been more than bitten, and chances are she too will become like that creature, if death has not claimed her. I want him locked in our most secure prison and I want her to be rushed to Vance as soon as possible. Tell him she has been bitten by a Necrosis, and to do anything he can to stop the spread of the bite."

"Yes sir," said the Combat Specialist.

Quiet soon returned to the streets as Bishop came to the end of his walk back to his quarters. Just as he opened the front door of the castle, he took one last look over his shoulder at his city.

*If only I were younger, I may have been able to save that poor girl. But that is why I am not younger. Her death was as absolute as this life I have been born into.*

He disappeared inside the castle with both rage and grief in his heart. Bishop returned to his quarters where he dusted off his old chess set. He began a new game moving one pawn forward three spaces to the middle of the board. He fiddled with

3

the locket in his hand and discovered an insignia on the back of it. He rose from where he had been sitting, and took one last look out his balcony window. After retiring for the night, he would soon fall victim to the woman's screams for help, which would haunt his dreams for the next few nights.

◆◆◆

Jude awoke to three knocks at his door. "Mom if you are waking me up at the crack of dawn again to go running with you, I will be very upset."

"Jude I cooked breakfast for you to jumpstart your first day at the Academy. Be downstairs in five minutes!" replied his mom.

Jude used both hands to rip back the covers over his head. "I think I would like to trade my breakfast in for a few more hours of sleep."

After a few moments passed, a voice from inside his room scared him from his sleep. "You have five seconds to get up before you become my breakfast!"

Jude sprung up from his bed in alarm thinking that he was in danger. The first thing he realized was that his utility belt with his vials was missing. It was his brother. He was wearing his black battle pants and a green wool sweater, along with his signature necklace of miniature skull heads around his neck.

"Do me a favor and do not tell anyone we are related until you can at least prove to be a threat," replied Jed.

"I can turn into a giant mountain lion and swallow you whole if I wanted to! You just caught me off guard that's all."

"When you are in battle, you are always off guard. Especially when your opponent is someone like me," replied Jed with a glare.

"Look give me a break. You caught me off guard and could have ripped my head off or turned me into one of you or whatever, I get it. It won't happen again you can be sure of it; especially now that I am old enough to start training at the Academy."

"First things first. There are meat and eggs down there that are making me sick by just the smell alone. You better get down there and eat it before I throw up all over this house. Afterwards, I will walk you to the Academy. I have an adventure to tell you about," said Jed.

"Now you are talking!"

Jude ran into the washroom and brushed his teeth and washed his face. He put on a black tunic and beige pants that had been passed down through the family for generations. He took one last look in the mirror at his jet-black hair, green eyes and tan face.

"Ready!"

"I wish you were that quick when I 'caught you off guard' just a second ago," said Jed.

"Are you seriously going to ride me about that all day? I have actually been doing a lot of reading and experiments, and I think even someone like you will be proud once you see me on the battlefield."

"We will see," said Jed.

Jed was off the bed and down the stairs in half a second. The speed of his older brother gave Jude pause. He always thought he was completely unaffected by the fact that his older brother was a Vampire, but sometimes he forgot just how fast his brother could glide across a room.

Jude hurried down the stairs towards the kitchen. Just as he left the last step, Jed and his mother, Aileen, greeted him. At the corner of his eye, he noticed a tangle of blonde hair, before realizing his best friend, Eli, was there as well. He was wearing a brown and tan belted tunic and beige war pants his dad had smithed for him.

"Eli! What are you doing here?"

"It's our first day at the Academy, my dad is finishing up smithing some weapons for Ivor so your mom invited me over for breakfast. I hope that's okay."

"Well of course it is okay," replied Aileen.

"Thanks Ms. Bray," replied Eli.

"You are basically family anyways," agreed Jude.

As all four of them sat down for breakfast, the three of them connected hands before Jude looked to Eli for his.

"Oh yeah I forgot," said Eli.

"Now Eli, you know we always give thanks for all of our meals that the Three Brothers have given us," said Aileen with a wink. Aileen led a short prayer before giving the okay to eat. It was Eli who broke the silence.

"So did any of you hear the screams or know what happened last night?"

Jed's translucent white eyes went directly to Eli's. Eli instantly noticed the glare and his fork froze in mid-air as he was about to take another bite of his eggs. Jude had to fight back the urge to laugh.

"No I don't believe I did, but I am a very heavy sleeper," laughed Aileen.

"What happened?" asked Jude.

"Well from what my dad told me, a Necrosis attacked the Western Hold last night. A woman was seriously injured."

"Oh my goodness!" replied Aileen bringing her hand to cover her mouth. "Is the poor thing okay?"

"Well the creature had been taking bites out of her so..."

"Okay I have officially lost my appetite," replied Jude putting his fork down.

"That is a problem I never have," replied Jed.

"Well anyways, Bishop was the one that found her and a meeting is supposed to be happening as we speak."

"Well that gives me more reasons to ask Helena from down the street to put some magic wards on our door," said Aileen.

"Don't worry mom, now that Eli and I are training at the Academy, no one will dare touch either one of our houses."

Both the boys looked at each other grinning, before finishing their meal, and departing the house—accompanied by Jed.

# A FACELESS ENEMY

As the doors to Council Hall closed, the attendees all took their respective seats. Bishop of course headed the roundtable, followed by Anya on his left and Vance on his right. The remaining attendees were Ivor, the mentor for the Weapons Master Agents, a few well-respected Agents; and last but not least Lynn, the Combat Specialist mentor. Anya was the current General of Bishop's armed forces and one of his dearest friends. Vance was also one of Bishop's dearest friends and was the mentor for the Magi Agents. One seat remained empty at the stone table.

"Now that mostly all of us are here, I believe we can begin. An incident occurred last night a few blocks from the entrance to this castle. I heard a scream from my balcony window and reacted hastily to the cry for help. As I stumbled across the source of this scream, I was alarmed to find out that I was too late. I do not know if any of you have heard, but a Necrosis ran freely through our streets last night," announced Bishop.

Commotion erupted in the room followed by gasps and wide eyes.

"I was just as shocked as you all are now; even more so when I witnessed the agility and hunger within this creature. Now in all my travels across these lands, I have never seen a Necrosis move with the speed that this one had. I had the girl sent over to Vance right away but, well Vance, I will let you take over from here."

All eyes swept to Vance as the Magi mentor rose from his seat. His purple eyes stood out against his pale skin and short white hair. He wore a royal blue tunic and matching pants.

"In all my years I have never seen an attack from a Necrosis this bad. Now it is true that it is common for all living dead to have a hunger for flesh. However, that is just it, this creature did not only eat her flesh, he ate everything from her toenails to her organs. As you all know this is uncommon considering the fact that ingesting anything other than flesh usually proves harmful to the creature. I was perplexed by what I saw, so I decided to take a trip to the creature's prison only to find out that he had eaten most of his own limbs. The hunger of these creatures is staggering and unmatched. In my opinion, they would eat anything and everything. He could have gone berserk and decided to eat everyone in the whole land! I just have to be grateful that Bishop was able to get to the creature before anyone else was harmed. Unfortunately the victim sustained too many severe injuries and lost too much blood, not even blood magic could save her now. We have identified the victim and sent word to her family," explained Vance.

Anya was the one to break the silence that seized the room. "My question is why was no one on watch in the Western Hold? There should have been at least one Weapons Master and one Magi in that hold."

"I have called a meeting with all of our Agents for this afternoon Madam General, for I had the same question," replied one of the Agents.

"Well I plan to attend that meeting because I have some questions of my own. I want all the information on that meeting as soon as this one is adjourned. I want to know time, location and who all is attending. Got it?" replied Anya.

"Yes Madam General," replied the Agent.

"While I do appreciate the initiative, we can point fingers all day; that still will not help the fact that there may be more of these creatures on the loose in our lands. So our next question has to be where did this creature come from?" asked Bishop.

Anya was quick to respond. "We don't even have to ask that question, we know it is those filthy Necroborns in the Immortal Lands. That's all they do is desecrate the dead."

"Now while that is of course the most common assumption Anya, we have to trust the fact that we are allies with Lord Egon, the ruler of the Immortal Lands. We cannot afford to doubt the alliances that our men have died to help create. However, I am not saying that we should dismiss Egon's involvement altogether. This is why I am proposing that we send a small squad to the Immortal Lands to meet with their Lord. I want to know if he has any knowledge of this attack or the origins of these creatures."

Anya sprang from her seat with a purple summoned blade in hand. "Sir I would like to volunteer for this mission."

"While I do appreciate it Anya, and I know that you are more than capable of leading this team on this mission, I also know that you are not too fond of the inhabitants of the Immortal Lands. So I have decided to send Fox."

"Sir?" asked Anya.

The Council Hall doors creaked open as a dark figure strutted through its doorway. The figure appeared to be male with short, dark, and spiked hair. He was tall with an athletic build and perfect posture.

"Fox at your service your excellence," said the man.

"Ah Fox, you finally decided to join us. I hope the marshlands treated you okay," replied Bishop.

"Eh did not care for them one bit. Too smelly and the locals would not stop trying to eat me for dinner. But I mean who could blame them? I am simply delicious aren't I?" replied Fox with a wink.

A light chuckle sounded around the table.

"Well your timing of course could not be more perfect, even though we started a while ago. I will have Anya fill you in on the details that you missed."

Fox shot Anya a smirk while Anya replied with a glare that said, *I will skin you alive.*

"What I will tell you," Bishop continued, "is that you will be traveling to the Immortal Lands to seek an audience with the lands ruler, Lord Egon. You will be accompanied by two Weapons Masters and a Magi."

"Let me stop you right there," interrupted Fox. "I don't need the whole team. I work better alone as we both already know." Anya looked at Bishop as if confused by the comment.

Bishop felt his energy boiling in his veins. After a couple of deep breaths, he continued. "I am aware that you are fond of working alone, however this mission proves to be extremely delicate, and I cannot afford for you to get 'lost' on another one of your journeys."

Fox chuckled. "Fine well said, but can I have a Combat Specialist instead of one of the Weapons Masters. They tend to be the only Agent that is worth anything in battle, with me anyways."

One of the Agents changed his position in his seat while glaring at Fox.

"So be it," agreed Bishop. "But know this, if you fail even the smallest portion of this mission after the ridiculous requests you have just presented here today, I will have you living out the rest of your life under the impression that you are a butterfly. Do I make myself clear?"

"Will I be a pretty butterfly?" Fox asked with a smirk. A silence hung in the room. "Alright alright, yes I understand your excellence."

"Good," replied Bishop.

"Now if you will excuse me, I smell like swamp, vomit and handsomeness," replied Fox as he strutted out of the Council Hall doors, closing them behind him. Before the doors were all the way closed, he snuck a quick wink at Anya, who was both glaring and grimacing his direction while he exited.

"Now that brings us to the last order of business," continued Bishop. "We cannot believe so blindly that Egon is the only possible option for why this creature showed up in our lands. After further conversation with Vance, we believe it could be a possibility that the Spirit Lands could have had something to do with this."

An awkward silence hung in the room. No one moved, and breathing was so silent, that the entire table seemed to be mute.

"But sir," replied one of the Agents finally. "If the Spirit Lands are responsible, then that means you suspect a possession."

"I do not like to rule out any possible options. While I fear that my theory could be correct, I have to explore all possible threats."

"Yes sir. Of course sir."

"This is why I am sending Anya to the Spirit Lands. One Magi and one Combat Specialist will accompany her. However, I must express caution. Your only mission, and I must emphasize that, your only mission is to go to the border of the Spirit Lands, and see if you detect any trace of dark magic or more Necrosis. Venturing any further than the border is not authorized. I do not want to risk any of you losing your bodies, minds or souls there. You will stay there no longer than a few hours and return immediately. I shall look forward to your report when you return."

"Yes sir!" replied Anya.

"Now this meeting is adjourned. As I believe Vance, Ivor, and Lynn have Agents to groom; and I believe I am late for another meeting. Good luck to all of you. May the Three Brothers guide you." With his closing speech, The Council exited, except for Bishop and Anya.

"My Lord?" asked Anya.

"What is it General?"

"I am just curious as to why you chose Fox to go to the Immortal Lands instead of me. While I trust your judgment completely, I am just confused. Have I failed you in any way?"

"No of course not. It is simple actually. The Spirit Lands mission requires my orders to be followed perfectly. The Immortal Lands mission does too, however if Fox does not follow my orders there, I am sure Lord Egon won't need my help in setting him straight. While I trust Fox with my life, I know at times he can be a tad bit reckless and display behavior that makes me question his intentions. I know you will follow my orders flawlessly, and your mission will be a success."

"But sir," replied Anya. "If you don't trust Fox, then why send him on missions? Why trust him with your men?"

"Let's just say that I always give the men going with him specific instructions to abort the mission if they expect any foul play, or if Fox is venturing from the main goal. Fox is an amazing Agent we both can't doubt that. His skills at hand-to-hand are unparalleled and he is definitely an asset to my team. He is just an asset that I have to keep an eye on."

◆ ◆ ◆

"Wait, so explain to me again why you are able to walk in the sun? I thought the sun and Vampires hated each other," said Jude.

White brick walls and cobblestone streets stretched on for miles around them. Statues of some of Kismet's greatest Agents and Operatives decorated the corners of many of the streets. Small descriptions of the Agent's greatest accomplishments were etched in their bases.

"Hate is such a strong word. I think we just don't see eye-to-eye on anything. If the sun could just stop trying to prevent me from existing, I am sure we could come to some neutral ground," replied Jed.

Eli laughed slightly at the reply. He had always told Jude that he thought Jed was an awesome Agent and brother. However, now that he was also a Vampire, Jude found Eli uncomfortable at times around the immortal. Jude got the sense that Eli always wanted to have an older brother, sister, or any sibling. However, Jude felt like Eli, Jed, Aileen, and Eli's dad Marius, were all a part of his family, and as far as he was concerned, Jed was Eli's brother as well.

Eager to hear the rest of the story, Eli took the initiative to jumpstart the tale. "So what happened next Jed? Did you run behind him with your super speed and pin him down?"

"No actually I just decapitated him. Yeah taking an arrow to the forehead at close range can be extremely infuriating. I became so engulfed with rage I, well let's just say I was a little overly-dramatic. I see that now."

Both Jude and Eli laughed hysterically. "You still never answered my question about why you can walk around in the sun without blowing up," said Jude.

"Well to begin with, I hardly believe I would blow up, just probably go into convulsions. My eyes would want to roll back in my head and I would for the first time feel excruciating pain. At least that is what the books in the library claim. The answer to your question is neither I, nor anyone here, knows why I can walk around in the sun. It is true that the effects of the sun are not as immediate as people think. Vampires were known to be able to walk around in the sun for maximum an hour before the sun took its toll. Lynn has been researching different theories since I came back from the war. Unfortunately, she has not been able to come up with anything. I have no proof, but I believe it has something to do with my blood before I was bitten."

"I already know why you can live in the sun," said Eli with confidence.

Both Jude and Jed whipped their heads to hear what the blue-eyed boy was saying.

"It's because you're a total badass!" continued Eli. "You were already an amazing Agent before you were a Vampire."

Jed said nothing to Eli's compliment. His fangs extended and his bottom lip quivered, as if signaling the presence of an overwhelming and uncontrollable sensation.

"Hey Eli," said Jed.

"Yeah."

"You got any rats at your house?"

Jude joined Eli's stare and confusion. "Why do you want to know if he has rats at his house? It is kind of a rude question to ask someone," said Jude.

"Rude? How is that rude? Look, Jude's house is out of rats and I am starving. So do you got any or not?"

"I haven't seen one so I'm pretty sure we don't," said Eli. His gaze slowly turned ahead of him, making Jude believe that his friend felt overwhelmingly uncomfortable.

"Why don't you just—you know— hunt," said Jude.

"Because I am hungry now, and would have to leave the city in order to catch someone. Plus I have business in the city I cannot be late for." Jude was sure that Jed saw the look of disgust on his face, because as their eyes met, a smile formed at Jed's mouth. "Forget about it, there are plenty of dogs that runaway in the Eastern Hold. I will check there."

Jude tensed and felt the unease begin to flow, when the sight of his adolescent nightmare strolled into sight.

"Hey, isn't that—."

"Yes shh," whispered Jude in an attempt to quickly silence Eli's awkward observation. Jed appeared to be uninterested by the small commotion between them. Jude was ready to breathe a small sigh of relief when the short light-brown hair continued on through the crowded streets before stopping.

"Jude? Jude Bray?"

*Oh no.*

"Hello. Will," said Jude reluctantly. He had been trying to avoid this conversation for the past few years and realized that his time was up.

"Hey! How have you been? Long time no see!" said Will with a smile. His voice was a lot deeper than Jude remembered and his light-brown hair stole the attention away from his dark brown eyes. His thicker body, which Jude had come accustom to over the years, was replaced with a more athletic and leaner frame.

"I have been well, and yourself?"

"Great! Today is my first day in my advanced classes, I will be out on the front lines soon," said Will with a noticeable amount of energy. "Eli! It's been a long time since I've seen you. How's the night fishing?"

"I've been good. Haven't had any downtime to go night fishing—you know what it's like—been training and stuff. Congratulations on the—on your advanced classes," said Eli. Jude could hear the discomfort in his friend's voice.

"How is it you were able to get into advanced lectures? You haven't even taken the introductory courses yet," said Jude. He was embarrassed to feel a touch of resentment in his voice.

"Yeah, my father pulled some strings at the Academy, and they allowed me to bypass the rookie stuff," said Will.

"Well the advanced courses expect you to be fully knowledgeable about *all* of the 'rookie' courses. So do you think it may be a little difficult?"

"My mom always says the Three Brothers always make good things happen to good people. So I think the gods will have my back," said Will staring at Jed. Jude looked to Jed and saw that his extended fangs were leaking saliva. His starving eyes were fixated on a small dog that ran alongside its owner, up to a café that sat at the end of the Market District. "Well I've got to get to my lecture—you know—my *advanced* courses. It was nice seeing you guys again."

Jude felt himself snarl as he watched Will exit the Market District and ascend the Academy steps. His short brown hair appeared to shine and showed that an effort had been put into its grooming.

"Wow, that was uncomfortably intense," said Eli turning his attention back towards Jude.

"I really hope that running into—that guy—won't be a sign of how my first day will go," said Jude.

"Do either of you know where that little dog lives?" asked Jed. When no one responded, Jed continued forward towards the Academy. Jude met eyes with Eli, who looked equally unnerved, and then soon followed after the immortal.

Three long ceramic pathways stretched parallel towards them from the Academy. The statues of the Three Brothers stood tall at the entrance. The first statue was of the brother Rune, and marked the beginning of the left-most ceramic path. The path, a bright royal blue, appeared so calming and so pure, that it resembled the surface of the stillest and purest oceans. A statue of the brother Pith marked the right-most ceramic path. Its ceramic path was a slate-black that was void of any imperfections, and sparkled in the rays of sunlight that poured down the white stone-walls of the Academy. The middle ceramic path divided the previous two. A statue of the brother Aegis headed it and its path was of a fiery red that stood most prevalent among the three. Banners signifying each of the three statues, fell from the white and black stoned walls that housed two large wooden doors.

"This is it. The day has finally come where I can finally master my Weapons Master skills and become the best Agent this land has ever seen. I feel sorry for anyone foolish enough to go toe-to-toe with me!" said Eli

Eli and Jude had waited for this day ever since they were young. They would both practice their respective abilities against each other in fake battles. Of course back then Eli could only summon half an arrow and Jude could only turn into a small kitten. Eli always asked Jude why he was always one step ahead all the time. Jude felt like he never had an answer. It was uncommon for anyone under the age of twelve to be able to transform into anything without the proper training. Everything was different now. They both finally reached the age of twenty years old, and they were old enough to enter the Academy to be trained by real Agents. It did sadden Jude that due to their different bloodline abilities, they would not be in the same lessons; but he was sure that they would both see each other somehow.

"Well this is where I leave you," said Jed.

"Thanks for walking us J," replied Jude.

"Yeah it definitely helps motivate me more now that I was walked to my first lessons by one of the best Agents in Kismet," agreed Eli.

"Some advice for the two of you," said Jed.

Both Jude and Eli turned eagerly towards Jed. All that stood before them were the three ceramic paths and no Jed.

"Your brother is weird," said Eli. "Weird, but badass," he continued.

"Come on," started Jude. "We don't want to be late."

# IVOR
# THE TERRIBLE

*I would rather face-down one of those Necrosis right about now.*

This was the first thought that passed through Eli's mind, after five minutes of lessons in Ivor's classroom. The classroom was made entirely of granite with extremely high ceilings and wide walls. Hundreds of blades, bows, axes and arrows decorated the walls of the classroom. The Weapons Master mentor was an older gentleman with short black hair, pale skin and dark brown eyes. He went by the name of Ivor and had a voice that was loud with impeccable clarity. Ivor stood dead center at the front of the classroom in front of a statue depicting Aegis. The area he stood on appeared to be a medium-sized sparring area equipped with starting lines and boundaries. The statue was fearsome with a quiver of arrows on his back, a sword in his left hand, and a dagger in his right. The movement of the statue said, *I'm going to destroy you!* Ivor's posture was perfect to say the least. He stood in his granite-colored battle tunic and black war pants with both hands planted firmly behind his back.

"There will be no talking in my class," the mentor started. "If you had something to say that was of any value, our roles would be reversed."

Professor Ivor started his lecture with the topic of the Three Brothers. He explained that the Weapons Master bloodline comes from the oldest of the Three Brothers—Aegis. According to Ivor, the Three Brothers acted and decided as one, but that if there was a leader of the three, Aegis would be considered it. The subject lost Eli's attention immediately.

"In combat, Weapons Master Agents are almost always the offensive aspect of the squad, and in some cases, the leaders as well," said Ivor as he circled the class slowly with his hands frozen behind his back.

*I have no problem with being the leader.*

Ivor soon returned to the subject of the Three Brothers and how some of Aegis' most powerful abilities were attainable with proper training. As Eli looked across the classroom of the thirty or so peers that sat at their desks facing the front of the classroom, he wished that Jude was there with him. Returning his attention ahead of him, Eli noticed a man in granite-colored clothes blocking his view. Eli looked up to discover Ivor staring down at him.

"Anything interesting?" the mentor asked with stern eyes.

"I'm sorry sir I was just—," but before Eli could finish, Ivor had hoisted him up by the collar of his tunic, and pushed him to the front of the classroom. Eli looked down and realized that he was standing on one of the two starting lines that he had observed earlier. Ivor was standing on the opposing line.

"What is your name?" demanded Ivor.

Eli stood frozen in a panic. His mentor looked even scarier standing face-to-face than he had when Eli was in his seat.

"I believe I asked you a question. If you refuse to obey my wishes and answer me, then why are you even here? Why are you in my class seeking my knowledge and lessons?"

"Eli. My name is Eli Brassie."

"Eli Brassie is it? Okay Eli, legs a shoulder length apart, hands at the ready, and eyes on me. Now in a few seconds I am going to attack, and you will defend yourself. Ready?"

Eli went into shock. He had never been in a real battle before, only play battles with Jude when they were kids.

"Wait your going to—," but before Eli could finish, Ivor's eyes turned black and his hands came together. Burning arrows materialized as the hands separated.

"Sir I am not sure what to do," said Eli quickly.

"Defend silly boy, even a toddler could understand that. Defend!"

Soon the attack pelted Eli from all sides. He could think of nothing better to do than to close his eyes and put up his hands to shield his face. His face felt burned and scratched and he smelled burning leather. Shortly after, he looked up to see Ivor glaring at him. Eli looked behind him to see the barrage of arrows depicting a perfect outline of his entire body on the wall. The arrows still burned bright with flames. The outline perfectly showed a figure cowering in fear.

"How did I defeat you?" asked Ivor.

"Huh?"

"It seems as though you are both incapable of defending and hearing, are you sure you are in the right class? Now I will ask you again. How did I defeat you?"

Eli was already embarrassed. He had made a fool of himself in front of the entire class. All he ever wanted was to go to the Academy and train to be the best that he could be. Now he was face-to-face with the one man who could help him achieve that, and Eli had angered him.

"I'm not experienced enough," replied Eli.

"Ah that is half of it." Ivor turned to the class and in a powerful voice asked, "Can anyone in here tell me why, besides experience, did I defeat Mr. Brassie?"

No one moved, spoke, or even looked like they breathed from where Eli was standing.

"Really? No one? It seems I got the 'special' students this year." Ivor turned back to face Eli. "I beat you because yes you are not experienced enough; but also because you have not yet learned to let your bloodline aid you in battle. If you had, you would have instantly summoned some sort of shield to defend, or if you were experienced enough, a barrage of the same number of arrows to precisely counter my own."

Eli's head began to hurt. Why couldn't his mentor just say he was better than him? He knew it, Eli knew it, and the whole class knew it. But he had to go out of his way to point out the many options that Eli had but did not know. He was humiliated.

"You may return to your seat."

Eli quickly returned to his seat avoiding any eye contact with the other students. He was sure he would see some kind of snickering, pointing or ridicule.

"Oh and Mr. Brassie," continued Ivor.

"Yes sir?"

Pointing to Eli's feet Ivor smirked, "Do put that out would you?"

Eli looked down to find that one of the arrows had lit his left combat boot on fire. That was not all, because as Eli looked down at the inferno growing up his leg, crimson liquid fell from his cheek onto his pants. It was at that very moment that Eli realized how bad his face hurt.

"Here," said a voice behind him. A rugged thick cloth came into view over his right shoulder. Eli took the cloth and padded the flames. To his surprise the flames went out instantly. Eli then used the back of the same cloth to wipe the blood from his face. Afraid to turn around and risk being caught, Eli under-handedly passed the cloth back in the same direction and whispered, "Thanks."

The last half of the sermon was much better than the first half. Eli learned a lot from Professor Ivor. He learned that his bloodline was the descendant from the oldest of the Three Brothers. He also learned that since he hadn't been in battle, his bloodline wasn't trained to adapt to present conditions, and once it did, he would be a master of almost any weapon. The idea motivated him to win back the respect of his mentor.

"Can anyone tell me the difference between a Weapons Master with a weapon and a non-weapons master with a weapon?" asked Ivor.

Silence took the room as Eli looked around to see if anyone had the courage he did not have to raise their hand. Ivor sighed before pointing to a student a few rows away from him. "Yes, you."

"Is the answer long-range assault?" said a boy with dark brown hair that covered his face. The boy screamed as a dagger left Ivor's hand and uprooted the boy out of his seat. The entire class turned around to find the boy hanging from the back-wall by the dagger that pinned him in place.

"Anymore fatuous answers?" asked Ivor scanning the classroom. Eli noticed that the mentor's gaze set on another student, but Eli was too afraid to turn to see who it was. "Yesssssss?"

"What does fatuous mean?" asked a young girl. The hall filled with a high-pitched scream. Eli joined the class as everyone turned around to find the young girl pinned by a dagger to the back-wall alongside the first student victim. Both captives struggled in place in an attempt to free themselves from the wall they hung from.

"If either of you remove yourselves from the justified punishment from which you hang from," started Ivor as a wall of hovering arrows materialized in front of him. The arrows shined with a danger while readying to attack. The noises of the recent struggles soon fell silent, and a few seconds later, the arrows dissolved. "How about you in the back," said Ivor pointing to a girl sitting in the last row.

"The brain of a fully realized Weapons Master completely masters all uses and techniques of a weapon within a few minutes of it being summoned. A non-weapons master, such as people of the Erudite bloodline, will actually have to train with each individual weapon they plan to use; and still they will not be as skilled or be able to use the abilities that a Weapons Master can use," said the girl.

"Correct for the most part," started Ivor. "When a person fully unlocks all of their abilities as a Weapons Master, weapons will no longer be just weapons. Unfortunately for you, until you better yourselves as Agents, these new techniques will remain a secret."

Eli listened attentively while Professor Ivor lectured on the dangers of using abilities in combat.

"Each bloodline heir has a secondary supply of energy called blood energy. This energy is directly tied to your physical endurance and is used to activate your bloodline abilities. If your blood energy is ever fully depleted, the Agent cannot only be rendered unconscious, but also suffer brain damage, paralysis, and sometimes even death. The more inexperienced you are, the less blood energy you have. That is why it is imperative for Agents to stay in tune with their blood energy level at all times," said Ivor with a smirk.

A student closeby began to raise their hand, but when Ivor responded with an instant glare, the hand retreated.

"Homework for tonight," continued Ivor. "I want you to go home and select the weapon you are most skilled with. That is, which weapon you *think* you are most skilled with." The mentor released a small chuckle before turning to the doors of the classroom and exiting.

As soon as the doors behind the mentor closed completely, it was as if the world began to breathe again. Eli's peers instantly broke into commotion discussing today's teachings. A few students scrambled to help free the two students that still hung from the back-wall by Ivor's daggers.

"Well I have to say I am surprised you came out of that alive," said the same voice from behind Eli.

Eli turned around to find similar blue eyes staring back at him. The voice came from a young man that appeared to be the same age as Eli. He had messy, tangled black hair. He was wearing a white battle tunic and matching white leather and mail pants.

"You and me both," replied Eli. "Thanks for the cloth by the way, it was a lifesaver. It's really strong against fire. Where did you get it?"

"From my sister. She has Magi blood and put a fire resistant enchantment on it. She thought I might need it after the horror stories she heard about Professor Ivor." Both the boys laughed briefly.

"I'm Eli by the way."

"Zane."

"Your sister is pretty smart to think to give you that cloth," complimented Eli.

"Please don't let her know that. She thinks she knows everything. I was actually reluctant to take it. If she hears that she was right I will never hear the end of it. To be honest I thought Ivor was going to ignite you on fire instead of the arrows."

Eli's stomach sank. "He would do that?"

"Well that's what he did to a girl last year for sneezing during one of his sermons," Zane continued. "She had to be rushed to the healing wing right after class."

"After class?"

"Yeah. Ivor said it was rude to leave during one of his lectures," Zane went on. "Matter of fact, why don't you keep the cloth just in case."

"Are you sure?"

"Yeah just in case he decides to pick on you again."

"Thanks, I will probably need it. But are you sure your sister won't mind?"

Zane rolled his eyes. "Should I care?"

Both the boys exited the large wooden doors and walked the halls discussing the day's lessons.

"What weapon are you bringing tomorrow?"

"I haven't decided yet. I am thinking it will either be my throwing daggers or my long bow. What about you?" said Zane.

"I was thinking either my sword my father forged for me, or my long bow."

"Well I have to meet up with my sister in Magi Hall, so I guess I will see you tomorrow."

"Do you know where the wing is for Combat Specialists?" asked Eli.

"You mean Combat Hall? Yeah it's right next to Magi Hall on the other side. I'll show you."

The two boys walked the Academy grounds making small talk. Eli was amazed at how many students-in-training there were in the Academy. As Zane and Eli exited out two wooden doors to an exterior courtyard, Eli was instantly hurled forward and landed face first onto the lawn surrounding the courtyard. Immediately students passing by broke out into laughter.

Eli looked up to see Zane offering a hand up. "Are you okay?"

"Today just isn't my day. First I'm attacked and set on fire, and now I'm being pushed around—literally." Zane chuckled slightly while helping Eli to his feet.

"I am so sorry about that. I was aiming for someone else," said a voice behind the two boys.

Eli turned around to see a young girl around his age, maybe a year or two older, with straight long black hair. She had similar blue eyes as Zane but was somewhat taller than Eli's peer. Her voice had a ring that seemed to echo every word that fell from her mouth.

"What are you doing here? I was just coming to get you," said Zane to the girl.

"Lucky me," she replied.

"Hey if you don't want me to walk with you home anymore all you have to—," said Zane before the girl quickly interrupted.

"Who's your friend?"

"I'm Eli, it's nice to meet you."

"Wow aren't you the polite one," she replied smiling. "My name is Meara."

Just as the two had exchanged names, a young girl appeared next to Meara.

"There you are!" said Meara.

"Sorry I had to talk to Professor Vance about something," replied the girl.

Eli's throat dried, his heart raced, and his eyes froze at the stranger. She was beautiful. She had light purple eyes, long dark brown hair, and tan skin. She had a slender body and wore a tight-fitting skirt and sleeveless shirt. She looked around the same age as Meara but much prettier if Eli had to say so himself.

"Is this your brother?" the girl asked towards Zane.

"Who? The corpse? Yes, unfortunately," replied Meara.

"I could tell because he has the same blue eyes as you."

"Whatever," scowled Meara. "This is his friend Eli."

"Nice to meet you," said Eli and the girl in unison.

She smiled. Her voice was both light and sharp at the same time; making Eli intrigued and intimidated simultaneously.

"I am Sia Wyatt. It is a pleasure to meet you."

*Pleasure to meet you?*

He wanted to stay and talk to Sia but knew that he had to meet up with Jude in Combat Hall. "Well it was nice to meet you Sia and you too Meara, but I have to meet a friend." Eli turned to Zane, "So I will see you tomorrow?"

"You shall, I will be looking forward to you being pelted with daggers this time," Zane smirked.

Meara and Sia exchanged confused looks as Eli headed towards a huge archway that had a black medallion with a vial intersecting two fists etched into it.

# A DIFFERENCE OF BLOOD

Jude's first day was going just as he expected. Aside from the fact that there were not as many peers in his class than he had imagined, he enjoyed his first lesson, and especially his mentor Lynn. She was slightly older than his mom, and had black hair, dark skin, and dark brown eyes. She was of medium height with a small frame. Her voice was light and pleasant to listen to, and she was very knowledgeable. The first topic she talked about was how rare the Combat Specialist bloodline was. She explained that this was the reason why there were only around fifteen students in Jude's class. The first few minutes of the lecture were a challenge for Jude to concentrate. He kept thinking about his run-in with Will Keating.

*It is infuriating that he feels comfortable enough to walk up to me and act like nothing happened.*

Jude and Will had been good friends back in Jude's younger years. Besides his best friend Eli, Will had been one of Jude's closest friends. What Jude liked most about Will, was the fact that Jude felt like he could be himself around Will; as well as the fact that both of their families were struggling financially. Even though Eli was Jude's best friend, and never seemed to judge Jude for his deprivation, Jude found it more comforting to have a friend like Will who was going through the same things that he was. They had been friends for four years when Will's parents had kicked him out of the house. Jude could not bear to see one of his good friends on the streets, so he begged his mom to let Will stay with them for a little while. Aileen reluctantly agreed to allow Will to live with them for a few weeks, but made sure to assign him his fair share of chores. Jude was giddy with excitement to be living with one of his good friends. The days seemed more promising and their friendship seemed to grow.

Then one day Aileen came to Jude and told him that she was noticing things missing from around the house, including fifty gold from her room. Her antique jewelry box, which Jude's father had given her, was also missing. Jude was sure that the items would turn up eventually, until Will's parents had allowed him back home. Jude and Will had been hanging out in Will's room, when Jude noticed his mother's jewelry box on Will's desk. His father's signature was carved lightly into its side. After Jude confronted Will about his mother's stolen property, Will and Jude's friendship ended in an argument where Will had called Jude "selfish, greedy and a horrible friend." They had not seen each other since, and Jude made sure to do anything in his power to avoid running into his old friend.

*It is amazing how the gods rewarded him with a promotion in his rank, when he has done so many awful things to good people.*

"Now, does anyone know where the source of all the three bloodlines' power comes from?" asked Lynn.

Jude felt a smirk come across his face at the easy question.

*I read about that when I was like seven—easy.*

A lone hand darted up to the left of Jude.

"Yes you!" said Lynn pointing to the boy.

"The power of all three bloodlines comes from the three gods, or Three Brothers, whatever you choose to call them. The Weapons Master bloodline gets their power from Aegis, the god of might. The Magi bloodline gets their power from Rune, the god of magic. The Combat Specialist bloodline gets their power from Pith, the god of lineage," he said.

"Excellent!" said Lynn clasping her hands together.

She went on to explain that no one knows why, but that for some reason, less and less people are being born with the Combat Specialist bloodline. Lynn also informed the class that the next day they would be meeting outside in the Academy courtyard to start their movement training. Jude loved being outdoors and around nature, so he looked forward to the upcoming lessons.

At the end of class, Jude hurried to meet with Eli, to share the news about how rare his bloodline was, and how his first day had went. As he exited through the wooden doors of his classroom and into the inner sanctum of Combat Hall, he was surprised to find Eli waiting outside for him already. The first thing he noticed was a cut across the left side of his face and damage done to his left pant leg and boot.

"What happened to you?"

"Ivor is what happened to me," replied Eli.

The boys started walking towards the entrance of the Academy to head home. "Come on he cannot be that bad."

"Jude the man threw a barrage of flaming arrows at me during the first thirty minutes of class."

"Wow I guess his reputation proceeds him," replied Jude with a frown.

"What? You knew he was crazy and you didn't tell me?"

"Hold on, hold on, I didn't want to scare you on your first day. Plus I was not completely sure what I had heard was true. You know sometimes people have a tendency to make stuff up about people they are not particularly fond of."

"I guess," replied Eli. "How was Professor Lynn?"

"To be honest, she was awesome. She told us about how my bloodline is rare and less and less people are being born with it."

"How rare?"

"Let's just say there is ten to fifteen students in my class."

"You got to be kidding me."

"No joke. We look like insects in that big classroom," said Jude.

"That is crazy," replied Eli. When the two boys arrived at the front door of Eli's house, the sound of hammering and metal vibrated through the door.

"Do you want to come in?" asked Eli.

"Sure! It has been a while since I have seen your dad since he is usually at the Academy." As Jude and Eli entered the house, the volume of the hammering increased. Eli closed the door behind them. Jude's eyes began to adjust to the low light of the familiar home. The dark stonewalls and wooden floors were just as he remembered, along with the dozens of various weapons that decorated the walls. Weapon cases inhabited the corners of the living room.

Eli's dad, Marius, stood hunched over his workbench hammering a sword vigorously. Marius turned around glimpsing the two boys, and a smile crept over his face.

"Jude my boy! How have you been?" asked Marius while simultaneously moving in for a bear hug. His hugs always nearly crushed Jude's arms when he was a kid.

"I have been doing pretty good Mr. Brassie. It is nice to see you too. I rarely see you anymore." A small amount of sorrow came across Marius' face. However, it was enough for Jude to realize that he had hurt the man in some way. "Sorry Marius, all I meant was I missed the three of us hanging out."

A small smile came over Marius' face. "As have I my young friend. How is your mom doing?"

"She is doing well. She still works over at the Academy library, and she is still gardening."

"Your mother always had the most beautiful garden. Probably the most beautiful garden I have ever seen in all my years," said Marius.

"Yes she always says there is a secret that I am too young to understand; and that she will teach me someday," replied Jude.

"It is a secret worth the wait if I do say so myself," said Marius with a smirk.

"You know the secret dad?" asked Eli.

"I have a hunch. Your mother and I went on a few missions together when we were younger Jude. I learned a lot from her." Marius disappeared to the kitchen, and returned with a plate of chopped strawberries, grapes and apples on one plate, and bread with cheese on the other.

"Now are you boys hungry from the long walk from the Academy?" asked Marius. Both boys ambushed the two plates stuffing their faces. Shortly after, Marius erupted into laughter. "I guess that is a yes. Well I have a pot of hot cider on the stove. Why don't you boys run along and I will bring it up shortly."

Jude and Eli retreated to Eli's room upstairs. It was exactly how Jude remembered it. Bright white stonewalls similar to the ones that made up all the buildings outside. There was a big window with no shutters in the middle of the room, which is the best place to catch the morning sunrise. There was always something so peaceful, bright, and positive about the location of Eli's room in relation to the other rooms in the house. On the wall a sword made out of wood and bark hung on the wall. Jude remembered it as the same sword he helped Eli make when they were younger.

"Are you okay?" asked Eli.

"Huh? Yes I am fine. It has just been a while since I have been in your room. You are usually always coming over my house."

"I'm sorry. I don't mean to be a burden if that's what you mean," replied Eli with sorrow in his voice.

"No! No that's not what I meant. I love you coming over. I always tell everyone you are my second brother. It's just I miss coming over here. Your house is like my second home. I practically grew up here just like my house."

A smile crept over Eli's face. "I feel the same way about your house."

The two boys sat on two leather seats that they had made when they were younger.

"So tell me what happened with Ivor the crazy," laughed Jude.

Eli recounted his lessons with Jude from earlier today. Even though Jude was not of the Weapons Master bloodline, he found learning about another bloodline fascinating. In the midst of Eli's story, Marius dropped in to drop off some hot cider but did not stay long. He retreated downstairs and the slight sound of hammering began again.

After Eli's story was over, the boys made a few jokes about making some Magi friends, so they could make Eli fire resistant. Afterwards Jude recounted his lessons to Eli. Eli had always told Jude that he was fascinated with the Combat Specialist bloodline. Jude's mom used to tell Eli and Jude about her missions with various comrades that had Combat Specialist blood.

Aileen also used to tell them both stories of babies being born with blood that encompassed too much of all three bloodlines. The blood was so diluted that the carriers gained no abilities. The healers called them Erudites. They had to train with standard weapons and had no abilities to aid them on the battlefield. She always told them that they should be proud of their bloodlines, and Jude was.

Jude got a faint feeling that Eli was jealous, when he heard that Jude was going to be spending his next lesson outside. Jude and Eli both loved exploring together.

*Spending my day outside instead of indoors with a mad man like Ivor makes me feel spoiled.*

"Well I think I should be heading back home. I have a lot to read up on before tomorrow's lesson," said Jude.

"You have homework too? I have to pick my most skilled weapon for tomorrow's lesson."

"Well I do not exactly have scheduled homework, but homework I do have."

A puzzled expression came across Eli's face. Jude began to laugh and was amused at Eli's expression. The expression was familiar and meant Eli was trying hard to decipher the meaning of his words.

"I am sorry," said Jude. "I have been hanging around my brother a lot lately and the riddle talk is contagious." Both the boys laughed while doing their best Vampire impersonations.

"My plan for becoming the best Combat Specialist is to always stay one step ahead of my competition, including my allies. I feel like as long as I know more than my opponent, I have a good chance at success," said Jude."

After exchanging goodbyes with both Eli and Marius, Jude departed for home. The streets were quiet and the night was still, except for the last minute stragglers and stray animals scurrying about. Jude enjoyed the quiet. It gave him a chance to recount past information and events, as well as thoughts. He was greeted by the large statue of the Three Brothers in the center of the Market District. A few shopkeepers finished tidying up their respective shops before retreating indoors. Jude loved this part of the town. The moonlight seemed to hit the statue perfectly giving the impression of glowing eyes in all three statues. As his eyes ran over all of the familiar details of the statue, an anomaly became visible. There was no water in the base of the statue. Jude was confused by this discovery, but soon departed towards the direction of home. His mom would be giving her garden one last sprinkle of water before getting ready for bed. As he neared the corner of his house, a slight gust of wind, so faint that it was almost unnoticed, brushed past him. Jude stopped.

"Whoever you are, you picked the wrong one to rob tonight." Just as he yanked a vial from his utility belt, a hand was on his shoulder.

"Now that is what I like to see, an Agent ready for battle," said Jed.

"You find a lot of amusement in sneaking up on me don't you," replied Jude.

"You can call it amusement if you like, but I am trying to teach you something."

"You are? What are you trying to teach me?"

"In my experience, telling someone what you are trying to teach them, is counterproductive to having them figure it out themselves."

Jude thought long and hard about Jed's words before opening the door to his house. His mom was blowing out all the candles when he came in.

"Hi boys!" said Aileen smiling. "What did the two of you do today?"

Jude was the first to respond. "Well I had a good day at the Academy today. It went really well. Afterwards I hung out with Eli at his house."

"Oh you did? Did you get a chance to see Mr. Brassie?"

"Yes he made snacks for us. It was nice seeing him again," replied Jude.

"Yes he is a nice man. What about you Jed? How was your day?"

The expression on Jed's face did not change. In fact, Jude realized that his expression hardly ever changed, except when he was alone spending quality time with Jed. "Same old, same old."

"Well that's good," said Aileen.

"I do believe the night calls for me," said Jed opening the front door.

Jude hated that his older brother stopped sleeping at their house ever since he became a Vampire. He understood that Vampires did not sleep, except for during a solar eclipse, but he still missed the presence of his older brother down the hall.

"Jude I am going to plant some new veggies before I go to bed. Do you mind helping me?"

"Um, I can only help for a little because I really need to study," said Jude hoping he was not hurting her feelings.

"Oh it will only take a few minutes. I will meet you at the garden," said Aileen heading to the storage closet.

Colder air than Jude remembered, hit his face as he opened the front door. When he turned towards the garden, he came face-to-face with a variety of fruits and vegetables. Strawberries, watermelon, cucumber, carrots, and potatoes lined the outer wall of the house. A lone water bucket sat on its side next to the porch. Jude picked it up, placed it under the outdoor faucet, and filled it up. The door swung open next to him.

"Good, you already filled up the bucket," said Aileen as she closed the door behind her. She instructed Jude to dig a few holes next to the carrots. She handed him a small hand tool before picking up the bucket and watering the already-sprouted fruits and vegetables.

"So how did your first day go?"

"It went really well! Professor Lynn is very nice and tomorrow we are spending class outdoors," said Jude as he tossed a pebble out of the hole he was digging.

"That's good! I know you will excel at everything just like your father once did."

The mention of his father caused Jude to stop digging. He looked over at his mother who was continuing to water her garden as if unaffected by the topic.

"Hey mom."

"Yes Jude," said Aileen without looking up.

"When I was younger, you never told me how dad died. You always told me that I was too young. I am twenty years old now, so—can you tell me now?" For the first time since they had began, Aileen ceased movement. Her head turned slowly towards his direction but kept her gaze low.

"Oh you don't want to hear that story, it's much too sad. Besides, the gods would frown on us for turning such a beautiful night into one of sorrow," said Aileen as she moved on to water the potatoes.

"I kind of need to know."

"And why is that Jude?"

"Mom he *is* my dad. I miss him so much, I mean, you know how close we were," said Jude not understanding her hesitation.

"I am not saying that your dad did not love you or that you two were not close, but you were young Jude, you guys were as close as a father and son could be at *your age*."

"Will you just tell me," said Jude feeling angry.

"You know the Three Brothers will punish you for talking back to your mother. You dishonor yourself—and how do you expect to get into heaven without honor?"

"But I did not talk back, I just raised my voice a little," said Jude confused.

"You are talking back to me now, and the gods do not like that, or when children raise their voices to their parents."

Jude said nothing to her comment. He did not understand where her hostility came from.

"Well if you must know, your father was a very honorable and skilled Operative. We were very happy together for many years. However, your father's dream was to become a Special Operative, and he could not do that since he had a family. So he eventually decided to leave us so he could fulfill that dream. He was killed a couple of years later on one of his missions. The gods do not take too kindly on father's who abandon their children," said Aileen. The bucket made a loud noise as it hit the floor.

Jude felt hurt by his mother's words. He felt like her recount of passed events was filled with so much negativity. He always remembered his dad as being a great father. He always played with Jude, took him fishing, and helped Jude train for the day when he would join the Academy.

*I remember him as always being there for me. He never acted like we were ever in his way. He even went on Jed's first mission with him against the advice of The Council.*

"I remember dad always wanting to help everyone even when they did not want the help," said Jude laughing.

"Yes he did that too."

"Do you miss him?"

"Are those holes finished Jude?"

"Yes."

Aileen walked over to Jude and examined his work. A smile plastered across her face as she bent down next to him. She reached into her pocket and took out some seeds. "Good job Hun! Now lets put some of these in there."

Jude realized he was not going to get any more information from her. She had always been distant when it came to the topic of his dad. He was afraid she would never be open to talking about him. After he was finished, Jude retired to his room where he lit one candle and set it on his work desk. He opened a book he picked up from the library a few weeks ago. "Okay, prepare yourself *Advanced CS Techniques*. You have met your match," he said aloud. He finished all but the last twenty pages of the book before deciding to retire for the night. He said a quick prayer to the Three Brothers to protect his family, his friends, and Kismet; and soon found himself drifting away into a weightless world of dreams and confusion.

# AN UNWANTED
# ALLY

"I believe we have our winners!" exclaimed Professor Lynn.

A thunderous applause vibrated from the class, as students ran fourth to congratulate Jude and Bree. Bree joined Jude amongst the crowd and gave him a quick shoulder nudge.

"Not bad princess," teased Bree. Jude smiled back.

A lone distant applause began from one of the archways of the courtyard. Lord Bishop soon appeared in a blue tunic with matching pants. A white cape blew vigorously in the wind as he approached the wide-eyed students before him.

"I must say that was truly an entertaining and skilled battle," said Bishop.

"Ah Lord Bishop! Thank you very much for the compliment. The students are learning about adapting to different battle situations, along with utilizing acrobatics to help give them an edge on the field," replied Lynn.

Bishop approached Bree and Jude with both hands folded behind his back, and the friendliest of smiles on his face. "You two are definitely a very talented and skilled duo. May I ask your names?"

As eager as humanly possible, Bree seemed to take the opportunity to make the best first impression. Jude knew who the ruler of his province was, but he was never able to officially meet him.

"Bree Braunstone my Lord!"

"Very nice to meet you Ms. Braunstone," replied Bishop.

He soon turned his gaze to Jude, who was thinking of all the ways not to embarrass himself, or insult Bishop.

"Thank you very much for the compliment sir. My name is Jude Bray."

"It is definitely a pleasure to meet an aspiring Agent who is quick on his feet," complimented Bishop.

"Thank you sir."

"May I ask you a question Mr. Bray?" asked Bishop.

Jude's stomach sunk.

*Great I already insulted him. I can kiss my spot on the armed forces goodbye.*

"Why did you choose to save Ms. Braunstone from your Professor, when you had a clear opening for victory?" asked Bishop.

Bree was quick to interject. "But I saved him first! He would have been unconscious if it wasn't for me!"

Bishop regarded her with a light smile before returning his attention back to Jude.

"Well sir, I saw my opening. Due to the size of Lynn's form, I could have exploited the gap between her hooves. It's just my comrade was in trouble, and I could not bring myself to sacrifice a comrade for victory. It just did not seem right," replied Jude.

Bishop's smile seemed to broaden for a second, before dissipating.

"May I ask you one last question Mr. Bray?"

"Sure, anything sir?" replied Jude.

"Why do you want to become an Agent for our lands?"

Jude did not even need to think about Bishop's question. He answered immediately after Bishop was finished. "I want to fight to defend my mother and my older brother; and the income will help my mom a lot. She won't have to work all day all the time."

"An honorable man," replied Bishop.

Turning his attention to Lynn he asked, "First years?"

"First years!" smiled Lynn back.

"And they were able to take you on in your troll form— amazing!" Bishop turned so he was facing the whole class. "Keep up the good work!"

"Class dismissed! Tomorrow we will be meeting back in our usual room. Jude and Bree come with me please!" said Lynn.

The class dispersed while commotion broke out amongst them. Jude and Bree followed Lynn back to her classroom. Jude was ecstatic trying to think of what their prize could be. As they entered the classroom, the familiar smell of wood, stone and embers filled the air.

"I have to say, I am very impressed with the teamwork you two displayed today," Lynn started. "I do have to say that it is a shame that neither of the other students tried to use their vials or the acrobatics lesson we learned today," said Lynn with a touch of disappointment in her voice.

"In all fairness, you were pretty intimidating," said Bree.

"Was I?" asked Lynn.

"Yes, I have to agree. I will probably have a few sleepless nights coming my way after today," replied Jude.

The three of them erupted into laughter. Lynn stopped in front of her cabinet that hung inconspicuously in the corner of her classroom. She placed a hand on it, and the cabinet vibrated. Soon one of the doors of the cabinet opened. Lynn opened both doors to reveal hundreds and hundreds of vials full with numerous liquids. Jude and Bree watched in awe, before Lynn closed the cabinet and held out a vial to each of them.

"A reward for your bravery today," said Lynn. "Remember, it's not the power of the blood in the vial that matters, it's the power of the heart that guides it."

"Is this blood?" asked Bree.

"That is correct Ms. Braunstone," replied Lynn.

"But from what or whom?" asked Jude.

"Now that is something that not even I have the answer to," Lynn replied with a wink. "I will see you both tomorrow."

Jude and Bree both exited, cradling their prize in their hands as if they were holding a newborn. Just when Jude turned to say something to Bree, the blue-eyed girl took off in the opposite direction.

Stammering and not knowing what to say, Jude quickly yelled, "Hey!"

Bree stopped and turned around.

"Good work today. See you tomorrow," said Jude. Bree smiled a flirtatious smile and continued on her way, before disappearing from view.

"You have got to be kidding me," said Jude. "This is where you go in the middle of the night? To some bushes?"

"Just when I think you have taken one step forward, you take two steps back," replied Jed.

He lifted his arm and pushed aside the wall of brush and trees. The first thing Jude noticed was a large moon camping above a large watering hole. The watering hole was enormous, stretching wider than Jude could imagine. The water was as still as can be, perfectly showing the moon's reflection on its surface. Crickets chirped softly in the background, as fireflies glided low along the surface of the water.

"This place is amazing," said Jude amazed.

"Yeah it's alright."

"When did you find it? How did you find it?" asked Jude.

"Maybe a month or so after I died."

"Died?" The words shook Jude to his core. "You did not die. You are here with me, right now."

"Right..." An awkward silence hung in the air for a few minutes. The crickets seemed to chirp louder in Jude's ears.

"Why don't you stay at home during the night? I know you do not sleep but you could still stay."

Jed's eyes scanned the surface of the water, as he took in its entirety as if for the first time. "Because that is not my home anymore."

"Of course it is your home!" snapped Jude. "It will always be your home." Jed rustled Jude's hair playfully.

"Don't do that!" snapped Jude.

"Do what?"

"Condescend to me with your big brother gestures as if I cannot understand. I am not a kid anymore. I am twenty years

44

old. I can understand!" Another awkward silence hung between them. Again the sound of the crickets seemed to increase as time passed amongst them.

"Mom does not want me there. She does not want me around you guys," replied Jed.

"That is not true. She misses you like I do."

"She misses me, but I don't think it's the way you think."

Jed picked up a stone and skipped it across the waters' surface. Ripples interrupted the calmness of the water. "Mom misses me the way someone mourns somebody. She mourns my death."

Jude said nothing.

"After I was turned into an immortal, I returned home to mom thinking I would find support there. She was all the support I had after father died. I remember the first time she laid eyes on me. Her eyes widened and she let loose a small scream before her hand covered her mouth. I went in for the hug I dreamt about every night when I was away on my mission, and she ran from me. I believe you were fifteen years old at the time. You were at Eli's house that night. So I took off. I found comfort in the night. The night seemed to watch over me. I do not know how to explain it. I just feel *right* during the night. My senses are stronger, my mind is clearer, and I feel rested like I used to feel when I would sleep as a human. I didn't return home for weeks. Mom put on a fake sense of happiness to see me when you were around, but funny thing about being a Vampire is, you can taste and sense the fear of those around you. To this day she still fears me."

Finally Jude found his voice.

"I used to think that you hated me when we were younger. We were so close before you went off on your missions, and when you came back, you were so distant. You rarely visited the house, and mom would not let me go out to find you. She told me that you no longer wanted to be apart of our family. Eli and the others would ask about you, and I was embarrassed to have to tell them that I didn't know where my own brother was, or if he was coming back. I am sad to say that for a few months I began to hate you for making me feel this way. You were the closest thing I had to a dad after father passed away. But then suddenly you started coming around more, and I remembered how close we once were."

Jed listened to everything Jude said before speaking.

"I apologize for leaving you in the dark for so many years. What mom said about me not wanting to be apart of our family anymore is not true. I believe she only said it to keep you away from me. If it is any consolation, I came back because of you."

Jude looked up at his big brother, and for the first time, Jed returned the stare.

"I realized that mom did not have the right to keep us apart, and it was not your fault that her and I were at odds. I thought about you every night I was gone. As scary as it sounds, sometimes I would follow you at night just to make sure you got home safely," Jed went on. "I never left your side."

"There can be no more secrets between us. Agreed?"

Jed met Jude's stern gaze. "Agreed."

"Is there anything else you have not told me?" asked Jude.

"Besides my underworld abilities, nothing."

Silence returned to the night, as the movement of the water became audible.

"I was on fire today at the Academy you know."

"Really? You don't smell like it?" regarded Jed.

"Very funny."

Jude told Jed about all of the events that happened earlier today in regards to Professor Lynn. For the first time in a long time to Jude, Jed cracked somewhat of a smile when he heard his little brother turned into a swamp snake to take down a troll. Jude felt like things were back to the way they used to be.

"So what do you do when you are not on missions?" asked Jude.

"Hunt."

"Alright this is the end of the vague answers, at least with me," snapped Jude.

"We both know what I hunt, so what is the point of saying it?"

"Because it seems as though you are avoiding it by not saying it—that's all."

"I hunt nearby travelers and enemy soldiers. I usually try to venture outside of our land of Kismet. I never want to kill any of our own people. I try to only kill people of other provinces. It is my way of trying to keep a shred of any humanity I may have left. However, sometimes I cannot make it all the way across our borders, so I hunt the travelers and farmers that live along the borders of Kismet. It also helps me to keep watch over anything suspicious coming in and out of our lands."

"Does Lord Bishop know you are doing this?"

"Yes, he feels like he owes me for the many battles I have helped him win. He is actually probably the only one in our town that does not look at me like a monster. When he looks at me, he sees me for the Agent I was before—this."

"I do not agree with the last thing you just said," replied Jude. "I have never looked at you as a monster. As far as I am concerned, you are the same big brother I have always had; whether you are a Vampire or not. To be honest, the fact that you can go on living in our lands being the only Vampire in it, says a lot about you. I know it must be hard to hang around us humans all the time, but I am glad you do. I do not know what I would do without you."

Jed showed a bit of a smile again. "You humans are not too bad. You guys just stink as much as your food—that's all."

"How did it feel when you were bitten? You know, by the Vampire that changed you," asked Jude.

47

Jed slowly turned his head, and stared deeply into Jude's eyes. His white translucent eyes calmed Jude, and made him not want to move a muscle.

"It was horrific. I would not wish it on anyone."

"Explain it to me," Jude pleaded.

"I had just finished transforming back from a mountain lion. My team had basically won already. We were facing an enemy that we call the Amorphous."

"What is an Amorphous?" asked Jude.

"Amorphous are a race of people that have existed longer than our race of people. No one has ever seen their true form. That is because they always take on the form of the last person or animal they killed. They are a very cruel race. We were lucky that there were only a few of them during our mission. Anyways, after returning to my human form, I noticed a quick movement at the corner of my eye. Before I could turn around, I felt a sharp pain in my neck. I was in the arms of what appeared to be a man, while his fangs sank into my neck. The first sensation of course was pain from the bite. He took a bite and then ran off just as quickly as he got there. The bite paralyzes you. Soon your lungs just stop processing air, they just shut down while you are still alive. You begin to suffocate while you are coughing up blood. The pain reaches such a staggering level, that you begin to lose the feeling in your face. Just when the pain becomes too unbearable, you finally suffocate from the lack of air. Lying there among all the dead corpses of both my men and enemies, I shed the last tear I would ever cry. Just as quickly as that tear fell, darkness poured in from all corners of my vision. That is when I saw what I had only heard whispers about for many years. I saw myself being pulled down into the fires of the underworld by every demon you could imagine."

"But why would you see that?"

"Vampirism came from the fallen brother Anim as a curse on mankind before he was imprisoned. It is said that when someone becomes a Vampire, Anim immediately claims it, casting the soul down into one of the many realms of his underworld. That way, if the Vampire dies, there is only one place he can spend eternity. When I awoke I was in the outskirts of Kismet. I discovered that due to my vampirism, I lost all of my abilities as a Combat Specialist. That was probably one of the worst results of what had happened to me, besides the loss of my comrades and friends. I feel like my honor died with me that day as well."

"Does that scare you?"

Curled brows showed Jude that Jed did not understand the question. "Does what scare me?"

"Feeling like you have lost your honor," said Jude.

"No—why should it?"

"Mom used to always tell me that being a good person and helping others builds honor, and honor is your ticket into heaven when you die," said Jude.

"Sounds like garbage to me. Even if by some farfetched chance she was correct, I do not believe all of the honor in the world could save me from an eternity in the shadows of Anim's realm of excruciating hell. Anyways, whomever the Vampire was that did this to me, they will suffer for their cowardice. You can count on it."

# STRIKE TWO

Eli was determined to master this technique if it meant being late to class or not. Eli thought about what Jude had said a few months ago, about him always wanting to be one step ahead of both his opponents and allies. That sounded like a genius plan to Eli. Why had he not thought of that? He has spent the past ten years of his life telling everyone he had ever met that he was going to be the best; and he did not even have a plan of action.

Eli had gotten up bright and early before the sun had risen. He had been training in the city's forest for a few hours, before he began to think it was all in vain. He decided it would be foolhardy to anger his mentor for the second time, so he set off for the Academy so he would not be late. The walk back through the forest was enticing. Eli loved exploring, not necessarily nature, but the unknown. However, nature had always been something his mother had loved; and whenever he was with her, he felt that he loved nature as well. As he thought about his mother and the time they spent together, a memory flashed before his eyes:

*"Catch me mommy! Catch me!" A young boy stood on a small rock that littered the ground of a beautiful forest that was home to a variety of colorful flowers. As the boy jumped, he was swooped up by the comfort of the woman's small hands, before he was spun around and around. Her long blonde hair blew effortlessly through the wind as she hoisted him high up into the sun's rays that showered him with warmth and comfort.*

A bird perched by singing a tune caught Eli's attention. It was not the first time that Eli had thought about his mother. She swam in his dreams and sometimes his conscience from time to time. He both welcomed and loved the memories of her. They both comforted and taunted him at the same time. When the white-stone pillars of the city's walls came into view, he was comforted with knowing that he would make it to class on time. He passed through two Erudites standing guard at the gates as he entered.

*Ha! Erudites. What a joke.*

Making his way through the Eastern Hold of the city, he noticed the sun's rays were hindered by the pillars of the city's gate; which casted a gloom over that part of the city. The tall lavish buildings still screamed luxury, but also mystery as well.

As the Academy loomed up behind the elaborate houses, Eli noticed movement to his left. A tall light-stoned house with double doors came into view; and then he saw her. Sia looked even more beautiful than the last time Eli remembered seeing her. The wind blew strands of her long dark brown hair creating shadows across her face. A small scratch marked her left cheek but it too looked beautiful to Eli. She wore a tight-fitting short white dress, black combat shoes, and a thick black belt that clung to her thin waistline. Even though he fancied her appearance, he thought that she looked a little over-dressed. Her purple eyes, duller than he remembered, fixated on him.

"We have met, haven't we?" she asked.

Eli's stomach began to do somersaults as he celebrated the fact that she had not forgotten him.

"Yeah. I mean yes, we have," he replied with a smile.

"Eli is it?" she asked.

*Oh man she remembered my name.*

"Yeah and you are Sia right?"

He needed no confirmation. He had thought about her every day since they had met in the Academy courtyard.

"Correct," she replied with a friendly smile. "Care to walk to the Academy together?"

"Sure!" Eli said eagerly. "I mean I wouldn't mind," he corrected himself.

As the two of them continued down the lively streets toward the Academy, Eli could not help but sneak glances in Sia's direction. Trying to be as covert as possible, he quickly shifted his attention away from her every time he saw any hint of movement from her head or eyes.

"Crap!" yelled Sia.

Eli looked around hastily, in an attempt to identify what had startled her. "What? What happened?" asked Eli. He looked over at Sia as she stopped dead in her tracks. She was looking hastily into a small mirror that she gripped firmly in the palm of her hand.

"Nothing!" she said turning her back to Eli. After a few moments, she turned her gaze back towards his direction. Her skin looked even smoother than before. The scratch he had noticed from earlier, was now covered with what appeared to be fresh, smooth new skin.

"How do I look?"

Eli felt himself blush as he became more aware of how dry his throat felt. He swallowed a couple of times before responding.

"You look good—great I mean," said Eli as he adjusted the collar of his tunic. "You always do."

"That is nice of you, but I know I had that ugly scratch under my eye. My stupid cat scratched me and left the ugliest mark."

The silence hung thick for a few seconds, before they continued their walk towards the Academy.

Eli and Sia headed for the Academy footsteps landing on the familiar ceramic path that led to the Academy's double doors.

"If you do not mind me asking, why were you in the Eastern Hold today?"

*Oh great she thinks I'm stalking her now.*

"I'm sorry, I didn't know you were going to be there. It wasn't intentional," he hastily replied.

Sia appeared taken back as if she just withstood a small earthquake. "No I mean usually everyone else takes the Market District road. The only people who ever venture into the Eastern Hold, are the people who live there or have family there."

"Oh. Well I have been doing a little bit of training and I didn't want to be late, so I figured the Eastern Hold would get me to the Academy faster," he replied bashfully.

"Oh whereabouts were you training?"

"Nowhere special, just the forest border outside the city's walls," he replied embarrassed.

The two of them arrived at the double doors leading into the Academy. Holding his head down, Eli opened the door for Sia hoping she would appreciate the gesture. She stared at him for a few seconds before entering.

"I have not been to the forest since I was a little girl. I was scared of the forest back then. But I miss the trees and animals that live there," she said.

"There's nothing to be scared of, I have been going there by myself for a while now."

"I am not a little girl anymore, and I am *not* scared of it— if that's what you are implying," said Sia.

*You are going down in flames and she will laugh while skipping through your ashes.*

"No I wasn't implying anything, I was just saying it's nice there," he said in attempt to recover.

When he looked up at the red medallion with two intersecting blades, he realized he was already at the door to his hall. He cursed himself for having such long strides. "Well this is me. I mean this is my class." He took a deep breath. "It was nice walking with you. Hopefully I will see you around?"

Sia studied him for a while. To Eli, the dullness that was once present in her light purple eyes had lifted, and was replaced with a piercing shade of neon purple. "See you around."

*That was painful!*

Entering his class, he found Zane reserving a spot for him at the front of the class. Eli nearly fell over laughing when he overheard Zane tell one student, that attempted to sit there, that he would "charbroil your mother if you even think about sitting there" to a tall student with a soldier build.

"Is this seat taken?" asked Eli sitting down.

"Actually I'm reserving that for someone, and if you don't want to end up a rug in my room, I suggest you relocate yourself."

Eli froze in shock.

"I'm just kidding," teased Zane.

"You really had me I have to admit," laughed Eli. "Hey you know that girl that hangs out with your sister?"

"Who? Sia Wyatt?"

"Yeah, her," replied Eli elated that Zane knew who he was talking about.

"What about her?"

"Do you know if she is, you know," said Eli.

"If she is what? I'm not a Magi and I don't even know if they can even read minds. Out with it!"

"Single! There I said it!" exclaimed Eli.

Just as the words left his mouth, a slow smile crept over Zane's face. Before Zane could respond, Ivor stormed into the room slamming the doors behind him.

"The next student I find leaving my doors open even the slightest after entering or exiting them, will find themselves crafted into the finest shield of my career. Do I make myself clear?" scowled Ivor.

"Yes sir!" said the class in unison.

Ivor soon began a lecture on the logistics of using their abilities in battle. Eli was not surprised when the mentor explained that summoning weapons requires blood energy, and the less blood energy the caster had, the more taxing it was on the body. Eli discovered this during his training in the woods. On one occasion, he had summoned so many weapons, that he found himself passed out face-down with a series of frogs leaping over him in a straight line. What did surprise Eli was Ivor's next topic explaining that firing arrows with a bow, took nearly half the energy as firing arrows without one. That hit way too close to home for Eli. He was not entirely disappointed since he found himself skilled with the bow, and had better accuracy and range when using one.

"I will now teach you a technique that will allow you to be able to attack and defend simultaneously," announced Ivor.

Excitement dispersed within Eli. He thought perhaps he could solve the riddle of why he was not able to successfully pull off what he had been training in the forest the past few weeks.

"First I will need a volunteer. Who of you is brave enough to face me in the arena?" asked Ivor amused.

"Eli is!" said a voice across the classroom.

Simultaneously Zane and Eli whipped their heads around to see whom the voice belonged to. It was the tall student from earlier that Zane prevented from sitting in Eli's seat. The boy grinned trying to contain his laughter.

"Ah excellent idea Mr. Nysell! Mr. Brassie will you please join me up front please," smirked Ivor.

"I'm going to charbroil his whole family now," whispered Eli over his shoulder to Zane."

"I'll bring the butter," replied Zane quickly.

Eli walked to the front of the class and positioned himself at the same starting line as before.

"Now before I teach you this technique, I want to first show you the result of a battle without this technique," announced Ivor.

*Bullcrap! You just want to humiliate me in front of the whole class to prove you know more than me.*

"Ready yourself!" exclaimed Ivor.

However just as the words left his lips, Ivor was already hurling an attack at Eli, who in turn dove out of the way. The class erupted into laughter at the acrobatics of their peer. Even Ivor seemed amused by the antics judging by the smirk on his face.

Rage burned inside Eli.

*You're my mentor. No matter what personal feelings you have towards me, you are not supposed to be bullying me. I'm here to learn.*

More determined than ever, Eli took his place at his starting line again.

*You asked for it!*

"Again!" exclaimed Eli at Ivor who appeared taken back.

"Perhaps after I teach you what you will need to even stand a chance in battle," laughed Ivor.

"No! With all do respect sir, I won't need it to face someone like you."

Ivor's eyes changed to slate black as he rolled up the sleeves of his robe. A war blade appeared in front of him, hovering above the ground for a few seconds, and then launching itself at Eli.

Adrenaline coursed through Eli's veins while a series of undecipherable phrases ran through his mind. His hand flew up, summoning an identical blade as his mentor's. Both of their blades met in the middle of the sparring arena before redirecting back at Ivor. A series of gasps erupted throughout the classroom

*Wait. How did I do that?*

Eli was ready to panic until the dual blades, which were inches away from skewering his professor, dissolved before making contact. Ivor's cape came to life as if some kind of gale force had entered the hall. A bombardment of arrows darted towards Eli, and just when Eli was ready to repeat his previous attack, nothing happened. A girl somewhere close by screamed. Eli panicked, not realizing what was going on. When the arrows hit with a direct attack, Eli released an internal plea for aid. The attack halted digging into his shirt, before redirecting itself back at Ivor with double the original projectiles. Eli's vision blurred and his throat closed. He had not realized that he had fell to his feet. He felt nauseous and dizzy, and was uncertain of what was going on. He lifted his head in panic and watched his attack, which looked inevitable, barrel towards Professor Ivor.

*There are too many. He won't be able to dodge it.*

"Professor..." he said.

A shield walled up in front of Ivor. Explosions shook the hall around Eli, causing him to fall to the floor. He propped himself up only to catch his attack exploding on contact with Ivor's shield. Black residue pillaged the shield before the weapons dissolved, leaving no trace of their existence. The shield vanished, bringing Eli face-to-face with his mentor once again. Smoke rose from various areas within the sparring arena they stood on. The nausea and dizziness still crippled Eli. He found it difficult to breathe, and even more difficult to focus.

*Please. Please don't attack again. I don't think I can defend against another attack.*

Ivor glared at Eli for what seemed like minutes. "You are dismissed Mr. Brassie," said Ivor pointing to Eli's seat.

Eli forced himself to his feet. He had to regain his footing when the tilting world around him nearly made him fall. Once his vision was somewhat clear, he scurried to his seat, keeping his eyes to the floor along the way.

"That was incredible," whispered Zane over Eli's shoulder.

"Thanks," replied Eli still fixated on Ivor.

"What are you going to call that move?" asked Zane.

"I hadn't thought about it. Since it replicates any threat targeting me, maybe threat replication?"

"Badass!" whispered Zane.

"Mr. Nysell, will you please join me up front?"

Eli glared as his peer took his position.

"Since you are someone who appears to be more disciplined than Mr. Brassie, I will teach you this technique."

*Whatever.*

Ivor taught the class a technique that both summoned a weapon and a shield simultaneously at half the effort. He explained how the shield could only protect the caster, but was capable of shielding anything in front of the caster, as long as he or she had sufficient blood energy to maintain the shield. Eli did not care that Ivor intentionally chose not to teach him this technique directly. He still took detailed notes and was determined to try the technique out on his own terms back in the forest, at a later date.

"Now, all of you get into hopeless pairs of two and find a empty space for the two of you. You will need enough space for light sparring so choose wisely," said Ivor. The class remained motionless for a few seconds before the commotion began. Eli and Zane found a spot in the back of the classroom next to the doors. They believed that drawing the least amount of attention from Ivor as possible was best.

"That will not be happening today gentlemen," said Ivor crossing the room until he was next to Eli and Zane.

"Huh?" asked Eli confused.

"The blind will not be leading the blind in my class. Keating come here," said Ivor.

Eli felt ambushed when he found himself looking into the eyes of Jude's old friend. He had been going to the Academy for a few months now, and not once noticed that Will was in his class as well.

*I thought he was in advanced classes now. Why is he in my class?*

"Zane, you pair up with Mr. Nysell. I am pretty sure he can at least attempt to salvage what little skills you may have," said Ivor. Eli heard Zane mumble something under his breath as he left, but he could not make out his words. Eli never though he would be afraid to see Ivor leave, but when the mentor left him with the crazy nightmare that Eli had heard so much of, he kicked himself for not clinging to Ivor's pant leg as the mentor departed.

"Hey..." said Will as he changed his posture.

"Hey how's it going?" said Eli. He felt like every word he spoke was a nail in his own coffin.

"Pretty good," said Will.

"Now, I want each of you to summon a blade and engage in civil sparring. We are not trying to kill one another—as if any of you were even capable of inflicting a pinch—but are honing our skills in close combat. Daggers, axes, and any other blunt weapons are allowed. I will be coming around in an attempt to mend all of the mistakes you all will inevitably make," said Ivor.

Eli held out his hand and soon a blade appeared. He thought back to when it seemed impossible to summon any kind of weapon. After he had turned sixteen, his dad had taught him how to summon a few of the basic weapons, and that had made all the difference. He looked up and noticed Will staring back at him with both of his hands on a blade that was held above his head—ready to strike.

"You may now engage," said Ivor loudly.

Will was the first to attack, bringing his blade down firmly in a vertical slash. Eli's horizontal blade immediately halted the attack, forcing Eli to connect eyes with his opponent. He pushed Will's blade away and twisted into a back-slash. He felt his blade get knocked away before his feet were knocked out from underneath him, and soon his back collided with the smooth hard floors of Master Hall.

"Whoa what's your deal? Professor said light sparring," said Eli angrily. The back of his head hurt from the impact with the floor, and he felt a non-visible cut on his leg. His pant leg began to soak up the trail of blood that had begun to run.

"Civil sparring is what he said, and that's what I'm doing," said Will assuming a fighting stance.

Eli returned to his feet, and instantly felt the burning of the cut at the back of his leg, and applied pressure with one of his hands. "Professor," said Eli. After a short minute, Ivor appeared next to them. Eli noticed an unwarranted smirk appear on Will's face.

"Yes Mr. Brassie, how can I be of service to an upstanding and sophisticated gentleman such as yourself," said Ivor with a roll of his eyes.

"My partner refuses to follow your directions and have a civil sparring session. Can I switch partners?" said Eli. Ivor stared at Eli for a few seconds. His gaze stayed rock-hard and ice-cold. No personality whatsoever seemed to be present behind his dead eyes.

"Oh I see. You are *that guy*," said Ivor with a small smile and a shake of his head. Eli waited for any kind of clarification to Ivor's words, since he was unsure of their meaning. "Let me guess, Mr. Keating proves to be too powerful of an opponent for you. So instead of taking the honorable Agent route and strategizing ways around his high-level skills, you decide to be *that guy* and tell on him for being too much for you. Typical."

A small covert laugh escaped from Will's lips.

"Why is he even in this class? He's supposed to be in advanced classes," said Eli. He felt angry towards Ivor for insulting him instead of seeing that Will was going against his original directions.

"He *is* in advanced classes. Why he is in this class is none of your business. So continue," said Ivor and soon he was gone.

"It's funny," said Will laughing. His laughter caused him to lower his blade so he could hold his stomach. After he was done, he returned his blade to its offensive position. "Now I understand why Jude always called you his best friend, and not me. You're both weak, and the weak need the weak in order to feel strong."

"Jude said you were garbage, and I guess he was right," said Eli. He charged Will with a lunge of his blade, but failed to anticipate the bash of Will's newly-summoned shield in his other hand. Eli felt himself slide across the hall's surface, until his head collided with an adjacent wall. The staggering high ceiling was what made up his view until Will hovered above him—with his sword at Eli's neck.

"I won. You lost. The end," said Will smirking. Eli felt his rage assert control. Will was garbage in his eyes, and he did not understand how Will could be rewarded with a promotion in rank, after he had done Jude so wrong. Above all, he hated the smug look on Will's face—the look of victory and superiority.

*I'm going to bash your face in.*

The dagger hit Will's shoulder as soon as Eli had thrown it. The brown-haired boy dropped his sword—which dissolved instantly—and grabbed his shoulder with a grimace. Eli leaped to his feet and slashed Will's leg, who fell to his back quickly. The look of anger and fear was present in Will's eyes when they found Eli's. Eli grabbed the top of the hilt of his blade and began to smash the pommel into Will's face.

"No! No! You didn't win! I won! Do you hear me? I won! Not you! Me!"

An arm wrapped around Eli's waist and tugged him away. Will staggered to his feet, wiping the blood that fell from the side of his face and nose.

"Man what are you doing?" asked Zane. He had climbed to his feet and extended a hand down to Eli. Eli accepted Zane's assistance, and instantly felt the blinding rage dissipate.

"I—I don't know," said Eli.

"I will tell you what you did," said Ivor taking a firm stance next to Zane and Eli. Eli had not noticed the Professor's presence, and was surprised by the scowl on his face—at least surprised for a few seconds. "You disobeyed my directions and dishonored both my hall and this Academy with your savagery."

"Me? What about," started Eli but stopped at the rise of Ivor's lone stern finger that rose instantly. Ivor turned on the balls of his feet with an enraged elegance, and soon returned to the front of the classroom.

"Let me make myself perfectly clear," started Ivor while he clasped his hands firmly behind his back. "There is no room for dishonor, disobedience, savagery, arrogance or insubordination in my hall. Mr. Brassie has shown me that the hope for a class full of nothing but honorable and obedient students is asking for too much. The next student who decides to disrespect me, or this Academy again, will find themselves banished from this Academy forever. That is strike two Mr. Brassie. Class dismissed!"

When the class was over, Zane and Eli were the first to leave the hall.

"I am officially convinced that Ivor has it out for you," announced Zane.

"What was your first guess?" replied Eli sarcastically.

"I mean you would think he would be happy you were able to pull off such an advanced move at the beginning of class; and clearly you won in your sparring with that Will guy. I mean you're his student. But it's like he doesn't want you to learn anything. It's very strange."

"It doesn't matter, he's probably just bitter because he is dead last on the favorite mentor list," replied Eli.

"No argument here. So about Sia," replied Zane with a smirk. "She is single, and I was actually going to ask if you wanted to hang out with Sia, my sister and I later on this evening. We are going to this spot that serves hot cider among other things," Zane went on with a wink.

"Sure, who's all going?"

"Originally my sister had just invited Sia and I, but I can still tell what kind of night it will be. It will be a night full of 'You think he is single,' 'Oh he's a bad boy,' and 'Go talk to him,' all night. I find it wise to bring an ally with me," said Zane with an annoyed expression on his face.

"Do you think your sister will mind?"

"Do I care?" fired back Zane.

Both boys laughed heading for the main gates of the Academy. Eli agreed to hang out with the group later on that evening. He was both excited and nervous to be seeing Sia again. He was determined to make a better impression this time. After setting a time and location to meet up, Eli exchanged farewells with Zane. Wanting to get home in time to wash, groom, and change clothes, he sprinted towards home. Closing the door behind him, Eli was surprised to see that his father was not smithing in the front room.

"Father?"

"Eli is that you?" came a voice from the kitchen.

"Yeah it's me," replied Eli venturing into the kitchen. To his surprise he found his father cooking dinner. He even had an apron on. "Um what's going on?"

"I wanted to make dinner for us. It has been a while since we both sat down to the table together like we used to. How was training at the Academy today?"

Both surprised and confused, Eli set the table while recounting his run-in with Ivor.

"That man has some serious issues and you can tell him I said so," scowled Marius.

When they both sat down to the table, Eli was blown away by the amount of food there was. Steak, Chicken, buttered bread, cooked carrots, squash, peas, potatoes and for dessert, his dad even had made a pie. "Father what is all of this? Is something going on? Whatever it is you can tell me."

Their eyes met and a silence fell upon them.

"Son look, I know I have not been there for you like I should have been these past couple of years. I have been spending more time working than with the one thing that means more to me. That is you son. I think the primary reason why I have been so invested in working all the time is so—," Marius' voice trailed off as he cupped his face in his hands.

Eli reached his arm across the table rubbing his father's shoulder for support. "It's okay father."

"I do it so I don't have to think about your mother," he continued as tears began to stream down his face. "I try to fill her spot but I can never take her place."

*A young boy hid under a dark brown table pulling the tablecloth down behind him. "I wonder where he is," said a man walking closeby. "Hmm I think I know where he is," said a woman, as her voice grew louder. The tablecloth flipped up as a pair of hands snatched the boy up. He laughed and laughed as kisses rained down from both sides. "Mommy and daddy love you Eli," said the woman cradling the boy in her arms.*

A tear formed at the corner of Eli's eye as he dropped his head. Getting up from his seat and closing the distance between them, Eli hugged his father in a tight embrace. "You are right father, you can't take her place. No one can. But you have done an amazing job. I do think of her a lot, but you do so much, that I can honestly say that I'm okay father—I am."

Marius lifted his head and stared into Eli's eyes. "I promise I will be there more for you son, you have my word."

Eli knew he should have been getting ready to go out with Zane, but he could not leave his father. It was true he felt a distance between him and his father the past couple of years. Eli spent more time over Jude's house than his own, because his father was so obsessed with work. Jude's family was the only support he had at times. However listening to his father's words, gave him hope that things could finally go back to the way they used to be. He knew they could if effort was made on both ends.

"So there's this girl at the Academy," started Eli while finishing his dinner.

"Oh! That's my boy," said Marius with a grin on his face. "I want to hear all about her!"

A smile swept across Eli's face. "Well she's around my age. She's a Magi and has light purple eyes and long dark brown hair. I know most of the Magi have purple eyes, but her purple eyes are different. When she looks at me I can't move or breathe. All of my defenses come crashing down. At times I feel like if I was under attack while looking upon her eyes, I would willingly withstand whatever was being thrown my way."

"She sounds like a treasure," said Marius.

"Yeah but whenever I see her, I always say the wrong things. I don't even think she knows I like her."

"You know I think I have the solution to your problem. Now bare with me, it's from ancient times and it may sound crazy, but I think it will work," replied Marius.

"What is it?" asked Eli eagerly.

"Just tell her how you feel!" laughed Marius.

"It's not that easy."

"Let me tell you something. When I first met your mother I was blown away. She was beautiful, extremely smart and very kind. I had feelings for her for years and never told her. We went on countless missions, your mother and I. I remember Bishop would be sitting with me at the campfire—."

"Bishop? You mean Lord Bishop? You guys were friends?" asked Eli shocked.

"Yes and we still are. He knew how much I loved your mother and gave me the same advice I am giving you."

Eli looked down at his hands. They were sweating and fidgety. "So let me guess, you told her that night and she liked you back, and you got married, and lived happily ever after."

"No not necessarily like that. I waited until I felt the time was right. We had been held up outside of enemy lines for days. We were all hungry and tired, and honestly we did not smell too well. But one day when we were setting up camp, I asked her if she would mind taking a walk with me. We walked the nearby forest climbing the trees, crossing streams, and so on. She loved nature. I found that when I was with her, I too loved nature. It was then I told her how I felt. To my surprise she had the same feelings. After we returned home from our mission, we started dating. It was the happiest period of my life. We soon got married and had you."

"Wow! But see you were lucky because she liked you back," replied Eli.

"More than liked," teased Marius with a wink. "But my point is, you will never know until you take that first step. Who knows, you might find out you liked her more than you thought, or didn't like her as much as you thought you did. Now time to get down to business! Get upstairs and wash up, that is an order soldier!"

Eli washed up and was halfway through shaving, when his father stepped into the room.

"No no not like that," said Marius. " Let me show you a secret shaving technique that my dad taught me."

"A secret shaving technique? Are you joking?"

Marius showed Eli the shaving technique his father showed him. Shortly after, he left and came back hiding behind the door. "Now you can take your socks off now, or I can knock them off once you see our secret weapon," teased Marius. He stepped through the door with a dressy black long-sleeve sweater with silver stitching. The sleeves naturally cuffed at the wrists and had tiny silver swords sewn into the exposed cuffs.

*This has to be expensive.*

"Father where did you get it?"

"Your mother made it for me when I was away on one of my missions. She was a woman of many talents. Try it on."

Eli tried on the sweater, and to his surprise, it fit perfectly. Marius handed him some expensive looking black slacks as well. Eli retreated to his washroom, tried them on, and realized they fit as well. Looking in the mirror, he was surprised at how good he looked. Opening the door, he walked over to his father and hugged him.

"Thanks dad, I love them."

"I am glad son. Now hurry or you will be late!"

Eli grabbed his shoes and headed for the Market District, where he knew that he would find Zane waiting for him.

# STATUS REPORT

Fox did not anticipate the journey back taking as long as it had. He was relieved to see the city's tall white-stoned pillars and lit torches from the distance. Bishop would be furious by his tardiness, but it was something Fox was actually looking forward to. He enjoyed pushing his ruler's buttons. As he ventured through the front gates, he received stares from the Erudites posted there, but neither said anything. Passing through the Market District, he decided to take a break at the Three Brothers fountain in the center of the town. Sitting down on the small wall that surrounded the fountain, he washed his hands in the fountain's water supply. As he gazed up towards the moon, he thought of how good a warm cup of cider would taste right about now.

"Out for an evening stroll," said a voice behind Fox, who quickly jumped to his feet and turned around, legs parted, and hands at the ready. A tall young man with long white hair and white eyes stood arms crossed before him.

"Something like that," replied Fox never coming out of his fighting stance. "Have we met?"

"No we have not, at least up until now," replied the stranger. "Weren't you sent out on a mission recently to the Immortal Lands?"

"That information is classified, and even if it wasn't, you are not exactly the kind of guy I would like to sit around the campfire and gossip with—no offense," glared Fox.

A silence hung in the air as the stranger glared into Fox's eyes. "No I suppose not. One last question and I will let you get back to your 'campfire' you love so much."

"No I won't sleep with you—sorry. My lady's warm sheets are already calling for me." The stranger appeared unaffected by Fox's humor, which gave him pause. Fox studied the stranger, never taking his eyes off of him, as the stranger turned his back, and walked away from him into the moonlight.

"Weren't you sent with three other men on your mission? Where might they be?"

*This is Jed Bray. Ex-Combat Specialist and the town's lone Vampire. Why didn't I realize it before?*

"Like I previously stated, that information is classified, and if you don't mind, I have a date with a cup of hot cider and a even hotter young lady. Good night," said Fox gathering himself and heading in the direction towards the castle. While Fox walked further away from the Market District, he never lost sight of the stranger that was still there watching him. When Fox turned the last corner leading up to the castle, he made a mental note to keep an eye on Jed Bray.

◆ ◆ ◆

Bishop had received word of Fox's arrival shortly after returning from the Academy's library. He was disappointed at how long it had taken Fox and his team to return from the Immortal Lands, but he knew punctuality was not one of Fox's strong points. Waiting in Council Hall, Bishop poured two cups of hot cider, before taking his seat at the head of the roundtable. Soon the doors to the hall opened, as Fox strutted through with a small limp, and a few scratches on the right side of his face.

"You have finally returned. Please sit, I have poured us some hot cider," said Bishop. Fox accepted the cup of hot cider and sat down next to Bishop.

Bishop gazed at the door expecting to see the other three men from Fox's team walk through the door any minute.

Sipping his hot cider, Fox broke the silence. "Is something wrong?"

"No I do not believe there is, I am just curious as to the whereabouts of the rest of your team. It is not like them to be this tardy."

"No I guess it isn't. I assure you they wouldn't be this tardy—if they were coming."

Bishop's eyes went straight to Fox. He had not heard of any news that Fox's mission went wrong in any way. If the other Agents had decided that it was acceptable to just postpone their report on the mission until the next day, they would soon find that they were mistaken. "And why aren't they coming?"

Fox took a sip of his hot cider before answering.

"When we arrived at Lord Egon's court, everything appeared to be fine. We were cared for and fed by Egon's people. I asked the Lord if he had any knowledge of any fugitive Necrosis or knew of anyone who had been seen reanimating any corpses. He assured me that this was the first time he had heard of any fugitive Necrosis. He also assured me that he would check with the Necroborns, who kept a residence under his care in his province, to make sure they had not heard of anything as well. He promised he would send word to you as soon as possible. On our last day there when we left, we were ambushed by fifty or so Necrosis on the roads miles from Egon's castle. We were too far away to return to his court for help and too far away from Kismet to seek help here. Unfortunately we were outnumbered, and once my last Agent fell, I knew I would soon be next. It seemed wise that getting word to you about the threat was more important than anything, so I fled."

Bishop studied the core of Fox's eyes deeply. He had no reason not to trust Fox's report. Fox had been under his command ever since he was young. He had given shelter and a safe haven to Fox after his people were killed in the massacre and his village destroyed. Fox had done many missions that most Agents would find unnerving; and he always kept discretion.

"Do you remember which direction the Necrosis attacked from?"

"No it was dark and we were setting up camp when they attacked. All I know is they were headed for Kismet," said Fox with a drop of his head.

"How many?"

"Hundreds sir," replied Fox. "I am sorry sir, I have failed you."

"No no you did not fail me Fox. On the contrary, I appreciate your wise thinking of fleeing to bring word to me, instead of taking your chances with those Necrosis. I know how much you like a battle that is tipped in your opponent's favor," smiled Bishop.

Fox returned the smile and finished the last drop of his hot cider. "Well if you don't mind sir, I am very tired and would fancy a hot bath."

"Of course of course. I will send word to Lord Egon and make sure he keeps his people off of the roads," replied Bishop. Fox got up from his seat and bid farewell to Bishop. Just as he was almost at the door, a hand grabbed his shoulder. Fox looked up into Bishop's eyes. "Good work out there Fox." Fox stared back for a moment before responding.

"Thank you sir. You can always count on me."

# THE FORGOTTEN FOREST

Eli was overwhelmed by the depth of the forest Zane had led him into, after leaving the comforts of the city. Millions of tall trees went on for miles in every direction further than the eye could see. There were so many trees, that after stumbling a few times, Eli found himself completely lost in the maze of nature that they had traveled through. As the sound of a distant owl let loose a hoot that made Eli's skin crawl and teeth chatter, he finally gave in to the inevitable truth that he was scared out of his mind.

"Are you sure you know where you're going?"

"Kind of," replied Zane. When Eli returned an alarmed expression, Zane quickly recovered with, "I do not need to know exactly how to get there, I just need to know the direction. Once we get close, we can just follow the music."

As Eli continued to follow Zane throughout the endless maze of trees, a sound broke his concentration. It sounded like a mixture of water, drums, wind and chimes. The combination of sounds was so staggering at first, but as the boys ventured closer into its grasp, Eli found himself empowered with more energy and excitement. When the two boys slowed their pace, they soon came across what appeared to be an extremely large tree that blocked their way. A large cloudbank hung low around the tree and gave it a sense of mystery. The height of the tree far surpassed the height of the others that Eli had seen along the way. On either side of it were a series of smaller trees that had more of an artificial texture than the rest of the forest. As Zane moved in closer, Eli's vision became more and more clouded as he followed. The fog was thick and vast. When Eli caught up with Zane, he was in complete shock when the ground around him began to rumble. The large tree in front of them submerged until there was no trace of it left.

"Here we are!" announced Zane.

The first thing that Eli noticed about the Forgotten Forest, was how large of an open space it was. Hundreds of trees perfectly outlined a large square and green meadow. Slightly hidden in their branches was an array of small shapeless lanterns that hung throughout every tree giving the meadow a slight glow. The music, that Eli had heard earlier, blasted loud in all directions and had no clear source. Dead in the center of the meadow was the largest tree trunk Eli had ever seen. The tree trunk was so tall and large, that it was impossible for Eli to see the top of it from where he was standing. Each individual piece of the trunk's medium-brown bark was as big as an average door to a house. Connected to the right side of the trunk was a staircase made out of the same wood as the trunk, which spiraled from ground level all the way to the top of the trunk's surface.

As Zane and Eli continued forward towards the trunk, Eli noticed a small river that began at the back of the meadow, and ended in a large lake right beside him. Dozens of people his age were crowding around the lake swimming, talking, and socializing. Eli thought he recognized a few from his class, but he could not be sure. On his left, Eli noticed a smaller segregated area with piles of large logs, wooden dummies, and large boulders. Many people also crowded this area socializing. When Eli looked closer, he noticed a small crowd circling around two guys that were fighting in a heated sword fight.

"Man what the heck!" Eli shouted pointing in the direction of the battle.

One of the fighters was tall and muscular with short messy brown hair. He was wearing dark shorts and a black long-sleeve shirt. In his right hand he carried a glowing purple sword and in his right a purple shield. Looking poised for battle, he charged at his opponent, driving his sword in the direction of his opponent's heart. His opponent parried with his sword with a backwards swing, knocking the brown-haired warrior off balance. His opponent wasted no time taking advantage of the opportunity and counter-attacked. The brown-haired warrior took the full force of the hit, tumbling backwards and landing flat on his back with a *thud*. The summoned shield and sword dissolved leaving no trace of their presence.

Eli and Zane took a closer look at the end result of the battle, and soon Eli noticed that the fighter's opponent was not human at all, but a wooden dummy. The detail of the dummy was so precise and accurate that it even appeared to have dimples and eyebrows. There appeared to be a sense of some sort of life emanating from the wooden figure. While the dummy retreated back to a line of four other similar figures, it went back into a ready stance, losing all sense of the liveliness that it once exuberated. The fighter returned to his feet, and was greeted by three other guys who patted him on his shoulders sharing a series of laughs and explosive gestures.

"Pretty awesome huh?" asked Zane.

"Well first of all, what was that thing he was fighting?"

"Pretty life-like huh? Compliments of Professor Vance. It's a dummy carved completely out of the wood from the trees that surround the city. Vance enchanted them with a spell that allows them to come somewhat to life and engage in battle. They are really awesome to practice against, but they are also really challenging. They are really advanced and have also been enchanted with a spell that allows them to learn different moves and techniques from opponents they face, and remember them for future battles against other opponents. I think the record for the longest someone has lasted in battle with them, is seventeen seconds," informed Zane.

"Seventeen seconds?"

"Hey those things may not look like it, but they kick some major ass," replied Zane.

"I bet I could last way longer than that."

"Yeah that's what all the victims say," replied Zane with a grin. "There is also a sparring field for people who want a sparring match, as well as these devilishly heavy tree trunks that people used to test their strength. I would not recommend the tree trunks. The first time I tried lifting one, I blacked out from the strain of overexerting myself. Those trunks are no joke," he informed with a worried expression on his face.

As the two boys headed back towards the large tree trunk that erupted from the center of the meadow, Eli realized it was taller than he had thought, and a lot wider as well.

"This is my favorite part of the Forgotten Forest," said Zane. Eli followed his friend as they climbed the wooden staircase along the side of the trunk. Countless stairs appeared in front of them as they climbed higher and higher. At one point Eli looked over the edge of the staircase and briefly succumbed to acrophobia. As the two boys finished the last few steps at the top of the large trunk, they were greeted with a breeze of fresh air that swept across their face. Tired from the journey up, Eli welcomed the breeze as it cooled his body down before departing.

"They call this place Inzanity," informed Zane. "They serve hot cider, mead, tea and a few off the menu items—if you know what I'm saying," he said winking.

The first thing that Eli noticed about Inzanity was the large circular rings on the surface of the tree trunk they were standing on. The rings in the middle were smaller and grew bigger the further away from the center they were. Inzanity was covered with trios of tree trunks. A medium sized trunk, which people were using for tables, was surrounded with two to four smaller trunks used for seats. Rows and rows of these set ups occupied Inzanity's grounds. As Eli and Zane walked through the many occupied tables, Eli became aware of a large wooden counter operated by a lone figure; with an assortment of the familiar trunks lined in front of it.

"I swear if you weren't my brother I would have incinerated you years ago," said a voice behind Eli.

Eli turned around to discover Meara standing before them. She was dressed in black pants with a matching shirt. A few pieces of jewelry hung from her neck and ears. Her hair hung neatly to the side.

"Nice to see you too," replied Zane.

Eli thought he noticed Meara give a smile his direction, but he figured he had to be seeing things since Meara always appeared to be scowling even when her voice sounded happy.

"I got us a table, and I have to say that both Sia and I believe that both of you need training in punctuality," said Meara leading them both to a secluded table on the edge of Inzanity's surface. When Meara took her seat next to Sia at their table, and Zane and Eli took their seats on the opposing side, Eli's eyes were immediately drawn to Sia; who had been gazing peacefully at the meadow beneath them. From what Eli could tell, Sia was wearing a tight-fitting dark green dress that made her bare shoulders look both smooth and delicate. Her hair sat whimsically contained in a neat ponytail across one of her bare shoulders. She looked more mature and sophisticated than he remembered. It was at that time that Eli realized how great a view Inzanity provided over the whole meadow. The silver moon shined bright within the clear and calm sky over their heads.

"Sia the tardies are finally here," said Meara. As Sia withdrew from her thoughts, she looked at Zane and Eli as if for the first time. Eli noticed her light purple eyes shining bright in the moonlight that covered their table.

"Sia what is up with your right eye, it's all puffy. You may need to lay off of the heavy makeup; and why are you so dressed up? You know no one is getting married right," said Meara.

"I do not wear heavy makeup," replied Sia. "It must be the stupid trees and plants around here; and don't worry about me, my emerald dress and I are just fine."

"Whatever," said Meara.

"Hi guys, I am glad to see you found the place okay," said Sia.

"Nice to see you too Sia. How have you been?" asked Zane.

Sia took a beat before answering. "I have been content, and yourself?"

"Same I guess."

Eli could not keep his eyes off of Sia. He felt creepy. Every time he saw her, she looked more and more beautiful than he remembered. Her amazing eyes and delicately small pink lips only outmatched her clear and flawless face. As his eyes traced every inch of her face from her lips down to her chin, and finally to her neck and shoulders, he finally returned to her light purple eyes that were staring effortlessly back at him.

*Oh shoot. Was I staring at her? Did she say something to me?*

"I'm sorry did you say something," asked Eli to Sia.

"No. I thought you were going to say something since you have been looking my direction for a little while now."

*Crap she noticed.*

"Oh I was? I'm sorry I was lost in thought." Eli looked over at Meara and Zane to see if they had noticed as well, and to his relief, they were both looking at a menu.

"May I ask you what you were thinking about?" asked Sia. Caught off guard, Eli scrambled for something, anything he could say he was thinking of besides the truth. He knew he always had a habit of saying the wrong thing to Sia before, and it always ended with her being put off by his comment. The last thing he wanted to do was tell her that he had been admiring her and thought she looked more beautiful than any goddess he had ever heard of.

"I'd rather not say," he replied.

Looking taken back, Sia's only response was, "Oh."

*Stupid! Stupid! What's wrong with you! Why not just tell her to jump off this tree why don't you!*

"So what will you be having?" asked Meara towards Eli.

"What do you mean?"

"For a drink. Zane and I were going to treat the first round."

"He will have the Liar's Poison," replied Zane for him with a grin. Both Meara and Zane smirked at each other.

"What about you Sia?" asked Zane.

"I'll just have a Doppelganger," replied Sia.

"You always get the Doppelganger. How boring," said Meara.

"Hey, I need to make sure everything on me is kept in check."

"You're at Inzanity and out with your friends. Let your hair down," said Meara.

"It *is* down," said Sia holding her ponytail up. "See."

"You know what I mean."

"Wait what's a Liar's Poison," asked Eli.

"You'll see," said Meara and Zane simultaneously as they both stood up from the table and headed over to the counter he had seen earlier.

"Aren't you in for a treat," said Sia with a smile.

"Why is that?"

"I would rather not say. It would ruin the surprise."

Sia's eyes seemed to wash over him examining every inch of his face. If anyone else had been looking at him as hard as she was, Eli would have felt uncomfortable; however with her, he felt calm and content under her gaze.

"Does your face normally change colors like that?" asked Sia.

"My face is changing colors?"

"Yes it goes from normal to pink, then back to normal—every now and then."

*Crap*

"Um no it usually doesn't, it must be the trees."

"Are you allergic to them?" asked Sia.

"No. No I don't think so."

"Ok then," she replied with a smile. Eli watched Sia as she ran her small fingertips over the top of one of her smooth bare shoulders. "So, Eli."

"Yeah."

"Do you have a last name?"

"Brassie," he said feeling confused.

"Sounds some-what familiar. Brassie, does that name come from some sort of legendary warrior?"

"No clue. No one has ever asked me that before."

"Oh, my apologies. I did not mean to offend you in any way," she said.

"What about yours?"

"Wyatt? It comes from one of the ancient tomb keepers that used to watch over hallowed land. Our family tree is filled with many respectable and honorable ancestors that were entrusted with the safekeeping of sacred knowledge."

"Oh."

"My great, great, great grandfather also fought in the War of the Heavens, and was an honorable Operative that was instrumental in the salvation of many lives," she continued.

"The War of the Heavens?"

"Yes, the war between Anim and the Three Brothers," she said.

"Oh that."

"I am assuming that you know it, right? I mean everyone does," said Sia beginning to giggle.

"Yeah I heard of it. Doesn't mean I believe in all of that mess." Both tension and silence seemed to descend upon the table. A few seconds later, Zane and Meara returned with four brown ceramic cups in the shape of tree trunks. As Zane handed Eli his cup, Eli quickly examined it closely, before smelling it. He had never heard of a 'Liar's Poison' before, and he was sure that no one there was going to tell him what it was.

"Let's propose a toast," announced Meara holding up her cup.

"To you finally brushing your teeth?" replied Zane with a smirk.

"Don't make me give you the back of my hand," said Meara.

"Whatever. Lets propose a toast to having a great night filled with hasty comments, regretful actions, and a great time!" announced Zane. When all four of their glasses touched, Eli tried to decipher the meaning behind Zane's toast.

"Bottoms up!" said Meara downing a portion of her drink. When Eli, Zane and Sia followed, Eli was relieved that his drink actually tasted good. It tasted like a mixture of berries, honey and herbs. As he continued to drink more, he noticed that his anxiety disappeared almost instantly—and for the first time—he felt like he was having a good time.

"Shall we have a waiter bring us cards so we can play number?" asked Zane.

"What's number?" asked Eli.

"It's a card game. Basically everyone picks a random number between one and twenty-five and writes it down on a piece of paper that gets flipped down. No one tells the other players their number. One random card from the deck is placed in the middle of the table along with a piece of paper that depicts what the current number of the center is, and each person is dealt four cards. The object of the game is to get the number in the center to equal the random number you wrote on your piece of paper. Red numbers subtract from the total and black numbers add. You can only place one card down at a time, but if you decide to draw a card from the deck instead of playing a card, you can go twice the next turn. It's a game for thinkers basically," said Meara.

*Sounds like a game for Jude.*

"It sounds difficult, but it is actually fun once you get the hang of it. Usually people bet money. If you play that way you have to put in money equal to the number you picked," said Zane.

Eli tried to go over the rules and object of the game in his head, but found himself getting a headache. "Hmm maybe next time."

"Good choice," started Sia with a wink. "I think they are trying to take advantage of you."

"We are not!" said Meara and Zane in perfect unison. The four of them talked about training and an upcoming Academy examination called the Trials of Magic, Might and Lineage that Eli was unaware of. He did not ask for any further explanation on the exam, he was not here to talk about training or his crazy mentor Professor Ivor. As more and more time passed, he noticed that Meara's face turned from dark green to dark blue, then to hot pink and back to normal—within a span of two minutes.

"Okay it's official, I have been drugged and you guys plan on taking advantage of me," said Eli. The whole table erupted into laughter.

"What are you talking about?" asked Zane still laughing.

"Meara's face keeps changing colors, and if I am the only one seeing it, then I'm assuming it's because of my drink. What's in it?"

"Oh yeah her drink does that to her. She ordered the Bamboozle. It changes the color of her face based on her mood or her reaction to the conversation," informed Zane.

Eli was instantly embarrassed. "Why would you drink something that changed the color of your face like that?"

"Because it's the bamboozle!" yelled Meara.

"Oh no we have lost her," replied Sia smiling.

"Speaking of 'bamboozle," began Zane. "There are some lookers around here!"

"Speaking of lookers," said Meara with a grin. Eli do you like anyone at the Academy?" Eli was caught off guard by her question, but did not think that anyone had noticed. He knew that no one but Zane knew about his feelings for Sia, and he wanted it to stay that way.

"Nope no one besides Sia," he replied. Just as the words left his mouth, his eyes widened and heart stopped.

*What the heck? Why did I say that?*

Sia's eyes widened as her cup stood frozen in mid-air awaiting a sip. Zane and Meara erupted into laughter.

"I'm sorry. I don't know why I said that," said Eli.

"Because it's true!" replied Meara. Eli felt himself blush.

"It's okay buddy, everyone knows Sia's a looker," said Zane giving Sia a wink, who replied with a glare.

"A looker? She's the most beautiful woman I have ever seen," replied Eli feeling insulted. Meara choked on her drink before erupting into more laughter followed by Zane.

*What the heck is wrong with me? I need some fresh air!*

"If you will excuse me. I am going to get some fresh air to help stop me from sharing any more intimate feelings about Sia," said Eli. His eyes widened before he sped off nearly tripping over Zane's chair. He could hear Meara and Zane laughing hysterically behind him. As he walked back up to the counter people were getting drinks from, he hastily leaned over the counter.

"Excuse me!" he yelled at the gentleman working the counter. The man was wearing a fire-red tunic and black pants.

"What can I do for you?" the man replied.

"What's in the Liar's Posion?"

The man let loose a small chuckle before replying. "Virgin to the world of Inzanity drinks are we? Liar's Poison temporarily makes you incapable of lying or beating around the bush on anything you say. In other words, your brain and heart are an open book!"

Eli's stomach sunk as he stared at the man who had just returned from serving drinks to a couple. Desperate to get out of the view of Sia, who he was sure was repulsed by him and embarrassed by his announcements, Eli ran for the stairs that led down to the meadow. When he got to the bottom, he headed passed a small patch of trimmed grass where people were dancing. One girl kept curling her finger at him trying to get him to join her on the dance floor, but Eli kept towards the lake. He was positive the girl's dress was not only inside out, but also backwards. He took one last look at her face and noticed her tongue was putting in extensive overtime in moistening her lips.

The lake's dark surface soon calmed as many people retreated from its depths and camped out along its shore to dry off. Eli found a secluded spot away from most of the crowd and sat down with his knees curled up.

*Why would Zane make me drink something like that knowing what it would do? What an idiot! Freaking idiot! I am going to have a few words with that guy tomorrow.*

When his mind began to clear, Eli found himself tapping his foot to the music that was playing overhead. The music they played in the Forgotten Forest was so catchy, that Eli wondered if he was subconsciously always partying along to the music. After a few moments, a figure sat down beside him.

"Care for company?" asked Sia.

Eli's heart skipped a beat as his mouth opened but no words came out. When Sia took a seat next to him, Eli was even more aware of the soft curves of her face. The moon's light danced in her eyes as the purple in them went from light to dark, and back to light again.

"Sure."

"You know there is something about the water that makes me feel calm and at ease. It has a healing essence to it."

"It does," started Eli. "It helps me think when I have a lot on my mind."

Sia took a look towards the area where everyone was dancing and then back to Eli. "You know everyone looks like they are having a pretty fun time over there."

Eli kept his focus on the lake's calm surface before him. "I know. I'm sorry if I'm not as fun to be around."

"Wow, how embarrassing," she replied.

"What is?"

Sia began looking around hastily, as if she was desperate to find something. "I was hoping you would ask me to dance."

Eli became confused by the conversation they were having. "Why not just ask me instead of dropping hints?"

"*Me* ask *you*?"

The conversation felt stale and pointless, and Eli soon found himself wishing that he was at home under the secure covers of his bed. "Nevermind."

"It's fine, you do not have to ask me to dance if —."

"Would you like to dance?" he asked quickly. Eli stood up and reached out for her hand. She took it and followed him to the dance floor. More people than he remembered were having a good time dancing along to the catchy music that ran infinitely throughout the meadow's air. Sia pulled Eli towards the center of the dance floor. He thought she moved beautifully as she held her arms over her head and circled him, while moving to the beat around them. Eli tried his best to keep up, but found himself extremely self-conscious. He figured Sia could sense his apprehension because she soon slowed down, grabbing both his hands, and guiding him through an easier and slower-paced dance. Before long he found himself laughing and dancing with Sia without any care for who was watching. To him she appeared to be having just as much fun as he was, and that comforted him. He soon forgot about his awkward announcement of his feelings for her, and soon fell into the hypnotic rhythm that the crowd was immersed in.

◆◆◆

Eli was glad that Sia was more knowledgeable about how to get back to the city. He was sure that he would get them completely lost if she was as clueless as he was. Sia had decided to head home because she wanted to get a good night's sleep before training the next day. Eli was faced with a decision to either return to his table with Zane and Meara, or walk back with Sia. He was proud of himself for having the nerve to volunteer to walk her home. The two of them talked about many things on the way back to the city. Eli asked Sia about the Trials of Magic, Might and Lineage. He was alarmed when he found out that it was in a few days, and that the examination pitted all three bloodlines against each other to see who was ready to join the armed forces as a Bloodline Agent.

"I have a lot of training to do then. Why didn't Professor Ivor tell me about this exam? I mean it's a pretty important thing to tell everyone."

"It's because it's supposed to be a surprise. I only found out because my father used to be a Professor, and he told me that he had heard talk of it around the Academy," replied Sia.

"Wow your dad must be a pretty important person."

Sia kept her expression vague and emotionless.

"Something like that."

"Are you nervous about the exam?"

"What is there to be nervous about?" she said.

"I don't know. Maybe losing."

"The Trials are not about who wins and who loses. They are about earning honor for yourself. Those who do not pass are the ones that are not ready or worthy to fight for our people. If you do not pass, then you should not be upset that you are not an Agent; you should be upset that you did not train as much as you should have. I mean if you are not in the Trials to gain honor, then why are you in the Trials at all? What is your purpose?"

Eli was taken back by her answer and even more confused by the shift in her mood. Sia was beautiful and wonderful to be around; but at times he felt like she was also harsh and distant. It was hard for him to believe that someone so beautiful could be so cold sometimes.

"Oh no! She was right! And she made an announcement in front of everyone! That hyena!"

"Huh?" asked Eli feeling confused again. He looked over to find Sia looking sternly into her small mirror as she padded the area under her eyes with her finger.

"Nothing," she said putting the mirror away. "Sorry, I am just tired." While Sia went on about some of the different Trials of Magic, Might and Lineage the Academy had hosted in the past, a cold shiver fell on him. He found himself looking behind him constantly while trying to pay attention to what Sia was saying. Just as she finished her sentence, Eli heard the snap of a branch behind them, and instantly jerked around. Sia grabbed his shoulder and turned him back around, while pushing him to keep walking.

"Yes we are being followed," she whispered. "I do not know who they are or how many of them there are, but I have been smelling a foreign odor the past few minutes, which seems to be trailing us."

Eli was both anxious and alarmed. The first thing that came to mind was what weapon he should summon. His first idea was his blade since it would prove to be effective at close range. However he didn't know how many enemies there were, and did not want to risk being surrounded; so he figured a bow might be more appropriate. He figured with the bow he could pick off a large number of enemies faster before they had a chance to reach him. Just before he could make a decision, he was shoved face first to the floor beneath him. Leaves and mud were instantly shoved into his mouth as he came crashing down.

"On your right!" screamed Sia.

Eli looked up to see what appeared to be a group of men charging for them. Eli closed his eyes and threw out his hand. When he opened his eyes, a bow materialized before him and hovered in midair. He snatched the bow and then met the enemies' charge with a charge of his own. When he got closer he discovered that some of the men were missing eyes and limbs. That was when he realized that these were not men, but Necrosis. Eli fired countless arrows exploding the head of the closest Necrosis, and impaling the one next to it to a nearby tree. Growls and snarls hissed from their mangled and decomposed mouths and soon one by one they fell to Eli's bow.

The ground suddenly shook violently causing Eli to fall to his feet. His bow dissolved from his hand, as he rolled uncontrollably across the forest, and crashed into a nearby tree. He looked up quickly to catch Sia surrounded by a horde of Necrosis. She stood motionless while the horde charged her.

*How could I leave her like that?*

Sia's eyes opened suddenly, and instantly turned from light purple to dark. Her small pale hand pushed the air in front of her, causing the Necrosis to be propelled back. Spears of rock pierced the floor just in time to skewer the Necrosis in place, bringing Eli front and center to a line of suspended bodies, hanging motionlessly in the spot they once threatened.

Eli quickly returned to Sia's side frantic with panic.

"Are you okay?"

"Yes. I am okay," she replied.

Just as she smiled, Eli saw a dark figure appear behind her. Sia let loose a scream as a stray Necrosis grabbed her from behind and brought his fangs down for a bite.

Suddenly the Necrosis stood motionless with its fangs no more than an inch from Sia's neck. A purple arrow was buried deep between his eyes. Blood flowed from the arrow and dripped slowly down Sia's soft pale neck. Eli was unaware of what had happened until the Necrosis collapsed to the forest ground, and that was when Eli noticed his out-stretched hand. He didn't remember moving his hand. The last thing he remembered was Sia screaming and the horrific sight of the creature attacking her. He soon felt Sia's presence beside him as her soft hand grabbed his wrist, and pulled it back down to his side.

"We need to report this to Bishop and The Council at once. There may be more," she said. Speechless, Eli simply nodded, and the two of them continued towards the city. Both of them remained as silent as the night around them.

The walk back from the Forgotten Forest seemed far shorter than the walk to get there. Both relief and sorrow swarmed inside Eli when the familiar cloudbank, leading up to the city's sturdy white-stoned walls, came into view. Eli was happy to be out of the forest after the recent attack, however he was disappointed that his night with Sia would soon be over.

Eli and Sia went straight to the castle after returning to the city. Long royal blue banners fell from the castle's walls embroidered with the land's insignia. The insignia always confused Eli every time he crossed its path. After constant interrogation by the castle's guards as to why they needed an audience with Bishop at such a late hour, Eli and Sia soon became discouraged and gave up on convincing the guards. As they were halfway down the castle's stairs, Eli heard the doors to the castle open.

"Good evening my friends," said a voice. Eli turned around to see Lord Bishop standing in the entryway to the castle. Eli was elated to see Bishop, and hoped he would not be cross with him for disturbing him so late in the night.

"I told them they would have to come back at a decent hour," said the guard that declined Eli's request to see Bishop.

"My door is always open for anyone who needs to see me. Please remember that Sho," said Bishop.

"Yes my Lord."

Bishop ushered in Eli and Sia into the castle. As the three of them took their seats in the sitting room outside of Bishop's chambers, Eli marveled at its décor. It was a large square room with white walls, red curtains, and a large single glass window that led out to a terrace. Dozens of bookcases, filled to the max with assorted books, outlined the walls of the room. Three fire-red couches surrounded a dark cherry wood coffee table. Sia and Eli sat on one of the couches and Bishop soon joined them on the opposing couch. On the table sat a white ceramic teapot with four matching teacups, along with a glass chess set that appeared to have been recently used.

"Can I get you some tea?" asked Bishop. His face was content and his voice heavy.

"Yes please," replied Sia. Eli nodded when Bishop came to him teapot in hand.

"Were you in the middle of a game sir?"

"I actually was my boy," said Bishop.

"Who were you playing against?" asked Eli.

"Myself my dear boy."

"Why do you play against yourself? I'm sure there are plenty of people in the castle that you could play against."

"Because it takes a disciplined and skillful player to be able to outsmart themselves," replied Bishop. Eli thought about Bishop's words for a moment. "Do you play?"

"No, but my father does. He tries to teach me when I'm not training."

"Ah your father is probably one of my greatest opponents," Bishop replied with a smile.

"You and my dad play chess together?"

"We sure do. Your father is one of my best friends. We used to go on countless missions together." Eli remembered his dad telling him that him and Bishop used to go on missions together, and that it was Bishop who helped Marius tell his mom how he felt.

"Yeah he told me. He also told me you knew my mother too."

Grief showed on Bishop's face before he spoke. "I did. Mya was a beautiful woman and fierce Operative. She had the hearts of many men including your dad. However your dad was the only one that had her heart."

Eli took a sip of his tea.

"Sir, Eli and I were attacked this evening in the Forgotten Forest," informed Sia.

Bishop's eyes widened as he placed his cup on the table. "Attacked? By whom my dear?"

"By a small group of Necrosis," replied Eli.

"My goodness are you two okay?"

"Yes sir, we were able to dispose of them, but if there were more of them, I am not sure how lucky we would have been," said Sia.

Bishop stood up from his seat on the couch and paced across the room briefly. He soon came back hovering over the chess set. He moved one of the pawns forward so it was threatening an opposing rook, before taking his seat. "I am grateful that you two are okay and no harm came to you. I am also grateful that you reported news of this to me as soon as possible. I am pretty sure that the two of you have heard of the first incident we have had with these creatures and a woman. I was hoping that the first incident was just an anomaly, however I can no longer support that theory. You both have my word that this will be handled. I cannot have the safety of my people in jeopardy."

"Thank you sir. We just wanted to make sure you were aware just in case there are more," replied Sia.

"I will dispatch Agents at once to root out any other Necrosis and dispose of them. I *will* get to the bottom of this—you have my word."

Both Eli and Sia declined when Bishop offered to have a few guards escort them home. Since they were within the city's comforting walls, the two of them felt they would be able to handle the walk back home. Eli and Sia were surprised but comforted when Bishop hugged both of them and told them that he was happy that they were safe. After exchanging farewells, Eli and Sia headed towards the Eastern Hold. The night was cluttered with bits of the cloudbank that spilled through the cracks of the city's walls. Clouds partially covered the face of the moon when Sia's house came into view. When Eli walked Sia up to her door, the realization that he may never hang out with her again, dawned on him—and he soon succumbed to sorrow. He looked down at her face. Her eyes carried an exhaustion that he knew matched his.

"Well thank you for walking me home," she said.

"You're welcome Sia," he replied. He could feel the sadness in his own voice.

"What's wrong?"

"Nothing. Why would anything be wrong?" Her eyes examined every inch of his face before returning to the sadness that filled his eyes. "It's just despite that one incident with the

Necrosis, I had a good time tonight. I think I am just disappointed that it's over—that's all," he said.

When Sia opened her mouth to respond, Eli found himself soaring through the air before crashing down into the cobblestones that filled the streets. A hot pain filled his arm as he tried to regain his composure and return to his feet. He looked up to see a large pale man with a black tunic and matching pants staring down at him.

"Daddy what are you doing!" screamed Sia as she looked on in horror. Eli felt a heavy pressure inside of him when his feet left the ground making him hover further away. When the large man clenched his fist, an icy-cold pain erupted throughout Eli's entire body, and soon his body began to convulse. His head jerked up from the pain, and for the next few moments, the cloudy sky was all that swept across his vision, as tears streamed down his face.

"Daddy stop!" Sia screamed as she began to beat on his shoulder.

"How dare you lay a hand on my daughter you filth!" the man said. His voice sounded proper and clear, but lined with a sharpness that was both intimidating and terrifying. Eli fought through the pain, as he forced his gaze towards Sia.

"Daddy it wasn't him! We were—." Sia was unable to finish her sentence before she was lifted off the ground by an invisible force, and hurled into the house—the door slamming closed behind her.

"I didn't. I swear," was all that came out of Eli's mouth while the convulsions increased, along with the pain that came with them.

"Don't—lie—to me! If you ever come anywhere near my daughter again, I swear I will skin you alive," replied the man before flicking his wrist, and tossing Eli into the door of the neighboring home.

When Eli hit the ground, the convulsions stopped. He staggered to his feet, and quickly gazed at Sia's door hoping to see some trace of her. All he saw was the glow of her porch light and a lone fly that hovered aimlessly around it.

The site of the Lin Kitz statue embraced Eli with warmth and comfort. The night was full of so many ups and downs, that Eli felt himself mentally exhausted after the night he endured. Walking up to the statue, he took in its entirety. Smooth white stone sat carved in unmatchable perfection, into the shape of one of Kismet's most admirable and powerful Operatives. Both hands wielded one of his blades of legend, and stood ready in front of him. His infamous bow, which some say always stayed summoned to his back even when he was not in battle, was carved with a brilliance that made Eli marvel.

Turning for home, Eli wondered what it would be like to have his statue amongst Kismet's greatest warriors, with his many accomplishments carved at the base. His head looked up towards his house, and his adrenaline instantly made him anticipate battle. A lone figure stood motionless outside of his house, staring into one of the living room windows.

"Hey! What are you doing?" yelled Eli.

The figure turned around with a slowness that gave Eli his own confirmation, that the figure was an enemy.

"Only what fate has commanded me to do," said the figure acknowledging Eli. His voice was hollow and enigmatic, but his lips never moved. He was younger than Eli, maybe sixteen from what Eli could tell. His tangled white hair hovered slightly over his shoulders while his skinny and small frame, barely kept the rags and hood he wore from falling. His hands never left his un-visible pockets.

*I must be seeing things.*

"Are you the stranger I will soon know oh so well?" asked the stranger. His lips remained still through every word he spoke.

Eli felt his brain tell him to either run or attack. He did neither. Instead he found himself lost in the utter darkness that was the stranger's eyes. Every inch of the stranger's eyes was completely black, void of any mortality whatsoever.

"You're a Necroborn. I can tell by your eyes. What are you doing here?" asked Eli.

The stranger returned his gaze to one of Eli's living room windows. A small smile crept across his face. "Just one card is all I need, to bring this city to its knees. Just one card is all I need, to return this city to its glory."

"What are you doing outside of my house? Why don't your lips move when you talk?" asked Eli.

The stranger's head tilted slowly, keeping his gaze glued to Eli. "It is in the cards, that this will soon be my home. It is in the cards, that this will soon be my city. It is in the cards, that you and I shall meet on the battlefield."

Eli felt his pulse quicken. The way the stranger delivered each and every word without moving his lips was chilling. Eli turned around, searching frantically for any Agents or soldiers, even Erudites, that he could alert of the stranger. The streets were dark and bare, and void of any life. Eli returned his gaze to the stranger and saw his house instead. His eyes searched around desperately for the whereabouts of the stranger, but found nothing but empty cold air all around him. Eli felt nervous and vulnerable. He felt like he was seven years old again, and a monster was on the prowl, ready to strike when he least expected. He ran for his front door, placed his key in the lock, and looked over his shoulder.

# ADVERSARY
# OR ALLY

Jude had gone straight to the Academy from the watering hole, the morning after hanging out with Jed. He was happy that he had made an effort to hang out with his brother that night, and he felt that their bond was stronger than ever. On the other hand, he scolded himself for forgetting to thank the gods for his victory over Professor Lynn, the previous day. He said a quick prayer thanking the Three Brothers for watching over him, and again asked them to watch over his family, friends and Kismet. His mother flashed in front of his vision for a few seconds. He felt himself frown at her face. The more he thought about her, the angrier he got.

Professor Lynn had done a lecture on the art of human blood. Jude had learned that when taking on the form of another human, that any abilities acquired are not as strong as the original's. What Jude was most interested in, was Lynn's lecture on transformations without vials, which seemed to catch the attention of his peers as well. Lynn talked about how even after a transformation, the blood of the last person or creature you had transformed into, lingers in the blood making it possible to transform back into that form without an additional vial. She also explained how when a Combat Specialist is close to death, the body automatically transforms into the most powerful form it was subjected to. Lynn said the scholars refer to it as, "The Beast Before Death." Jude was quick to raise his hand to this.

"Yes Jude," asked Lynn.

"So what if you transformed into lets say a dragon only once in your life, and it was years ago. Would your body automatically transform into a dragon when you are severely injured, if that was the strongest creature you had ever turned into?"

"That is correct. It is unknown why, but our bloodline in particular has a survival instinct to it, that tends to always fight to stay alive. Because of this, when a Combat Specialist is turned into its most powerful form, due to the severity of his or her injuries, instinct takes over and it can be difficult to distinguish friend from foe," informed Lynn.

"What if someone breaks your neck or stabs you in the heart? Something that would normally automatically kill someone, will you still transform, or just die?" asked another student.

"I really do not like to get too far into talking about death all the time. Hopefully this will never happen to any of you. However, to answer your question, any injuries that are absolutely fatal will automatically kill you like they would any other person," replied Lynn.

Jude's class was given a homework assignment to go out into the surrounding forest and study the movements of their favorite transformation. Lynn believed that they would better understand how to move and attack as the creatures they transformed into. Jude had been way ahead of the class, and had been studying the nature and movement of many insects and animals the past couple of days. He found out that his favorite was the forest spider that was native to their lands. He found the creature to be quick, cunning, and powerful. His second favorite had to be a black raven that he found perched in a tree. After spending a few days flying with it, Jude mastered the agility and movement the bird possessed.

After class, Jude had went to Eli's house to hang out and tell him what he had learned from his brother, in regards to his mom. He was still upset about it and needed someone to talk to. He was shocked when Eli's dad told him that Eli had went to a party in the Forgotten Forest. Eli and Jude had always done everything together, and this was definitely the first time that Eli had not at least invited him to an event or party he was going to. Jude figured that it had probably slipped his mind or there was some sort of logical explanation so he didn't worry about it. He left word with Eli's dad that he would come over in the morning to walk with Eli to school, and then he headed for home.

With Eli out at a party, and Jed busy for the night, Jude decided to spend the night training. He snuck in the back door in an attempt to avoid seeing his mother, and was relieved when he realized she was not home. After locking himself in his room, Jude experimented with mixing the blood of different specimens. After a few hours of trial and error, he was excited with his results. Turning in for the night, Jude was again haunted by night terrors that would carry on throughout the night.

◆◆◆

Jude awoke to a knock at his bedroom door. He knew it was his mom and decided to pretend he was still asleep. As the door slammed open, he nearly fell out of the bed, in an attempt to see what made the noise.

"So now you are ignoring me!" yelled his mom after entering his room. "So—disrespectful."

Ignoring her, Jude got out of bed and retreated to his washroom, closing the door behind him. He was surprised when his mom followed him inside. "What are you doing? I am in the washroom!"

"What are *you* doing? I am talking to you!" yelled Aileen.

"I don't feel like talking."

"You don't feel like talking? What has gotten into you? First you don't come home after hanging out with your brother, and then I don't see you all day. And now that I finally get a chance to talk to you after all of my worrying, your response is, 'I don't feel like talking.' Am I dreaming?" said Aileen with a scowl on her face.

"You lied to me!" exclaimed Jude turning to his mom. "You told me that Jed did not want to be a part of our family. You kept my only brother away from me for years. How could you? He is my only brother! I kill myself training every day and every night to become an Agent to protect you. To bring in an income so you do not have to work such long hours at the library every day. I do it all for you and Jed."

Aileen stood unresponsive as she pushed back the sleeves on her shirt. "I didn't lie to you. He doesn't want to be a part of our family; you see how he barely comes by here anymore. He is selfish. He doesn't need us anymore now that he is a monster."

Jude was speechless to see this side of his mother. She had always been so loving, caring and kind around him. She had always been there to tuck him in at night when he was a child, always was there to help him with his homework, and was always there to offer love and support in his time of need. Now she was standing in front of him calling his only brother, who he loved tremendously, a 'monster.'

Jude glared at his mother, anger rushing through him. "I wonder what else you have lied to me about. Are you even my real mother? Maybe I am adopted. Did father really die or did you chase him away too? Jed is not the monster, you are!" said Jude.

"Disrespectful!"

Jude was caught off guard as Aileen raised her hand and slapped him hard across his face. His ears rang for a few seconds. His mom had never hit him, even when he was a child. Jude had always followed all of the rules and always loved and respected his mother, until this moment.

The two of them stood frozen staring at each other, fearful to make any sudden movements. Jude put on his black tunic, grabbed his books, and exited the room—all without saying a word. As soon as the door to his house slammed closed behind him and the fresh air blew across his face, a tear dropped from his eye. As he quickly made his way towards Eli's house, he had already made up his mind that he was not coming back home, at least not for a while.

The sight of Eli's house brought comfort when Jude knocked on the door. Eli answered the door with a 'Don't ask' expression on his face.

"Ready?"

"As ready as I'll ever be," replied Eli.

Jude told Eli about the night he had spent with his brother. He was comforted to see that his friend was both interested and concerned about the things that they had talked about.

"Wow man that's tough! I'm sorry to hear that," replied Eli. "Have you talked to her about it yet?"

"Yes, our conversation erupted into an argument that ended with a slap across the face."

Eli's eyes widened. "Well if it makes you feel better, I finally got a smidgen of revenge on Will Keating."

"Wait what?"

"Will Keating has apparently been in my class these past few months. Anyways Ivor made me pair up with him in a sparring exercise. He was of course as crazy as you told me, so I decided to check him," said Eli.

"Check him?"

"Yeah, you know—teach him a lesson."

Jude thought about Eli's words, and began to teeter on the balance of feeling relieved or ashamed at what Eli had told him.

*I know I should not find joy in the suffering of someone who used to be such a dear friend of mine. But I cannot help but feel happy that some sort of justice has at least been attempted. I just do not understand how the gods can reward the evil.*

"I'll take your silence as a silent 'thank you,'" said Eli grinning. He rubbed his hands together quickly before returning them to his side.

"So, how was the party?"

"What party?" asked Eli. Jude looked at Eli confused by his response.

*What does he mean 'what party?'*

"The party in the Forgotten Forest."

"Oh yeah I was invited by my friend Zane, but I didn't go," replied Eli.

Jude was blown away that Eli had just lied about going to the party. He felt it was such a dumb thing to lie about, and was shocked that Eli, of all people, would lie to him. "Wow two for two."

"What?" asked Eli.

"Nothing."

Eli tried to make idle conversation with Jude on their way to the Academy, but Jude was not in a talkative mood after the morning he endured.

*Wow first my mom and now Eli. I wonder who else has lied to me.*

As the Academy's familiar statue came into view, Jude quickened his pace yelling, "See you later" to Eli, as he departed.

He headed to the library to do some research on creatures native to their lands that he was not familiar with. When he arrived, he was not surprised to see that the library was completely empty, except for a few stragglers. He knew today was his mom's day off from work; so that was at least one thing he did not need to worry about.

After searching through row after row of books on various creatures, one book titled: *Hybrids for Hire* caught his eye.

After glancing at a few pages, Jude decided to take that book and another titled: *Vial Customization*. He found a seat at a table close by the largest window in the library, and began reading the book on hybrids. The book was mostly a history book to his distaste. He was seconds away from giving up on the book, until he reached a section in the book titled: "Chapter 9 – Dual Transformations."

*BINGO!*

After gathering all of the notes he needed on the subject, he closed the book and set it aside.

"If I had your bloodline, I would check that book out," said a voice a few seats down from him.

Jude was so preoccupied with the book he was reading, that he was unaware of the stranger sitting next to him. The boy looked a year or two older than Jude. He had short black hair and wore a blood-red tunic with black pants. The arm holding the book the stranger was reading, looked like it was three times the size of Jude's arm. However, what immediately caught Jude's attention was the series of scars that trailed the stranger's neck and knuckles. They looked both painful and smooth at the same time.

"I'm sorry?"

"I said if I had your bloodline I would check that book out," repeated the stranger. His voice was rough and conflicting, resembling grinding stones one minute, and echoing caves the next.

"And why is that?"

"Because," said the stranger.

An awkward silence hung in the air as Jude thought whether or not to take the stranger's advice. He decided it could not hurt. "So what kind of blood do you have?"

"Red blood."

*Man I feel like I'm talking to Jed right now.*

"Well thanks for the advice," said Jude gathering his belongings and heading for the front counter.

He ended up checking out both books, and as he was halfway out of the library doors, he took a look over his shoulder towards the spot where the stranger was sitting, and noticed he was gone.

*Now I really feel like I was talking to Jed.*

The next day, the cloudbank filled the streets, giving them a haunting look. The skies were clear and the sun shined bright, clearing out some of the fog that inhabited the city. Jude had decided to head straight to the Academy after spending a restless night at the watering hole.

The loud commotion of the class, along with Bree's excessive poking, was what initially woke him from his nap. After a few minutes of idle chit chat with Bree, Jude was quick to notice that the class should have started over ten minutes ago, and Lynn was no where to be seen. The doors of the hall opened as a lone figure stepped through the entryway.

"Finally, I wonder what took her so long," said Bree.

"I get the feeling that this is not Professor Lynn," replied Jude.

The lone figure carried no books or belongings, but took a seat in the very first desk in one of the front corners of the classroom. It was the same guy Jude had seen in the library a few days ago.

"Who's that nut job?" whispered Bree.

"I don't know, I briefly saw him in the library a few days ago. I couldn't quite read him," replied Jude.

"That's because you're a guy," replied Bree before getting up from her seat and strutting over to the stranger's desk. After a few seconds, she quickly stomped back towards her seat with both arms at her side, and her hands balled up into fists. After plopping herself down into her seat, she crossed her arms and began to mumble under her breath.

"Well what happened?"

"He's a freaking lunatic, that's what happened," yelled Bree out loud. A few students turned around at her outburst, but they soon returned to their conversation. After a few moments, Professor Lynn came barreling through the doors, slamming them behind her. She took her position at the front of the class before speaking.

"I apologize for my tardiness. I am afraid we will not be having any lecture or training today. Lord Bishop has some grave news and has instructed an emergency gathering with everyone in the land of Kismet," informed Lynn. Many confused looks swept across the hall, followed by small commotion. Lynn ushered the class out of the hall and towards the castle. The class walked in straight lines next to students of both Magi Hall and Master Hall.

"What do you think is going on?" asked Bree.

"I don't know."

On the way to the castle, Jude observed thousands of people pouring in from all over the city. Men, women and children all joined the massive group of followers that frantically headed for the castle's gates. After reaching the courtyard in front of the castle, dozens of soldiers outlined the outer edges of the courtyard and all exits. Worry began to swim inside Jude as he desperately ravaged his mind for any clue as to what could be happening. Bree had found her mom and quickly abandoned Jude to meet her. Jude did not even attempt to look for Aileen. For one, he did not want to see her—and even if he wanted to— he believed it would be nearly impossible to find her in the massive ocean of people he was standing in. The commotion of the assembly was so loud and frantic, that it appeared that everyone was speaking in another language.

"Enjoying the chaos?" said a voice next to Jude.

Jude turned around to find Jed standing next to him. "You're here?"

"Of course I am here. Why wouldn't I be?" replied Jed.

"Do you know what is going on?"

"I have a guess, but I'd rather be sure before I say anything. I will say this, if I am right, we have a lot of work to do."

As the addition of more and more people came to a halt, the commotion fell to a whisper as the guards closed the gates around everyone. When Jude looked up towards the balcony that was covered with Agents of every bloodline, a lone figure parted the sea of soldiers, and took its place before everyone.

# AN UNSETTLING
## ASSEMBLY

Bishop was both proud and comforted to be standing before the people of Kismet. The very people he had sworn to protect, now looked up at him with eager eyes, waiting to hear his news. He had wished that this meeting was not tainted by the grave news that he would soon report. Fox soon joined him on the balcony. Bishop was both surprised and comforted by Fox's presence. Taking his spot among his Agents on the balcony of his quarters, Bishop gazed into the eyes of a farmer he had visited a few days ago. Clen was his name. Bishop's eyes soon found a woman named Myrtle, who he remembered had four young girls. Lastly his eyes found his good friend Marius, whose eyes still carried the grief from the passing of his beloved wife Mya.

Anya had finally returned from her mission to the Spirit Lands that morning, and with Bishop's blessing, elected to take her place among the people, instead of the balcony for Bishop's speech. Anya had reported that there was no abnormal activity during her mission to the Spirit Lands. Following Bishop's orders, they had ventured to the border of the Spirit Lands—stayed no more than a day—and then returned home. Bishop was both relieved and disappointed at this news. Taking a deep breath, Bishop found the courage he needed, and began.

"People of Kismet, it warms my heart to see the faces of each and every one of you here today. Please forgive me for the news I am about to share with you. We have received word that a large group of Necrosis have assembled in the West, and as we speak, they make their way to the border of our lands."

Bishop paused as the expected commotion broke out among his people. He let the commotion carry on for a few seconds, before raising his hand and continuing.

"Sources tell us that they will be at our borders in five to six days. So this is why I have made a decision to send a group of Agents to meet them at our borders before any harm is carried over to our homes. Unfortunately, we will need capable Agents both defending our borders as well as here in the city defending our homes. I am saddened to say that after the loss of our brothers and sisters in the battle in the north sometime ago, our numbers have dwindled. That is why a rash decision had to be made. An open enlistment has gone into effect, for Academy students that are interested in joining our Agents that will be defending the city."

An even louder commotion broke out among the people. A few "boos" were audible from the crowd.

"But they are our children," screamed a woman from the corner of the courtyard. Bishop felt the grief he was feeling display on his face. He forced himself to assume a vacant expression before continuing.

"I know news of this is upsetting. I wish there was an alternative. On a brighter note, the Academy is once again hosting the Trials of Magic, Might and Lineage. I encourage everyone to join us tomorrow during these Trials. I have requested that the Professors of all three halls, volunteer their top five students for the Trials. These brave individuals will face each other in a series of battles to decide who will win the honor to have the opportunity to join the ranks of Kismet's Agents. The doors will be open to each and every one of you to give you the opportunity to support your sons and daughters, brothers and sisters, friends and peers. The three winners of the Trials, will join an elite squad that will personally assist our General in the battle against the Necrosis. I believe that the right individuals, along with our General's expertise, should be able eliminate the threat long before any lives are taken. There is something about the Trials of Magic, Might and Lineage that has always yielded individuals that bring more than just honor and modern skill to Kismet. The winners always seem to bring hope and contingency for a better future. For some of you, this is the chance you have been waiting for to fight for your people, for your friends and your family. For some of you, this is your shot at glory and immortality. No matter what your reasons, I hope you remember to fight with honor. It is the hearts of our honorable brothers and sisters, that will see us through these dark times and back to the light we once basked in. I have already sent word to our allies in Geminate and Praxis, as well as those in the Immortal Lands, for aid both here and in battle. I know we will prevail. May the Three Brothers watch over each and every one of you; and for our potential contenders of the Trials, may fate be your ally."

Bishop took his leave returning to the confines of his quarters, as his Agents closed the doors to his balcony. After his quarters emptied out, Bishop gazed at the dancing flames that inhabited his fireplace. With worry on his face and sorrow in his heart, he extinguished the flames that once lived there. Crossing the room to the sitting area, he gazed down at the potential threat from the opposing knight. He took the knight with a bishop, placing the opposing king in check.

# THE TRIALS
# DRAW NEAR

Jude spent the rest of the day training nonstop with Jed at the watering hole, after departing from the castle's courtyard. He was not sure if Lynn would volunteer him for the Trials, but he wanted to be prepared nonetheless. Jed informed Jude, that even with the extra help from the enlistment, as well as the winners of the Trials, they would still have a tough fight ahead of them. Jed spent the whole day with Jude, training him in speed and agility. Jude was grateful for Jed's assistance, but found himself exhausted when the sun began to set.

"Remember that a moving target is hard to hit," began Jed. "If you are going up against a Magi or Weapons Master using any sort of projectiles, never stop moving."

Jude committed every piece of advice Jed gave him to memory. He had decided that he would not let one piece of advice go unheard, since Jed had told him that people usually die in the Trials of Magic, Might and Lineage. Jude was not scared of the Trials. He had been training and studying nonstop for as long as he could remember, and he thirsted to be out there fighting alongside his brother in battle.

Jude had not seen Eli since their awkward walk to the Academy a few days ago. He wondered how his friend was doing with his training. Every now and then Jude would think about what he would do if he had to go up against his best friend in the Trials.

"When you were in the Trials, did you ever have to go up against a friend?"

"I did," said Jed.

"What happened?"

"I killed him." Jude stood frozen for a second. When Jed noticed the shock on his face, he continued. "You have to understand, this is not a demonstration in your training class or wooden swords in the backyard. This is a fight to the death. Sure sometimes if it is clear that someone has lost, The Council may stop the match before anyone is killed, but I would not count on it. Treat the Trials as if they are a mission."

Now Jude was worried more than ever about what would happen if him and Eli had to face each other in battle. Eli was his best friend. They had known each other since they were kids; and to Jude, Eli was like a second brother. Sure they were not on the best of terms right now, but Jude had already decided to show Eli that there were no hard feelings—next time he saw him.

"Hey!" said Jed snapping his fingers in front of Jude, who was deep in thought. "Pay attention! The night is almost over."

Jed trained Jude to use the abilities of the creatures he transformed into to his advantage. Jude had explained to Jed that he had been experimenting with a different form of vial.

"It has a permanently extended needle so it resembles a dart."

Jed looked at the vial Jude had handed him. "What is it for?"

"I filled a few with the blood of smaller more weaker creatures. I plan to turn any enemies into weaker creatures that are easier to take down," said Jude with a smirk on his face.

"It won't work unless your enemy is also a Combat Specialist. Any other enemies won't have your bloodline, so they won't have your ability," informed Jed.

"I figured that, which is why I mixed a very small portion of my blood with the weaker creature's blood. The smaller portion of my blood should temporarily allow for a quick transformation, if injected in close proximity to the target's vital organs."

Jed looked out over the surface of the watering hole. Jude guessed he was thinking about his words. "It has never been done, but if the right portion of your blood is added, it just might work. You just have to be careful not to include too much or your opponent may temporarily acquire your bloodline traits for longer than you would like," said Jed.

Jude and Jed experimented with vials containing different amounts of Jude's blood in them, along with the blood of some nearby rabbits. Jude began to feel a little dizzy from the loss of blood, so when they made six vials that all contained different amounts of his blood; they figured that it should be sufficient for their experiment. Jed quickly ran into the forest for a specimen and returned in less than ten seconds with a small fox. He injected the fox with the first vial. Nothing happened. After injecting the fox with the next three vials with no success, Jed let the fox go and went to find a new specimen. He soon returned with a badger.

"We don't have much time," started Jed. "When you were experimenting, what amount of your blood did you find to be more likely to work?"

Jude thought for a moment, and then picked up the very last vial that he had only placed two drops of his blood in—along with the rabbit blood. "This one, and after thinking about it, I am almost positive it will work."

Jude injected the badger with the vial and instantly the badger turned into a small gray and white rabbit. Jude could not be sure, but he was almost certain that he saw a look of shock on Jed's face. A swell of confidence came over Jude, as he watched the rabbit hop around for a few seconds, before turning back into the badger, and running off into the forest.

"That was ingenious," said Jed. "But how good is your throwing accuracy?"

That was one thing that Jude had not thought of. He would need to land a direct hit somewhere close to his opponent's vital organs, in order for the trick to work. Defeat crept up on him.

"Don't worry little brother, fortunately for you, I know a throwing trick you can master in a few hours. That is, if you are willing to agree to only four hours of sleep tonight," said Jed. Jude thought about what was more important, sleep or mastering this experiment that he had spent countless hours on.

"I'm in."

◆ ◆ ◆

Eli had spent the rest of the afternoon training in his usual spot in the city's forest after Bishop's assembly. He would have also used the morning to train, but Professor Ivor was the only mentor that required his students to return to class after the assembly. Professor Ivor spent half the class lecturing about instinctual defense, and the other half facing off one on one with each individual student to see how well he or she could perform the technique. Many students failed miserably and were humiliated by Ivor, before being allowed to return to their seats. Eli, Zane, Will and a student by the name of Joanna Marks, were the only individuals that successfully performed the instinctual defense that Ivor had taught.

After a few hours of training, Eli found it too difficult to concentrate. All he could think about was Sia. Thoughts of her haunted every inch of his mind. He still did not understand what had happened the last time he saw her. Determined to see her, he set out for the Eastern Hold.

When he arrived in the stone rows of elaborate homes, the streets were buzzing with people training. Eli had to duck a few times when a neighboring Magi had hurled a garbage container his way nearly taking him out. When the familiar view of Sia's doorstep came into view, anxiety overcame him.

*What if she doesn't want to see me? That would explain why she hasn't talked to me since the last time we hung out.*

He knocked on the door. After a few moments, the door creaked open, but no one was behind it.

"Hello?"

"Who are you?" said a voice beneath him. Eli looked down to see a small boy holding the door open. He had a very small frame, curly dark brown hair, and chubby rosy cheeks. He wore a royal blue tunic with beige shorts.

"Oh I'm sorry. My name is Eli, is Sia home?"

"Maybe. Why?"

Not sure how to answer, Eli just looked at the boy. The boy was so young. He looked like he was around eight years old, but Eli felt like he was talking to someone his age. His voice sounded young and eager, but his words carried a clarity and sophistication that was baffling.

"Mik who are you talking to," said a familiar voice from inside the house. Eli looked up to see Sia standing behind the young boy. Her eyes looked puffy and her face looked tired; but the puffiness in both her cheeks is what drew Eli's attention.

"Hi!"

"Hi," she replied slowly. "Mik go up to your room okay?"

"Are you sure? I can take him! He doesn't look so tough," said Mik.

"Yes I am fine. Go on."

After Mik was gone, Sia closed the door behind her. She wore a long light pink nightshirt with white shorts underneath.

"Hold on," she said disappearing into the house and slamming the door behind her. After a couple of minutes—the door swung open—and Sia appeared before him. The puffiness under her eyes was now minimal, and she had changed into a pair of tight-fitting white pants and a light pink top.

"What are you doing here?" she asked.

"I came to see you."

"I can see that, but why? The Trials are tomorrow, you should be training, not visiting me." Unsure of what to say, Eli just stared deeply into her eyes.

"Are you mad at me?"

"Look I can't see you. Please don't come by here again, I have training to do," said Sia going back into the house and slamming the door behind her.

A small pressure descended upon his chest. Each breath he took felt like it was not enough, as he gasped for more and more air. A warm breeze blew passed his nose. It smelled of marshmallows and spices. The scent reminded him of his mother. Turning around to head home, he told himself she was waiting there for him, even though he knew it was a lie.

Making his way up the stairs and towards his front door, the door swung open before he had a chance to reach for it.

"Son! What are you doing here? I thought you were training," said Marius. He was dressed in black combat gear with silver accents. His hair was neatly brushed to the side and in his hands he held two large cases.

"I was—I guess I am taking a break. That's all."

Marius stared at Eli for a few seconds. Eli hoped that his dad could not see through the illusion and into the pain that dwelled within.

"Well I am about to head to the Academy. I am teaching a lecture for the Erudites today."

"A lecture? Wait, you're a Professor? You never told me that!"

"It is somewhat of a new thing. I am pretty sure I *have* told you a few times—whether or not you were listening is unknown," said Marius with a smile. "Wanna come?"

Eli felt like a few hours in his warm bed was just what he needed. The situation with Sia and the stress of the Trials, made his whole body feel like it was just getting over a cold.

"Please!"

"Sure dad. I guess it's time that I see what you are always so busy with."

"Great! I am sure the kids will be ecstatic to meet you! Grab one of these cases will you," said Marius. Eli grabbed one of the black cases that Marius had been holding, and instantly felt a small pop in his back.

"What in the name is in this?"

"Assorted weapons—for the class."

# THE FOURTH
# BLOODLINE

Eli was positive that they had to be lost, as they made their way through a dark and strange corridor within the Academy. Eli and Marius had already passed Master Hall, Magi Hall and Combat Hall; and Eli's arms began to grow numb under the massive weight of the large case he was carrying.

"Here we are," said Marius setting his case down in front of a single wooden door. The door appeared to be damaged and only hung on its top hinge.

"Give me a hand son."

Eli set his case down next to Marius, and helped his father with the door. It was surprisingly heavier than it appeared—and a lot older as well. After retrieving his case, Eli followed Marius inside. A round indoor courtyard stretched out in front of him. Crumbled stained pillars and debris littered the floor and walls. Dead grass so dry that it appeared to be burned, covered a large portion of the floor. Dozens of small and shaved tree trunks sat in rows in front of a long desk—that stood in the center of the room. A light breeze blew from above causing Eli to shiver. Looking up, Eli noticed that the roof of the courtyard was completely torn away with only a few fragments of the ancient and distant roof that once hung there.

"Dad, what is this place?"

"This, my son, is Erudite Hall."

"Erudite Hall? But I thought there were only three halls—one for each of the bloodlines," said Eli feeling confused.

"Depends on who you ask. You can set your case next to that desk right over there," said Marius pointing to the long desk that Eli had seen earlier.

"Dad, this place looks abandoned."

"I know—it is a shame. We clean up what we can at the end of every lecture, but I am afraid this part of the Academy is ready to surrender," said Marius opening his case. From the case he retrieved blades and daggers of all sorts.

"No wonder those cases were so heavy."

"Yes I guess they can be a little heavy if you are not used to their weight. I guess carrying them to lectures for the past few months has gotten my body used to it. At least it is good for my upper body," said Marius with a small laugh.

"You carry these all the way to the Academy every day?"

"Well not every day, you see The Council refuses to really give us any kind of funding for the Erudites. I am only allowed to use this room every two to three days to teach, even though no one *ever* uses this room. I think it is The Council's way of keeping the Erudites below the other three bloodlines. They refused to even give us our own hall when I first became their Professor," said Marius.

"Well what did they use for a lecture room before?"

"The Council made them learn in the forest."

"In the forest? While all of the other students get those large expensive lecture halls?"

Eli was waiting for Marius to tell him that he was just kidding around with him. The thought that certain students were not given the same courtesy as the rest, seemed a little hard to believe. However, all Marius did was set daggers, swords, and bows on the various stumps that sat in the center of the room.

"I am afraid so my son. You see—many people do not believe that Erudites can go on to be skilled Agents or Operatives. They believe that because they have no abilities, they are more of a liability rather than an asset. To be honest, many people kind of shun them and act like they are not even apart of the city. Anyways, when the last Erudite Professor was killed by that Necrosis, The Council debated on whether or not they should even find her a replacement. They believed that maybe they should devote all of their time into the education of the students *with* abilities, rather than the ones without. So I instantly volunteered myself for the position. When I saw their 'lecture hall,' I researched other options and ran across this place."

Eli thought back to all the times he had passed an Erudite soldier that stood watch in front of the city or around the castle. He never realized how much worse they had it than the other bloodlines. He grabbed a few daggers from the case Marius was using, and began to place weapons on the stumps as well.

"No no, that is Brayden's seat, he doesn't get any blades or daggers," said Marius when Eli placed a sword and dagger on one of the front trunks.

"Oh, how come he doesn't get blades but the others do?"

"Well Brayden is focusing on long-range attacks this week. He has been doing very well with close combat, and he asked me if it would be okay if he learned more about the longbow this week," said Marius.

"Learned?"

"Yes son, you see, Erudites do not have the same type of blood that you and I have. They are unique. When they hold a weapon in their hand, their brain does not automatically analyze every technique and use for it like yours does. They have to learn how to use whatever weapon they have before they use it." When all of the trunks had a variety of certain weapons on them, Marius took a step back and examined all of them. "Perfect! They should be here in a few minutes as well."

"Howcome class is so late in the day? There was hardly anyone in the Academy when we got here."

"The Council refuses to let them have their class at the same time as everyone else I'm afraid. It is really quite cruel. They do not believe that they are on the same level as the Weapons Masters, Magi, and Combat Specialists; so therefore they are not allowed to have their lectures at the same time as everyone else."

"And Bishop stands for this?"

"I am afraid he was overruled on the subject. Only Lord Bishop and Professor Lynn believe that the Erudites are just as capable of becoming skilled Agents and Operatives. The others don't, so they were overruled."

"But it looks like you do," said Eli feeling slightly angry.

"Yes—but I am not on The Council. So it does not matter what I believe."

"Oh. I see."

"You see son, Erudites may not have the same abilities as you and I, but they are still just as capable of becoming powerful Operatives and Agents. They just have to work harder than you and I," said Marius.

"But who would want to? It seems like so much work, and why would you want to become an Agent for a city that doesn't respect you?"

"That is probably the reason why my class is so small. Many parents of Erudites refuse to let them come to lectures because they do not believe in what they are capable of. They know how The Council feels about their children, and they just don't want to get their hopes up. My goal is to one day have every Erudite in our city coming to class, training, and eventually competing in the Trials of Magic, Might and Lineage."

"Wait," said Eli as he scratched his head. "The Erudites don't even get a chance to compete in the Trials?"

"I am afraid not," said Marius tilting his head down.

"But that isn't fair!"

"People aren't fair son. That is why I fight so hard to protect these kids—from people," said Marius grabbing Eli's shoulder.

Eli took a look around Erudite Hall a second time. Not only were the pillars that lined the walls cracking, but also the dead grass had holes in its surface. Moss grew in the corners and dead birds and flies seemed to have dropped from the roof, and lay scattered at various locations around the courtyard.

*This is no place for someone to learn.*

"Why don't you join me at my desk—I have a second seat. I will introduce you to the kids when they come in," said Marius taking a seat behind the long desk that headed the trunks. Eli took a seat next to his dad and sat eager to see what kind of students would walk through the destroyed door ahead of him. A few minutes passed before many footsteps sounded from the hall outside. A small knock sounded.

"Come in!"

The door slowly pushed open and a small group of both boys and girls erupted from the door. Eli counted around twelve students that looked around fifteen years old. The class was a buzz with laughter and conversation, as the students took their seats. Eli noticed that all of the students filled up the seats in the front of the class, and left the back rows empty.

*There are way more seats than students.*

Marius stood up from his seat with his hands planted firmly at his sides. "Good afternoon class!"

"Good afternoon Professor Marius," said the class in perfect unison.

"The young man sitting next to me is my son Eli. He is of the Weapons Master bloodline."

"Good afternoon Mr. Eli," said the class.

Eli rose to his feet feeling embarrassed. "Good afternoon!" Eli quickly took his seat feeling like he was taking too much of the attention away from Marius.

"Did all of you have a wonderful day so far?"

A lone student raised his hand.

"Yes Sal."

"My dad took my throwing daggers away again. He told me I should quit and become a farmer with him," said a brown-haired boy.

"I will forge you some new ones—some special ones. Come by my house tomorrow after the Trials and they will be ready," said Marius.

"Thank you Professor!"

"So today we will be talking about what happens when your opponent disarms you and leaves you with no weapons at your disposal. First and foremost, you must remember that your weapons are an extension of yourself—especially blades. When in battle, you should cling to your weapon like you cling to your life. Now those of you on the longbow may experience this problem more than others since there are only so many arrows you can carry at a time."

Eli listened attentively to Marius' lecture. He was surprised to see how eager and attentive the students were to his dad's lecture. Marius talked about how long-range Agents on the bow should conserve as many arrows as possible, and use a handheld arrow as a dagger for close combat when possible. He then went into detail about using the environment around you to attack your enemy when you are disarmed. The information was both entertaining and beneficial when Eli thought about all the ways he could use the environment to his advantage when in battle. After an hour or so, Marius separated the students into pairs. Each student practiced being disarmed and defending against an attacking opponent. Marius walked around assisting each pair with the various exercises, and Eli followed. Eli was surprised at how passionate each of the students were. They all helped each other with the lessons and congratulated each other afterwards.

*It feels like they are a family and a team. They don't compete against each other like my class does.*

Eli looked over and noticed a lone redhead firing arrows at a target that hung over a large crack in one of the walls. Eli walked over to the boy and observed. He was having difficulty holding the bow steady, and was not able to even touch the target in front of him.

"Do you mind?" asked Eli holding his hand out towards the boy. The boy turned around and looked at Eli as if noticing him for the first time.

"Um sure, thank you!"

Eli took the bow and a stray arrow from the floor.

"No problem. Okay first you want to make sure you are standing perpendicular to your target with your feet a shoulder width apart. Don't forget to balance your weight over the balls of your feet because that is very important. Try to keep your back straight but don't tense up too much because when you fire, you want your body to absorb the recoil of the shot. Now raise your bow to your enemy and put your arm that holds the bow into position, before turning your elbow out. When you fire, make sure to follow through with the hand that released the arrow as if the arrow is still in its grasp." Eli released the arrow and hit the center of the target. He breathed a big sigh of relief.

"Wow that was great! Now let me try," said the boy. Eli gave the bow and a couple of arrows back to the boy. The first arrow made it to the target, but barely. The second arrow made it a lot closer to the center, but was still far off.

"This is my first time hitting anything! My name is Brayden Taddea," said the boy extending his hand.

"Nice to meet you Brayden—name is Eli," said Eli shaking his hand.

"You are so lucky having Professor Marius as your dad!"

"Yeah he is great."

"He's more than that! He is the reason I have a shot at becoming an Agent. My mom and dad always tell me that I will be lucky if I am able to get the opportunity to stand watch over the front gates," said Brayden.

"Well watching any of the gates isn't that bad—it's still a great honor."

"Yeah I guess. But my dream is to be out on the battlefield with my friends, taking down enemies and going on adventures—not standing watch at the gates."

"I understand, that is my dream as well."

"You have nothing to worry about since you're one of the favorites," said Brayden with a grim look on his face.

"Favorites?"

"Yeah, you have Weapons Master blood. You have powers and abilities that I can only dream of. At least everyone will give you a chance to become an Agent. People laugh at me and tell me I should give up when I tell them I want to be an Agent. Professor Marius is the only one that believes I can become an Agent. He even told me that if I work hard, I can become an Operative someday," said Brayden.

"No he isn't the only one. I believe you can become whatever you want. I have dreamed about joining the Academy all of my life. I not only got to join, but I may get the opportunity of becoming a contender in the Trials of Magic, Might and Lineage. Don't let anyone tell you to give up on your dreams. Your dream is all the power you need."

Brayden stared back at Eli for a few seconds before wrapping his arms around him. Eli bent down a little to hug the red-head back.

"So I see you have met Mr. Taddea," said Marius.

"Eli taught me how to use my longbow Professor! I was able to finally hit the target!"

"Nice work Brayden," said Marius clasping the boy on his shoulder.

Marius soon instructed the class to break into groups in order to help clean up the courtyard. To Eli's surprise, the kids were eager to help clean up their hall. All of the students ran to clean up the debris, dead insects, and moss that covered the room. Marius soon ushered everyone back into their seats before he returned to his seat. Eli quickly joined him.

"Great work today class! Now for your assignment I want you to analyze twenty non-weapon related items, and come up with five ways you can use them as a weapon in battle. I will see you all after the Trials. Dismissed!"

The students took the weapons, which Marius had handed out, with them on their way out the door. When Eli asked his father about it, he explained that he always allowed his students to bring weapons home from each class. He also explained that many of the students' parents tend to hide their kids' weapons in order to discourage them.

"I am not trying to disobey any of their parents in any way. If their reasons behind their actions were just because they want their child to follow in the family business or become something else for positive reasons, then that would be fine. However, when they discourage them because they do not want them to pursue their dreams, that is when we have a problem."

"Do the parents get mad at you?"

"Sometimes, I mean, I have gotten some nasty letters," said Marius with a shrug. "The day the kids stop coming to class is the day I know the parents are putting their foot down, and that is when I respect their wishes."

Eli took a look around at the rows of seats in the back that were never occupied. Eli followed Marius through the hanging door and into the halls of the Academy. As they passed by two large wooden doors, Eli stopped and looked up at the insignia above the doors. A vial and two fists intersected each other on a round medallion. The medallion alone looked like it was worth half of a house.

*I never realized how good the other bloodlines have it.*

"Dad, thank you for allowing me to come with you today."

"Oh of course son. I loved having you with me today, and the kids were happy to have you as well. You are welcome to join us anytime," said Marius.

"I think what you are doing is amazing dad—really. I can't imagine how it would feel like to not have my abilities. You give those kids a way to dream."

When the fountain in the middle of the Market District came into view, Marius took a seat along its outer wall. Many civilians ate on outdoor patios of restaurants, shopkeepers socialized with customers, and stragglers came and went from the many buildings that surrounded them. Eli took a seat next to Marius on the fountain.

"I am going to tell you something that your mother told me on one of our missions, before we got married. 'When a comrade falls in battle, if there is even the slightest chance that they could be saved, you take it.' Mya told me that during one of our toughest battles long ago—it stayed with me. Even though the Erudites are not necessarily fallen, I see them as a portion of our people that are down right now. The Council and nearly everyone around them tells them that they cannot achieve their dreams, and that if they are lucky, the best they could achieve would be watching the gates for the rest of their lives. I believe the Erudites are just as capable of becoming Agents and Operatives as the other three bloodlines. I just want to show them how skilled they really are."

"You and mom must have went on so many adventures together," said Eli noticing his throat tightening.

"Too many to count, but each of them were special. There is something intimate and special about being miles away from home, surrounded by enemies, and fighting side-by-side for survival with someone you love."

"What happened when you guys had me?"

"That was definitely the happiest moment of my life. Words cannot explain how it feels to create a child with the love of your life. The connection when I locked eyes with you was instant. I instantly loved you when I first laid eyes on you; and instantly wanted to protect you with my life," said Marius.

"But how were you guys able to go on missions now that you had a child? Did you go on missions and mom stayed home?"

"When you were first born, neither of us went on missions. I took a leave from the Occult Operatives and started forging weapons to bring in income for us. Smithing did not bring in as much money as being an Operative, but since I had knowledge of legendary weapons, the weapons I smithed brought in more than enough money to support you and your mother. There is something about having your own child that makes you want to buy nothing but the best for them, especially your first—and we did. When you were old enough to go to school, we went on a few missions here and there, but for the most part we preferred to be as close to you as possible. Even though we left you with a trusted mutual friend of ours, there is a pain like no other that a parent feels when they are apart from their child—no matter how old the child is."

"So basically, I took away both you and mom's dreams," said Eli feeling guilty.

"Do not ever say that son, because it isn't true."

"Dad, you and mom loved to go on missions—especially with each other. You can't tell me that you didn't miss it after I was born."

"Son it's true that becoming an Operative was both of our dreams. I never dreamed that I would end up becoming an Occult Operative—ever. It is too hard to explain to you since you are not old enough to have a family of your own—however I will say this. There will come a day when you will find someone that is worth putting ahead of yourself—then you will understand," said Marius patting Eli on the shoulder.

Eli thought long and hard about Marius' words. He did not understand how Marius could throw away what made him happy in order to stay home. Being forced to give up on your dreams just because of a baby seemed pretty unfair.

*Having kids isn't for everyone and surely isn't for me.*

Marius stood up from the fountain, and Eli soon followed. When his home came into view, Eli felt as if he had just returned from studying something. He felt more knowledgeable but exhausted. He was glad that he decided to go with his dad to his lecture. Meeting Brayden and the rest of the kids, gave him a broader understanding of some of the aspects of their people's way of life, which he was unaware of.

*Just when you think you know everything about your home, you learn something new.*

# THE TRIALS OF MAGIC, MIGHT, AND LINEAGE

Eli did not get much sleep after returning from the Academy with Marius. His dreams were haunted with visions of his mom and dad the whole night. He was awakened by the smell of ham, eggs, and fresh bread, which left his room smelling like a bakeshop.

*Dad you're the best.*

Eli quickly did a few stretches before washing up and putting on his signature brown-belted combat tunic and beige pants. As he made his way downstairs, he summoned weapon after weapon in each hand, trying to ready his mind to react instinctually in combat. When he reached the living room, he went into complete shock. All his dad's weapons and materials were neatly put away in weapon cabinets, the floor was actually visible, and to top it off, there were countless banners that hung from the walls and ceilings that read:

"Good Luck Son! I am So Proud of You!"

"Well look who has finally decided to wake up early for once. It's the executioner!" said Marius with a smirk on his face.

Eli let loose a small laugh. "Dad you're awesome."

The moment Eli walked into the kitchen, his mouth dropped. Large platters of pork, hard-boiled eggs, and freshly baked bread, filled up the dinner table. As Eli took his seat across from Marius, he looked at the empty third seat that was always bare. Shaking off the pending grief, Eli forced himself to crack a smile.

"Thanks for all of this dad."

"I cannot have my boy storming the field on an empty stomach now can I? Now lets talk battle strategy!"

While Marius and Eli ate their breakfast, Marius told Eli some of his most successful battle techniques and strategies he had used on a few of his missions. Eli nearly fell over giddy when his father told him about a strategy he used to take down five men who had surrounded him while on a mission. Eli finally had let go of the grief he was carrying for his mother, and focused on the advice his dad was giving him. As the two of them finished their plates, they heard a knock at the door.

"Are you expecting anyone?"

"No," said Eli shaking his head.

While Marius cleared the table, Eli answered the door. He was surprised to find Jude standing outside his door dressed in a black belted tunic, similar to his own, with matching black pants.

"Nice, you're up," said Jude with a smile on his face.

"Yeah I just got done having some breakfast with my dad," replied Eli happily. Eli invited Jude in before briefly excusing himself to the washroom. When he came back, he found Jude reading the many "Good Luck" posters that Marius had put up for him.

*I wonder how things are with his mom.*

Marius soon joined the two boys in the living room.

"You two are going to bring down the house!" said Marius waving his fist in the air.

"Thanks Mr. Brassie. Will we see you there?" asked Jude.

"Of course! I will be in the front row!"

Eli and Jude bid a temporary farewell to Marius before leaving. When they closed the front door behind them, Eli noticed the cloudbank had cleared out from the day before, and the sun's rays poured down giving the day a warm and comforting feel. The boys made their way down Lin Kitz Street, passed the Market District, and through Amos Street. As Eli and Jude turned the next corner, they both stopped cold when they first laid eyes on the Coliseum. The building was a large circular structure that was so tall, that it partially blocked out the sun. It appeared to be made of stone—whiter than the freshest milk. A set of at least seventy wide stone stairs led straight up to the entrance of the Coliseum. The entrance was marked with the statues of the Three Brothers standing tall against its own tall white pillar. The brother Rune was on the left, Pith on the right and Aegis in the middle. Each pillar behind the statue held a long blood-red banner that carried the insignia of the corresponding statue. Hundreds of people ascended and descended the steps to and from the building's entrance. Some marveled at the statues, while others marveled at the Coliseum itself.

"This place is badass and we haven't even seen the inside yet!" said Eli ecstatic.

"I am afraid that I may have a stroke if I see the inside," replied Jude.

The two boys ascended the stairs towards the entrance, and soon Eli became a tiny bit more nervous as he took more steps. By the time he reached the top of the stairs, he felt slightly dizzy. Eli was surprised to see that the Coliseum had no doors, just an open entryway that led into the first inner chamber. Statues of countless Agents and Operatives lined the walls in the first room Eli came to. The floor was made up of a red ceramic tile that matched the red banners he had seen outside. Every five or so feet contained a different statue along the walls of the

Coliseum. Eli and Jude walked up to closest statue, which was of a Magi, and read the plaque that lined its base:

"Christian Hughes"

Bloodline: Magi

Age: 26

"I wonder what you have to do to get a statue of yourself in here."

"What makes you think they are statues? They could be living people trapped in stone prisons for all of eternity," said Jude.

Jude and Eli began laughing hysterically while they walked around the chamber they were in. It stretched all the way around in a complete circle, for what seemed like miles. At one point, Eli had asked a passing soldier how much longer before they reached the last statue. The solider laughed telling them they had not even walked a quarter of it yet. The two boys decided to return to the front of the Coliseum to await further instructions.

After about an hour of going over basic battle strategies, Eli spotted the three mentors of the Academy taking their positions against a tall wooden door, which appeared to go deeper into the Coliseum. Professor Ivor was wearing his signature granite-colored battle tunic with black pants. He appeared to have added a black cape that somehow kept the appearance that it was blowing in the wind, even though he was indoors. Eli recognized Jude's mentor Lynn, who wore a dark green top with matching combat pants. Professor Vance could always be counted on to wear his finest royal blue tunic, pants, and matching cape. Another woman—who Eli did not recognize—soon took her place next to Ivor.

"Attention!" screamed Ivor. All of the noise in the Coliseum came to an immediate stop.

"Thank you. To my right is one of the Academy's best healers Mrs. Moyen. Now I would like for all of the friends, family, and so on to follow Mrs. Moyen so she can take you to your seats. All of the potential contenders will follow Professor Vance, Professor Lynn, and myself, to the holding area where we will announce our picks for the Trials of Magic, Might and Lineage."

"All of the friends and family of our contenders follow me please," announced Mrs. Moyen in a pleasant tone.

When only students remained, Professor Vance clapped his hands, and the tall wooden door, behind the three mentors, swung open revealing a second large chamber within the Coliseum. As the students followed their mentors into the Coliseum, Eli stayed as close to Jude as possible. He didn't see Zane, Sia or Meara, and did not want to risk being left alone in a crowd of strangers he did not know. Eli found himself walking through what appeared to be a small sparring area. As the doors automatically closed behind the last straggler, Eli allowed himself to examine the room he was in. The holding area had the same red ceramic tile floor as the previous room, except for the sparring area, which had a granite-colored cobblestone floor. It also contained the same white walls that the recent chamber contained; however instead of statues, there were three rows of wooden benches. On the sidewall to Eli's right, was a medium-sized stone hut with the words: *Medicinal Quarters* engraved on its door. The sidewall to his left however, contained a large golden plaque, which appeared to be removable.

"We will now announce the chosen contenders that will be participating in this year's Trials of Magic, Might and Lineage. As we call your names, please step forward, and take your position next to your mentor. Professor Vance, would you like to start?" announced Ivor.

Eli watched as Professor Vance stepped forward with a small piece of parchment in his hand. "From the Magi bloodline, I have chosen the following: John Brills, Tillius Edwards, Katrina Wo, Sia Wyatt, and Pang Quarrels."

The five announced Magi took their places at Vance's side. Everyone's eyes, including Eli's, stayed fixated on the boy Pang Quarrels, while he took his place slowly alongside Vance. Eli recognized Pang and his scars from the Market District when he met Zane at the fountain, the night of the Forgotten Forest. Eli made an effort to commit the boy's name to memory and keep a mental note to keep an eye on him. When his eyes set on Sia, his stomach dropped. She wore a short, tight-fitting, royal blue dress with a matching cape. Her hair was neatly brushed to the side and her eyes glowed with a determination he had never seen in her before. Eli thought she looked perfect.

*She always seems to put a lot of effort into her appearance.*

He was filled with so much emotion, that he was not sure which one to allow himself to experience first. He was still hurt by Sia from the last time he saw her, but at the same time he was both worried for her safety, and wishing she would realize how he felt about her. However, he thought back again to how cross she was with him, and he asked himself if it was smart to have feelings for someone who could hurt him so badly.

When Vance stepped back in place, his five selected contenders took a seat at the first bench closest to him. Professor Lynn soon stepped forward, holding her own piece of parchment in her hands.

"From the Combat Specialist bloodline, I have chosen the following special people: Francesca Litta, Jude Bray, Raphael Pompeo, Serena Piera, and Bree Braunstone," announced Lynn.

"Looks like this it," said Jude smiling at Eli. "Good luck buddy, I'll see you out there." Eli watched his best friend take his position between Professor Lynn and the other Combat Specialists. He figured that Jude was extremely intelligent and would most likely dominate the Trials.

"So this is where you have been hiding," said a familiar voice next to him.

It was Zane.

"Hiding? No. Anxiously waiting? Yes!"

"Tell me about it!" agreed Zane.

Eli felt comforted that he was standing with someone he knew, right before Ivor made his announcement. His nerves were getting the best of him, and he was aware of the flips his stomach was doing as well. He did not want to let his dad down, but most importantly, he did not want to lose. His dad had always stuck by him and was so proud of him. He needed this. He had been waiting for the opportunity to show everyone that he was one of the best. When Professor Ivor returned to the front, Eli took a deep breath and prepared himself.

"From the Weapons Master bloodline, I have chosen the following: Joanna Marks, Dominic Adams, Lucia Magdalena, and Zane Humphrey," announced Ivor. The crowd remained silent and none of the chosen Weapons Masters moved, as they waited to see who was the fifth and final contender.

"That is all," said Ivor folding the parchment in his hands. "The four that I have selected, please take your seats at my side." A small bit of commotion broke out within the crowd, as the four Weapons Masters took their seats next to Ivor. Eli felt both enraged and embarrassed that his name was not called. He felt bad for bragging, but he felt like he was much better than the individuals, excluding Zane, that Ivor had chosen.

*He is doing it on purpose because he can't stand me.*

Eli looked over to Zane, who was giving him a *what the hell* look, from afar. Eli had already made up his mind that he would have a talk with Ivor man-to-man after this was over. Soon the doors leading to the front chamber of the Coliseum opened. Everyone in the room turned around to find Bishop standing in the doorway, arms neatly folded behind him. He wore an expensive-looking set of red and white dress robes with a matching red cape that was lined with expensive white fur at the shoulders. His smooth brown skin seemed to deceivingly mask his true age.

Bishop joined the three mentors at the front of the crowd, shaking hands with each of them separately. "Have we announced our contenders?"

"Yes sir," replied Ivor.

"Fantastic! Who will be competing in this year's Trials of Magic, Might and Lineage?"

Vance pointed to the five contenders he had chosen, that sat on the bench in front of him. Next Lynn did the same, showing her five chosen contenders. When Ivor showed his four chosen contenders, Bishop's expression turned from excitement to confusion.

"Forgive me if I am mistaken Ivor, but it appears you have only chosen four contenders. Is that correct?"

"That is correct sir. I feel like these were the only students that I felt were worthy enough—and at least somewhat intelligent enough—to have the honor of competing in this year's Trials of Magic, Might and Lineage, my Lord," replied Ivor. Eli felt the devil on his left shoulder assassinate the angel on his right shoulder.

*Oh you don't even know. You're so gonna get it!*

"Well we always pick the best, and would need at least three winners from these Trials since we have seven new recruits. If I may make a suggestion Professor," said Bishop.

"Of course sir," replied Ivor.

"Perhaps I should choose the last Weapons Master contender. I think I may know someone who would be perfect to participate in this years Trials," said Bishop with a smile on his face.

"Of course my Lord, I always value your input. Please make a selection," said Ivor. Eli was not sure if he was seeing things, but he was almost certain that there was a certain level of irritation and anger in Ivor's demeanor, when Bishop proposed choosing a fifth contender. The Professor was good at quickly extinguishing it, because as soon as Eli noticed it, the masked demeanor returned.

"Eli Brassie! Are you here?" yelled Bishop. Eli froze and was unable to respond to Bishop's calling. Some of the students around him turned around and stared, as Eli scrambled to respond.

"Yes sir!" yelled Eli stepping out from the crowd. Eli noticed a smile plaster across Bishop's face, while a look of disgust simultaneously, and covertly, appeared on Ivor's face.

"How would you like to be our fifth contender for the Weapons Master bloodline?" After fighting back the shock that was coming back with a vengeance, Eli quickly regained his composure.

"It would be an honor sir."

Bishop clasped Eli on the shoulder as his smile widened. "Then it is settled! We have our fifteen contenders! Good luck to you all and may fate be your ally," said Bishop before exiting out the same doors he had entered through.

When Eli took his place alongside Zane, Joanna, Dominic, and Lucia, he began to notice that many of the un-chosen students were staring at him whispering.

"Congratulations man! Just think of it, you and me wiping the floor with these amateurs," exclaimed Zane while putting his arm around Eli.

*I'm not going to let anyone ruin this for me. I have earned this, and Bishop has noticed all of my hard work. That is why I am standing here.*

"I know! Someone better warm up the MQ beds for these novices," replied Eli with a grin.

The three mentors had instructed the fifteen chosen contenders to standby in the holding chamber, while they escorted the remaining students to their seats within the Coliseum—alongside the spectators. Eli had tried to talk to Sia once the mentors had left, but she stormed away from him every time he approached.

Eli introduced Jude to his friends Zane and Meara, as everyone waited for the return of the mentors. Jude introduced Eli to his friend Bree, who was eager to meet everybody. The five of them stood huddled in a circle talking about what had transpired the past couple of hours.

"I still can't believe the nerve of that guy!" said Zane. "He just thinks he is the biggest badass in the world only choosing four contenders. Man get a hobby!"

"Told you he was crazy," said Meara.

"Well at least all of that waiting to hear whether I am competing or not is over," replied Eli relieved.

"Are you worried about the Trials?" asked Jude to Eli.

It was Zane who answered for him. "Nah why would he be, he's going to do great. Plus we have known about the Trials for some time now."

Jude looked a little taken back. "Oh you have? How long have you guys known about it?"

"Well the four of us talked about it at the party in the Forgotten Forest. So I would say three or four days."

"The four of you? Don't you mean the three of you?" corrected Jude.

"No the four of us: Me, Eli, Meara and Sia," said Zane pointing out Sia in a group of girls. Eli could not tell how Jude was taking the news. He just stood there emotionless listening to every word Zane had said.

*He looks like his brother right now, minus the white hair and creepy eyes.*

After a few minutes of talking about the Necrosis crisis, Jude excused himself to the washroom. Eli's heartbeat grew louder as he noticed Sia walking over to the Medicinal Quarters.

She appeared to be asking the healer that worked there a question.

*This is driving me crazy. I've got to talk to her.*

♦♦♦

Jude was relieved to have a few moments alone. After hearing that Eli and his new friends had somehow known exactly when the Trials were going to be, Jude figured it would not be long before he was unable to keep the expressionless masquerade he had been performing. He splashed some cold water on his face and studied his features in the mirror, before reaching for a towel to dry his face.

"Ugh! Dirty bloody sheets!"

*That is why he lied about going to the party. He did not want me to find out about the Trials. He needed some sort of an advantage over the competition—over me. I never thought in a thousands years that Eli would look at me as an opponent before looking at me as a friend. I feel like I can't trust anyone anymore. Everyone only looks out for his or her own well-being.*

When Jude exited the washroom, a familiar figure stood in the corner, admiring a painting. If it was not for the announcement of contenders, Jude felt like he would never learn Pang's name. The boy appeared to be very guarded and cautious when they talked in the library last. As Jude approached Pang, he began to wonder why the boy had decided to compete in the Trials completely shirtless, and with no armor whatsoever.

"Biding your time?" asked Jude while giving Pang's shoulder a light tap. When Pang turned around, he studied Jude for a while before answering.

"Perhaps."

"Congratulations on being a contender."

"Much appreciated—you as well," replied Pang with a dismal smile before continuing. "I plan on winning, so I would pray to all three of your gods, that you are not picked as my opponent." He returned his focus to the painting of what appeared to be a great battle.

"I plan on winning as well, and it would be smart for you to hope that I am not your enemy," replied Jude. When Pang turned around, Jude noticed he smiled somewhat of a normal smile for once.

"Pang is what they call me," he said reaching his hand out. Jude shook Pang's hand.

"Jude."

"Did you find that book, that I persuaded you to check out, interesting?"

"Extremely. It appears I owe you one," replied Jude.

"Hmm, it appears you do."

"So, you are a Magi? I would have never guessed."

"I am *not* a Magi," said Pang with an edge.

"But you were selected as a contender to represent the Magi bloodline by Vance."

"Yes well they don't know where to put me, which is why I travel from class to class. My techniques are a little different than everyone else's, and no one here has the knowledge to really mentor me on them. Vance is somewhat knowledgeable, which is why they put me with him for the most part."

"Well if you're not a Magi, then what are you?"

Pang studied Jude's face, and soon the smile he once had vanished. "A person. What are you?"

"I know that," began Jude. "What I mean is—."

"I know what you mean, and you will just have to wait until the Trials if you are looking to get an edge on the competition," replied Pang.

"That is not my style. Being one step ahead of my enemy—yes. But trying to get some unfair advantage is too low for me."

A small smile returned to Pang's face before he responded. "Dearly noted my friend."

# CHOSEN

$E$li had began to become restless, when the familiar sound of the holding area doors erupted behind him. Professor Ivor made his way through the center of the room looking straight ahead, and not paying any attention to the watchful eyes that stood perched around him. Lynn and Vance—who were friendlier to the contenders that both sat and stood around them—soon joined.

*Why couldn't one of them be my mentor? Why did I get stuck with the fiend?*

"Now for round one!" exclaimed Vance. His voice was upbeat but slightly raspy. He walked over to the golden plaque Eli saw earlier, and waved his hand over it.

A loud stone-grinding noise erupted around Eli causing him to jump. Alarm sprang throughout the room, as many looked around in an attempt to discover the source of the rumbling. When it ceased, Vance turned around to reveal a small black urn protruding from the wall under the plaque.

"Now if you all will line up single file in front of me please, we can begin." As everyone fell into formation, Eli wondered howcome Jude had not yet returned from the washroom. Eli found himself somewhat in the middle of the line behind Zane and Meara, but in front of Bree. Bree had told him that she wanted as much time as possible to analyze what was going on.

"Now all you need to do, is hold out one finger face-up in front of you over the urn," explained Vance as he demonstrated with his own. "You will feel one small prick before a sample of your blood is collected by the urn. There is no need to be nervous you will barely feel a thing, and it will be over in a few seconds."

The line moved forward, and soon Eli began to feel a tiny bit nauseous. He found himself breathing a little heavier as if he had been sprinting, and his palms felt a tad bit moist.

"Why are we giving samples of our blood?"

"It's how they decide the matches," replied Meara.

"You mean they couldn't just pick a number out of a hat?" asked Zane with a worried look on his face.

A few seconds went by before Eli found himself laughing at Zane's comment. Meara, Bree and Zane soon joined him in laughter. Eli noticed the line was moving faster than he expected, as students walked up to the urn one by one, and then exited the line—returning to either their seats, or waiting to the side for friends.

"Has anyone seen Jude?"

"You mean the weird one with the paralyzed hair?" said Zane.

"He isn't weird."

"He *is* kind of weird," replied Meara.

"He is my friend, and I would appreciate it if you all would stop bad-mouthing him. Thanks," said Bree glaring at everyone.

"I never thought I would hate to see the two of you finally agree on something," said Eli to Zane and Meara.

Bree pointed to the front of the line. "Isn't that him right there?"

Eli looked in the direction that Bree was pointing, only to find Jude stepping out from the front of the line. One other boy, that Eli could not identify, accompanied him.

*Well at least he didn't miss anything.*

When Jude walked passed, Eli finally discovered that it was Pang who Jude was walking with.

"Man if you didn't think your friend was weird before, what about now? I mean he's walking with the biggest reject in the Academy!" exclaimed Zane before breaking out into laughter. A few people in front of him turned around and joined him. Eli just watched as Jude and Pang turned around glaring at Zane.

*Why is he walking with him?*

Pang appeared to have whispered something to Jude, before Jude approached Zane face-to-face. Eli slowly separated himself from Zane by a few footsteps, and was stopped cold by Jude's glare. Turning his attention back to Zane, Jude said nothing. Eli could tell Zane was getting uncomfortable because he began to fidget and change his posture frequently.

"Have I done something to you? We were just all talking a few moments ago, and you appeared to not have a problem with me *then*," said Jude.

"Yeah, that was before I noticed how much of a freak you are," replied Zane laughing. Eli waited hastily for Jude's response, and quickly noticed that Pang had appeared right next to Zane with the same glare as Jude.

"You have serious problems. It is futile for me to sit here and argue against your empty claims and petty insults, because all you want to do is look good in front of your so called friends. Just to clarify something for you, none of you are *real* friends if this is what you find entertaining. You are all unintelligent tyrants," said Jude.

"Why don't you just go read a book!" said Zane.

"Do you even know how to read—fool?"

Zane's fist hung frozen in midair, ensnared in Pang's grasp. Everything happened so fast, that Eli was caught off guard when he came to grips with what was happening before his eyes.

"Assaulting another outside of honorable combat. Isn't that a crime in your land?" said Pang. Silence appeared to have trapped everyone before Pang continued. "Unfortunately for you, crimes are what I do best. This arm will soon be mine before you cower in fear before me cretin." Pang's red orange eyes stood out against his jet-black hair. Eli watched Zane, waiting for a response, but all he did was stare back at Pang. After Pang released his grip, Zane quickly returned his hand to his side. The movement of color in Pang's eyes seemed to freeze—suspended in time while life went on.

"The cold will ally itself with the merciless mind-numbing pain that will ravage every nerve in your body. Feel the nails on your fingers severe the binds of flesh that entraps them in the very pain they flee from. Feel the hammering on your spine as nails of gargantuan agony pour down your back like acid down the throat of submissive prey. When death's cold whisper sends chills down your shaking hands and trembling shoulders, you shall feel your eyes betray their purpose as they flee like cowards, back into the shadows of your fractured skull. I shall lather my body in your blood and dress my armor in your entrails," said Pang. His tongue ran slowly over every crack of his lips.

The sight made Eli's shoulders spring to his ears, shrouding his neck, and easing the chill. Pang's glare jumped from Zane to Meara. As the cold grip of the red and orange settled on Eli, time stopped all together. Pang's glare soon returned to Zane, and soon the silence finally lifted from the nightmare that left Eli frozen in time.

"Let the hunt begin," said Pang retreating to a painting that hung on the other side of the room.

As soon as Pang left, Jude and Zane stared at each other motionless. A few people behind Eli were yelling at them to move up. It was at that moment that Eli had noticed a large gap between them and the next student in line. Just as he was about to step in and tell Zane that they needed to go, Jude's glare switched to Eli.

"I thought we were friends," said Jude.

"Whoa, wait we *are* friends," replied Eli. He was confused by Jude's words and started to wonder if his friend was just mad at Zane, and taking his anger out on him instead.

"Friends do not let their friends talk badly about their other friends," replied Jude turning towards the direction Pang had went.

"Well our parents aren't supposed to slap us around *either* but that didn't stop yours," said Eli.

Jude stopped. Eli had expected Jude to respond or turn around, however, after a few seconds of idle movement, Jude continued towards Pang. For the first time, Eli felt like he was having an out of body experience. He felt like he had been watching Zane disrespect Jude and Pang, but could not bring himself to say anything. It was as if he was watching himself desperately grab for the voice to tell Zane to stop. To tell him that Jude was his best friend. But nothing came out. To think that Jude had the nerve to get mad at him for Zane's comments enraged Eli.

*I cannot believe that he has the nerve to get mad at me for no reason. He is the one that spouted that 'friends don't let their friends' crap to me. He is lucky I didn't say something worse. No wonder his mother slapped him, he is disrespectful— and kind of only thinks of himself.*

"I swear on my apple pie at home, that if you four don't move, you will all be personally introduced to the side of my blade!" yelled a girl's voice from behind Bree.

"Calm down she-devil!" replied Bree before turning around and cutting in front of Zane, Meara and Eli. Eli soon moved up in line alongside Meara and Zane, but remained quiet. The more he thought about Jude's ridiculous comment, the angrier he got.

"I rest my case that your friend is a nut job," said Zane with a smirk.

"Oh my gosh will you just shut up and let it go!" screamed Meara.

Bree was soon at the front of the line. Her long blonde hair flopped against her back, as she approached the urn. Eli watched her place her finger up. He noticed a small wince from her as a cut appeared on her finger, before the crimson droplet found its way into the urn.

"Is that it?" asked Bree.

"That's it," replied Vance who still held his position next to the urn.

When Bree exited the line and idly waited a few steps away, Eli no longer felt nervous about the selection process. Zane took his turn and then Eli. Taking his place in front of the urn, Eli noticed the delicate detail that ran along the neck and base of the urn, which gave the illusion that it was holding an inscription that said:

"A Life for a Life"

The urn appeared to be very old and almost ancient. Eli watched keenly while he held his finger face-up over the mouth of the urn. Suddenly he felt an invisible prick, and soon a small droplet of his blood dripped down his finger, before depositing itself into the urn.

"You are all done my boy!" said Vance with a smile on his face.

Eli joined Meara, Bree and Zane, who were still waiting for him a few feet away. The three of them appeared to be having idle chitchat when he joined. Eli made no effort to join in on the conversation or make his presence known. Instead, Eli looked over at Jude and Pang, who still occupied their corner of the room, and soon remembered a time when him and Jude were kids. Eli had gotten in trouble so his dad told him he could not leave his room; so Jude would craft different weapons out of wood and sneak them up to Eli's window at night. Since Eli's room was on the second floor, him and Jude always had to find some creative way to get Jude from the ground, and up to Eli's window.

*Friends don't let their friends talk badly about their other friends.*

"Uh oh, don't come unsheathed now Eli, here comes Sia Wyatt," said Zane.

"You are vile," said Meara.

Eli turned around to find Sia exiting from the front of the line. Her long brown hair bounced freely on the side of one of her shoulders. Her purple eyes examined every inch of the room. Soon her eyes fell on him, and that is when he felt himself stop breathing. While her eyes stood fixated on him, he began to believe that she might actually talk to him.

"Sia over here!" yelled Meara. A smile came to Sia's face as she walked over to greet her friend. The two of them gave each other a light hug.

"Hey guys," said Sia to no one in particular.

Everyone greeted her back in unison, except for Eli, who seemed to get his greeting out a few seconds earlier than the group's. Sia appeared to not notice, as she pulled Meara aside, before the two girls laughed and talked about something Eli could not makeout.

"I believe we are ready! Everyone please take your respective seats and we will begin," announced Vance.

Eli took a seat between Zane and Bree. Eli could not help but notice that Bree was also sitting next to Jude and Pang, and found himself oddly uncomfortable in close proximity to his friend. When all of the contenders were seated, Vance took his place at the front center of the room— with Ivor on his left and Lynn on his right.

The Magi clapped his hands twice before a black urn appeared on a small table in front of him. Eli looked over his shoulder to discover that the urn he had deposited his blood into earlier, was missing.

"Now all of you have deposited a droplet of your blood into this very urn. This urn has been used for the Trials for as long as I can remember. Its enchantment is said to have come from the god Rune himself. It is said to bring those destined to face one another, face-to-face in a battle of magic, strength, and blood. In a few seconds I will close this urn, and its enchantment will automatically select our challengers for round one of the Trials of Magic, Might and Lineage," announced Vance.

A swell of commotion broke out throughout the room. Eli watched in anticipation, as the options of who his opponents could be, cycled through his head. When Vance held both his hands out over the urn, as if holding something, a small black lid materialized in his fingertips. The lid came down over the urn, silencing the commotion that once filled the room.

A small blue essence sprang from the base of the urn before circling it. Suddenly a scream broke out from across the room.

"Oh my gosh she's gone!"

Eli jerked his head to look in the direction of the scream, only to find blue smoke slowly rising from an empty spot on a bench. Suddenly another scream broke out towards the front of the room. Eli looked back to see small amounts of the same smoke surrounding Lucia Magdalena, a girl from his class. She stood in shock on stage. However, instead of wearing the tight brown shirt and pants she was once wearing, she wore a tight-fitting red tunic with black scale armor plates on her shoulders, and red leather armor pants.

"What the heck! How did she get up there so fast?" replied Bree. Right as Eli started to respond, Bree appeared next to Lucia in the same blue explosion. Thinking his eyes were playing tricks on him, Eli returned his attention back towards Bree's seat.

"Hey Bree, for a second I thought that was you up—."

Bree was gone. Only a few strands of blue smoke hovered in the spot she had once inhabited. As Eli looked back towards Bree, he noticed a panicked expression on her face, along with the fact that she was now wearing a tight-fitting black tunic with silver scale armor, shoulder plates, and tight-fitting black leather combat pants. Eli looked over to see Jude respond with a panicked expression of his own.

"Go Bree!" yelled Jude.

That was when Eli noticed that nothing separated him from Jude on the bench they were sharing.

*Oh boy.*

When Eli returned his attention to the stage, a boy appeared right next to Bree in the same cloud of blue fog. Eli recognized him as Tillius Edwards; they used to play together, along with Jude, when they were all kids. Eli instantly looked over to see if Tillius' face displayed the same worry that Bree's did; however, as soon as he turned his head, Eli found himself looking into the light purple eyes that haunted every inch of his conscience.

*Sia.*

Her curves were even clearer than they were before, in the new navy tight-fitting combat dress she was now wearing. A long black cape fell from her neck and down her back. When Eli locked eyes with Sia, his heart fell. For the first time in a while, she did not look away, and neither did he. Eli searched her eyes for any sign of what she was thinking or feeling. When he looked down to her pink lips, he saw them smile.

"Looks like we have our round one challengers!" announced Vance. A mixture of applause, whistling, and shouts of support, rang throughout the room from the remaining ten contenders.

"I should have been in the Trials," said Meara crossing her arms.

"Sorry we didn't have enough time to plan your funeral," replied Zane.

"Will the five round one challengers please follow me into the next room, so I can prep you for your match," said Vance. He ushered the challengers on stage to a small door that suddenly appeared in the corner of the room next to a painting. While Eli took one last look at Sia before she entered the door, a small voice inside of him told him to go to her. He sat frozen. The top of the door slowly descended towards the ground, swallowing the five challengers whole.

"No!"

"What's your problem?" asked Meara. Eli said nothing, just stared at the place on the wall where the door once stood. Where she once stood.

"Alright, enough of that. If the rest of you will so kindly follow Lynn and myself to our right, we will show you to your seats among your family and friends," said Ivor.

Everyone assembled into three straight lines of Magi, Combat Specialists and Weapons Masters, before following the two mentors towards the same wall as the plaque. A slow rumbling erupted throughout the room, as a door appeared in front of the two mentors. When Eli looked over towards the golden plaque, he noticed it was no longer blank. Instead he found the five names of the challengers on their way to either victory or death. Out of all five of the names, the one that seemed to demand his attention was *Sia Wyatt*. The rumbling soon subsided, along with the presence of the five challengers. Frustration took the spotlight while worry was its stage. Before Eli could come to grips with the emotional foreign presence that fought to control his body, the familiar red orange pendulums of Pang Quarrels, pierced his conscience.

# SIA'S SONG

Jude found himself blown away by the chamber of the Coliseum he was in. The spectator area stood a few stories tall, overlooking a massive battle arena. Thousands and thousands of continuous stone benches—layered with blood-red cloth and pillows—circled around the spectator area. A few merchants went by with shirts, flags and signs of the different bloodlines. Jude purchased two black Combat Specialist shirts that had the CS insignia on the front and "Blood is Only the Beginning" on the back. He instantly put one of them on and saved the other one for Jed. He also bought a crowd sign to support Bree that had the CS insignia on it and said:

"No Tears Just Bring the Fear!"

The whole chamber appeared to be indoors, except for the giant oval opening that overlooked the battlefield—which was the most impressive. The physical ground of the battlefield itself was not made up of white-stone flooring like the spectator area; it was completely covered with shiny black sand, no more than a few inches high. Three large wooden doors stood equally spread out on the same level as the battle arena, leading out onto the sands. Above each of the three doors, was either the Magi insignia, Combat Specialist insignia, or Weapons Master insignia—as well as their respective god statues.

This was the first time Jude had ever been to any Trials battle, and he found himself both anxious and nervous to see the first battle. Jude knew that as soon as Lynn had chosen him and Bree as contenders for the Trials, they would soon be challengers. However, seeing Bree on the stage with the other challengers, filled him with worry. He knew Bree was an agile and smart fighter. He had fought alongside her against Lynn in the Academy courtyard. However, he could not help but realize that her four opponents had to be just as skilled or they would not have been chosen. Jude was especially worried about Sia Wyatt, since he had learned from Eli's friend Zane, that she too had known in advanced about the Trials before anyone else.

*I hate cheaters. However, I cannot ignore the fact that I know the gods want me to forgive them. I'd rather not and just endure the consequences.*

He tried his hardest to shake off any ill fillings towards both Eli and Sia.

*Three Brothers, please lend your protection over my friend Bree Braunstone. She is an amazing person, and I am so grateful that you have put her in my life.*

Jude had found a spot in the second row close to the battle arena, but soon relocated to the first row when he was spotted by Eli's dad Marius, and waved over. Jude loved Marius. He was like the father he wished for after his father died, and he respected him fully. However, since Jude knew he and Eli were at odds, he found it uncomfortable to be sitting next to Marius knowing that Eli would soon join them.

"You know the last time I was at a Trials of Magic, Might and Lineage battle, it was my own a little over twenty years ago," said Marius.

"How was it?" asked Jude. He was eager to gain as much insight as possible before his own battle.

"It was exciting! But it was also difficult and taxing," said Marius.

"Any advice?"

Marius looked over at Jude with a smile. For a second, Jude thought that Marius would not share any strategies or tips with him, since he probably wanted his own son to win.

"Never second-guess your instincts, and learn to react instinctually," said Marius. Jude and Marius idly sat in the first row, as last minute stragglers took their seats among them.

"How was it being in battle with friends and peers from your classes?"

A grave look showed on Marius' face before he responded. "It was hard. I had to make some pretty tough decisions while I was down there. But I have no regrets. The life of an Agent is never easy, especially an Agent that has a heart."

"Dad!" said a voice from behind them.

Jude looked over his shoulder to see Eli take the seat next to his dad. The father and son hugged and exchanged greetings before finally settling down. Jude took the opportunity to fully take in every inch of the Coliseum's detail. Across from them in the spectators area, where benches would normally be, stood a small, single squared area roped off with velvet ropes. Inside the roped off area was a seat resembling a throne, as well as three smaller chairs. The backing of the throne was made up of a red cushion backing, outlined by two large white bishop chess pieces on both sides of the chair. Jude marveled at the detail of the throne. Small red and white squares resembling a chessboard were what made up the actual seat of the chair. The area led out into a small balcony that branched off slightly over the sands of the battle arena.

"Doing okay?"

"Huh?" replied Jude.

"A lot on your mind I see," said Marius with a slight smile. "I asked if your mom was doing okay?"

Jude instantly looked at Eli. "She works a lot so I see her every now and then, but I think she is doing okay."

"I have not seen her in a while, and I was thinking of coming over to get some fresh vegetables from her amazing garden," said Marius.

"I think our tomatoes, cucumbers and potatoes are ripe."

"I think you have just bought yourself a visit from yours truly," said Marius.

"I am sure she would love the company," replied Jude with a smile.

*Alright, so clearly Eli has found some childish reason not to talk to me, even though he knows I did nothing to him. I guess I will have to be the bigger person.*

"Hey Eli, how are you?"

Eli turned his head slightly in Jude's direction before responding. "Hi."

*And it goes south.*

Jude turned his attention back towards the balcony he was looking at earlier. He watched as Bishop took his seat at the throne. He wore an emerald green dress robe that had white fur on the shoulders with a matching cape that flowed behind him.

*Wow, he changed just for the Trials.*

Professor Lynn, Ivor and Vance soon joined Bishop; and took their seats in the three remaining reserved seats in front of the Lord. A few guards soon filled in the space among the four of them. As Bishop rose from his throne, silence descended upon the entire Coliseum. The Lord approached the balcony that overlooked the battlefield, and rested his hands on the wall that surrounded it.

"My friends, we are gathered here today in the name of fellowship, tradition, and above all, honor. Through the Trials of Magic, Might and Lineage, we honor the gods with a tradition that has been passed down throughout generations of our land's ancestors. This tradition was not created for the sake of battle or for the death of your adversary. It was not created in the name of selfishness, disloyalty or ill will. This tradition was created as a way to celebrate the collaboration of the three bloodlines, and their loyalty to one another. It was the collaboration of the Three Brothers—our gods—that desecrated the evil one, and brought balance to the world. Furthermore, as we take part in yet another Trials of Magic, Might and Lineage, may us honor the Three Brothers, our land, our way of life, and above all, each other," announced Bishop.

The crowd responded with thunderous applause, whistling and support. Before long, Jude noticed the General of the armed forces, Anya, appear on the sands of the battlefield below.

"May I have your attention please!" announced Anya, her voice echoing throughout the Coliseum. When the commotion ceased and the spectators were still, she continued. "We will now begin round one of the Trials of Magic, Might and Lineage. Presenting the challengers of the Weapons Master bloodline." She pointed towards the first large wooden door on the sands, which was guarded by the Aegis statue. The large door slowly creaked open, revealing a dark passageway behind it.

"Dominic Adams and Lucia Magdalena," announced Anya. Jude watched the small versions of Dominic and Lucia make their way across the sands. Even though they were of the same bloodline, Jude noticed the separation between the two of them, as they ignored the presence of the other.

"Presenting the challengers of the Magi bloodline," said Anya now pointing towards the middle wooden door, which was guarded by the Rune statue. "Tillius Edwards and Sia Wyatt!" The door swung open revealing its challengers, who made their way onto the sands, taking their spots next to their opponents.

"Is that her?" asked Marius.

Jude looked over to Marius to see whom he was talking to.

"That's her. That's Sia," replied Eli.

"Ah son she is beautiful. I am happy for you," replied Marius.

Jude awaited a response from Eli but heard nothing. Eli just stared at the challengers. For a moment, Jude thought he saw sadness in Eli's eyes, but before he could be sure, Anya broke his train of thought.

"And last but not least, presenting the challenger for the Combat Specialist bloodline." She pointed to the last door, which was guarded by the Pith statue. "Bree Braunstone!" The last door swung open revealing its lonesome challenger, who took her position among the circle of competitors.

"Go Bree!" shouted Jude at the top of his lungs. He swung the sign he bought back and forth. He was relieved when Bree soon recognized him and responded to his cheering with a series of heroic gestures.

"Last one standing is the victor!" announced Anya.

Jude looked in Bishop's direction to hopefully catch any evidence of what was going through his mind. The only thing he saw was a blank expression and a snapping gesture from the ruler. Blue sparks trailed after his snap and Anya soon appeared at his side.

"Round one will be: Lucia Magdalena versus Dominic Adams versus Bree Braunstone versus Tillius Edwards versus Sia Wyatt," announced Bishop.

"Begin!"

◆ ◆ ◆

Eli watched in horror as Dominic charged Sia with his sword and shield in hand. Sia jumped back avoiding his back slice, but did not anticipate his shield bash. A loud *clank* echoed off of the walls, as Tillius' shield came in direct contact with Sia's face, sending her flying towards one of the walls—where she made direct contact before hitting the sands.

"Yeah, you gotta watch out for those shields, they'll do that to ya," said Dominic blowing her a kiss.

"No! Leave her alone!" yelled Eli.

"Stupid move Sia!" screamed a voice closeby.

Eli looked over to see Sia's father, Mr. Wyatt, sitting a few rows over from him—along with Mik. Eli felt his blood boiling as he recalled the night he walked Sia home from Bishop's castle after the Necrosis attack.

"Get up now!" yelled Mr. Wyatt.

The sword and shield that Dominic had been holding dissolved, and a bow and arrow took their place. He cocked an arrow, and appeared as if he was ready to fire. Suddenly a large troll appeared behind Dominic, before the mallet it was carrying sent him soaring through the air. Eli watched as spectators screamed, when Dominic's body came crashing down with a *thud,* right on top of them.

"Gotta watch out for mallets, they'll do that to ya," growled the troll in a grotesque deep voice.

Eli looked back to catch Sia returning to her feet.

"Earth Prison!" screamed Sia as her hand punched the ground. A tremor rippled throughout the Coliseum, as hundreds of spectators began to scream. A large trench opened up in front of Sia and darted out towards the troll. Rocks and mud crawled up the troll's legs trapping it, causing it to let out a monstrous howl. Lucia soon appeared at the trolls neck, burying a sword in its' neck, before jumping back down, and avoiding the troll's grab.

"Dagger barrage!" screamed Dominic from the spectator area. A large number of arrows formed in front of him, before shooting in the direction of the troll.

*Oh my gosh she's done for.*

The troll shrunk and Bree soon took its place. The arrows soared too far above her head to be a threat.

"They are all ganging up on her. That isn't fair," said Jude.

"Everything is fair down there I'm afraid my boy. Remind me to tell you a story about my first Trials, and you will understand," replied Marius.

A dagger soared passed Bree barely missing her, and sticking into the wall mere inches from Sia. Bree turned around to see Lucia throwing dagger after dagger from over her head. Now being able to move, Bree broke into a series of back flips that carried her in the opposite direction across the battlefield. Lucia took off in pursuit of Bree, unleashing countless daggers at the girl. Eli was shocked at Lucia's speed, as she soon caught up to Bree in mere seconds.

"My word! She is incredibly fast!" said Marius.

As Bree's flips carried her closer and closer to one of the walls, Lucia closed the distance between them, before summoning two swords.

"Get outta there!" yelled a voice next to Eli.

He looked over to see Jude on his feet, gripping the railing in front of him. Eli could see the worry in his green eyes.

"You're done!" screamed Lucia as she brought both swords above her head, before hammering them straight down at Bree.

Bree did one last back flip before propelling herself high in the air. A loud echo vibrated throughout the Coliseum, as

Lucia's swords made contact with the stadium floor. She quickly picked them up and assumed a fighting stance. Keeping her swords ready, she looked around and soon her head looked towards the Pith statue. Eli followed her gaze.

"You're going to have to do better than that Hun!" yelled Bree down to Lucia from atop the statue.

That was when Eli had realized he had forgotten all about Sia. When he quickly turned his attention back towards the spot he last saw her, dozens of Dominic's arrows ripped through the air towards her. She began to dodge before she was stopped cold, as a green glow enveloped her.

"Why isn't she moving?" asked Eli.

"Stop embarrassing me you stupid brat!" yelled Mr. Wyatt.

"It's Tillius, the other Magi. It looks like paralysis," said Marius.

Eli looked over to Tillius, and found him with his hands in a prayer position, while his mouth appeared to be mumbling something. Eli turned his attention back to Sia, who was still caught in the paralysis.

"Sia you can do it! Break free!" screamed Eli. He noticed her eyes look his direction, before she wiggled and fought against the spell that held her in place, but to no avail.

Sia soon closed her eyes as if accepting what was coming. Right as the arrows made contact, her eyes opened with a glow. The attack ceased, turned around, and hurled back towards Tillius. Tillius dove to avoid the attack, but was not fast enough, as two of the arrows buried themselves into his shoulder, and pinned him against the wall behind him. A scream released across the battlefield. He kicked and struggled in an attempt to break free. Dominic, who had returned to the battle, summoned his sword and shield again, and charged Tillius—who was helpless to move. Just when Eli thought that the Magi was done for, a roar erupted throughout the Coliseum. Many people in the spectator seats covered their ears as a giant gargoyle soared through the oval opening in the Coliseum, and descended upon the battle. It scooped up Dominic in one of its claws, as it soared over the heads of many spectators.

Eli ducked to avoid contact with Bree's tail. She flew back up towards the oval opening of the Coliseum, and tossed Dominic full force directly down towards the sands. Dominic hit the ground with a heavy *thud*. Eli thought he heard a small crack when Dominic came in contact with the ground, but he could not be sure. Eli looked up to see Bree, in her gargoyle form, pelted with arrows, as a few buried themselves in one of her wings. He looked down to see Lucia with her bow in hand, running around the outer wall of the battlefield letting loose dozens of arrows.

Soon Eli saw what looked like Sia, sprinting across the sands towards Tillius. Still in motion, her feet left the ground as lighting erupted from the bottom of her feet, propelling her off of the ground. The ground beneath her burned from the contact with the lightning as she propelled herself higher.

Just when she was level with Tillius, her hands openly pushed forward. "Creeping inferno!" screamed Sia. A cone of flames erupted from her hands, and as soon as the fire made contact with Tillius, the dark figure behind the flames began to convulse. Burning banners cascaded down from the Coliseum walls engulfing the black sands beneath them. The fire traveled around the whole outer wall of the battlefield until the challengers were trapped in a ring of blazes.

The cone of flames from Sia's attack instantly stopped, when a scaly long object swirled around her body, sending her crashing to the sands. Eli looked at the spot where Tillius had been impaled moments before Sia's attack. All that was left was a charred skeleton hanging by two arrows that penetrated its shoulder. Eli returned his attention to Sia, who was coiled up in a large red snake that wrapped around her whole body from head to toe. Its head loomed up above her, as its thin tongue ran across her face.

"Break free you moron!" yelled Mr. Wyatt.

"That is no way to talk to your daughter," said Marius to no one in particular. "I am really tempted to go over there and say something to him."

Sia kicked and jerked but the snake had her pinned. The snake opened its mouth and came down. It buried its fangs into Sia's neck, barely missing her face, before letting out a hiss and loosening its hold on her. The snake slithered away with an arrow protruding from its body. Eli looked over to see Lucia firing another arrow at Sia who dove and dodged. Just as Lucia prepared another arrow for Sia, a dark figure appeared behind her. A dagger let loose a gushing crimson trail, as blood fell from Lucia's neck. Her bow and arrow dissolved, and soon she brought her hand to her neck, pulled it away, and examined the blood. She dropped to her knees, while Dominic appeared behind her, with his dagger in hand. The dagger soon disappeared and a giant war axe appeared in his hand.

"I believe this is what they call overkill!" yelled Dominic as his axe swung down at Lucia's neck decapitating her.

Lucia's head propelled itself through the air landing in the lap of the women next to Jude. The women screamed hysterically as blood whipped across her face. She tried to push Lucia's head away but her fingers got caught in the bloody blonde hair that fell from Lucia's head. Eli returned his attention to the battle to find Dominic jumping to avoid a fireball from Sia.

*Come on Sia just two more.*

A large roar again erupted through the Coliseum, as Bree in her gargoyle form took flight around the battlefield. She swooped down slamming one of her wings into Sia, and sending her tumbling across the sands, before snatching up Dominic once again. Dominic squirmed in Bree's fist trying to break free. The gargoyle roared in pain. Dominic fell a few feet before landing firm on his feet with his dagger at the ready.

Eli heard lightning and looked up to see the sky rumbling through the oval opening of the Coliseum. The sky and clouds turned from blue to gray, as the winds from outside, poured into the Coliseum from the opening in the ceiling. Bree, still in her gargoyle form, swooped down and tried to snatch up Sia, who quickly laid flat on the sands, avoiding Bree's attack. When Bree circled around the Coliseum preparing to return, Sia started running towards Dominic's direction, who had forced his back against the wall to avoid being hit by one of Bree's wings as she circled.

"What are you doing? You are a Wyatt! Wyatt's don't run! Stop being a coward! Turn around and face her! Do you hear me? Face your adversary!" screamed Mr. Wyatt.

Just as Sia had reached the wall on the opposite side of the battlefield, Dominic noticed her presence and summoned his shield and sword, before meeting her charge with his own. Sia stopped and looked to her left to see Bree flying in quickly towards her. She turned back towards her right, and saw Dominic still charging at her. Nausea crept up on Eli.

*She's trapped!*

"You've just made your last mistake!" screamed Sia. She raised both her hands up in an arc. Thunder rumbled and the Coliseum shook, while bolts of lightning poured through the opening in the ceiling. The Coliseum emitted a blinding blue light, as lightning struck both Dominc and Bree simultaneously. The light was so bright, that Eli had to look away. When the flash had finally subsided, Eli looked back towards the battlefield, but went into a panic. Most of the battlefield had been set aflame, while clouds of smoke rose from the black sands. The air smelled of burning flesh and charcoal.

Bree laid flat in the middle of the battlefield. Smoke rose from her wings, tail and head, while her body was motionless. Eli looked around but could not find Sia or Dominic.

"Dad! Where is she? Where is Sia?" asked Eli

Both Marius and Jude looked around, along with the other spectators. "I don't know son."

The whole Coliseum fell silent, as spectators stared at the only challenger left on the field. Bree's gargoyle form began to shrink, and her familiar blonde hair and small frame appeared once more. When her entire human form had returned, Eli noticed she was lying on top of something.

"What is that?" asked Marius.

"It's Sia and Dominic!" yelled Eli.

A pile of bodies appeared while Bree laid motionless on top of Dominic, who was in the middle, and Sia, who was on the bottom. Just as quickly as hope and excitement swelled inside Eli, it left.

"Get up you halfwit!" screamed Mr. Wyatt. He quickly rose from his seat.

"Why aren't they moving?" asked Jude.

A small bit of movement shook the pile of bodies. Sia's arm pushed Dominic's body slightly off of her.

*She's alive!*

Bree and Dominic's bodies tumbled off of Sia as she struggled to return to her feet. Eli jumped up out of his seat, and just as he was about to jump down to the battlefield, a hand grabbed his wrist. He looked down to find Marius staring up at him.

"No son, this is a journey she has to do on her own."

Eli studied Marius's eyes for a while and then the battlefield. He remained standing with both hands grabbing the railing in front of him.

*I'm here for you.*

Sia attempted to return to her feet but collapsed, sending her face landing face first into the sands. A series of gasps soon followed.

"Get up you filth!" screamed Mr. Wyatt. Eli felt himself reach his breaking point. He had enough of hearing Sia's dad talk to her like that.

"Shut up she's not filth! You're the filth you pig!" screamed Eli. Many people who were sitting next to Sia's father turned their heads to look at Eli, who watched as Sia's father rose to his feet and calmly walked towards him. When he was finally standing face-to-face with Eli, he just stood there motionless glaring at him. Eli glared back.

*I'm not scared of you.*

"I am sorry I must have overheard you dog! What did you say?"

Eli saw a flash of movement, and before he could realize what was going on, his father was standing between him and Mr. Wyatt with a dagger at his throat.

"No one! And I repeat, no one! Calls my son a dog! I suggest you sit down before I put you down!" said Marius.

Mr. Wyatt studied Marius for a while before returning to his seat. Eli noticed Mik never turned his attention in their direction. Eli heard movement down below and instantly returned his attention back to the battlefield. Sia was crouched on one knee. When she pushed up from the ground, her hand instantly went to her chest as she let out a scream. She looked around the Coliseum until her eyes found him.

Eli smiled down at her. Even with the dirt and blood plastered across her face and in her hair, she still looked beautiful. She returned his smile, and as the smile formed, blood came pouring out of her mouth. Sia's eyes rolled back into her head. She swirled around collapsing to the ground, and her body was still.

# A FALLEN FRIEND

Jude felt numb to everything going on around him and inside of him, once the match came to an end. Seeing Bree's body, void of any life, brought about a grief so heavy, that Jude thought he would break if anyone even so much as touched him. Bishop had excused all of the spectators from the match as soon as it was over. He wanted to give the families alone time to mourn their losses, without any interference from any outside parties. Jude disagreed with Bishop's decision to an extent. He may not have been in Bree's family by blood, but he still felt extremely close to her. Even though Jude did not know or particularly like Sia, he felt a little worried about her condition. He knew that Eli had some kind of feelings for her. It was apparent every time he looked at her. However, Jude did not think the brown-haired girl would make it through her injuries.

During his walk back to the watering hole, memories of Bree's big blue eyes flashed across Jude's vision. He relived his battle alongside Bree against Professor Lynn time and time again. Out of everyone, Jude was sure Bree would be a winner in the Trials. She was confident, smart and skilled. It was hard for Jude to think that even that was not enough to save her. As the grief made a home in his heart, Jude thought about how he would feel if he had seen Aileen or Jed the way he just saw Bree.

*I think my body would instantly shut down and I would die if I lost them.*

When Jude began to imagine the pain that Bree's parents must be going through, he wandered across a familiar sight. Aileen stood hunched over her garden, watering a few patches as she hummed an indecipherable tune. Time seemed to stand still as Jude stared at his mother, and all of the memories of his childhood flooded into his vision. He sighed.

*She may have lied to me, but she is my mother, and I know she loves me.*

Just as Jude snapped out of his reverie, Aileen looked up and instantly stopped what she was doing. Neither spoke nor moved, and the only noise audible was the leaves of the plants in her garden, blowing in the wind.

"Hi mom."

"Hi Jude. Back from the Trials?"

"Yes," he replied.

"So did you win or did you—."

"Mom before you proceed to ask me how the Trials went, I think we need to talk. Can we go inside?"

"Sure Jude, I'll put some tea on."

Jude followed Aileen into the house and closed the front door behind them. To his surprise, he did not feel like he was home when the living area and kitchen spread out in front of him.

*What is it about having a disagreement with your parents, that makes you feel unwelcome in your own home?*

While he followed his mom into the kitchen, he gazed at the large family painting that hung on the wall in the middle of the living area. It was of him, Jed, his mom and his dad. He guessed he was around eight years old in the painting. When the daydream came to a halt, Jude continued towards the kitchen, where he found Aileen cleaning around a pot of water that was boiling on the stove. Jude took a seat at the table, and as he sat down, he remembered his first day at the Academy when Eli came over for breakfast and they all sat down together—even Jed.

*I never thought I would see the day when my mother and my best friend, both felt like complete strangers.*

Aileen placed a cup in front of Jude and a cup in front of the seat across from him. She kept her head low, never looking up from what she was doing. After retrieving the hot water from the stove and pouring both Jude and herself a cup of tea, she sat down with both hands clasped around her cup. Jude simply stared at the woman in front of him while she fiddled with a crack in her cup. He took a sip of his tea and instantly recoiled at the heat.

"Is it too hot?" she asked quickly.

"No it's fine."

*It's like drinking flames.*

"Look mom, I cannot do this with you anymore. I know we both have had our differences, but I just sat and watched a close friend die in battle in front of my very eyes. She was one of the kindest people I knew. What's worse about the whole situation is, I did not even get a chance to say goodbye or tell her that she was an inspiration in my life. I took her for granted all this time, thinking that she would always be around. I do not know if I will ever be the same after seeing what I saw today. However, what I do know is that I do not think I can live through seeing you or Jed in the same lifeless state that I saw Bree in today. I will not live through it. We both know you lied to me and I am pretty sure you have your reasons why you believe that it was the right thing to do. All I want to tell you is that Jed is my friend and my family, just like you are. No matter how much you may think he is a negative influence on me, know that I am an adult, and that I am responsible for my own actions. It would not matter if Jed was Anim himself. It is I who makes the decision about who I am going to be in this life. All I need from you is to just respect that, respect me, and to love me no matter what. Because honestly I cannot live without either one of you," said Jude.

As soon as Jude was finished talking, he watched as tears began to stream from his mom's eyes. She buried her face in her hands, and soon muffled sobs became audible. She got up from her seat, walked around the table, and wrapped her arms around him. Jude got up from his seat and wrapped his arms around her, rubbing her back as she sobbed.

"I am so sorry Jude—for everything. For lying to you, for hitting you, for not caring that you have not come home for the past couple of days. I just want what is best for you," said Aileen.

"I know mom, and I am sorry too for all of the mean things I have said to you. They were out of anger, but I was still wrong. I think we both just need to work on being more honest and open with each other, and I think we will be fine."

"Yes I agree," said Aileen still sobbing. She unhinged herself from their embrace and cupped Jude's face between her hands. "You are not my little boy anymore are you? You are all grown up. Now you are my big, brave warrior."

"Mom I will always be your little boy just like I will always be here to protect you." Aileen slowly began to sob again as she took Jude in another embrace. "Can you just do me a favor mom?"

"Yes Jude anything."

"Can you make an honest effort to get to know Jed? I mean really get to know him. He needs you like I do."

"Oh honey he doesn't need me, not anymore," replied Aileen pulling away from their embrace.

"He does mom, I have talked to him, and he has been in pain since you guys have stopped talking. He misses you and still loves you."

Aileen just stared at Jude for a while. "Oh my—you have really grown up haven't you? Okay Jude I promise."

Afterwards Jude made a quick trip to the castle to speak with Vance. He took one last look at the Three Brothers statue that stood tall in front of the Academy, before heading home to get as much sleep as possible. He was not sure if he would be chosen tomorrow. He actually hoped that he would go last so he could study some of the techniques of the other challengers.

Regardless of whether or not he was going to be chosen tomorrow, he wanted to make sure that he was ready.

◆ ◆ ◆

Eli felt a deep pain in his chest when he saw Sia's body hit the ground. His brain automatically told him to stop breathing, and the tears from his eyes soon felt as natural as blinking. Anya had appeared on the battlefield after Sia had collapsed. Professor Vance and Professor Lynn, who aided her with carrying the bodies to the healers, accompanied her. All of the spectators had been instructed to leave so the families could have alone time with their loved ones. Marius tried to persuade Eli to come home with him, but he had decided that he was not going to leave Sia. Eli had begged Bishop to let him see Sia but Bishop declined, due to Mr. Wyatt's request. Bishop did however, allow Eli to sit in the holding area outside of the Medicinal Quarters—where the contenders were chosen for the Trials.

While Eli made peace with the grief inside of him, he noticed a panic that erupted throughout the room. Mentors, healers and soldiers ran rapid in and out of the Medicinal Quarters, as commotion erupted throughout the room. When Eli began to approach the hut, his path was blocked by a tall figure.

"Where do you think you're going dog?" asked Mr. Wyatt.

"I just wanted to see what the commotion was—that's all.

"Whatever this 'commotion,' is, it does not concern you. So be a good boy and run along." Before Eli could respond, a healer dressed in an all white tunic with matching pants, sprinted up from behind Mr. Wyatt.

"Sir, if we are going to save her, we will need your permission to treat her immediately," said the healer.

*Save her?*

"She's alive?"

"Yes but not for long, she is bleeding internally and we may not be able to stop it. Not unless we act now," replied the healer.

"Very well, do what you must," said Mr. Wyatt.

A bit of hope found its way into Eli's heart, as he looked over Mr. Wyatt's shoulder, and saw a glimpse of Sia on a table inside of the Medicinal Quarters. Her body was wrapped up with bloodstained bandages and crisp white sheets. Her chest lightly rose and fell while the rest of her body showed no sign of movement. He walked closer to get a better view.

"You are *not* going in there dog, and the faster you learn to accept that, the better," said Mr. Wyatt.

"We're losing her!" yelled one of the healers operating on Sia.

*No!*

Eli sprinted passed Mr. Wyatt as fast as he could. He did not care what Mr. Wyatt said. He needed to help her.

"Guards remove this troublemaker at once!" screamed Mr. Wyatt.

When Eli walked into the door of the Medicinal Quarters, his heart sunk, as he watched Sia's body jerk violently atop her bed. Blood splattered out of her mouth and the bandages around her neck turned more and more red. Eli felt a hand close around both of his arms. He turned around to see two guards pulling him away.

"Please come with us sir," said one of the guards as they both pulled him away from the operating room and towards the main door.

"No! She needs me! Please!" screamed Eli as loud as he could.

"She does not need you silly boy," laughed Mr. Wyatt.

"What is going on out here," said Professor Vance walking out of the operating room. Eli broke out of the grip of the two soldiers and ran over to Professor Vance as fast as he could.

"Professor please! All I want to do is see her. She needs me! I can help her make it through this, I swear, just please let me stay. I'll do anything you want! Please!"

Eli watched as Vance looked over to Mr. Wyatt.

"Absolutely not! That boy is a menace and a troublemaker. I do not want him anywhere near my daughter. Out! I want him out!"

Vance turned his attention back to Eli, sorrow displayed on his face. "I am so sorry my boy, but that is her father, and we have to respect his wishes." He nodded his head towards the guards.

Eli found himself being pulled away again. He fought as hard as he could. "Please!" Desperate to escape the hold of the guards, Eli summoned a dagger in his hand.

"He's got a knife!"

Eli's head began to hurt severely as blackness caved in from all corners.

*No, what's going on.*

He felt dizzy while the blackness covered the last clear portion of his vision; and then all he saw was Sia on the battlefield smiling up at him, as blood fell from her mouth.

*Please don't leave.*

# ALL A DREAM

Jude had slept in his bed for the first time since his argument with Aileen. Even though his house did not feel like his home, his bed still comforted him with a stability that he had missed. Jude had woken up a couple of hours before dawn to attend the funeral ceremony for Bree and the other challengers. As he looked in the mirror, he wondered how he would be able to get through Bree's funeral and still be able to perform at his best, if he was named a challenger in today's Trials.

*Why can't they postpone the Trials to give us time to grieve?*

Jude had not been to a funeral ceremony before. When his father died, he was told that his dad's body was too badly mangled and disfigured to have a funeral. His comrades had made him a gravesite on the battlefield after the mission was over. Jed had suspected that Jude would be attending Bree's funeral ceremony, and dropped by to provide him with proper attire.

"Why is there a hood?"

"I can understand if you have never been to a funeral, but are you really completely oblivious to our customs?" said Jed.

"Mom used to shield me from anything having to do with death, she always said I was too young."

"It will be easier to understand if I explain throughout the ceremony."

Jude put on a slate black robe, with the symbol of Pith embroidered in silver on the back, over the slacks and sweater he had originally put on. Jed had explained that it was customary to wear the bloodline color of the deceased you are paying respects to, in hopes that their god would aid their spirit into the next life.

"Are you sure this is wise for you to attend a funeral, knowing that you may be a challenger today?" said Jed.

"I do not care if it is wise or not, she was my friend, and I want to be there for her."

Aileen had come in to check on them a little before they were ready to leave. She was not able to accompany them to the funeral, even though she stressed she wanted to attend. Aileen had picked up an early shift at the library so she would be able to attend the Trials later on in the afternoon, if Jude was named a challenger. Jude was grateful for the effort his mother was making and responded with a hug on her way out. He was surprised to see that she initiated an embrace with Jed as well, which ended in an awkward tangle of arms and hands.

An icy cold breeze blew across Jude's face as he opened his front door. The sun had not yet risen, and the darkness that enveloped the city, gave a sense of watchful eyes amidst the air. This was the first time Jude had felt nervous and uncomfortable behind the great white walls that protected the city.

*It feels like we are about to be ambushed.*

"We have to hurry or we will miss the pilgrim's path," said Jed closing the door behind him.

"The what?"

"Oh little brother, what would you do without me," said Jed exposing his fangs.

The wind created echoes throughout the side streets and alleys, when Jude accompanied Jed to the southern gates. Jed had instructed Jude to keep the hood of his funeral robe up at all times. Jude somewhat panicked when he put the hood up and it stuck in place, unyielding to any winds or movements. Jed had explained that the robe was enchanted, and that the hood would never come down on its own, only by the wearer. Anxiety and sorrow made their way in and out of Jude's heart as Jed explained what lay ahead.

"The pilgrim's path is a slow march from the main gates to the burial site. During the march, family and friends of the deceased, follow behind a group of men called Canaan Shepherds. The responsibility of the shepherds, is to carry the body from the city to the burial site. Before the journey begins, the shepherds make an oath with the gods to ensure safe passage of the soul of the deceased into the afterlife; in exchange for their word that no harm or defilement shall come to the body. If any does, the shepherds carry the shame into the next life where they will be tormented for eternity," said Jed licking his teeth.

"But why would someone want to take on that kind of responsibility with so much at stake?"

"I couldn't tell you. There is nothing really at stake for someone like me who is already damned for all of eternity. On the contrary, it would give me something different to do besides my usual massacres. If I had to guess, I would say that humans do it to have some sort of a shot at redemption for past bad deeds."

A cloud of black, blue, and red robes covered the path ahead of Jude, when he came around the last corner at the southern gates. Hundreds of people crowded around four different areas in front of him. Jude heard sounds of crying, mumbling and screams.

"What are they doing?"

"It is the final goodbye before the departure," said Jed.

Jude was comforted that Jed was there by his side as they passed through the crowd of people. Four transparent coffins laid spread out in a circle among the hundreds of hooded figures. To Jude, the coffins appeared to be made out of clear glass, but he could not be sure. As Jude came across the first coffin, his heart started racing and his stomach started turning, when he gazed upon the face of Dominic. Burns and scars were still visible on his hands and face, however majority of his injuries had been covered up somehow. He was dressed in a red cape with a matching tunic and pants. His hands were clasped over his heart around the pommel of his sword. He looked as if he might get up for battle at any minute.

Jude was disturbed when he came to Lucia's coffin and saw that her unattached head had been placed at her neck, as if it was still apart of her body. After passing Tillius' coffin, he knew what was soon to come, and in turn slowed his pace. A hand lightly grabbed his shoulder. Jude looked up into a pair of white translucent eyes that gave no signs of life. To Jude, his fangs appeared sharper than any blade in existence.

"You will be fine," said Jed retracting his fangs. Jude stared at Jed for a few seconds before turning towards the last coffin.

Bree's small frame laid flat on a bed of flower petals and large leaves. Jude recognized the larger leaves that made up most of her bed, as the black cherry leaves that hung from a group of trees in the eastern part of the forest. Dozens of white daisies lay scattered around Bree's body atop the cherry leaves. A few white daisies were scattered throughout her bright blonde hair that laid perfectly straight on either side of her flowing white dress. The coffin that she laid in was so clear, that Jude could not find its edges or surface. He found himself running his hand along where the top should be, to assure himself that there was anything even there.

*She looks like she is floating in midair.*

"It's not glass, if that is what you are thinking," said Jed.

"What is it?"

"To be honest, nothing. What you feel is the barrier between this world and the next. It is the greatest unsolved riddle of the world."

"What do you mean?"

"The barrier is supposed to protect the body from any demons or evil spirits that want to possess the body before it makes it into the ground. Once the body is in the ground, it is said that nature and the gods protect it from there on. Only thing is, the barrier does not appear for everyone, and no one knows why."

Slow chimes and bells rang softly behind Jude while Bree's big blue eyes flashed across his memory. When Jude turned around, he saw a group of men dressed in all white robes and pants with matching hoods, which covered the identity of their faces. They walked in two perfect lines never missing a beat. Small bells and other instruments hung from their hands, as they walked slowly in unison up to the group of people that crowded around the coffins. The crowd parted, opening a path in the middle of the sea of people, as the cloaked men crossed the path.

"It's the shepherds," said Jed.

The shepherds assembled around the coffins. The sound of the bells and chimes soon ceased, as the coffins began to rise in unison. Four shepherds carried each coffin towards the southern gate, as the large wooden doors creaked open revealing a long path that led into the darkness of the forest. The people dressed in the black, red, and blue robes soon assembled behind the traveling coffins. Tears were prevalent in their eyes, while they followed their loved ones into the trees. Jude found himself a few feet behind Bree's coffin, never taking his eyes off of her.

*Why did this have to happen to her? Why would the gods let this happen to a good person?*

The peacefulness of the forest did not comfort but taunted him with the fact that she would never rise again. The long dirt road went on for what seemed like miles to Jude, as the tall trees continued to overshadow its visitors on both sides. When the clearing opened up, the first thing Jude noticed was the abrupt change of his surroundings. Tall light pink cherry blossom trees went on for miles in all directions. Small pink leaves fell slowly from the trees as the wind brushed the branches of their captives. The shepherds continued on through the forest, never stopping and never slowing.

"I will never forget you," said a voice to Jude's right. He looked over to find no one but Jed walking by his side.

"What did you say?"

"I didn't say anything," said Jed.

"Are you sure?"

Jed just stared at him for a few seconds, before returning his gaze to the front of the group.

"Don't leave," said a voice behind Jude. He jerked his head around to find a few red-hooded figures marching behind him.

*I think I am losing my mind.*

When the march slowed and came to a halt, Jude looked up to find an open meadow that started from where the last cherry blossom tree ended, and then continued on as far as the eye could see. Four rectangular holes were laid out on the meadow, with two on each side. The chimes and bells soon continued as the shepherds let go of the coffins. Jude found himself alarmed, wanting to lunge after the coffins afraid they would break, once all of the shepherds released them. However, once the last shepherd let go, all four of the coffins remained suspended in the air, as if hands still guided them. The shepherds strayed away from the coffins, taking their positions along a corner of the rectangular holes in the lush grass.

The coffins slowly began to glide until all four of them hovered above their own hole, before slowly lowering into the ground. While Jude watched Bree's coffin slowly submerge until it was no longer visible, a hand cupped his shoulder.

"She will be at peace, never worrying about anything ever again," said Jed.

"But I just don't understand why the gods would take her. I asked them to protect her and they failed her; I failed her."

"It may be wise to consult a fellow follower on why the gods do what they do. Asking an immortal, who has an inevitable fate with hell, is prone to bias," said Jed.

"I just don't understand."

"Ease your mind little brother and watch."

Jude watched in awe as the holes began to bury themselves. Dirt filled up each hole simultaneously until only small patches were visible. A shepherd from each grave reached into his robe and pulled out what appeared to be a small plant. The plant was mostly small branches and contained only one small light pink petal. The plant was buried on top of the respective graves until only the pink petal was visible. As the shepherds and followers stepped back from the graves, a strong wind passed through the trees behind Jude and up to the graves. The small pink petal on each grave blew in the wind slightly before calming.

"Now you will see why everyone wears hoods," said Jed.

The sky began to brighten as the sun began to rise. Jude looked towards the horizon to see the familiar orange and yellow rays pour out across the edge of the sky. Jude looked down at the meadow as the sun's rays soon crept over the grass of the meadow. A clear line between darkness and light pushed closer and closer towards the crowds, until the sun's rays cast light upon everything around the attendees.

"The sunrise is the second birthday of the deceased. Today is the first day of the rest of their eternal life. The sun's rays are a blessing that can only be bestowed on the deceased, if their bodies are the first mortal things they hit. The hoods enchant the wearer with a spell that makes us invisible to the sun," said Jed.

Jude looked on as the graves lit up with the orange and yellow rays that rained down from the horizon. As Jude turned his attention towards the sunrise, an explosion of four light pink rays erupted from the sun. The clouds departed, as time seemed to stop all around him. It was the most beautiful thing Jude had ever seen. The pink rays directly hit their own grave, as the sun and the graves appeared connected for a few seconds; and then the pink rays were gone. Jude looked from the graves to the sun, but all that was left was a normal sunrise. The rays of sunlight hurt Jude's eyes when he looked directly into the sun, but he forced himself to look anyways. When the crowds began to retreat back towards the forest of cherry blossom trees and eventually home, Jude took one last look at Bree's grave. He kneeled down in front of it and took a deep breath.

"I will never forget you. You will have a place in my heart for as long as I live," said Jude. When Jude walked with Jed away from the graves, he took one last look over his shoulder. A second light pink petal occupied the plant on Bree's grave.

"It was a dream—all a dream," said an omnipresent voice.

# PREMONITION

Eli awoke with a severe headache that made it hard to open his eyes. He looked around noticing bits of red and white, but his vision still felt hazy.

"Ah finally bored of the inside of our eyelids are we?" said a familiar voice.

"Yeah," said Eli rubbing his eyes.

As soon as Eli was done rubbing his eyes, he found himself lying on the familiar red couch that sat perched in front of the glass chess set. He turned his head to find Bishop in a dark purple robe, hands firmly positioned behind his back. Eli sat and thought for a second. He knew where he was, but could not think of why he was in Bishop's quarters or how he had got there.

"What time is it?"

"I would say about an hour before sunrise," replied Bishop.

"What's going on?"

"I was hoping that you could tell me—Mr. Brassie. From what I have been told, you pulled a dagger on two guards with civilians present. Now that does not seem like something you would do, so instead of allowing you to become another victim of Mr. Wyatt's holding cells, I had you brought here," said Bishop.

"Wait, did you say Mr. Wyatt's holding cells?"

"Yes, he is head of our city's jails."

*Wooden benches, healers and Mr. Wyatt swam throughout his vision. "Absolutely not! That boy is a menace and a troublemaker. I do not want him anywhere near my daughter. Out! I want him out!" A blonde boy in a belted tunic being dragged out by two guards surfaced. He summons a dagger, and all goes black.*

"Do you want to tell me what's going on?" asked

Bishop.

When Eli's vision came back to the red and white quarters, he turned to see that Bishop had taken a seat on the couch across from him. Only the wooden table holding the glass chess set separated them.

"I did it sir."

"Did what my boy?"

"I pulled a dagger on the guards. Mr. Wyatt would not let me see Sia, and she was dying. The guards wouldn't even listen to me when they dragged me away." Eli clasped his hands in front of him, beginning to realize how foolish he must have looked. "I was desperate."

Bishop stared at Eli for a while before getting up from the couch and returning with a pot of hot tea and two cups. He poured Eli a cup and then poured himself a cup.

"I find myself to be a compassionate man. But I am also proud to say that I am a man that knows when being brash, is sometimes the best way to go about things. It is because of this, I find it in your best interest to be the first to tell you that the healers will no longer be treating Sia Wyatt."

"I'm sorry sir, I don't understand why they would stop. Last time I saw her, she was in critical condition and they were not sure if she was going to make it."

"That is correct, she was in critical condition which is why they have decided to stop treating her. Her condition far surpasses any of our best healers' abilities. Even if they were to find some farfetched way to aid her recovery, the chances are too slim. That is why Mr. Wyatt has given specific instructions to stop all treatments henceforth," said Bishop.

Rage instantly had hold of Eli as he found himself standing when he was just sitting a few seconds ago. "That is not up to him!"

"I am afraid it is my boy. He is her father and his word is law in this situation I'm afraid," said Bishop.

"So you're going to just stand by and let her die!"

"This situation does not involve me, so no I will not be standing by, I will be minding my own business—and I strongly suggest you do the same."

Eli heard doors opening behind him. Looking into Bishop's eyes, Eli saw resistance that showed no signs of weakness.

*He doesn't care.*

"You requested my services," said a voice behind Eli.

Eli turned around to see an unfamiliar dark haired soldier standing behind him. Unlike the other soldiers, this one did not wear any armor, just a black shirt, white utility belt, and black combat pants. His brown eyes were shrouded in both mystery and hostility.

"Ah Fox, I am glad you're here. Eli I would like for you to meet Fox, I have asked him to accompany you home tonight; just to make sure you make it home okay."

*No you just want to make sure that I go home, and not to see Sia.*

"I promise we will stop for milk and cookies on the way," said Fox extending his hand.

*Milk and cookies? Who does this guy think he is? Shake your own hand buddy.*

"Now Fox we won't be needing any of your mouth tonight, Mr. Brassie has had a long night," said Bishop.

"Yeah that's what they all say at first, but trust me, they eventually come around," said Fox licking his lips.

Eli knew it was not wise to anger not only the ruler of Kismet, but also his dad's best friend, so he took a few deep breaths to regain his composure. "I apologize for my outburst sir. I have been under a lot of stress due to the Trials, and I didn't mean what I said."

"It's quite alright my boy. A long nights rest is all you need," replied Bishop. He walked Eli out to the castle courtyard accompanied by Fox. Once Bishop was gone and the familiar Market District came into view, Eli started the countdown in his head of how long it would be before he got to his bed. He rated walking home with Fox as one of the top three worst moments of his life. Fox had already ridiculed him for his plan of action against the guards, as well as his current hair situation.

"You will never catch a stud like myself with hair like yours, let me be the first to tell you," said Fox.

Eli soon learned to ignore every word that came out of Fox's mouth. When his eyes found his house, Eli was beyond relieved.

"This is my house. Have a good night." Eli walked up to his door.

"I'm such a horrible babysitter, I totally forgot about the milk and cookies. Maybe next time," said Fox.

Eli glared at Fox but ignored him. As he opened his front door, a hand quickly grabbed his wrist. He looked down to find Fox restraining him.

"Don't forget to lock up," said Fox with a smirk on his face.

Eli jerked his wrist away and slammed the door behind him. He realized he probably only had a couple of hours of sleep to look forward to, before heading to the Coliseum; so he went straight to bed.

*Flowers and trees circled for miles. Purple, pink and blue roses scattered throughout the lush greenery. Frogs croaked and birds chirped from no clear direction. He knew it was her before she even turned around. As her light purple eyes stared deeply into his, the waterfall that flowed behind her turned as red as blood. He felt his nose moisten and went to wipe it only to return with a trail of blood.*

*"I don't have much time," she said. "He grows stronger each and every day. Soon no one will be able to stop him. He is coming for us." She let out a shriek as she dissolved before him.*

*He reached out to catch her, but instead slipped and fell into complete darkness.*

Hot air and moist skin was what greeted Eli when he peered at his bedroom window. Dozens of lights from surrounding homes gleamed dimly in the night air beneath the sheer shine of the moon. Eli took a few moments to catch his breath as he wiped his face dry.

*A dream. It was just a dream.*

Eli knew trying to get back to sleep after a dream like that would be useless. Ever since he was a kid, he could never go back to sleep whenever he experienced a bad dream. The only times he was able to actually return to somewhat of a slumber, was when his mother was there to sing at his bedside. He missed her dearly, and wished that he could talk to her like he used to.

He got out of bed and walked to his washroom. After splashing a few handfuls of water on his face, he examined himself in the mirror. Weary blue eyes and tangled hair stared back at him in his reflection. He splashed one more handful of water on his face, before drying it with a towel, and returning to his room. He slipped on a navy sweater and some black pants before leaving his room. The familiar sound of Marius snoring in the next room forced him to laugh slightly, which made him slap a hand over his mouth to muffle the noise. While he slowly made his way down the stairs and out of the front door, a brisk cold air swept across his face, while the smell of fresh grass lightly touched his nose.

*Well if I can't sleep, the least I can do is get some training in.*

Eli made his way down the familiar cobblestones and headed towards the city's main gates. The night was quiet except for the sound of running water behind him, which he knew came from the Three Brothers fountain in the Market District. Eli replayed his night terror over and over again. The first thing he wondered was what the place was that he had visited in his dream. He was completely sure he had never been there before, however there was still a sense of familiarity to the location. The last thing he wondered was whether or not there was any validity or credibility to Sia's words in the dream. He had never been one to take dreams too seriously in the past, but this dream seemed so real; and he had heard stories of people having premonitions about events that had not yet come to pass.

Eli received a couple of nods from the Erudite guards that stood watch at the gates, as the forest's lush greenery came into view. He made sure to greet both of them with a smile. Shadows crept at every inch of the forest concealing everything beyond its entrance. Eli felt a shudder pass through him when he ventured through the first few yards of trees. He headed in the direction of the Forgotten Forest but knew he had no idea of where he was going.

After traveling for a while, he came across a large oak tree that stood out amongst the other trees. Eli examined the shrouded blanket of leaves and branches that made the tree look sort of like a hut. As he walked closer to the tree, a curtain of the tree's leaves blocked his way. He casually pushed the leaves aside and walked under the tree's shelter. He could not explain the feeling, but he felt like he was being watched. The feeling should have alarmed him, however he found himself more intrigued than unsettled. He exited through the curtain of leaves he had originally entered through, and headed to his right. The tightly staggered trees went on for a couple of miles before opening up into a path.

Walking down the path, Eli noticed a change in the scenery around him. The familiar trees, which he was accustomed to seeing, were replaced by a confusing sight. To his left, every tree that lined his path was filled with royal blue petals, so vibrant and so piercing, that the longer he looked at them, the more lost in thought he became. He broke away from the sight only to find himself staring at the same trees on his right, which were filled with light purple petals. Eli noticed a transparent silhouette of Sia's face appear throughout the leaves for a short moment, before disappearing.

*They are the same color as her eyes.*

As Eli continued down the path, a light pink statue stopped him. The statue was of a woman with long hair and outstretched wings. Eli thought she looked like one of the beautiful angels that his mother had shown him in a book she had read to him when he was a child. The woman was frowning and worry seemed to swim in her eyes. He looked around and soon realized that the wall behind the angel marked a dead end. He looked at her again. This time he noticed she was holding something. As he walked closer, he soon realized that she was holding what appeared to be a heart. He looked back up at her smiling face. He shook his head thinking he must be seeing things.

*Wasn't she frowning a second ago?*

He sat cross-legged in front of her, staring at her unyielding eyes. He welcomed the drowsiness when his eyes began to flutter.

*I see your heart and it is true. You may enter.*

Eli awoke to a wet tickling sensation on his face. When his eyes opened, he found himself looking into the baby blue eyes of a small animal he had never seen before. It had white fur like some of the rabbits of Kismet, but its face and body were small and round. When he sprang up from where he was lying, the creature fled, before turning around to assault him with a series of squeaks. Its long orange tongue sagged loosely from his mouth, while his baby blue eyes returned Eli's gaze.

*What is that?*

As if responding to his thoughts, the creature took off running towards the direction of the statue. When Eli turned to see where it was going, he noticed something strange. The statue was gone. All that stood in front of him, was the same large wall with a large crevice in the spot where the statue once stood. While he continued down the path, the small creature continued to squeak as it scurried in front of him. When the crevice ended and the inner area branched out in front of him, Eli stopped.

*What is this place?*

# END OF THE LINE

Jude was both relieved and anxious when he was chosen to be a challenger in the second round of the Trials of Magic, Might and Lineage. He didn't think he could sit idly by in the spectator seats another round. Once the urn had teleported him to the front of the holding area, he knew his time had come. He looked down to find that his favorite combat pants and tunic were replaced with black leather armor pants and an all black cuirass. He had to admit that he felt more protected in the pre-selected armor, than in his personal clothing he was originally wearing. As he looked out over the crowd, he instantly noticed the tangle of blonde hair he was looking for. Eli returned Jude's gaze while he sat arms crossed on one of the benches in the holding area.

Professor Ivor came in and dismissed the remaining contenders, so that the five chosen challengers could get ready for their upcoming battle. The same door, which Jude had seen before, appeared along one of the stone-walls of the holding area. Professor Ivor led the way, ushering in the selected individuals. Jude walked nervously in the back, taking in every inch of the holding area as if for the first time. He noticed the ceiling was engraved with a depiction of some sort of battle. An Agent stood with one foot standing on top of a pile of fallen soldiers. In one hand was a sword, in the other hand was a severed head hanging by its hair in the grip of the Agent.

"Jude!" said a voice behind him.

Jude turned around to find Professor Lynn staring back at him. Her smooth brown skin complimented the brown dress robes she was wearing perfectly.

"Hi Professor."

Lynn just stared back motionless. Jude waited for a response or some hint of what his mentor was originally going to say. A hard rumbling echoed throughout the room. Jude turned around to find the door to the Coliseum sliding closed. He ran towards the closing door, in an attempt to not be left behind. Ducking under the stone slab, he looked back to find that Lynn had not moved from her spot.

"Be strong," said Lynn before her view was cut off by the cold wall that separated them.

The first thing that Jude noticed, was how cold and dark the corridor was, once the door had closed behind him. A few small lights hung on the walls, but for the most part, the room was dim. Jude quickly caught up to the remaining challengers after his brief interaction with Lynn. Ivor had been waiting for him when he entered the briefing room tardy. Ivor scolded Jude many times about honor and disrespect, but Jude ignored the Professor's words. The whole time that Ivor was talking, Jude began to reminisce about him and Eli as kids. They always dreamed about this very moment and it was finally here. The only thing they had not anticipated about this moment, was how much was at stake.

*We were clueless. If I lose—no—if I die, no one will protect mom or Jed from any future threats. The two of them will eventually return to not speaking to one another. They would go on living alone, absent of any family, for the rest of their lives.*

He felt it. He was ready. As he paced back and forth throughout the briefing room, he examined his current adversaries.

*I have not seen any of them in battle, so I don't know their strategies. Come on Jude think!*

While he was deep in concentration, Joanna walked by eying him. He returned her stare with his own, before dismissing the interaction, and returning to the riddle in his head.

*Well what I do know is that Joanna is of the Weapons Master bloodline. I should expect speed from her as well as close combat with blunt weapons. However, she may also be a long-range fighter if the bow fancies her. She is a wild card and I need to keep as much distance between us as possible; but also some dodging room, just in case she takes on a long-rage assault.*

"Nice to see that I am not the only Combat Specialist in this round," said a voice behind Jude.

Jude turned around to find a boy with the brightest red hair he had ever seen, standing before him. While Jude looked at him, the boy's bright red hair seemed even brighter in comparison to his pale white skin. He wore black-scaled pants and black metal-plated armor.

"Excuse me?"

"Sorry, the name is Raphael. I was talking about how last round that little blonde girl was the only Combat Specialist. That's probably why she got roasted," said the boy.

As Jude stared down into Raphael's stunned eyes as he laid on the floor, Jude was unaware that he had punched him.

"What's your deal!" yelled Raphael.

"That little blonde girl has a name. It's Bree, and she was my friend. Next time you talk about someone getting 'roasted,' I suggest you stop and think that maybe they are someone's child or friend." When Jude turned around, he was ambushed by the stares of the remaining challengers. No one moved or spoke; just stared. When Jude retreated to a secluded corner, he decided to ignore the remaining stares that followed his stride.

*So he is a Combat Specialist as well. Consider him number one on my list.*

Jude shook his head. He was aware that his emotions were getting the best of him. One thing that Jed had always taught him was to never fight with emotion. Emotion was like poison, "it clouds your judgment and hinders your senses and instincts."

*I have to make sure I always have an eye on him. I don't think he will be as versatile as me, but I cannot be too sure. Even with my training, I don't know if these abilities I have been experimenting with will even work, or if they will backfire and cost me my life. His role will change depending on how the battle is going, so I will just have to make sure he never leaves my sight.*

"Nervous?" said a voice. Jude had not noticed that a young girl was standing right in front of him. She was wearing black leather combat pants with royal blue stitching. She wore a royal blue tunic.

*I have already showed the others that emotion can get the best of me. The last thing that I need to happen, is for them to know that the incident was a rare occasion, and that I am actually as ready as I will ever be.*

"Yeah a little," said Jude purposefully tilting his head down.

"Hey it's okay. I'm sure we're all a little nervous. I'm mostly excited though, I've been waiting for this for all of my life," said the girl.

"I'm Jude."

"Katrina Wo. It's nice to meet you."

Jude stared at Katrina's battle tunic. It did not appear to offer that much protection, but he thought the deception might be the whole purpose.

*Why didn't I see it before? The urn reads your blood and places you in the battle attire that represents your bloodline. She is a Magi. Judging from Bree's battle, I cannot give her too much distance and risk paralysis like that Sia girl did. Close combat is probably her weakness. I will need to smother her with an ongoing assault.*

"Well I guess I will leave you to your thoughts. Good luck today," said Katrina as she joined Joanna and Raphael on the other side of the room.

*She is either really nice and in turn really stupid, since she just gave me something to use against her in battle; or she is cunning and she purposefully paraded her niceness around me to get me to lower my guard when I face her.*

As if hearing his thoughts, Katrina turned around and stared at Jude. She gave him a small smile and a flip of her long black hair, while continuing to return his gaze.

Jude returned a smile before taking up interest in a small statue close by. He looked around the room, taking in its entirety. It was a large room made up of dark stone all around. Three large wooden doors occupied the room, one on each of the three walls in front of him. Above each door was one of the bloodline insignias. Making his way across the room, he noticed a small shrine in the center of the room. The shrine was familiar in that it resembled the fountain of the Three Brothers. However, this shrine gave off a heavy energy that grew more unbearable the closer he got to it. When he finally made it to the base of the shrine, the energy he felt dissipated. The Three Brothers stood close together with their hands outstretched as if they were handing something to him. Jude raised his hand over one of the stone hands before noticing a small inscription at the base:

"A prayer is a prayer, no matter the outcome."

Jude said a small prayer to the gods to watch over him during his match. He studied the inscription for a while, before returning his gaze to the shrine. As he circled the statue examining every inch of it, he noticed a young boy with blonde hair meditating in the corner. He wore smoke gray battle pants and a light blue tunic with dark blue lacing. Jude recognized him as John Brills. He lived a few houses down from Jude's, but always stayed indoors. When Jude attempted to close the distance between them, the boy's eyes sprung open revealing the purple glow behind them. The glow quickly dissipated as the boy stared back at Jude.

*Magi. I will have to keep you and Katrina on my radar.*

"I am sorry I did not mean to disturb you."

The boy stared back at Jude for a few seconds before closing his eyes. "Let that be your last mistake," said John.

Jude turned around and retreated to his corner.

*One Combat Specialist, two Magi, and a Weapons Master; I have my work cut out for me.*

A faint echo of applause and cheering echoed throughout the room, as another stonewall—adjacent from the one that Jude had entered through—grinded open. Professor Ivor stepped through the door with his hands folded firmly behind him. A stern expression was plastered across his face.

"I find it amusing that some of you choose to mingle and socialize with the same individuals that aim to take your lives. I suggest you pray to the gods that your ignorance does not cost you in the end," said Ivor laughing hysterically.

*Now I know why Eli hates this guy so much. He is infuriating.*

"If you will all take your places behind your respective doors, the end of your lives can begin."

Jude found himself standing next to the boy, Raphael, from earlier. Silence hung throughout the room. Jude slowly turned his head studying the faces of each and every challenger in the room.

*But he is right. Each and every one of you aims to claim my victory. You wish to take from me what I need to protect my family and my home.*

The door in front of Joanna creaked open as light poured in around her. Jude watched as she ventured forward, before the door closed behind her. The roaring of a crowd erupted throughout the room, as Jude turned his attention back to the door in front of him. All of the anxiety that he was once feeling, was replaced with excitement and eagerness. The door in front of him creaked open, and a massive amount of sunlight temporarily blinded his vision. He felt himself smile.

*Fate, is my ally!*

# THE BEAST
# BEFORE DEATH

Jude made his way across the familiar black sands. Taking his place at the center of the battle arena next to Joanna and Anya, his eyes fell on the spectators above. All of the people in the audience appeared much further away from where he was standing, but their faces were still identifiable. He gazed around looking for any sign of Jed or his mom. Jed's snow-white hair was luckily a beacon among the crowd of spectators, and Jude was able to find him quickly. Jude felt himself smile when he caught sight of his mom sitting right next to Jed. She stood up waving both of her hands, when his eyes fell on her. Another set of hands next to his mom waved back at him. It was Marius with as much high energy as he always had. Jude wondered for a moment where Eli was, but he knew he could not expect his best friend to be there, considering how much Eli had been hanging out with his new friends. He had hoped however, that Eli would find time for his match. Jude looked over at Jed, and found a smirk on his brother's face. The presence of all three of them doubled the confidence Jude was already feeling, and at that moment, he thought he could not lose.

"And last but not least, presenting the challengers for the Magi bloodline," said Anya.

Jude quickly returned his attention back to the battle. Joanna was glaring at him and her hands were fidgeting.

"Katrina Wo and John Brills!" announced Anya.

Jude watched as Katrina and John took their places at the center of the arena. The tension in the air was palpable. Jude felt his heart abandon its post.

"Last one standing is the victor!" announced Anya before a cloud of smoke was all that was left of her.

"Round two will be: Katrina Wo versus Raphael Pompeo versus John Brills versus Joanna Marks versus Jude Bray!" announced a distant voice.

A few seconds of applause and cheering sounded around the Coliseum, before the unsettling silence returned.

"Begin!"

A huge explosion erupted and soon Jude found himself flying through the air. After coming in direct contact with the smooth black sands, he quickly leaped to his feet. His vision was blurry and his hearing seemed muffled for a while.

"Rest in pieces!" screamed a voice in front of him.

Jude focused just in time to find Joanna charging sword in hand. He did a back flip that landed both his feet high up on the wall behind him. Joanna's sword drove right into the stonewall and stuck there, before Jude leaped off of the wall behind her, and ran in the opposite direction.

*She's going to go on a long-range assault.*

Jude quickened his sprint searching around frantically for the two Magi. He found Katrina firing a barrage of orbs at Raphael that seemed to explode on contact. Raphael was on the defensive dodging and diving as fast as he could.

*Joanna is behind me, Raphael and Katrina are in front of me, but I can't find John.*

Jude took out his *plan b* vial on the right of his belt, and injected it into his shoulder. As he felt his body shrink and the peaceful feeling of flight come over him, he knew his raven form was complete. His vision sharpened, and as he flapped faster, he felt the onslaught of the wind quicken against his feathers. He heard what sounded like Raphael scream.

*So she finally got you.*

An explosion erupted on the wall next to Jude, which made his flying stagger. He quickly flapped his wings as fast as he could, as he circled around to find Katrina in hot pursuit.

*Where are you?*

Jude circled the Coliseum again, keeping Katrina at a distance, but also keeping her close enough to anticipate a paralysis spell. A barrage of explosions pelted him. Jude dive-bombed to dodge, and then quickly regained altitude.

"You won't get away!" screamed Katrina from below.

He swerved left and right in an attempt to dodge Katrina's assault. Then he saw him.

*Ingenious but cowardly!*

Jude dive-bombed down as fast as he could with both his claws open at the ready. He concentrated on size, and soon felt his raven form amplify, and soon he felt his tremendous size take over. He came down on Joanna, who dove to get out of the way—as he guessed. Jude felt his colossal claws grab onto John's shoulders as Jude kicked up for the sky. John's invisibility quickly wore off, and soon Jude saw two of the same orbs that Katrina had been using, appear in both of John's hands.

*Got ya!*

Jude quickly picked up a little more speed before dive-bombing towards the ground; hurling John full force at Joanna, who had her bow at the ready. Jude quickly returned to his normal form and did a front roll when he came in contact with the ground—as to avoid any impact.

A large explosion erupted behind him and soon heat crawled over his body. He was not surprised when he was not given anytime to recover, once he felt an excruciating pain in one of his arms. His body left the ground as it was hoisted into air. He let out a scream of pain when he looked up to see a giant stinger impaling his right arm. The buzzing that surrounded him, made his ears feel like they were going to explode. Jude had no time to engage the giant wasp. His face came in direct contact with something cold and hard, which made nausea creep over him. He turned over on one of the spectator benches to catch the giant wasp readying its stinger, and then it attacked. Someone screamed behind him.

*Please let this work.*

As the stinger came down, Jude rolled to the side and evaded the attack. He quickly returned to his feet and stabbed the wasp in its side with a vial. When he felt the sands beneath his feet after jumping down from the spectators area, he quickly looked up and was relieved to see that Raphael was not in pursuit.

*No time to check.*

He injected himself with one of his vials but resisted the transformation. The pain in his right arm intensified making him stagger slightly. He sprinted in no particular direction.

*A moving target is hard to hit huh Jed? Lets hope you're right.*

While he sprinted and surveyed the area around him, he quickly found Joanna, who was deep in combat with Katrina. While Katrina dodged one of Joanna's swords, the other sword parried and made direct contact with her. The force of the attack tossed the Magi across the sands, while blood stained the sands beneath her.

*Perfect timing.*

"Bombs away!" screamed Jude. He took out a vial and hurled it at Joanna. An opaque green cloud of smoke erupted around her, and soon she fell to the ground screaming. He quickly covered his nose and mouth and ran over to Joanna, who lay on the ground shaking. He injected an empty vile into her neck, and just as it was almost full, he felt the wind knocked out of him. He tumbled backwards across the sands. Returning to his feet, he saw Joanna staring back at him. The determination was prevalent on her face, as she tried to return to her feet, but soon collapsed. He smiled and put the new vial in his utility belt.

*You will come in handy later.*

Jude released the resistance on the transformation, just as his acrobatics propelled him into the air. Both Katrina and Joanna looked like ants for a few seconds, before he felt his six additional legs and his four extra eyes, fall into place. Jude felt the whole Coliseum shake and heard the screams all around him, while his arachnid form made contact with the sands below. His line of sight fell on Jed, before he sped off in the opposite direction towards John. After throwing the vial at Joanna, Jude had seen John returning to his feet. He got to him in mere seconds thanks to his extra legs, and when John looked up at him, his eyes widened. John clapped his hands together and soon Jude found himself looking at an empty space. He returned to his normal form and felt enraged.

"Coward!" screamed Jude in no particular direction.

*Is this coward going to run and play invisible the whole match?*

A small cat jumped down from the wall and crawled over to Jude. He looked at the animal confused for a second, before laughter found his lips. The pain in his arm returned again. He applied pressure with his hand.

"Here kitty kitty kitty!" said Jude.

The cat shook violently until Raphael took its place. He stood staring at Jude with wide eyes, not making a sound. "How did you do that!"

*I'll never tell you. But maybe I can use you to my advantage.*

"Do you really want to know?" asked Jude walking in a circle around Raphael. Raphael quickly readied both his fists and followed Jude's every move.

"First I add a little water into a vial, then some of those rare cherry blossom leaves, and then—."

"And then what?" asked Raphael growing impatient.

Jude felt a faint wind behind him. He smiled as he quickly turned around and punctured a vial deep into John's chest. Jude felt his vial make contact with the Magi's body, even though he did not see him. A few seconds passed and then John's body became visible. His eyes were wide and wild, and his body shook violently until he was gone, and a rat took his place. Jude quickly stomped as hard as he could on the rat, until he felt a *crunch* beneath his foot.

"It's over!" screamed a voice.

Jude soon found himself tumbling across the sands. He quickly jumped to his feet just in time to sidestep a slice from Joanna. He noticed she was moving slower. He knew it was a side-effect from the poison he had doused her with.

"What did you do to me!" screamed Joanna as she sliced over and over again at Jude.

Jude sidestepped left and right repeatedly in an attempt to out-maneuver Joanna. She was still too fast to get an opening.

"Who me? Well the little present I gave you is attacking your nervous system. The more you fight the more it takes over. Soon you won't be able to even stand!" said Jude.

Joanna let out a growl as she swiped Jude's feet with the back of her heel. Jude soon saw the oval opening in the roof before landing on his back. Her sword came crashing down next to him, as he rolled to the side and quickly returned to his feet. He snatched his new vial and injected himself with half of it. When he turned towards Joanna, his body felt foreign. He felt no chaos and no heaviness like he usually felt.

"What's wrong? Your meds not working?" gloated Joanna as she charged him.

"Actually," said Jude holding out both of his hands. A sword materialized in both of them. "They are working just fine!"

Jude met Joanna's charge with a charge of his own, and soon parried her attack with his new blades. She performed a back slice that Jude in turn parried and then went for a lower attack. She sidestepped his attack and retaliated with a hit from the pommel of her sword. The attack took Jude by surprise. He shook off the pain but failed to see Joanna's lower slice to his torso. Jude felt the coldness of her blade followed by the staggering pain it inflicted. He dared not look down at his stomach, even though he knew that there would be a lot of blood waiting to greet him.

*You got me. You expect me to panic and look away, and that will be your opening.*

He looked straight into her eyes. A glint of amusement seemed to twinkle inside of them. She brought down both swords. Jude held both his swords up in a cross to halt her attack.

*This is new to me. I am not used to fighting with her abilities as much as she is. Her brain masters her weapons as she summons them, mine tries to adapt as I go. She has the advantage.*

He dropped a sword and injected his side with a vial. Joanna screamed as Jude's gargoyle form picked her up and hoisted her into the air.

*This one is for you Bree.*

Jude flew through the opening in the roof leaving the Coliseum behind.

"Let me go you freak!" screamed Joanna.

Jude locked eyes with her and let loose a roar, before diving straight down towards the opening in the Coliseum. When he tossed her down towards the sands, he roared when she made contact with the ground. He landed a few feet from her body before returning to his normal form. Joanna's body twitched briefly, before she sat perched on one knee, swords in both hands.

*Wow, she still continues to fight. She has been poisoned and thrown to the ground, but she doesn't give up.*

He injected himself with the remainder of the vial, and summoned his swords again.

"I am afraid this is the end of the line for you!" screamed Jude. He endured the pain of his injuries and charged her. He brought down his left sword and was quickly stopped between both of Joanna's swords. She breathed deeply as both of her swords remained locked, holding off Jude's attack. Jude quickly swung his right sword at her neck—and just when he was sure that he would see her head rolling—his body gave way as her new shield bashed his hand. His sword sliced her shoulder, causing her scream to echo throughout the Coliseum. Joanna immediately took to the offensive. Jude let go of his swords and summoned a throwing dagger. He quickly tossed it at Joanna's injured shoulder and was relieved when it buried itself into her shoulder, pinning her to the adjacent wall. She let out a scream when she tore the dagger out of her shoulder, and fell to her feet. Jude felt his body return to normal and knew the effects of Joanna's blood had worn off.

*It looks like no more swords for me.*

Joanna slowly walked towards Jude until she stood over him. Two swords gleamed in her hands as she tightened her grip on them.

"How dare you come here today thinking that you can take my blood and use my abilities against me. You know what you are? You're a cheater! But believe me, you will never cheat again," said Joanna. She brought both of her swords down. Her hands came to a halt as Jude grabbed both of her wrists. He felt himself gritting his teeth as he tried as hard as he could to overpower her. Blood ran down her shoulder from her injury, but she showed no signs of pain. Jude felt blood running down his leg from his torso, before the pain in his shoulder made him weaken his hold on her wrists. She pushed her swords closer to him.

*She's too strong. Close combat is her strength, even in her condition. New plan.*

He instantly stopped his resistance, which caused Joanna to tumble on top of him. They both rolled across the sands and separated, before coming to a halt. When Jude returned to his feet, he was not surprised to see that Joanna was already on her feet with her shield and sword in hand. Jude looked at his utility belt.

*Only six left.*

He took a vial and injected himself. He searched his brain for the power, and when he found it, instantly let it take over. The faces of spectators soon were at eye level once his arachnid form took over. Joanna kicked sand behind her, as she walked in place preparing for her next attack; first with her left foot, then with her right. Jude mimicked her movements with all eight of his legs.

*I hope you're ready, because only one of us will walk away from this.*

"You will fall by my hand!" screamed Joanna as she raced towards Jude.

Jude jumped up and down before charging her. The Coliseum shook and screams were audible as both of them closed the distance between them. Joanna screamed as Jude charged her, knocking her swords out of her hands, and climbing on top of her. He pinned her down with all of his weight, as his web spun quickly around her legs. Jude saw a dagger form in one of her hands. The severed arm was flung to the side after leaving his mouth. Joanna screamed as tears fell from her eyes.

*There's no escape!*

Jude came down on her neck as his pincers gnawed at her throat. He felt blood and fluid all over the hairs on his body. His attack bore deeper into her abdomen. He felt her body convulse from the attack, which for some reason angered him. He went into a frenzy, instinctually wanting her body to stop struggling.

He lost track of time until he suddenly tasted sand. He came up from her body only to find nothing but a pair of legs. He felt nauseous. Returning to his normal form, his stomach settled. He quickly realized that he had let his guard down, so instead of turning around, he picked a direction, and ran. The sound of a large object made contact with one of the walls behind him. He kept running.

Jude ran as fast as he could but soon felt a burning pain in both his stomach and his shoulder. He looked down to see a trail of blood dripping down his moving legs; and then to his shoulder, and noticed it had started swelling.

*I have to end this quick. I won't last long.*

He turned around to find Katrina leaving the mouth of a large crocodile, before tumbling across the sands. Raphael returned to his normal form as he stood over Katrina's body.

"I believe the score is The Raph, twenty-three, and you, zero," said Raphael kicking Katrina in her stomach. Just as Raphael brought his foot down over Katrina's head, his leg stopped. He stood there motionless in the same stance. Jude observed as a purple glow gleamed in Katrina's eyes when she turned over. She returned to her feet and held out her hand—as if telling Raphael to stop.

"You dare kick me while I'm down!" screamed Katrina. Raphael still stood motionless. When Katrina raised her hand, Raphael's body left the ground, and was soon frozen. "You will suffer for your impudence!"

Raphael's scream broke the silence as he was hurled from wall to wall. Katrina's hand flew left, right, up and down while her magic flung Raphael all around the Coliseum. Screams broke out among the spectators when Raphael's body was dragged through the crowds and the concrete benches they were sitting on.

"Eat dirt you filth!" Katrina brought her hand down dragging Raphael across the sands. Sand poured out of his mouth and blood ran down his face. Her magic lifted his body slowly.

*She's strong and will be difficult to beat alone.*

"Die you coward!"

Jude sprinted at Katrina. Once the back of her neck was close, he executed a front flip, landing on her shoulders. Raphael's body dropped to the floor. Jude quickly locked his legs around Katrina's neck and forced his body backwards despite how heavy the weight was. His hands found the ground as his legs hammered Katrina's head into the ground. He quickly got up and sprinted towards Raphael's motionless body. He leaped over it and returned his gaze towards Katrina. Katrina staggered while struggling to her feet. Raphael's body still remained still. A lone vial still hung by his waist.

*So much for that plan.*

"So one versus one is it?" said Katrina.

"It appears so," replied Jude injecting himself with a vial. Silence soon took control over the battle arena.

"You will lose!" screamed Katrina. Her hand targeted him. Jude felt his body leave the ground. Katrina looked smaller as she held him higher above the battle arena.

*Come on Lynn! I listened! Where's the beast?*

"I win!" screamed Katrina.

A thunderous roar rang throughout the Coliseum. The roar was so staggering, Jude found the feeling return to his body—as he was let loose from Katrina's magic—and began to lose altitude. He curled into a ball—and when he felt the impact with the ground—he rolled to his feet. The Coliseum continued to shake. Jude looked up to find three sets of red eyes staring back at him.

The three heads of the Cerebus towered over Jude while screams erupted from all around him. The creature had all black fur and enormous paws. Two of the mouths opened up and darted down at Jude. Jude dove to the side and dodged the attack but was soon swept up off of the ground. The third head bit down on his injured arm while it held him higher into the air. Jude felt himself scream. Piercing pain ran down his arm and his back, before joining the pain in his stomach. He felt himself vomit. He took a vial from his utility belt and stabbed the head that was holding him. The beast roared and then threw him at one of the walls. Sparks formed in Jude's vision and soon his body began to feel heavy but comfortable. He was ready to give in to the slumber. An image flashed before his eyes.

*Long blonde hair disappeared between the legs of a troll. The troll shrank and a woman took its place. The blonde hair soon returned, approaching him slowly. He knew her. Her blue eyes glistened in the sunlight as her smooth skin came into view.*

*"Not bad princess."*

*The girl winked and then there was blackness. A large pink tree loomed up before him. Its light scent was pleasing to his senses.*

Black sands surrounded him when Jude forced open his eyes. Screaming pierced the air while he forced himself to his feet. The Cerebus planted one of its paws firmly down on Katrina, as all three heads slowly descended upon her.

"You will suffer for your impudence!" growled all three heads.

*No! Not yet, I still need her.*

Jude tried to run as fast as he could to save Katrina, but found himself limping. The pain in his stomach finally became unbearable and soon he collapsed to the ground. He heard Katrina scream. Just when he thought he was close, he looked up only to witness the three heads brutally descending on Katrina's body. Body parts were flung in every direction as the beast ravaged her. A heavy object hit Jude in the face causing his head to drop to the ground. He opened his eyes to find himself staring into Katrina's. He quickly rose up, knocking Katrina's lone head aside. When Jude returned to his feet, he saw the

Cerebus turn away from him and let loose a roar to the audience. Dozens of spectators tried to flee while the Cerebus' heads snapped at the people in front of it. A lone object caught Jude's attention. He limped over to Katrina's mangled torso and fell to both knees. He covered his mouth and injected the torso with an empty vial. Fresh blood filled the vial until it was completely full. He thought about Eli and all of the fun times they had once shared. He knew his best friend was not there. He had looked for Eli right after seeing his brother and mom. Jude was surprised that he was not angered but saddened instead.

*Wherever you are, I hope you know I tried my best to protect our family.*

The Cerebus turned around and roared. The roar knocked Jude off of his feet and onto his back. The ground shook as Jude heard the panting of the monster heading for him. When Jude sat up, he grabbed a vial from his belt, and injected himself.

"You win," said Jude. He looked up just in time to see the jaws of all three of the heads, descending upon him.

# ONE VIAL LEFT

Jude felt the coldness of the shadow that surrounded him when the Cerebus' body blocked out all of the light and sun around him.

"Earth Prison!" screamed Jude. The ground beneath him opened up, and soon he fell through a trench that appeared beneath him. He tumbled beneath the surface until his hand finally grabbed a piece of rock close by. Pain erupted throughout his arm while he dangled from the crumbling earth. The dark crevice went on further than he could see. Jude forced his other hand to reach up and grab whatever it could find. He found a small cliff and lifted himself up. Pain ripped through his body but he ignored it. He climbed higher and higher until sunlight shined above him. He pulled himself up and over the edge, until the familiar black sands crunched beneath him. He quickly turned himself around and gazed upon the entrapment of the Cerebus. Mud and earth crawled up the paws and legs of the monster, trapping it in place. Piercing howls ripped through the air as the three heads wailed in unison.

Jude stood up and slowly closed the distance between them. The Cerebus rocked back and forth fighting the prison. Jude closed his eyes and pictured the pillars amplifying. Hundreds of pillars shot up from the ground causing the Coliseum to rumble. Earth spears circled around the Cerebus until even its heads didn't even move. The ground began to tremor.

*No way!*

Bits of rock exploded everywhere as the earth prison shattered. Jude felt himself hit the sands as boulders and earth rolled passed him. Jude forced himself through the pain and to his feet. All three of the heads roared. Jude held out his hand.

"Paralysis!"

The Cerebus charged towards him.

"Come on! Paralysis!"

The Cerebus raised his paw and came down on Jude.

"Enough! Debilitate!" His mouth seemed to speak the words without his consent. The large black paw froze inches from Jude's face. He looked up to see three sets of clenched teeth staring back at him. Saliva fell from the monster's teeth forming a thick puddle at Jude's feet. Jude walked away from the beast and collapsed.

"You can do it honey!" screamed someone.

Jude recognized the voice but could not identify it. His eyes opened slightly. The Cerebus still stood motionless.

"Bring him down little brother," said a voice from above.

Jude searched the audience and soon found his mom and Jed. Jude's eyes were hazy but he thought he saw worry on Aileen's face.

*Mom. Jed.*

He returned to his feet.

*Let us end this.*

He took a vial from his belt, closed his eyes, and injected himself. For the first time he welcomed the pain. He flung open his eyes and barreled towards the Cerebus. Pain erupted throughout his entire body, but he used the feeling as energy to propel himself forward. The Cerebus broke free from the paralysis and matched his charge. Jude soon came to the monster's eye level when his troll form finished its growth. The Cerebus instantly stopped and let loose a roar from one of its heads. Jude returned the creatures' challenge, with a challenge of his own and then attacked. The monster rolled to its side and returned to its feet. The Cerebus circled the battlefield gaining more speed before pouncing. Jude's mallet connected heavily. The Cerebus broke the roof as its twirling body exited from view. Jude quickly followed.

Fresh cool air and warmth from the sun, greeted him before the Cerebus' large body came into view. Jude used a combination of his mallet and enormous legs to apprehend the creature. He let the rest fall into place until gravity caused their descension. They picked up more speed as their combined weight sliced the air around them. Jude tightened his grip when the Cerebus roared and staggered in an attempt to free itself. The collision with the battlefield formed a crater beneath their combined weight. The Coliseum shook violently causing screams to echo around them. Rock fragments assaulted Jude during his return to his normal form. His violent cough splattered the ground beneath him with blood. A cough sounded closeby. Jude's gaze fell on Raphael's limp body. Both challengers regained their footing.

"You know I could have killed you after you collapsed from Katrina's attack," said Jude breathing deeply.

Raphael's red hair, which was caked with blood and dirt, stuck to his forehead. His chest rose and fell abruptly. "We both know that. The real question is, why didn't you?"

"I was counting on the 'Beast before death' theory."

"Smart. Didn't feel like fighting Katrina alone did ya?"

"Why go through the trouble of fighting a frazzled Magi when I can have my enemy do it for me," said Jude with a smirk. Jude saw a small smile appear on Raphael's face for a few seconds before disappearing.

"So what happens now? I'm out of vials and have no more power in my blood," said Raphael.

Jude studied Raphael for a while. "I know. You are defenseless."

Both of them laughed in unison.

*Okay.*

Jude began to close the distance between them. Raphael made a quick movement and then Jude felt a small prick in his leg. He looked down to see a vial embracing him. "What's this?"

"I lied, I had one vial left," said Raphael laughing hysterically.

"I know," said Jude.

"Wait! Why aren't you transforming into a bird?"

"So that's what is in here. I assume you never intended to use this on me. If I had to guess, you brought it as a defensive strategy to flee from a close combat situation—maybe Joanna," replied Jude.

Raphael glared. "It isn't possible to use vials on opponents. What happened earlier with John and I was just a coincidence. Dumb luck!" Raphael's eyes started to blink constantly alongside his quivering lips.

"Let us just agree to disagree," said Jude.

"What do you mean 'agree to disagree?' Are you telling me that you know how to turn others against their will?"

"Well I would not worry so much about that, I would worry more about the poison that continues to ravage your vital organs by the second," said Jude.

"Poison? Are you mad? What—," started Raphael before his eyes fell on the vial that erected from his thigh. Jude felt himself smile while he watched Raphael's eyes widen.

"I knew you had one vial left. When you collapsed from Katrina's attack, I noticed it at your side," said Jude.

"So you just know everything don't you?"

"Not exactly. What I did not anticipate happening was you using it on me. I figured you would use it as an attempt to set up one final attack to take me down, and I was ready. I would have never guessed that you would be so desperate to win, that you would inject me with your own vial, in hopes that it would 'coincidentally' turn me. Regardless of what you chose, I knew that all I had to do was make sure my vial made it into your bloodstream; and make sure to waste as much time as possible, as to give it time to take effect."

Raphael fell to his knees as his left eye began to twitch irregularly. Jude knew this meant the poison was taking effect. He began to close the distance between them.

"You know, the poison is very unique. It is similar to the one that I used on Joanna earlier, however this one is a little less merciful. While it does become more potent as you move or fight against it, like Joanna's poison, this one I'm afraid is actually fatal. The more you fight, the more your body resists; and in turn, the more you suffer. The less you resist its effects, the easier it is for the poison to find your heart—and stop it!"

Raphael fell to his back and soon his body went into spasms.

"It was an honor to face you in battle. I have never met such an obstinate adversary," said Jude. He turned away from Raphael.

*Don't do it. No more pain. No one deserves to suffer.*

Jude felt a slight wind touch the base of his neck. Jude instantly intercepted Raphael's attack—and seized his wrist—the second he turned around. The dullness of his red hair matched the dullness in his eyes. The spasms became more violent. Jude followed the blood that ran from Raphael's mouth, nose and ears. Tossing Raphael over his shoulder, Jude recoiled when Raphael's body collided with the sands. Raphael's attempt to rise was short lived, after he was pinned at his throat by the bottom of Jude's heel.

"Be smart," started Jude as he felt the *crunch* beneath his heal. "Stay down!"

"Winner!" announced a familiar voice from above.

Applause and cheers erupted above Jude. He looked up and instantly found Jed and his mom. Marius and Aileen both sprang up from their seats and hugged one another. He looked around at the lifeless bodies of the challengers he once faced. His body screamed pain and his head felt light, as he made his way to the center of the Coliseum, and closer to Raphael. The pain intensified when he lowered to one knee. His hand met his heart and his forehead met his knee. He closed his eyes and ceased all movement.

Jude had read a book on the history of the Trials of Magic, Might and Lineage. He remembered an interesting chapter where some victors would take a knee in order to honor those they had fought in battle. This was not supposed to be a repetitive gesture used for every battle, however, Jude felt as though the challengers he had faced today, were not only skilled, but honorable; and deserved recognition alongside his victory. He did not know if the spectators had any insight on why Jude laid atop his knee in the center of the Coliseum, and if they did, he was unsure if they had joined him in honoring his fallen adversaries. The thought quickly left his mind when he realized the only thing that was important to him, was the honoring and recognition he was currently displaying.

He rose to his feet and was shocked to see all of the spectators kneeling by their seats. He felt light-headed as the Coliseum began to spin. He looked down and found his entire armor drenched in blood. He fell to his knees. He braced himself as he felt his body falling forward. A hand caught his wrist. He looked up to see Professor Lynn holding him up. She wrapped his arm around her neck and hoisted him to his feet. He was embarrassed when he noticed his blood dripping down her neck. Blackness closed in from the corners of his vision.

A hand squished his cheeks.

"No! The eyes stay open! Do you hear me? Open or I will fail you like no one's business!" said Lynn.

Jude forced his eyes open and was soon staring at a cheering crowd. He felt himself smile.

Eli was relieved that he was not chosen as a challenger in the second round of the Trials for many reasons. For one, he did not want to have to face Jude in an all out death match where winner takes all. However, his primary reason did not become apparent until Ivor had dismissed the un-chosen contenders. Eli had snuck into the Medicinal Quarters in an attempt to check on Sia's condition.

The all white dimly-lit hut brought back painful memories of Eli's visit here after her match. Tall plain white walls decorated with assorted generic paintings, stood tall behind the perfectly made single beds that covered the room. When Eli walked down the main aisle that separated the beds, he pulled down the sleeves on the belted tunic he wore. A couple of healers had walked passed Eli as soon as he had entered, but neither paid him any attention. While Eli walked through what appeared to be the last square archway in the hut, a small group of people rose up in front of him. Sniffling and sobbing leaked from the group, while Eli quietly approached from behind. A large man, dressed in all white, entered the room and lowered a sheet over the bed.

"I'm sorry. There was nothing we could do," said the man.

An older woman, dressed in all purple, collapsed to the floor while covering her face. "No! You killed my baby! How could you kill my baby! My baby!" She began to repeatedly hit the healer. The energy behind her attacks was so minimal, that Eli could not picture her doing any real damage.

"Can I help you?" The voice came from behind Eli. He turned around to find a young woman dressed in all white staring back at him, with a confused look on her face.

Eli looked back towards the group of people, and noticed that they all had turned their attention towards him as well. A group of puffy—and seemingly angry—eyes glared at him. Eli turned back towards the woman in white.

"Are you one of the healers?"

"Yes, I am Fey. Can I help you?"

"Yeah, I'm sorry. I'm looking for someone. Sia Wyatt. She checked in about a day or so ago."

"Hmm, follow me."

Eli followed Fey back down the main aisle that he had ventured through earlier. Her blonde curls bounced across her back, as she strutted down the aisle giving nods to other healers that passed by. When she came across a tall counter, she grabbed a clipboard that hung on a nearby wall.

"Just as I thought. Wyatt checked out early this morning," said Fey.

"Checked out?"

"Yes. As in, she went home."

"I don't understand. She was in critical condition like a day ago. They weren't sure," said Eli before stopping himself.

Fey cocked her head to the side and studied him.

"They weren't sure if she was going to make it," continued Eli.

"Well it was a thirty percent chance, due to her injuries. However, Vance is an amazing healer; and we were just lucky that he happened to stop by to help her when we needed him."

*Vance. He saved her?*

Eli remembered the sorrow in Vance's eyes when Mr. Wyatt had told him that Eli could not see Sia.

*He actually cared.*

"Young man?"

Eli returned his attention back to Fey.

"My records show that she was approved to go home. If you want to see her, that is where you will find her."

Eli felt himself smile. "Thank you! Thank you so much! You have no idea how much—just thank you."

"Young man! Wait a second!"

Eli turned around to find Fey standing with a small bouquet of light purple flowers in her hand.

"I had originally picked these flowers for the little girl in the room down the hall today. But you see—well lets just hope that your timing is better than mine was—and these help you the way I had hoped they would have helped her."

Eli took the flowers from Fey's hand. The purple reminded him of Sia. "Thank you." As he exited the Medicinal Quarters, his eyes had a hard time adapting to the dimness in the holding area. He heard the sound of crowds cheering and tons of applause above him.

*Looks like it's about to start.*

Eli quickly exited through the tall double doors, and eventually through the Coliseum's main doors. Golden rays of sunlight made the familiar cloudbank appear like tiny ghosts drifting harmlessly by. As Eli descended the stairs of the Coliseum's courtyard, a cold chill briefly touched the nape of his neck; and soon the sun's warm rays soothed it. He made his way towards the Eastern Hold, and decided to smell the flowers in his hand that demanded his attention. They had a soft berry spice scent to them, which made Eli take another whiff. The tall and lavish stone houses surrounded him, after passing by the Academy. Sia's front door created a shadow of uncertainty and nefarious intent. A brief memory of the night him and Sia were attacked by the Necrosis crossed his mind. He quickly dismissed the thought, and was irritated by his brain's tendency to hold on to things that could not help him in the present. He walked passed the first couple of houses, and up the stairs of Sia's house. He gazed down at the flowers and gave them one last whiff. He raised his closed fist to the door, and froze. He thought about the possibility that Mr. Wyatt could be home. He thought of the many times that Mr. Wyatt had made it clear that he did not want Eli around.

*What if he calls the guards?*

He sat and stared at the door for what seemed like minutes.

*Maybe I should just come back later. I'm sure she is probably resting anyways.*

When he turned around and retreated down the stairs, he heard a loud crash that made his shoulders tense. He turned around and ran back towards the door. Lightly placing his ear on the door, he waited. *Crash. Thud.* The flowers fell to the floor while Eli's shoulder easily barged through the unknowingly open door.

Demolished bookcases, broken vases, fallen chairs, and raining papers were the first things that greeted Eli, when he entered the Wyatt house. He looked around through the haze of slowly falling papers floating aimlessly down to the floor. A large grandfather clock caught his eye. He tripped over a broken table on his way to the clock, but quickly recovered. A large pendulum swung back and forth within the dark brown belly of the clock. While Eli studied its hands, he noticed something strange. None of the hands were moving. The time was also completely wrong. The clock read three o' clock in the morning, when in reality it was closer to noon. He stepped back and made sure the pendulum was still moving. It was. He returned his gaze to the hands, and became perplexed when they still showed no signs of movement.

*That's odd.*

He looked around the room he was in, and began to marvel at some of the art and furniture that decorated it. Large luxurious white couches and pristine emerald green décor displayed effortlessly throughout the room. Trophy cases filled with assorted awards and photos lined the walls demanding attention. Eli walked over to a photo that sat perched in a glass case. Before he could reach it, he heard a scream. It came from the hallway to his right. He quickly walked down the hallway opening and closing the many doors that surrounded him. Each door he opened was a luxurious dead end.

*Who needs this many rooms?*

A duo of tall white doors marked the end of the hallway. One was slightly cracked open. A scream escaped from the crack in the door.

"Daddy please! I'm sorry!"

Eli quickly pushed open the doors and froze at the paralyzing nightmare in front of him. The room was large, and was decorated with a canopy bed that laid perfectly atop the fluffy light pink carpet. A tall man stood in the center of the room—across from the bed—with his back turned, and his head tilted down towards the non-visible area in front of him. After a few seconds, Eli realized the man was Mr. Wyatt.

"How dare you embarrass me in front of the whole city!" screamed Mr. Wyatt.

A pair of crutches laid haggardly by his feet as a small pale hand reached out to grab one of them. Sia's arms and legs wobbled, when she attempted to use the crutches to help herself up. Tears streamed freely down her face. She wore a pair of short, tight-fitting, black shorts with a matching tank top.

"Daddy I—."

Mr. Wyatt kicked one of the crutches out from underneath her, which sent her tumbling to the ground.

"I did *not* give you permission to get up you vermin!" screamed Mr. Wyatt.

The sight of seeing Sia lay helplessly at her father's feet was staggering. Her puffy terrified eyes gazed inadvertently up at his face.

"Daddy I swear! I did my very best! The Combat Specialist would have overpowered me. I had to run, I needed a—."

The hand that came down across her face quickly silenced her. The impact sent her tumbling across the pink carpet—and landing face down.

"Don't—lie—to me!" hissed Mr. Wyatt.

"Stop it! Just stop it!" screamed Sia. Her voice was muffled by the pink carpet that gagged her.

"You little filth, come here!"

Mr. Wyatt quickly covered the space between him and his daughter. Eli watched Sia crawl desperately towards a door on the other side of the room. Fear and sobs sounded in her voice, while her pale body scurried across the floor.

*What are you doing? Help her!*

Eli tried to move but failed. His brain was screaming at his legs to move, but it was as if his body was unconscious while his brain was active.

When Sia's hand finally touched the door on the opposite side of the room, it opened. Her eyes stared at the opening door, when Mr. Wyatt snatched her ankle, and reeled her in. She screamed frantically while squirming and struggling to get away. Her father flipped her over before the back of his hand sent tangles of brown hair flying across her face.

"Daddy stop! You're hurting her!"

The voice sounded from across the room. Eli looked up to see a barefoot young boy in shorts, sprinting across the room towards the scuffle. Eli instantly recognized him as Sia's little brother Mik. His tiny body leaped on his father's back, causing a deep scream to penetrate the room. Mr. Wyatt swung Mik around in circles, while the little boy's fingers clung to the man's eyes. Sia slowly returned to her feet, grabbing a lone crutch next to her, and fleeing in Eli's direction. She passed by him as if he was invisible, and when he turned around to see where she was going, she was heading back the same way she had come.

"Leave him alone! He's my brother! He's just a child!" Sia collapsed to the floor in a helpless display of inevitability and submission. As soon as Mr. Wyatt ripped Mik from his back and gripped the young boy's neck, Eli's body went from feeling like it was paralyzed, to feeling like he was in combat. Adrenaline coursed through Eli's veins, at the sight of Mr. Wyatt's hand holding Mik by his throat.

"To think a son of mine, born a worthless Erudite. Oh, and to top it all off, he has the nerve to raise his hand to me—his superior, loving and honorable father," said Mr. Wyatt.

Tears ran down Mik's face when the green glow crawled across his face. Eli's gaze soon found the green aura that glowed from Mr. Wyatt's other hand.

"You will never raise that hand to me—again!"

"Drop him," said Eli.

The glow dissipated from Mr. Wyatt's hand before he turned his head slightly in Eli's direction. Sia still laid across the floor between them, and also turned her head towards Eli, as if noticing him for the first time.

"Is that you dog?"

"No, it's Eli."

Eli slowly walked towards Sia. Her purple eyes stared innocently up at his. Her smooth brown hair stuck to the side of her face, while her eyes were both haggard and puffy. She was beautiful. Being this close to her made his stomach feel funny and his heart race. He looked into her eyes and smiled when he offered her his hand. She accepted his help and soon found her footing, with the aid of his shoulder. He noticed one of the crutches close by and retrieved it for her. As she propped herself up, her mouth opened, but nothing came out. He turned back towards Mr. Wyatt and noticed that Mik still hung hostage in his grasp.

"I said drop him! I won't tell you again!"

When Mr. Wyatt loosened his grip, Mik fell to the floor. He returned to his feet quickly, and ran passed Eli towards Sia. Eli watched as the brother and sister tightly embraced one another. He approached Mr. Wyatt, growing more and more aware of how tall and built the man was. His biceps appeared to fight to escape from the gray shirt that clung to his body.

"Breaking and entering I see. I could have your head for this," said Mr. Wyatt.

"Is that all?"

Mr. Wyatt curled his lip for a second before turning his attention behind Eli. "Mik! Sia! Get over here now!"

Eli turned around and was surprised to see Mik's small bare feet trudging towards them. He walked a few steps before a hand grabbed his tiny wrist.

"No," said Sia holding Mik's hand.

The little boy looked up at his sister and soon turned his gaze towards Eli and Mr. Wyatt.

"You dare defy your father! You are my children! You were put on this Earth to honor your parents! To honor me! I said come here! Now!"

"You're right," said Eli cutting off Mr. Wyatt. "They are your children. We depend on our parents to love us not hurt us. You're supposed to help us through life's obstacles, not be one of them. The fact that you can sit there and treat your children like they're nothing is disgusting." Eli felt his heart race and his patience fade.

"How dare you disrespect me," said Mr. Wyatt.

"I don't mean to disrespect you. That isn't my intention. I respect that you're their father. But if you plan on hurting them again, you're going to not only have to go through me, but take me down!"

Right as the words left Eli's mouth, they surprised him. Mr. Wyatt terrified him. He knew everything was in the man's favor. Not only was the man powerful, but also Eli was trespassing in his house; and if Mr. Wyatt wanted to, he could claim Eli was responsible for the attack on his kids. He continued to stare into Mr. Wyatt's unyielding and unflinching eyes.

"I'll see you suffer," said Mr. Wyatt raising his hand.

Everything went into slow motion when Eli heard Sia scream somewhere in the distance, when the wall of flames appeared in front of him. The flames blocked his view of Mr. Wyatt, while simultaneously increasing the temperature in the room tremendously. The attack launched itself straight at Eli, bringing intense warmth and blinding light with it, as it closed in.

*What? What's going on?*

Eli felt an itch at the back of his mind, when the open palm of his hand independently rose, as if to hold off the attack. He felt the burning of the flames on the palm of his hand as it closed in fast. Sia screamed.

"Retaliation!" said Eli. He was confused as to why the word even crossed his mind. The incoming attack redirected towards Mr. Wyatt. The flames dissipated, and soon Mr. Wyatt's eyes locked with his. No flames or burns appeared to have touched him.

"My turn! Delimitate," said Eli.

A large net came up from the carpet beneath Mr. Wyatt's feet. The net instantly captured the large man, before pinning itself to the ceiling. The net rocked back and forth in response to Mr. Wyatt's futile struggle. As a glow appeared in the area of his hands, a small rope coiled down from the pink curtains that hung from the windows in Sia's room. It slithered up the wall, crossed the ceiling, and eventually entered the net. The sound of feet sounded behind Eli, and soon Mik and Sia stood at his side.

"Halcyon trance," said Sia with a cross gesture.

"I'll have you—," started Mr. Wyatt. His words were abducted by snoring.

Eli turned to Sia and studied her. A few strands of hair stuck to her neck and shoulders. He felt himself blush at the sight of her bare and smooth legs. Her head quickly turned his direction making him look behind her.

"You have to get out of here! When he wakes up, he will be furious," said Sia.

He looked into her eyes. They were still a little puffy, but the purple glow mesmerized him.

"Eli! You have to leave! Now!"

Eli looked down at Mik, who was already staring up at him. His eyes were puffy too, and his nose looked moist. Eli returned his gaze to Sia. "Are you hungry?"

Sia's eyebrows curled while a confused look passed over her face. "What?"

Eli rolled up his sleeves and smoothed down his hair.

"Are you hungry?"

Sia said nothing, just stared back at him. For the first time, he did not feel awkward staring back; and no longer felt the itch to look away when too much time had passed.

"A little," she said.

Eli felt himself smile before turning his attention to Mik. "What about you Mik? Are you hungry?"

The young boy stared up in Eli's eyes. "My favorite food is breakfast. Can we have breakfast?"

"It is 'my favorite meal is breakfast' Mik," corrected Sia. She looked down at him with a delicate smile. Eli found himself studying every inch of her smile.

"Sorry Mr. Eli. My favorite meal is breakfast. Can we have breakfast?"

Eli dropped down until he was on both knees and at eye level with Mik. "You can call me Eli—just plain old Eli. Did you know that back at my house, I make the best boysenberry flapjacks and sausage in the world."

A wide smile displayed across the boy's face. "You promise?"

"Promise."

"Oh boy! Now I'm really hungry," said Mik as he tilted his head back up towards Sia. "Can we have flapjacks at Eli's house Sia?"

Eli returned to his feet and anxiously waited for Sia's answer. She studied him for a while. "Oh please! Oh please! Can we Sia?" asked Eli. A smile formed on his face. He was happy when she returned the gesture.

"Go get dressed Mik, and when you come back, I will have an answer okay?"

"You mean you will have a yes," said Mik as he scurried out of the door he had originally entered through earlier. He slammed the door behind him, causing the net that held Mr. Wyatt, to rock back and forth. Snores still leaked from the nets vicinity.

"Have you forgotten about my father? What will you do when he wakes up? He will call the guards I'm sure of it!" she said.

"It's okay."

"What do you mean it's okay? You don't know what he is like! What he will do!"

"Just trust me."

"Trust you?"

"Yes. Just trust me that everything will be okay. Just come over, and everything will be fine."

The doors on the opposite side of the room flew open. Mik returned to his spot next to Sia. "Alright! All ready!"

She stared down at him. Eli could see the worry on her face. Mik's lip slowly poked out.

"We *are* going, right Sia?"

Sia turned her attention back towards Eli. "Yes Mik. We have to taste these legendary flapjacks."

# A PERFECT
# WELL-KEPT SECRET

The sky was clear and the streets were busy with life, when Eli opened the door to leave the Wyatt house. Before they left, Sia had asked for a few minutes to get ready and change clothes, which gave Eli and Mik some time to properly get to know one another. Mik showed Eli his room, which to Eli's surprise, was just as big as Sia's. The only difference was the dark blue carpet, black walls, and shield and sword décor. Eli enjoyed seeing the many depictions of weapons painted on the walls of the young boy's room. He pictured him decorating his room the exact same way, if his family had the money at the time they moved into their house.

Once Sia was ready, the three of them stepped out onto the streets, and locked the door behind them. Soldiers, merchants, everyday citizens and small children covered the Eastern Hold's district. Eli felt his stomach drop every time a soldier passed by. He had noticed that in addition to the new red dress that Sia had changed into, she also changed her hair. Both Mik and Sia took a bag of clothes and supplies with them, since they did not want to spend too much time at the house—in fear that their father would soon awake. The three of them took the backstreets to Eli's house, in attempt to avoid any chances of running into anyone from the castle. A couple of times Eli and Mik found themselves walking too fast for Sia to keep up, since she was still on crutches, so Eli offered to lend her some support. She instantly declined saying she did not need any help, and instantly tried to quicken her pace. Eli purposefully slowed his pace in an attempt to not make her feel left behind, which to his relief, appeared to work. Sia explained that since her father was head of the city's jails and and an ex-professor of the Academy, he had friends all around those areas.

Mik did most of the talking on the way to Eli's house, and for the most part, was in pretty high spirits. He talked about games he won at school and subjects he did not particularly care for. Eli was perplexed but happy that the young boy could be in such a cheerful mood after what he had went through. Sia on the other hand, seemed even more distant and quiet than he had ever seen her.

*Crap! I forgot to clean the kitchen!*

Eli didn't know what made him think of it, but mentally he was kicking himself. When the familiar Agent statues on the corners rose up ahead of him, Eli was both relieved and annoyed. He was happy that they had made it to his neighborhood without any problems, but he was loathing the sight of the kitchen that was soon to come. A man and a woman passed by on the opposite side of the street, as well as a tall lean man jogging by. The neighborhood appeared to be just as normal, quiet and peaceful as it usually was.

"I like it here," said Sia.

It was the first thing she had said since the three of them had left the Eastern Hold.

"It's calming," she continued.

"What are those statues?" asked Mik.

"They are of great Kismet Agents. They are on every corner of the Western Hold. When I was a kid, I always dreamed about my statue being on one of the corners of my street," said Eli.

"That would be awesome if they put a statue of me up in our neighborhood Sia!"

"The Eastern Hold does not allow any form of alteration to the hold's street architecture. That is the reason why we do not have any statues of our own. But if we did, you would be the second because I would be the first," said Sia with a wink.

"I would challenge you for that title," said Mik with a grin on his face.

Walking up the steps to his door, Eli thought back to how nice and expensive Sia's house had looked, and he instantly felt worried. He loved everything about his house and never felt ashamed, but he didn't know if Sia would think it was as amazing as he did. As he opened the door, he let Mik and Sia enter the house first, before entering and closing the door behind him. Luckily the living room was still neat and tidy from when Marius had cleaned up and made breakfast—for the first round of the Trials of Magic, Might and Lineage.

Mik dropped the backpack he was carrying, and ran to a sword that lay against a wall in the corner of the living room. "Whoa cool!"

"Mik don't touch," said Sia.

"No it's okay, my dad won't mind. To be honest, he would probably be excited that Mik's excited," said Eli.

Eli and Sia watched Mik try to pick up and swing the sword. The boy looked defeated when the sword barely budged from its spot.

"Give it up sword, you're going down," said Mik.

"Maybe that is the problem Mik, don't you want the sword to go up? I mean you are trying to pick it up right?"

Mik stopped for a moment and passed Sia an irritated look.

"It's okay Mik, it isn't your fault," started Eli as he approached Mik. "That sword is made out of Osmium, which some consider to be the heaviest and most dense metal in the world. Even I have a hard time moving that thing."

"Cool! So it has to be the strongest sword in the world, if it is the heaviest," said Mik.

"Hmm I don't know about that. Like my dad used to tell Jude and I when we were kids, 'even the weakest weapon is the deadliest in the right hands," said Eli.

"No way! With this sword I would be the strongest Agent in the world," said Mik.

"Not if you can't lift it," said Sia.

Mik passed her another annoyed look.

"Well I promised you both some 'legendary flapjacks,' so I better get started. If you want to shower or wash up, there is a guest washroom up the stairs on the right, and also one in my room—which is up the stairs and at the end of the hallway."

"That sounds nice," said Sia.

"I'm good," said Mik crossing his arms.

Eli had to fight to hold back his pending laughter.

"No you're not! You stink and it's embarrassing me. Now get to washing," said Sia pointing upstairs.

Both Eli and Sia watched Mik retrieve his backpack and march his tiny feet up the stairs. Sia turned her head back and stared at Eli, who felt himself still smiling.

"We won't be long. I promise," she said.

"Take your time. When you cook 'legendary' food, you need a legendary amount of time."

When Sia carried her bag up the stairs, Eli could not help but watch every step she took. He analyzed every inch of the tight red dress she was wearing, and determined that it had to be made for her.

*"When you cook legendary food you need a legendary amount of time," what the heck is wrong with me? Next thing I know I will be reciting poetry.*

When Eli entered the kitchen, he was surprised to see that the kitchen was not as bad as he had pictured. He quickly wiped down the counter tops and the kitchen table, before retrieving the pots and pans that he needed. As he warmed both pans, he began to wonder about which washroom Sia was using. He wondered if she chose his and was in his room right now.

*Did I make my bed?*

His hand accidentally touched one of the pans on the stove, which resulted in muffled swearing. He hoped neither Mik nor Sia had heard him. He began with the sausage. He figured three per person should be enough, and when the last three went into the pan, he breathed a sigh of relief.

"Hey Eli," said Sia from upstairs.

Eli quickly ran out of the kitchen to the living room.

"Yeah!"

"Where are the towels?"

*Um—towels?*

Eli ran upstairs and hung a left to his father's room. He was relieved to see that Marius had a large stack of clean bath towels in his washroom, and he hoped his father would not mind. When he closed his dad's door behind him, he placed a bath towel and a washcloth in front of the guest washroom, and then headed to his room. He hung his head down and knocked on the door.

"Yes," answered Sia.

*Oh man she's in my room. Sia Wyatt is in my room.*

"I have," started Eli as his throat made him cough. "It's me, I have—towels."

The door slightly cracked open as a bare pale hand, caked with water droplets, reached openly through the crack. Eli felt his heart start racing. As he handed her the towels, she opened the door a little more to fit the towels through the door, which made him look away.

"Thanks E," said Sia closing the door.

"No problem."

*I swear I am two seconds from having one of those strokes Jude talks about. Wait did she just call me E?*

When Eli turned around and began down the stairs, panic shook him. "The sausage!"

Taking off down the remaining stairs, he hung a tight right around the corner, and nearly fell into the kitchen. Big puffs of black smoke began to erupt from the pan, as the smell of burning sausage ambushed him. He quickly grabbed the pan and was instantly burned. After a moment of swearing, he retrieved a towel and used it to remove the pan.

*I can't let her know I burned something as simple as sausage.*

He opened the kitchen door that led out into the backyard. He found a small corner behind some bushes, and left the pan filled with burned sausage behind it. When he entered the kitchen, he kept the door open in an attempt to clear the kitchen of the remaining smoke. Opening the freezer, he noticed there were still three more pieces of sausage left—and after retrieving them—he felt an urge to dance. After the sausage was finished, he breathed a sigh of relief once again. The flapjacks would be simple. He had made boysenberry flapjacks with his mother for as long as he could remember—before she died. She was the one that had taught him her secret recipe. He decided to make each person three flapjacks to match the three sausage they were getting.

"Hey Eli," said Mik from upstairs.

"Yeah!"

"Where are the," started Mik as Eli heard the washroom door upstairs open. "Oh never mind, found them!"

When Eli dropped the last flapjack into the pan, a calm washed over him. He found himself whistling and thinking of Sia and Mik's face once they tasted everything. When he went to scoop up the last flapjack from the pan, it refused to move. He dug deeper under the flapjack in an attempt to loosen it up.

*Oh no you don't! It's not gonna happen!*

He used all of his might, and soon the flapjack lifted, leaving pieces of itself on the pan and the fork in Eli's hand.

*Really? Really!*

Eli scraped the remains of the flapjack into the trash, washed the pan, and tried again. The second time the flapjack came up with ease, which caused Eli to pass a smirk at the flapjack in the trash. He went into the top cupboard to get his dad's serving china, that they only used during celebrations and ceremonies, and placed the flapjacks and sausage on the table. As he examined the spread, he realized something was missing. He went into the refrigerator and took out a carafe of pineapple juice and a pitcher of water. He placed them on the table and examined the table again. He still felt like something was missing. He went into the refrigerator and looked for some fruit. The only fruit he could find was a handful of strawberries and two oranges. He peeled the oranges and then washed the strawberries, before placing them on the table in a small bowl. He then emptied all of the dishes into the sink that he had used, and started washing them.

*I haven't washed dishes in a while. This is weird.*

"Smells good," said a voice behind him.

"Thanks how was your—," started Eli. He turned around and stopped at the sight in front of him.

A short, burgundy and tight strapless dress latched firmly around her small waist. Her hair hung neatly over one of her bare shoulders, while her smooth legs looked even softer under the kitchen's low hanging light.

"My shower was perfect. Thank you for opening your home to us," she said.

Eli's mouth opened to tell her it was no problem, but nothing came out. He stood with his mouth open for a few seconds before Mik broke the silence.

"Whoa! Looks freaking awesome! I'm sitting here!" Mik piled into the seat that Eli usually sat at during dinner with his dad. Sia took Mya's old seat in the middle, which left an opening for Eli at her right.

Eli washed his hands quickly and then joined them at the table. He served everyone a serving, leaving himself for last. "Well dig in."

"Alright flapjacks, you've met your match," said Mik diving into his stack of flapjacks. After a few bites, his eyes widened. "These are amazing! Sia you have to try them!"

Eli picked up the fruit bowl and first passed it to Sia.

"I also washed off some fruit if either of you want any."

"Oh. Thank you," said Sia grabbing an orange and placing it on her plate.

"She hates oranges," said Mik in between chewing.

*Of course.*

"Oh I'm sorry. I didn't know."

"It's fine. I mean, I like the way they taste, they are just undisciplined and difficult that's all," she said.

"Undisciplined and difficult? We are still talking about fruit right?"

Mik erupted into laughter before inhaling half his glass of pineapple juice.

"Yes it's just, after they are peeled, they squirt everywhere once you bite them. They are messy and just a hassle—that's all."

"Okay. Well there is also some strawberries in here as well," said Eli passing her the bowl again.

"She hates those too," said Mik as he picked up a sausage and started gnawing on it.

Eli looked at Sia who looked embarrassed. Eli smiled. "Okay what did the strawberries do to you?"

"Nothing. They used to be my favorite fruit," she said.

"Why 'used to be?'"

Sia tilted her head down. "My mom used to have them every time she cooked breakfast. She is gone now."

Eli felt like excusing himself from the table so he could drown himself in the Market District fountain. He knew it was not his fault that he did not know her mother had passed away, but he still felt guilty for making her relive those memories.

"I'm sorry. I didn't know."

"No no it is ok. But thank you," she said picking up her fork. "Now let's try these flapjacks of yours." She took a few bites before calmly putting down her fork and then wiping her mouth with her napkin.

*Great, let me guess, she hates boysenberries now too.*

"Eli these are amazing," she said.

Eli felt all the anxiety melt away as she took another bite. He took a bite of his sausage and then a few bites of the flapjacks. "Thank you. It's my mother's recipe. I used to help her cook it when I was a kid."

"I will definitely have to remember to compliment her. Will she be home soon?"

Eli felt a lump in his throat. He swallowed many times, but the lump refused to budge. He was aware of Mik and Sia's frozen gaze, so he sipped his glass of water.

"Um no. My mom passed away a few years ago."

"Nice going Sia," said Mik pouring himself some more pineapple juice.

"I am so sorry. I did not mean to..."

"No it's okay. You couldn't have known. I'm glad that she was able to leave me with her recipe, since I enjoyed it a lot when I was younger. It helps me to stay close to our memories of cooking together," said Eli.

Sia stared at Eli for a second, and for the first time, he did not feel like staring back. Sia continued her gaze before breaking the awkward silence. "What about your dad, will he be home soon?"

"That's a good question, I don't know where my dad is. I do know that he has a small shipment of steel swords he needs to make by tomorrow for the Academy, so he should be home in a couple of hours I think."

Silence abducted the room as the sound of forks and eating echoed throughout the kitchen. Eli looked to Mik and was happy to see that he seemed to still be enjoying the food. Sia on the other hand, was more difficult to read. She sat straight up in her seat with her shoulders back, and never placed more than a small portion of food in her mouth at once. Eli looked back over to Mik. He too sat straight up in his seat with his shoulders back—but he at least cracked a smile at the end of each bite—and was not shy about putting normal to larger portions of food in his mouth at a time. Eli did not know why he was quiet. He kept thinking about his mom and how she used to tell him that eating fruit with every meal would help him become quicker and more accurate on the battlefield. Eli took a couple of strawberries from the bowl and added them to his plate. He noticed Sia look up at the movement, but her attention quickly returned to her plate.

After everyone appeared to be done eating, Eli quickly retrieved everyone's dishes and put them in the sink. Shortly after, Eli figured a game would be the best way to eliminate the awkwardness he was feeling after breakfast. Since there were only three of them, Eli and Sia decided on playing Egg Roulette in an attempt play a joke on Mik. Sia helped Eli hard-boil some eggs, while Mik stayed in the living room looking through all of the weapon cases and armor. They purposefully cooked twenty eggs and set aside one raw egg, since there were three of them and they knew Mik would never want to go first in a game he was not familiar with. After all of the eggs were in one bowl, Eli and Sia had invited Mik back into the room to help draw faces on them.

"I don't understand," started Mik. "Why are we drawing on the food?"

"Don't worry you will see," said Sia grinning.

Eli nudged her in an attempt to silence her laughter, but even he had a hard time not laughing when he saw the sinister grin that was plastered over her face. He thought she looked really devious. The mood in the kitchen completely changed halfway through the egg decoration. Some of the faces that Sia and Mik were coming up with made Eli laugh so hard, that he choked a couple of times. When all of the eggs had faces, the three of them moved the game into the living room.

Eli put down plenty of pillows to make sure that everyone would be comfortable. Sia reconfirmed that the raw egg was on the very bottom of the bowl, so that way Mik would surely be the one to grab it. After explaining the game to Mik, Sia and Eli exchanged looks of satisfaction when Mik volunteered to go last. Eli brought a bag of small candies he had received for his birthday from his room. He figured everyone deserved some sort of treat after breaking an egg on their face—especially Mik. After everyone had went once, the front door opened. Marius walked through the door with a large black pouch over his shoulder. He wore a black jacket and blue pants.

"Hey dad."

"So this is where you have been," replied Marius.

Eli could not help but think that he heard a small edge in his dad's voice, but he quickly dismissed it as a mistake before responding. "What do you mean?"

Marius dropped his pouch against the wall next to him, and joined the group, after closing the front door behind him. "I kind of expected you to be at the Trials today, but I guess you had—other plans."

"Well I *was* there, but I wasn't selected in the blood ritual—so I left."

"You didn't want to stay for round two?" asked Marius.

"Not really. I mean I have no reason to be there anyways if I am not competing." Eli was confused by the expression on his dad's face. Marius did not respond right away to Eli, which confused him.

*Why does he care if I stayed or not. It's not like I was chosen for battle and then chose to leave.*

Marius cleared his throat before turning his attention towards Mik and Sia. "So who are your friends?"

"My name is Sia Wyatt, it is a pleasure to meet you Mr. Brassie. You have a beautiful home."

"Thank you, and you can call me Marius. It is very nice to finally meet you as well. I saw your battle in the Trials, and I have to say that you blew me away. I was most impressed," said Marius.

"Thank you so much Mr. Brassie—I mean Marius. That means a lot coming from you."

"I have to say that I have been anxiously awaiting to meet you for some time now. Eli has told me such nice things about you," said Marius. He shot Eli a quick grin.

*Dad, I am going to straight murder you.*

Sia appeared to almost recoil at the statement. Her eyes moved from Marius to Eli, before returning to Marius.

"Really?"

Eli felt himself blush under Sia's gaze.

"Yes mam," said Marius.

"This is my little brother Mik," said Sia giving Mik a slight kick.

Mik quickly got up and walked over to Marius. "My name is Mik, nice to meet you sir."

"You can call me Marius."

Mik quickly shook Marius' hand when he extended it. Eli could see the grin on Mik's face, mirrored on Marius' face; a few seconds after they had shook hands.

"You have a very strong grip. That is the sure sign of a skilled Agent. What do you want to be when you grow up Mik?"

"A master bowman Mr. Marius sir. I like blades but I love the bow."

"Well you have come to the right place. I work on weapons all the time, and Eli is pretty skilled with a bow. Maybe he can give you some tips," said Marius eyeing Eli.

"Oh will you Eli? Please! Please! Please!"

"Mik don't beg, it's rude," said Sia.

"Of course I will," said Eli. He actually looked forward to teaching Mik a few things about the bow. The bow had always been Eli's favorite weapon, even though he was trying to expand his knowledge of other weapons. He figured that it would do his mind good to go over basic knowledge of the bow with Mik. "You know my dad knows a few healing tricks." Eli thought he saw Sia tense at the statement. "Maybe he can help you so you won't have to use the crutches anymore."

Marius and Sia's gaze met simultaneously.

"A little sore after the battle?"

"Yes, Vance told me that I will be okay, but the impact of the last half of the battle, may have slowed the healing process in my legs."

"Well between you and I, I know some techniques that even Vance does not know," said Marius with a wink. "May I?"

"Um—I don't know," said Sia.

Mik was quick to tease her. "Come on Sia! Don't be a baby! You're boring when you're crippled!"

"No no, it's okay Mik. I would not want to do anything that she was uncomfortable with."

Eli watched as Sia stared at his dad for a while. No one moved or said anything.

"Sure. I mean, yes I am comfortable." Sia laid down on the floor next to Marius, who propped her head up with a pillow.

Eli gave Sia a towel to throw over the end of the dress she was wearing, hoping to make her feel more comfortable. Eli and Mik took a couple of steps back to give Marius some space, but still observed closely. Marius placed one hand lightly on her ankle and then used two fingers on his other hand to slowly push into the back of her leg. Sia made a couple noises of discomfort, but for the most part, was perfectly still and quiet.

"There you are," said Marius as he moved both hands to the center of Sia's leg.

A loud *crack* sounded throughout the room. Eli instantly looked to Sia to see how much pain she was in, but she just laid there. Marius switched legs and did the same thing with Sia's other leg. Another loud *crack* erupted throughout the room, but Sia showed no sign of discomfort.

"All done! Try them out now!"

Eli jumped to his feet and extended a hand to Sia. He was surprised that she again declined it, but he didn't read too much into it. As she slowly rose to her feet, Eli realized he had been holding his breath. She took a few steps around, before turning to Marius with wide eyes.

"What did you do?"

"It's a special healing technique that I learned from Eli's mother Mya a few years back. The body typically has its own pace at which it heals. There is a bone in the leg that is free from any nerves or muscles in your legs. When the bone is slightly injured, it can trick your brain into thinking your legs are severely injured. This makes your brain accelerate the healing rate in that area to a staggering rate. Your legs are, for the most part, nearly healed. Now I would not go out and start jumping buildings or anything like that. However, I do believe that in one or two days you should be fit for battle."

Eli smiled when he saw Sia throw her arms around his dad's neck. She hugged him tight before regaining her composure.

"Thank you very much Marius. I do not know how to thank you."

"The real person to thank is Eli's mother Mya. She was the most skilled and beautiful healer, as well as Weapons Master, I have ever met in my life. She taught me so much."

Silence took the room before Eli clasped his dad's shoulder and shook him from his thoughts. Marius soon turned towards the bowl of eggs that still lay inconspicuously at their feet. "So what are you guys up to?"

"Roulette the eggs," said Mik.

"He means Egg Roulette," said Sia.

"Sounds fun! How do you play?"

Eli and Sia went over the rules and object of the game with Marius. To their surprise, he elected to play as well, and took a spot at second to last—right before Mik and after Sia. Eli found it refreshing to see his dad having so much fun and laughing at the faces of the eggs. Eli had a few flashbacks of how fun it was when he, his mom and his dad would all sit around the kitchen table and play small games that he would always win.

*Now that I think about it, I always won. Hey wait a minute...*

There were two eggs left and it was Sia's turn. She grabbed an egg and smashed it against her face. Besides a small *ouch* from her, nothing happened.

*Hmm, she's good. You wouldn't believe that she was in on everything.*

Marius grabbed an egg while inching closer to the bowl. "My turn!"

"Ah man, that's the last one. I don't get to have a turn now," said Mik.

"Hmm, I do not think you will want a turn my friend—trust me," said Marius.

"I do! It's not fair that I am the only one that does not get my last turn."

"I think you should let him have it dad."

"I agree," started Sia with a smile. "If he wants it, give it to him.

"Alright Mik, it's all yours," said Marius handing Mik an egg that had a pair of hypnotized eyes with its tongue sticking out.

Mik quickly snatched the egg and smashed it on his face. Slimy yellow yoke and egg white ran down his face. An expression of complete shock stayed frozen across his face. "You tricked me!" Mik's arms quickly crossed in front of him.

"All in good fun my friend," said Marius putting his arm around Mik.

Eli found himself laughing hysterically alongside Sia. Mik joined the laughter after a short moment of pouting. Marius went into the kitchen and came back with a cloth, which he handed to Mik.

"That means you won the game Mik," said Eli.

After wiping his face clean, Mik's face sprung up from the towel he was holding. "It does?"

"Yeah, whoever cracks the raw egg on their face wins. You would have lost if you would have refused to crack it on your face," said Eli.

Mik's demeanor completely flipped, as he danced around the three of them. "Yeah! I beat all of you! What do I get?"

"Hmm, how about a tour of my weapons room? I have some of the most legendary weapons of all time downstairs," said Marius.

The floor shook under Eli's feet, once Mik decided to run around the room in a frenzy.

"Yeah! Can we?"

"That is, if it's okay with your sister," said Marius looking to Sia for approval.

"Of course, as long as you listen to everything Marius says Mik," said Sia.

"I promise! Lets go!" Mik ran towards the kitchen. He came back a few seconds later with a confused look on his face. "Wait, which way is it?"

Everyone in the room, except for Mik, erupted into laughter.

"This way my friend," said Marius leading Mik down a hallway, and eventually downstairs.

Eli looked back towards Sia, who was still gazing at the spot that Mik and Marius had been.

"Do you want to go up to my room?"

"Sure," she said.

While Sia followed Eli up the stairs and towards his room, he became more and more aware of her footsteps and proximity. His hands began to sweat, his heart quickened, and he found himself breathing a little deeper than usual. When he opened the door, he was relieved to see that his bed was made. Sia entered behind him and took a seat on his bed. Eli took his chair from his writing desk and placed it in front of her, before sitting down.

"You know, I never got a chance to see you after your battle."

"Well I was a little preoccupied, as you know," she said.

"No I know. What I meant to say is, I never got a chance to tell you how amazing you were."

Sia stared at Eli for a while and then rose to her feet. She took interest in a painting on his wall that he drew when he was a kid. It was a painting that he drew of a dream that he had of a chest that contained a powerful weapon. The picture showed the chest buried underneath the Earth.

"If I had did amazing, I would not have ended up in the Medicinal Quarters with a concussion, a bruised rib, and internal bleeding. Clearly I did not train hard enough," she said.

"That's not true. You were up against four other really skilled opponents. I was there, I saw how amazing you were."

She turned her head to look at him for a few seconds, and then turned her attention towards a small mirror that hung on a wall in Eli's room. Eli watched Sia examine herself. "So since you were there, you must have heard my father and his— support."

"Yeah we all heard it. Sia I am so sorry, I hate the way he talks to you and how he—."

"Stop right there! The first thing I don't need is your pity. I do not need you to sit there and judge me just because you saw my dad on a bad day. He was just tired and under a lot of stress. He is an awesome father. He feeds us, gives us a roof over our heads, and clothes to wear. So do not sit there and feel sorry for me and think that I need you to come rescue me. I don't need your help. Is that clear?"

Eli thought about how helpless Sia looked at her father's feet, when he had walked into her room. "Has he done it before?"

Sia walked into his washroom and examined the mirror that hung against its wall. "Done what?"

"What he did earlier today. Hit you."

"That is none of your business! Oh dear Aegis! How dare you ask me a question like that! Does your father hit you? Should I be worried for my little brother's safety right now? I knew it was a mistake coming over here. You are just like everyone else!" Sia stormed out of the washroom and headed for the door.

Everything happened so fast—and not how Eli had intended—that he quickly rose up to stop her. "Wait! I didn't mean it like that," said Eli grabbing her wrist.

The ringing sounded for a few seconds before it stopped, after the initial slap. Eli stood shocked after it was over.

"Don't you ever touch me! Do you hear me?" She exited his room, but not before slamming the door behind her.

Eli still stood frozen in disbelief at what had just happened. He took a seat on his bed and stared at his hands. After he was sure that Sia had already grabbed Mik and left, but not after telling his dad about what he had done, Eli went to the washroom mirror. His face was a little pink, but for the most part it was normal.

*I didn't mean to upset her. I want to help but she won't let me. I don't know what to do.*

A brief memory of Jude, Jed and Eli walking to the Academy came to mind.

*Jude would know what to do.*

Eli splashed some water over his face, and after drying it, headed downstairs to begin the explanation to his dad in regards to why Sia left in a rage. The hallway was still dark, but light filled the remainder of it, once the stairs came into view. As Eli walked down the stairs, he rubbed his face with both hands in an attempt to get the fresh feeling of being slapped off of his face. When he pulled his hands away, he froze at what he saw. Sia sat on the last step looking up at him. Her eyes looked like she had been crying, but no tears appeared to be present. He was confused as to why she was sitting there. He was positive she would be long gone by now, telling everyone how much of a horrible person he was. Still confused, he took a seat next to her.

*Being a screw up at life—take two.*

"I'm sorry for what I said and—touching you. I didn't mean to upset you."

"All the time," she said.

"Huh?"

"He hits me all the time. Mik too." She buried her face in her lap.

He thought about all of their encounters that carried the secrets, the scars and scratches, and above all, the pain that she had been enduring. "Can I ask you a question?"

Sia looked up into his eyes but did not respond. He returned her gaze.

"Will you go somewhere with me?"

# AMETHYST

The way back seemed a lot shorter and less difficult to find. Before leaving his house, Eli and Sia went down to the weapons room to check in on Mik and Marius, and let them know that they were going out for a while and would be back soon. Marius had been training Mik on some basic sword techniques, so the young boy barely noticed Eli and Sia's presence when they entered and exited the weapons room. Eli was a little shocked that Sia had agreed to come with him. He had remained hopeful before asking her, but had already braced himself for the *no* he had expected.

As the two of them made their way through the many lush trees, Eli felt a growing feeling that someone or something was following them. He didn't know if Sia was aware of the same presence, but if she wasn't, he had no desire to frighten her.

*I think I would be afraid before she was afraid. She never seems to be scared of anything.*

Sia had remained quiet for most of their journey. A few times she asked where they were going and if they were lost, but Eli assured her that he knew exactly where they were. Many different oak and maple trees stacked on top of each other, making it difficult to pass in between them, as they ventured on. However, Eli was aware of the quietness that surrounded them, and he welcomed it.

"Your dad is really nice," said Sia breaking the silence.

"Thanks. I think he really likes you—both of you. It has been a long time since he has played a game with me."

"Well he is really fun to be around. He is very positive and all smiles. It's comforting," she replied.

"Well you are welcome over anytime."

When Eli received no response, he looked towards Sia from the corner of his eye to see that she was staring at him. He slowly focused his attention ahead of them in an attempt to act like he didn't notice her stare. When the giant oak tree appeared, Eli felt a smile come across his face. He turned to his left and continued on for a few more steps until he realized that he did not hear the familiar sound of Sia's footsteps next to him. He turned around to see that she was still at the large oak tree that they had just came across. He returned to her side but said nothing, just stared where she stared. Her small hand pushed aside the curtain of leaves before she entered. He followed. As she walked towards the tree, her hand moved slowly over its surface without touching it. He took a seat on one of the giant roots that laid uprooted from the ground.

"Eli where are you taking me? What is this place?"

He rose to his feet and extended her his hand. She accepted it just long enough to make it over the root before she unclasped it. As they walked a few more steps, the trees began to part as the familiar path came into view. He looked to his left and found the trees with their blue petals blowing in the light wind that passed by them. Eli looked back towards Sia who was admiring the trees on her right, which were caked with purple petals. She walked over to one of the trees and gazed up at the purple petals that hung from it. A light scent of honey and mango glided through the air as Eli took a spot next to her. When the two of them gazed up at the overwhelming number of petals that hung from the tree, one detached itself and glided softly down in front of Sia. When it was eye level with her, it stopped descending and held its position, turning slowly round and round. Sia's head jerked towards Eli, who returned her gaze a few seconds later. She turned her attention back towards the petal that still hung suspended, and held out her hand. The petal continued its descent and softly landed in the palm of her hand. She slowly brought the petal up to her nose and smelled it.

Eli continued on down the path, knowing that Sia would soon follow when she was ready. A rustling behind the trees on Eli's left, made him ready himself. Sia soon joined him with her hands extended. A few seconds went by before a loud squeak erupted from behind them. Both of them turned around simultaneously to find a small pair of light blue eyes staring up at them. The creature's soft white fur seemed even softer than the last time Eli had seen it. He crouched on one knee and held out at his hand. A thunderous roar sounded, as the creature exposed its rows of large razor-sharp teeth. Eli jumped to his feet. The creature looked up at him with no teeth or hostility present. Sia laughed lightly.

"Ah how cute," she said extending her hand.

"No don't!"

The furry creature wobbled over to Sia's hand and sniffed it with its tiny nose. Suddenly it started repeatedly hopping up and down from one foot to the next. It squeaked a pleasing noise before climbing into her hand. She brought it up to her face and rubbed his fur on her cheek.

*Of course it only likes her.*

"Eli look. He is friendly now," said Sia holding it out to him. Right as the creature turned towards Eli's direction, the razor-sharp teeth and growl erupted again. Eli recoiled, nearly tripping over a root from one of the trees.

"Looks like he only likes me," she said. She scratched the top of its head before putting it down.

"He was nicer to me the last time I was here. Maybe he was just using me to get to you."

The creature disappeared between a few huddled trees. As the two of them continued down the pathway, they came across a large light pink statue that blocked their path. Her face no longer smiled or was filled with worry; it was expressionless.

*It's the angel again. She's back.*

"Now last time I was here, the angel disappeared shortly after I fell asleep at its feet."

"It's not an angel," said Sia shaking her head.

"Sure it is. See—she has wings," said Eli.

"Just because a beautiful woman has wings, doesn't mean she is an angel. Besides, angels don't have faces. Their faces are absent of any physical characteristics. It's just—blank."

"Who told you that?"

"I just know. What were you dreaming about before you woke up?" said Sia.

Eli began to blush and diverted his attention in every other direction besides Sia's.

*You. Always you.*

A rumbling penetrated from beneath them as the statue swung inwards. Sia's gaze flew to him as her eyes widened. "What did you do?"

"Nothing. I just thought about what I was dreaming about the last time I was here."

"Which was?"

"I'd rather not say," he said.

As he walked down the pathway, the familiar large stonewalls rose up on both sides of them. The smell of honey and mango tickled Eli's nose, while his eyes closed to appreciate every second of the scent.

"Oh my. Eli look!" screamed Sia from next to him.

Eli's eyes flung open and took in the scenery that left him speechless the last time he was here. The greenest meadow Eli had ever seen radiated out from his feet into a wide arc. Dark purple, royal blue, and hot pink flowers stood a couple of inches up from its green surface. The familiar blue and purple trees, from the pathway they had just walked, surrounded the entire area. Eli looked passed the greenery and noticed what appeared to be smoke rising somewhere behind the meadow. He started towards the smoke. He did not know why, but after a few steps he decided to remove his shoes and socks, and set them aside. The green meadow was as soft as cotton beneath his feet. He stopped for a few moments and curled his toes in hopes to caress the softness. Continuing on towards the smoke, a large rocky wall rose up ahead of him. After a few more steps, Eli found the source of what he had seen earlier. A wide, steamy light purple waterfall parted the rocky wall, and cascaded down into what appeared to be a crater.

*Badass.*

The water left Eli speechless. Its purple color flowed as if water was naturally that color. Taking a few more steps, he noticed that the large light purple waterfall did not empty into a crater, but into an enormous hot spring—that radiated a cloud of steam in every direction. Around the hot spring was a pattern of the same royal blue, dark purple, and hot pink flowers that littered the meadow. Both of his hands rested gently on the outer lip of the hot spring. Steamed brushed passed his face making him sneeze. Large lily pads—big enough to sit on— slowly drifted throughout the hot spring. Small purple and blue rose petals floated alongside the lily pads.

*Where did this place come from? It's like something out of a book that only Jude would read.*

Eli was so amazed at his surroundings that he had completely forgotten about Sia. He looked over his shoulder and quickly realized she was standing right next to him, taking in the hot spring as well.

"Eli I am..."

"Yeah?"

"I'm speechless," she said.

"Want to go for a swim?"

"I do not think I have the proper attire for swimming," she said.

"Come on. It's only you and me out here—no one else. Look around us; trees stacked on trees go on for miles all around us. You're safe." Eli took off his belted combat tunic and pants so that he was only wearing his shorts. He ran towards the rocky wall on the side of the waterfall, and after finding a few shelves in the rock, started climbing.

"Eli wait!"

Eli looked down to see Sia in small pinks shorts and a matching bra, climbing up after him.

*Oh man! Honorable thoughts! Honorable thoughts!*

Eli felt himself begin to blush as he forced himself to climb higher.

"Wait," said Sia.

He stopped and looked down. She was having a hard time climbing up a shelf and looked stuck. He reached his hand down to offer her a hand. Her face looked grim.

"I don't know about this. What if I fall?"

"Don't worry I won't let anything happen to you," he said.

She stared up at him for a while and then flung her hand up. He quickly grabbed her hand and hoisted her up. She clung to his shoulder and found her footing on a nearby rock, before passing him and taking the lead.

"Hey!"

"Sorry E! You really need to learn how to see through a trap."

He climbed after her, but finished last, as he climbed over the last shelf of the wall. Sia was sitting with her legs dangling over the edge of the waterfall. She sat looking out over the hot spring and meadow. Eli found a safe spot next to her and joined.

"You know," he started as he dusted his hands clean. "I don't like people beating me at something as simple as rock climbing."

"Where did you find this place?"

"By accident."

"How?"

"It was after your match. I went to see you at the Medicinal Quarters, but they didn't let me," he said.

"Who didn't let you?"

"Your father."

Eli thought he saw her face turn into a scowl for a second, but he could not be sure. "Anyways, he called the guards on me. All I wanted was to see you. I didn't know if you were going to make it. I was desperate so I—I pulled a dagger on the guards. So they knocked me unconscious."

"Why would you do that? How stupid and dishonorable pulling a weapon on the guards like that. You are sullying your name with such reckless and immature actions. You could be in jail right now you know that?"

"I know that now. But I still don't regret my decision," he said looking into her eyes.

She did not look away, just stared at him for a while. After a few seconds she finally turned her tension towards the hot spring that boiled beneath her. "Then what happened?"

"I woke up in Bishop's quarters. He persuaded your father to not put me in jail apparently. He wanted to know why I did what I did, so I told him. He was like you. He scolded me for my decisions and basically made me feel like an idiot—like a child. He ordered one of his people to escort me home. He claimed it was for my safety, but I knew it was because he didn't want me to try to see you again. When I got home I tried to sleep, but couldn't. I had a nightmare so I decided to go for a walk. I kind of got lost in the forest and stumbled upon that giant oak tree with the veil of leaves we passed earlier. Shortly after that, I found this place. I didn't fully go in, I stayed at the entrance. I felt like I didn't have time to go exploring since the Trials were in a few hours. So I went home to try and get some sleep. I knew I would come back, I just didn't know when."

Silence hung in the air for a while. The only noise came from the running water next to them, which soon radiated the sound of splashing down below.

"Bishop was right, you should not have done what you did," she said.

Eli felt for a second like he had just been slapped again. He turned his attention towards her to see if she had planned to elaborate, but she kept her gaze away from him. "And why is that?"

"Because it was foolish, reckless, and could have resulted in major consequences. You should know better," she said.

*Foolish and reckless huh? After all I did to see you, to make sure you were okay. You tell me that I'm being foolish and reckless.*

"I feel sick," he said.

No response came from Sia. Eli felt belittled and hurt for a while. He recounted everything that had happened since he had met Sia.

*She has no idea of the pain I went through when I thought she was gone. Either that or she doesn't care.*

"So are we jumping down or..."

"Sure—whatever," said Eli rising to his feet and jumping down before she could reply.

He was so high up when he jumped, that the fall was longer than he imagined. Warm steam accompanied him on his way down, which he found comforting. When he looked down, he saw the haze of warm steam above the hot spring part. The large light purple basin soon came into view beneath him. Heat, silence and serenity were what greeted Eli when his body entered the world beneath the surface of the hot spring. Upon entrance into the water, Eli felt as if he had left his body at the surface, and only his soul now explored the depths underneath the purple utopia. As his eyes opened hesitantly, he realized the water did not bother his eyes at all. On the contrary—the water comforted his eyes and tickled his face—causing him to smile. While he looked through the water's depths, he found it inhabited by what appeared to be fireflies. He was confused by what he saw, and believed his eyes were playing tricks on him. The fireflies swam throughout the water as smoothly as if they were flying in air. Thirst for breath stabbed his mind. Warm and cool air simultaneously greeted his senses when he pierced the water's surface. He looked around and found no trace of Sia.

"Great, you didn't drown," said a voice above him.

He looked up to find that she had not jumped yet.

"Nope I'm still alive."

*Not that you would care.*

"Alright I'm coming down!" she announced.

*Be my guest. You can slap me again while you are at it. I like the pain.*

The surface rocked less than Eli had expected, when Sia's body came in contact with the water. While the giant lily pads and flowers rocked back and forth, some floated by him, tickling his back and shoulders. Another lily pad floated by. Eli grabbed a hold of it and leaped on top, expecting to sink the minute he sat down. A light rocking was all that greeted him when he sat motionless on the pads surface.

*Oh yeah!*

He looked around the green meadow and noticed that along the edges lined with trees, were what appeared to be fruit. He made out a banana and maybe some strawberries. A croak closeby startled him. He looked beside himself, and found a small frog floating by on a smaller lily pad.

*What the heck!*

The frog was different than any frog Eli had ever seen. Its skin was completely purple and its eyes were baby blue. However what caught Eli's attention the most, was the light purple glow that pulsed around its body. The frog hopped away from one pad to the next, when Sia's head erupted from beneath the water's surface.

"It's breathtaking down there!"

Eli reached his hand down to help her up.

"No thanks, I don't need any help—I got it," she said hoisting herself up next to him.

His hand hung there as if still waiting for her to grab it. He waited a few seconds before putting it down.

*I can't believe you have the nerve to call oranges difficult. Clearly you don't own a mirror.*

Eli sat cross-legged next to Sia, as he watched her examine the meadow and trees around them. Small fireflies, similar to the ones that Eli had seen underwater, buzzed about landing on the water's surface—before flying off towards the meadow. That was when Eli saw it. A purple glow emanated from everything in his surroundings. It glowed in a pattern similar to a breathing gesture or a heartbeat. Everything had it. The trees, the flowers, the animals, even the outline of the water and rocky wall that stood behind them. He wondered how come he didn't notice it before.

*This place is insane.*

Eli heard Sia say something but he had missed it. "I'm sorry did you say something?"

"I said I am sorry," she said.

"For what?"

"For saying Bishop was right."

Silence cloaked the air as the rocking of the lily pad became more apparent. Eli realized that he had been holding on to a bit of anger. Anger he was not aware of until she had apologized. He took a deep breath. "It's okay. You both are probably right."

"You know I was happy that you decided to stay for my match," she said.

He looked at her as she tucked a piece of hair behind her ear, and pulled up the strap on her top. "Why?"

"I don't know. It gave me peace of mind."

"Oh," he said. He noticed her take a few deep breaths before diving off the lily pad and into the water.

*This is painful. I'm in this amazing place and I feel like I'm being emotionally tortured here.*

Eli watched a blue and purple butterfly flutter by and land on a pink flower. Its wings flapped slowly, rocking the flower it sat on. It was soon joined by a pink and white butterfly, which landed next to it. As Eli heard the splashing of water behind him, the two butterflies flew off together, flying in a small revolving circle towards the entrance of the meadow. The lily pad rocked slightly as Sia's presence returned beside him.

*I have had feelings for you ever since I first met you. You kidnap my thoughts during the day, and haunt my dreams at night. Your safety and happiness dictates my happiness. And the whole time I'm jumping over hurtles and through pain, you idly remain unaware of the effect you have on me; which leaves me suffering in silence.*

She brought her hand up to her mouth and made a faint noise next to him. "Do you mind telling me about your mother?"

"Huh?" He felt slightly ambushed, and was unaware of how he should take her words.

"Your mother. What was she like?"

"Amazing. Wonderful. I guess everyone says that about their mom. To me, mine was the most amazing person in the world. I don't remember one time when I didn't see her smiling. I remember her reading to me at night and playing games with me every chance she got." Eli felt himself giggle slightly but Sia remained silent. "She loved cooking and writing poems. Every meal that she cooked, she would do something special with it. I remember when I was little she made sandwiches that she propped up and built into a castle. The castle even had a flag, made out of cheese, on a toothpick at the very top."

Eli and Sia both laughed simultaneously. When Eli realized this, he stared at her. She looked at him and then looked away quickly.

"What about her poems. What did she write about?" she asked.

"Everything. It wasn't what she wrote about, it was how she wrote them. She used to keep a little journal with her on her missions. I used to stay at a family friend's house. When her and my dad would get back from one of their missions, she would read me the poems she wrote before bed, about her adventures. I can't remember all of them, but I remember every time I heard one, I felt like I was picked up and taken away to whatever place she was describing."

"She must have been a very skilled writer. Did she leave you any of her poems, you know, before she passed?

"Her whole journal. There were still blank pages left. She used to help me put into words what I was feeling, and write poems like she did. I tried to continue to write once she was gone—but it was too—it was hard. Her last poem was to me. She told me that I gave her heart permission to beat, and her lungs the right to breathe. It said no matter what happened to her, as long as I was okay, she would be at peace forever. But it isn't fair because now that she's gone, I feel like I will never be at peace," he said feeling his eyes water.

Eli quickly looked away and wiped his eyes before any tears could fall.

She rubbed his shoulder. "Eli I am so sorry. Really I am. I miss my mom too. She was everything to me—to all of us, including my dad. I always remembered her taking me outside when I was young. She used to tell me that nature was alive and breathed just like me. She used to tell me this story about how when the gods departed this world in order to protect it, they left a piece of themselves in the very earth we walk on. She used to say that it was the gods' way of protecting us. I would go on so many trips to forests, mountains, everywhere with her. However, there was one specific spot that was especially special. I don't go there anymore. It's far too painful," she said.

"What about your dad. Did he come?"

Sia shifted her position before continuing. "He did at first, but then slowly he stopped coming along. He was a Professor back then specializing in training Erudites," she said.

"I heard your dad call Mik that the other night in disgust. I personally don't think that there is anything wrong with being an Erudite," he said.

Silence.

"Do you know what makes a person an Erudite?" he asked.

"We all have all three bloodlines in our blood. However, our primary bloodline makes up ninety percent of our blood. The other two bloodlines only make up the remaining ten percent, which is why we gain no abilities, power, or insight from them. Sometimes when someone is born, too much of the other two bloodlines are present—so the person's blood is diluted with so many bloodlines—that they have no abilities. They are basically what the scholars call 'anomalies in life."

"So let me guess, you think that he can never become an Agent—right?" he asked feeling his voice rise.

"Not exactly. He can but he has to train twice as hard as everyone else. He can't use magic like my family. He can't use any Combat Specialist abilities. The only thing left is to be a Weapons Master, but he doesn't get any of the Weapons Master abilities. So..."

"So his brain won't automatically be skilled or master the weapons he uses—I know. That does not make him a lost cause or any different from you and I."

Silence.

"Well does anyone know why it happens?"

"None of the scholars know. Same way they don't know why the Combat Specialist bloodline is becoming so scarce," said Sia.

"So lets say he trains very hard and passes his Trials and all of his tests. What then? Will your father finally accept him?"

Sia scratched the top of her head. "I don't think so since Mik will probably end up standing watch at the gates or castle for the rest of his life. The Council never puts Erudites in battle unless we are desperate for men like we are now. They feel like the Erudites will be at a disadvantage."

"That's not true. They can be a big help in battle. That is unfair to punish someone for being born a way that they had no control over," said Eli rising to his feet on the lily pad. "I'll train him!"

"Eli no. You shouldn't get his hopes up. Even my dad told him that he is doomed to stand watch over the cracks of the castle walls for the rest of his life. There is no use."

"Well your dad is wrong. And if you believe him—so are you. Mik and I will show both of you!"

Sia rose up and grabbed both of his hands so they were looking at each other. Just when he thought she was going to come closer, he was falling head first into the warm water below. As both of them kicked and swam underwater, Sia threw him a wink before quickly swimming away. He followed her through all of the bubbles and fireflies that swam passed. When he caught up with her, she had her back against the wall facing him. She was beautiful. Fireflies floating by, casted a dim light over her face drawing attention to her dark purple eyes that pierced through the purple of the water. Her dark brown hair swayed peacefully in the water while evading her face. He swam up to her. His left hand tucked around her waist and grabbed her side. He looked up at her, but she did not move. Her eyes stared backed at his. He tucked his other hand around her waist. He saw bubbles leave her mouth, which made him smile. He turned around and wrapped her arms around the back of his neck. She hung on tight as they broke the surface of the water, gasping for air.

After Eli wiped his eyes, he returned his gaze to Sia, and was greeted with a splash in the face. "Hey!" He wiped his eyes anticipating a burning that never came. He heard her laughter become feint. Looking around the hot spring, thick steam radiated everywhere, blocking his view. He called out to her. "Where are you?"

A voice on his right caught his attention. "I'm over here!"

He took off swimming to his right. He was confused when he eventually came crashing into the wall there. A voice on his left now caught his attention.

"Now I'm over here!"

He swam to his left and was soon greeted with another wall. He dove under the water's surface and looked around. He found her smooth legs kicking beneath the water's surface in the middle of the hot spring.

*Time to play sea monster!*

He swam quietly and gently through the water until he was upon her. He quickly grabbed her sides and thrust her up out of the water. He heard her scream hysterically as his head breached the surface of the spring. He laughed as she slapped his shoulders repeatedly while continuing to scream. He placed her on the edge of the hot spring so that only her legs were in the water.

"Cheating is a sign of weakness you know," she said with a scowl on her face.

Her bare skin seemed to glow more than usual. The water laid in small water droplets on the surface of her shoulders and her neck. Her water-soaked clothes clung to her warm smooth skin, as his eyes ventured up to the pools of piercing purple eyes that stared back at him.

"I know all about weakness," he replied.

"I do not understand."

He gazed up into her eyes, and studied the details of his dreams. "Why is it that the eyes of other Magi are only dark purple when they are using their bloodline abilities, but yours— yours stay light purple even when your not using your abilities?"

She stared at him. Her eyes ventured to one of her shoulders, which she scratched lightly before returning his gaze. "They were a gift from my mother. Her pregnancy with me was not easy. During labor, she accidentally activated her blood energy, causing the change in eye color. She did it because she way dying. Her body was straining and struggling through the labor. When I was born, I was born with half of the Magi glare still active. That is why my eyes stay purple. Since I am the only one of our people with this condition, the healers say it is a defect."

"They are wrong. It isn't a defect. It's a gift—and it's one of the many things that drew me to you, on that warm clear day that you walked into my life. Those eyes stay with me, even when you're nowhere to be found."

Her brows curled tightly before releasing. "Why?"

"When you see me, when you look into my eyes, do you see the madness behind them—the madness that is my feelings for you?"

Her eyes did not move. They did not flinch or shy away. Her breathing was quiet and her lips were still.

"I need you so much that it hurts," he continued.

She stared back at him never moving or making a sound. He placed a hand on the edge of the hot spring—on both sides of her—and hoisted himself up. He stared in her eyes as his lips inched closer. He looked for any sign of rebellion but found none. As soon as he felt the breath that came from her lips, he kissed her. Her lips tasted sweet and warm at the same time. Just when he felt his heart beating faster, he stopped kissing her. After dropping back into the water, he stared back up at her.

"What's wrong?" she asked appearing puzzled.

"I never thought I would ever get a chance to be this close to you. I dreamed about it ever since we met in the courtyard of the Academy and it hurt. Now that I feel like the pain can finally stop, it's replaced with worry that I will never be this close to you again. I feel like you will find a reason to leave."

She said nothing, just stared back at him. Eli was sure that she would not understand what he was trying to say.

"What's that?"

He followed her finger as it pointed towards something. Eli looked over to feel a splash of warm water hit his face as he heard her laughing. He wiped his eyes to catch a glimpse of her running away from him down the meadow. He quickly hoisted himself up, and when he found his footing, he fell backwards into the water. Water shot up his nose for a short time. When he found the edge of the hot spring, he tried again and was successful. He ran to the center of the meadow and looked around. A few frogs hopped by an all white monkey with purple eyes that sat gnawing on a banana.

"Sia?"

She didn't respond. He heard a squeak at his feet and looked down. The little creature with the baby blue eyes looked up at him.

*Why don't you have any purple on you?*

"I don't suppose you know where she is do you?"

The creature nodded its head twice before turning for some nearby trees.

*You've got to be kidding me.*

Eli found himself following the furry creature through countless trees and bushes, until he found it standing still in the middle of two trees. It turned around and stared at him.

"Well, where is she?"

The creature pointed a small finger upwards. Eli looked up to see Sia. Two trees strangely shared a large wide branch that Sia was laying on. He climbed one of the trees and found her lying perfectly still. Her chest rose and fell slowly. He lay down behind her and soon heard a squeak above his head. He looked up to see the furry creature staring back at him.

*As long as you don't ruin this for me, I don't care if you sit and watch.*

Eli looked down at the gentle rise and fall of Sia's body as she breathed. He wrapped his arm around her.

"Help!" She screamed violently as she tried to free herself from his arm.

Eli got up to a fury of slaps and punches as he covered his face from the attack. Hey! Hey! Ouch! What are you doing? Ouch! It's me."

"Just leave us alone! Stop it! Stop hurting us!"

Eli finally caught her wrists and felt aggravated as he locked eyes with her.

"Get off of me! Let me go!" she cried. She turned her head away from him. "I won't look at you! You can't force me," she said.

"Hey! Look at me! Look at me!" He shook her wrists until her violent behavior ceased. After a few seconds, Sia's eyes returned to him. "I'm not going to hurt you. It's me—Eli."

She said nothing, just studied him before turning her back to him. Confused by her reaction, he moved next to her and sat down. Goosebumps infested her arms and legs. He could see a light shake vibrated from her body. Her troubled eyes gazed off in every direction.

"Hey. What's going on? Talk to me."

"You touched me," she said as she stirred in her seat.

"I put my arm around you, but I—." He saw her shutter at his words. "I'm sorry. I didn't mean to scare you."

"It's okay," she said. Her shaking soon subsided, and the person he had been swimming with a few minutes ago, returned.

"Are you okay?"

The goose bumps on her arms began to disappear. "No," she started as she rubbed her arms. "I will never be okay."

"Talk to me. What's wrong?" He lifted his arm to rub her hand. Her body recoiled at his movement, causing him to abandon his plan of touching her. "I'm sorry," he said.

"My mother did not always take us with her when she visited nature. She did most of the time. But she did take us to many places. I loved every second of our time together. It was always quiet, except for the nature around us, which I welcomed. She always made an adventure out of everything we did. One night Mik and I woke up early in the morning to the smell of breakfast. I was seventeen and Mik was five. She cooked everything you could imagine. There was even a large bowl of flawless bright red strawberries at the center of the table. We all sat down and ate, including my dad. It was our day to do chores, so Mik and I started them right after breakfast. Mik's chore was to draw my mom and dad a picture. My mom said she was going to a spot in the forest to paint the sunrise. I was excited to see her painting because she always painted such beautiful art. Anyways, when the sun had set I was worried. I had sat at the windowsill in my room watching for her return, ever since I was done with my chores. It was all in vain though. She never came back. When I got a little older my father told me that she was unhappy being a mother, and that she probably went to find her own life."

Eli fought back the urge to comfort her throughout her story. The pain in her eyes and the heaviness in her voice, made him feel like he needed to do something to comfort her.

"For a child, especially a daughter, to have their mother abandon them is probably the single greatest pain they will ever know. To go on through this labyrinth we call life without a mother is just—hard. I stopped sleeping. Instead I stayed up every night asking myself what I did wrong to make her leave. I wondered if I had said something to hurt her feelings or if I was just not being the daughter I should have been. After a couple of years, I came to the conclusion that my mother just did not want us anymore. I realized that we were in her way of doing what she really wanted to do. I did not know what it was that she desired. It could have been something with nature, exploring, or whatever—but we were in the way. So we turned to my dad for support, which we did not get. He had just become head of the Kismet jails, and his entire personality changed after mom left. He never talked to us unless absolutely necessary. He worked all of the time, which meant we had to spend a lot of time at Ms. Lowell's house. It was as if we lost two parents instead of one. But the most drastic change was his temper. He had no patience with us—ever. I remember one time when Mik was six years old, he placed the milk on the bottom shelf of the refrigerator because he could not reach the top shelf. My dad beat him for two hours with a piece of the trip wire the soldiers use for landmines. From there it just got worse for us. "

Eli became more aware of all of the small noises around them, once Sia's story was over. The movement of distant animals, the soft movement of the leaves blowing through the wind, and even the sound of falling water far away, all bore at his attention.

"Have you ever told anyone?"

She looked up at him as if in disbelief. "No! Never!"

"Did your mother leave any clues or notes behind as to where she went?"

"No. No clues, just the family painting in the living room. I have tried to be strong for both Mik and I since she left, but sometimes I just need a day to break down you know? I just need a day to cry and let out all of my pain and stress. I get tired of always having to be strong for both of us."

*Oh man. It's now more than ever that I really need to say the right thing and not something stupid.*

"What can I do?"

As she stared back up into his eyes, a bit of softness returned. She studied him slowly, starting from his legs, and ending with his eyes. "Don't leave me." The hue of her eyes appeared indecisive—not wanting to decide whether or not to remain their normal shade, or to succumb to the darker hue that pulsed in the center.

He lightly touched her hand, never leaving her stare.

"Never."

# LIN KITZ

Eli awoke to not one but two sets of eyes staring at him. The baby blue eyes of the furry creature, that seemed to be following them around, joined Sia's light purple eyes. He quickly rose stretching along the way.

"What's going on?"

Red caved in from all angles of her eyes. The light purple eyes that he always dreamed of, were swallowed whole by a destructive force of blood red coats that carried with them the shadows of rage and destruction. Her mouth opened with the intensity of a savage predator.

"I have seen her soul—and it is mine!" Her hand clasped around his neck holding him off the ground. He struggled to break free, but her grip was too strong.

"Sia! What's going on? What's wrong with you?"

Her eyes returned to their normal purple and her face regained its softness. "You promised me that you would protect me—but you have failed."

He awoke in a cold sweat. When his body jerked up from the branch, he startled the furry creature that had apparently been sleeping next to him. It scurried down the tree, and once it reached the ground, it exposed its razor sharp teeth and roared up at him, before scurrying away.

"Eli what's wrong?" asked Sia stretching.

"Nothing. Just a bad dream."

Eli had slept with a safe distance between him and Sia. After witnessing her reaction from being touched, and hearing her story, he didn't want to do anything to make her uncomfortable. She rolled over and looked up at him through a tangle of dark brown hair that covered one of her eyes. He returned her gaze.

"We have to get back to Mik and your dad," she said after giving him a light kiss on the cheek.

"K."

She stared in his eyes for a while before returning to her feet. Eli soon joined her before helping her down the tree. They both found their clothes along the edge of the hot spring and got dressed. Eli found it difficult to keep his eyes off of Sia while she was dressing, but kept his back to her so she would not be uncomfortable.

"You can turn around now," she eventually said.

He turned around to find her dressed and staring back at him with a smile on her face. "Okay—cool."

She closed the distance between them and gave him a quick kiss on the lips. Eli felt himself blush again. She laughed at the sight. "Now I know why you change colors."

On the way out of the entrance they had arrived through, Eli and Sia gave one last look at the hot spring. The furry creature ran to the middle of the meadow and stopped, staring back at them. As the two of them exited out from underneath the high walls of the entrance, they heard a rumble. Looking over their shoulders, the light pink statue returned to her spot. A small smile was present on her face.

Eli thought the return home was way too fast. When the main gate came into view, he kicked himself for not walking slower. Sia continued to talk about her match and what she would have done differently next time she was in battle. Eli absorbed everything she was saying knowing that it could prove useful at a future date.

*Crap! Trials are tomorrow and I haven't been training at all!*

266

His stomach sank as Sia talked about ways to recover from falls quickly.

*I am in the last round of the Trials so I have had more time than anyone to train—and I didn't.*

When the two of them came closer to the guards at the main gate, Sia widened the distance between them. When she noticed Eli's confused expression, she explained that the fewer people that knew about them the better—at least until she could sort out the issues with her dad. Eli still did not understand her reasoning. Her father had to already know that they hung out. Eli had come into their house unannounced just to see her. He knew that Mr. Wyatt was a lot of things, but an idiot was not one of them. He felt the excitement that had been dancing around in his stomach, shrink slightly at Sia's decision to keep their relationship on the low.

The corner statues gave Eli a sense of calm as he realized that his bed was closeby. When his front door rose up ahead him, he knew their special night was over.

"Wait a minute. Where will you and Mik stay? You can't go back to your dad's."

"I know. I plan for us to stay at a family friend's house for a while. At least until we get things figured out," she said in a matter-of-fact tone.

"Why not stay at my house. We have a guest room downstairs. I'm sure my dad won't mind."

"No Eli we can't. My dad would expect it. He will be waiting for us, and I can't get you and your dad mixed up in all of this."

"In all of this? What do you mean?"

"I don't know. Just give me some time to figure it out. Everything will be fine—I promise," she said kissing him on the cheek.

He didn't feel assured, but believed she would keep her word. He knew after tonight, being away from her for too long would be even more painful.

"Okay. I'm with you. As long as you promise not to keep anything from me or hesitate to ask for my help if you need it," he said.

"I promise E."

The front door to Eli's house creaked open as the two of them entered. After Eli closed the door behind him, he heard a pair of feet running up the basement stairs.

"Sia!" Mik tucked her in a tight embrace when his eyes found her. Sia smiled while she hugged him back.

"How was training with Mr. Brassie?"

"Now how many times do I have to say it—it's Marius."

"It was awesome!" said Mik going into a fighting stance. "I learned some cool moves that will make me unstoppable in battle!"

"Well after the Trials and after we take out all of the Necrosis, I plan on teaching you a thing or two about the bow, so be ready," said Eli with a smile.

Sia turned to Eli and shook her head.

"Really? Oh yeah! I will be able to take anyone on! Even you Sia!"

Sia said nothing just stared down at her brother.

"I'm pretty sure a battle between you two would be the show of the century," said Eli.

"Well we have to get going Mik. We will be staying at Ms. Lowell's tonight so grab your stuff," said Sia retrieving her bag by the couch.

"What? Why can't we stay here? Ms. Lowell is boring," said Mik folding his arms.

"Mik you know that is not nice, now grab your bag."

"Man," scowled Mik retrieving his backpack.

"Don't worry Mik, next time I see you, I can teach you how to counter an attack with a sword," said Marius. He patted Mik lightly on the shoulder.

"Wicked!" said Mik as he curled his hand into a fist.

"Mr. Brassie, I mean Marius. Thank you so much for your hospitality, as well as watching my brother for me. I really appreciate it, and if there is anything I can do to repay you—."

"No no it is my pleasure. Just promise me it won't be the last time I see you both."

"Not a chance!" screamed Mik. He scurried out of the door as his backpack repeatedly slapped his back on the way out.

"If you ever need a place to stay, or even just some company, don't hesitate to come by," said Marius putting a hand on Sia's shoulder.

Sia stood motionless staring up at Marius for a while. Eli was not expecting the hug she gave him shortly after. After hugging her back, Marius waved a goodbye out the door to Mik. As Sia exited through the door, Eli went to follow, but was grabbed on the shoulder by Marius.

"Just make sure to hurry back. I have a few things I would like to discuss with you," said Marius.

"Like what?"

"You will see when you get back."

Eli was confused by his father's words. He thought maybe his dad had some advice for his match tomorrow. He could surely use any advice he could get—considering the fact that he had not trained in what seemed like forever. As Eli walked with Mik and Sia, he began to worry about the upcoming battle with the Necrosis.

Sia noticed his worried expression. "What's wrong?"

"Nothing, I'm just worried that I won't be prepared for when we face the Necrosis. From what I have heard, there is a outrageously large number of them."

"If I were you, I would focus on your match first, and the Necrosis threat second. I mean, your match is tomorrow you know," she said.

"But the Necrosis threat is more important."

"Just remember that if you don't win tomorrow, you won't be on Anya's squad. If you don't win your first Trials, you won't move on to more advanced classes, which means you are further away from your goal of becoming a Weapons Master Agent. That is, if you still want to be an Agent."

Eli thought long and hard about her words. He realized she was right. When the Three Brothers fountain rose up in front of them, Eli was confused as to why they were in the Market District.

"Alright we are here," said Sia.

"Your family friend lives in the Market District?"

"She's a shopkeeper. No one knows that she has a house on the other side of her shop. She thinks it helps her keep an eye out for thieves."

"Well I would feel safer if I walked you to her door."

The three of them walked towards a desolate and large wooden building that hung in the back row of the shops. It was one of the few buildings that Eli had seen that was not made up of the white stone that covered nearly the whole city. As they arrived at the doorstep of the building, Mik knocked twice. After a few seconds, the door opened slightly. A lone eye stared back at them before the door opened completely. An older woman— significantly older than Eli's dad—smiled back at them. She had long white hair that reminded Eli of Jed's hair. A few wrinkles were present on her otherwise smooth brown skin. She wore a long white dress and a small gray sweater.

"Sia! Mik! It is so good to see you," said the woman as she wrapped her arms around Mik and then Sia.

"Hi Ms. Lowell, it is good to see you too. I hope we didn't wake you," said Sia.

"No! No! Of course not," said Ms. Lowell buttoning one more button on her sweater.

"It is worse this time. Probably the worse it has even been," said Sia.

"Well then you two can stay here for as long as you need. And who is this young man?" Ms. Lowell nodded her head towards Eli.

"I'm Eli Brassie. It's very nice to meet you Ms. Lowell, and thank you for helping Sia and Mik. I really appreciate it."

"Well isn't he a living, breathing heart-stopper," said Ms. Lowell.

Eli fought back a pending laugh, but was powerless to stop the smile that instantly jumped to his face.

"Eli was nice enough to let us stay at his house for a while. Him and his dad were too kind," said Sia.

"Marius taught me how to use a sword," said Mik.

"Did he? Well Eli and Marius sound like they are priceless to have around. You know I just got done making some blueberry cheesecake cookies Mik."

"Cookies! Awesome!" Mik ran under Ms. Lowell's arm and into her house.

"I better make sure he doesn't eat them all," said Sia turning to Eli. "Thank you for everything. I will see you tomorrow?"

"I would like that."

"Good luck tomorrow. I will be in the first row cheering you on," she said kissing him on the cheek.

When Sia disappeared behind Ms. Lowell, Eli felt his heart grow heavy. He felt a hole open up in a foreign place in his chest. He took a deep breath before realizing Ms. Lowell had been staring at him.

"You must be a really kind man to help those kids," said Ms. Lowell.

"Well they are really special people."

"They definitely are special. I assume that you have met their father?"

Eli was caught off guard by her question. He didn't know how much Ms. Lowell knew about Mr. Wyatt, but he didn't want to be the one to expose Mr. Wyatt's behavior to anyone that Sia had not approved. "I have. A couple of times."

"Just be careful with him. He is a man who knows what he wants, and will do anything—and I mean anything—to get what he wants," said Ms. Lowell.

"Thank you for the advice. Oh and please if there is anything they need, please don't hesitate to ask. I'm the first house on the west side of the street on the Lin Kitz corner."

"Lin Kitz huh? I knew him," she said.

Eli was taken back by what she said. Lin Kitz had been one of Eli's many idols growing up as a kid. Him and Jude used to dream about becoming a Special Operative just like him. "You did?"

"Yes, very honorable man. Could take out fifty soldiers in sixty seconds while mentally making his grocery list. Gave his own life to save those he cared about," said Ms. Lowell shaking her head.

"It's amazing that you knew him."

"I agree," she said with a chuckle. "Well I won't keep you. Thank you for making sure the kids got here safely."

"No, thank you, and please if there are any problems, please let me know."

"You have my word young man," she said.

"Eli. My name is Eli."

# HEART TO HEART &
# HAND TO HAND

Eli felt a little better since he knew that Sia and Mik had a safe place to stay. He would have felt better if they were staying over his house, but in hindsight, he realized it would probably be too weird and too soon. As he passed the Three Brothers fountain and turned onto the main street, Eli almost missed his presence at the corner of his eye. He summoned two throwing daggers before darting to his right. A lone figure walked slowly towards him.

"Who's there?"

The figure said nothing but continued to close the distance between them.

"Stay where you are! I won't tell you again!"

The figure continued to close the distance. When he was less than ten feet away, he raised his hand. Eli attacked.

"Blunt force!" A duo of spinning war axes launched towards the figure. The figure leaped out of the way, rolled on the ground, and then returned to his feet. As the war axes missed, they boomeranged around and came back for a second attack. Just as Eli thought the figure was oblivious to the pending attack, he flipped backwards, barely missing the axes, but just in time to grab them by their hilts.

"Nice try," said the figure walking closer to Eli.

Eli summoned two blades and prepared for a close combat assault. Just when he was ready to strike, the streetlight illuminated the stranger's identity.

Fox wore all black combat pants with a black sweater. The war axes dissolved as he threw them to the ground. A white-gold pinky ring shined on his right hand, as he pushed a short strand of hair behind his ear.

"What are you doing sneaking up on me like that?"

"I'm sorry, did I scare you? I forgot I was approaching a novice," said Fox with a smirk.

Eli turned his back to Fox and continued his walk towards home. He didn't care to engage in any conversations with Fox. The guy seemed to love to push people's buttons and Eli was not about to let him ruin an amazing night. As Eli continued down the main street, he heard Fox's footsteps hot on his heels.

"Will you just leave me alone," said Eli without turning around.

"So, how was she?"

Eli nearly fell over at the question. "What did you say?"

"The Wyatt girl—how was she?" Fox widened his grin.

Eli charged him with a dagger in both hands. Fox just stood amused, and just as Eli got close, Fox dodged his attack.

"There it is," said Fox kicking the back of Eli's calf.

Eli felt a numbness cover his right leg. The feeling made him collapse to the floor. When he tried to order his brain to move it, nothing happened. Fox charged him head on.

"Arrow barrage!" A large group of arrows materialized in front of Eli.

"Not quick enough," said Fox as he sidestepped, before eventually maneuvering himself behind Eli.

Eli felt a punch to the back of his arm before the whole left side of his body went numb. Fox swerved around until he was completely behind Eli, and then all Eli could see was street. Pain flared from every inch of his face, while the taste of blood clouded his senses. He felt himself teetering on the edge of unconsciousness, but he fought to stay awake.

"Well well well, looks like Eli Brassie and Sia Wyatt are a thing now. I wonder if daddy knows. I would guess that he would go ballistic if he found out," said Fox. He placed his foot on Eli's back.

Eli tried to force himself to get up, but the feeling of numbness imprisoned his entire body.

"I don't know what you're talking about!"

"Sure you do. You've just confirmed all of my theories, mister 'why not stay at my house.'"

Eli's stomach sank. He felt the worry take over his mind. He began to wonder if the person he felt following him and Sia on the way to the meadow, had been Fox the whole time.

"You followed us."

"Maybe. Maybe not," said Fox lifting his foot off of Eli's back. "You should regain use of your body shortly. Good luck tomorrow."

The sound of Fox hysterically laughing sent Eli into a rage that threatened to destroy him if he let Fox get away.

"I won't lose to you! Come back here! I'm not finished with you!"

"You have already lost—Guardian!"

Seconds felt like minutes while Eli laid on the cold cobblestones of the street. The cold wind seemed to go by every five seconds. He repeatedly tried to regain the feeling in his body, but wasn't successful. Instead, he decided to recount the events of today to try to find out how early Fox had started following him, and what all he could have heard. When the thought of Fox hiding out in the meadow watching him and Sia came across his mind, he felt nauseous.

*Why would he follow me? And did he just call me Guardian?*

Eli thought back to when him and Sia first had entered the forest and he had felt as though someone was watching them. He quickly dismissed the thought when he realized that he had felt the same feeling when he had ventured to the meadow alone; and when he had went to the Forgotten Forest with Zane.

*He could have been following me then as well.*

Eli felt a pain on the left side of his body. He tried to move his leg. The end result was the curling of a couple of his toes. He concentrated all of his energy towards his legs. The feeling slowly returned, as he struggled to one knee. When he rose to his feet, his legs wobbled as if it was his first time learning to walk.

*I've never seen attacks like that. I got to find out what he did to me.*

When Eli finally began his walk back home again, he kept a closer eye on his surroundings. Rows of lightly lit houses rose up on both sides of him. When the Lin Kitz statue came into view, he breathed a sigh of relief. He opened the door to his house, quickly slamming the front door behind him. He looked through the window to see if he was followed.

"Son! Is that you?" Marius' voice seemed to come from the kitchen.

"Yeah it's me."

"I'm in the kitchen. Just made some fresh hot cider."

Eli made sure the locks on the door were all the way locked, before heading towards the kitchen. When he entered the kitchen, he noticed that two steaming cups were placed on opposite sides of the table.

*Oh no. The last time I saw two cups placed on the kitchen table like they were about to duel, dad had found out that Jude and I had gotten into his weapons room without permission.*

Eli took his normal seat at the kitchen table behind the closest cup.

"They make it home okay?"

"Yeah, they are staying with a family friend in the Market District. A Ms. Lowell, do you know her?"

"Hmm, I don't think so," said Marius taking a seat across from Eli.

"So what did you want to talk to me about?"

"All I ask, is for you to let me talk, before you respond son."

"Okay. Go ahead. Shoot."

Marius took a sip of his hot cider. "Now you know I am not one to go putting my nose into your personal life son. But when I feel like you are making decisions that will either hurt you or make you regret them in the future, I feel like it is my responsibility as your father to let you know."

*Great he hates Sia.*

"Can I ask you a question?"

"Sure," said Eli with a shrug.

"When is the last time you hung out with your friend Jude?"

Eli was taken back by the question. That was probably the last thing that he had expected his dad to ask about. "Um, I don't know. I saw him at the beginning of the Trials."

"No, I know you both are bound to see each other there since you both are in the Trials. What I am asking is, when is the last time you hung out together?"

Marius blankly stared at Eli over his cup. Eli thought back to the last time he hung out with Jude. He could remember the last time he had seen him. It was when Zane called him and

Pang weird. But he could not remember the last time the two of them had actually hung out together.

"I can't remember right now. I have a lot on my mind."

"What is sad is, I don't even need to guess about what's on your mind. If the situation was different, I would be just as happy as you are with what you're thinking about right now," said Marius.

"I don't understand what you mean. What's going on dad?"

"Son when is the last time you went over any of your friends' houses?"

Eli thought about it, and again came up blank. "I don't remember. Why does it matter?"

"Do you want to know where I was today?"

"Where?"

"The Trials. I went to support you, and when you were not chosen and Jude was, I stayed to support him. What's sad about the whole thing is, I instantly knew where you were when I did not see you in the spectators area," said Marius with an edge in his voice.

"Just because you decided to go and 'support' him does not mean that I have to," said Eli. When he realized that his dad had nothing to say in response, he decided to continue in hopes of ending the conversation. "Okay, so I was with Sia. What's wrong with that?"

"There is nothing wrong with that son." His tone inferred that Eli had missed the point.

"So then why bring it up!"

"Calm down son. We are just talking—that's it. All I want to know is, after you found out that you were to be in round three and not two, did supporting Jude ever come across your mind?"

"No and why should it?"

Marius stared back at Eli as if he was giving him time to think about it. Eli felt done with the conversation.

"Look dad, Jude and I aren't on speaking terms right now okay. I don't know what his problem is, but he seems to be getting along pretty good without me. So I don't know why you are asking me so many questions about us, as if I am the one to blame."

Marius finished the rest of his cider and then went to the stove and poured him some more. When he raised the kettle offering Eli some, he declined. As Marius took his seat again, he took another sip before responding. "You know he instantly knew you weren't there before the match began—Jude did. I watched him find his mother, Jed and I in the spectator seats. His eyes lingered on the empty space next to me, and I knew he was looking for you."

"Alright I'll talk to him first thing after my Trials. Okay?"

"Do you want to know why Sia is still alive?" asked Marius quickly, as if ignoring Eli's statement.

Now Eli was really getting irritated. It was as if his own dad was against every decision he had ever made. "Yeah Vance saved her—so."

"You are partially correct. Vance was busy at the castle preparing the Magi Agents for the battle with the Necrosis. We are low on men, so he spends extra time out of his schedule to make the Magi Agents as prepared as possible. Anyways, Sia's condition was dire according to what Vance had told me. He was not aware of how bad it was, so he assumed that the healers at the Coliseum could handle it. It was Jude who came to the castle and begged him to at least check up on her. Vance said he had never been so easily persuaded by a twenty year old before. Vance said he promised Jude that he would check in one time on Sia's condition, before he had to return to his projects. According to Vance, if he had arrived any later, she would not have made it. Her heart would have given out."

Time slowed as Eli remembered Sia's fragile body on the table in the Medicinal Quarters. He remembered the bloodied bandages that clung to her neck and chest, as well as the violent convulsions he had seen her endure. Eli was confused. As far as he knew, Jude did not even know Sia that well—let alone care about her. Eli actually thought that Jude did not particularly like her, Zane, or Meara at all, after Jude had found out that all of them knew about the Trials before anyone else.

*Why would you go through the trouble to help her?*

"I didn't know. I will have to thank him first thing in the morning," said Eli folding his arms.

"I am afraid that won't be possible."

"What do you mean it won't be possible? What's going on dad? Stop giving me short sentences and just tell me!" Eli's fist hit the table, causing the dishes that rested on it to rumble. Marius just stared back at him. The worry on his dad's face sent chills down his back.

"Jude is in the MQ son. Vance and all of the healers are doing everything they can."

Eli's heart felt like it stopped. He found himself gasping for air. He began to choke so he forced some cider down. Every time he went to speak, his throat was too dry, so he kept drinking.

"What's wrong with him?"

"He faced four very tough opponents. If I am not mistaken, they are calling two of his opponents prodigies. He took out two of the prodigies and another highly skilled opponent. I have to say that I don't think anyone, including myself, could have done as well as he did against those opponents. They were both skilled and knowledgeable. But Jude, he used some abilities and techniques that no one has ever seen. Scholars are constantly trying to interview him to gain insight on how he did some of the things that he did in that match. They named him, 'The Prodigy of Pith.' Poor thing, he probably won't even get the chance to be congratulated."

Marius looked at his cup and shook his head, before returning Eli's gaze.

"What do you mean he won't get a chance? Dad what's wrong with him? Tell me!"

"He suffered a lot of severe injuries which caused internal bleeding. Also, a few of the nerves around his spine were damaged from a fall. He engaged in a battle with an enormous Cerebus that resulted in the two of them falling from the Coliseum roof. The impact with the battleground caused a small fracture of his spinal cord, which damaged a couple of nerves that allow his brain to function properly. Luckily he is not permanently paralyzed. Vance is trying to both stop the internal bleeding and heal the nerves, before either his brain gives out, or he bleeds to death," said Marius sniffling.

"But he's going to be okay dad. Right?"

Eli choked as he saw a single tear run smoothly down his father's face. Marius quickly wiped away the tear and took a sip of his cider. The sight made Eli want to cry himself. This was probably the second time in his life that he had ever seen his father cry—besides his mother's funeral.

"Vance is only one man. He is skilled, but there is only so much he can do. I just want you to hope for a happy ending, but be prepared for the worst. Son I know Sia means a lot to you. I remember the first time I met your mother, she had a way of putting me under hypnosis with just a glance. All I am saying is don't forget about the people who have been there for you from the start. These are the same people who have stuck it out with you through all of the good times and the bad. Those are the people who truly care about you son. I know you see Jude as your best friend or at least you used to. I see you both as my sons. You are my number one and that will never change no matter what, but I have seen both you and Jude grow up together. If it was not my house you both were at, it was Aileen's, so I am sure she feels the same. I know nothing can replace the family that we once had with your mother. But haven't Aileen, her boys, and I, always been there for you?"

Eli stared motionless down at his cider as he thought about Marius' words. It was true that Mya, Marius, Aileen, Jude, Jed and Eli had always been one big family. When Eli's mother had passed away, Jude's family was the first to come over to offer anything they could. They had helped Eli and Marius through many tough times and vice versa.

"Yeah dad. You guys have."

"Son I have nothing against Sia. I think she is great, and so is her little brother Mik. All I am saying is, I have noticed that ever since she has come into your life, everything has been put on hold. Your friendship with Jude, your training, even your other friends you originally started hanging out with. I never see you hang around anyone anymore son. It is always where is Sia? What is she doing? I mean, you used to dream about becoming the best Agent of Kismet. To fight for our people like your mother and I have. Is that even still your dream son?"

Eli thought about it and realized his dad was right. He had been putting everything on hold. He just didn't realize it.

"Yeah dad it is."

"Are you sure son? You're in the last round of the Trials, and I don't remember the last time you trained. Now, you could have been training on your own and I could have just been unaware. Is that what has been going on?" said Marius.

"No dad. I have been hanging out with Sia. I completely abandoned training and my match is tomorrow. And if my match is even close to as difficult as Jude's, I'm afraid I won't be ready." Eli felt himself overwhelmed with emotion. He felt self-loathing, fear, anger, and even worry for Jude. He had not realized that Marius had left his seat, but when he felt the embrace of his dad's hug, he welcomed it.

"You will be ready son. I believe in you. I will be there with you the whole way. You are not alone in this. I will be in the first row cheering you on, and I'm sure Aileen and Jed will be there too. I am sure if Jude could, he would be there as well."

"Why would he?" Eli's head dropped on its own.

"Because he's your friend son. You guys are basically brothers," said Marius cracking a smile.

"No dad you don't understand. He and my friend Zane don't get along and I feel trapped in the middle. I have been blaming Jude more for their disagreement than I blamed Zane. I just hate confrontation and I don't like dealing with it." An image of Eli and Jude playing in the backyard flashed in front of him.

"There is nothing wrong with hating confrontation," said Marius.

"Then to top it all off, Zane was talking badly about him because he was hanging out with this guy named Pang that everyone thinks is weird."

Marius continued to rub his shoulder. "But it's okay, you were not the one doing it, so you can't blame yourself for other people's actions."

"I know. That's what I told myself. But I sat there and let him do it. Then when Zane and all of my other friends laughed at Jude and Pang, I kind of laughed too. I felt awkward. I didn't know what to do. Then Jude was like 'I thought we were friends.' And I told him that we were, but he said, 'friends don't let their friends talk badly about their other friends.' I knew he was right, but I didn't want to make Zane feel bad either. I felt caught in the middle. Since I felt like Jude was mad at me, I decided to be mad at him. I had no reason, I just decided because he was mad at me I would be mad at him. Feels childish now that I think about it."

"You know what son. You are going to feel caught in the middle of many challenging situations in life, and have to make some pretty tough decisions. As long as you do what you know is right, and not what is easy, you will be fine," said Marius.

"I'm just upset that I was blind to how Jude was still a friend to me even when I stopped considering him my friend. I can't believe I am telling anyone this, but Zane, Sia, Meara and I all knew about the Trials beforehand, even though we were not supposed to."

"You did?" asked Marius appearing shocked. "How?"

"Sia's dad told her, so she told us when we all hung out. The worse part about it is, I purposefully didn't tell Jude about it. I have been lying and playing dumb like I simply forgot to tell him."

"Why son? That isn't like you," said Marius appearing hurt.

"I know alright. You just don't understand, none of you do. Everything is so easy for him. He basically knows everything—or at least it feels that way. He even gets to have the better mentor, while I am stuck with Ivor. I needed an advantage over him, just in case we faced each other."

"An advantage huh? An advantage for what—to kill him?"

"Don't give me that look! You know there can only be one winner! You know it, I know it, and even Jude knows it!"

"You are absolutely right. Shame on me for forgetting that," said Marius slapping himself on the wrist. A grim expression briefly washed across his face.

Eli took a big gulp of cider, which was now room temperature.

"Need to be warmed up?" asked Marius quickly.

"No, I'm good. So—any advice for tomorrow?"

"Keep a weapon in hand and a projectile ability in your mind. You never know when you will have to quickly switch from a close combat assault, to a long-range one, especially when going up against a Magi or Combat Specialist. It is definitely easier said than done. At my first Trials, I stayed up for countless hours the night before, planning out every move for every situation. The minute the match started, straight destruction broke out everywhere. I ended up forgetting everything I had pre-planned, and had to adapt to each opponent as they came at me," said Marius.

Eli committed this to memory, while he took another swig of his room temperature cider. As his dad began to exit the room, Eli thought about all they had talked about.

"Hey dad."

"Yes son."

"Thanks for everything," said Eli.

"I charge a small fee. It is probably more than you will ever make, until you are put on the front lines. So until then, just do me a favor and remember that friendships only work, if both parties are committed to them. If one party is always the only one putting forth effort, the friendship will suffer, and eventually so will that person." A reoccurring display of joy and sorrow ran across Marius' face for a few seconds after he was finished. When neither said anything, he continued. "Just pay me back in full by winning tomorrow."

"It's a done deal!"

"Oh and son."

"Yeah dad."

"There is a pan with burnt sausage in the bushes out back. Do you know anything about it?"

# BREAKFAST WITH
# A PREDATOR

Eli found it difficult to sleep the night before. He kept having a reoccurring dream about going to Jude's funeral, and watching him lowered into the ground. After a few unsuccessful attempts at trying to fall back to sleep, Eli decided to utilize the remaining time before his match. He headed to his training spot in the outskirts of the forest. He left a note on his dad's door, just in case he awoke before Eli returned.

The grass was taller and the spot he had wore into the ground had vanished, when he returned to his familiar spot next to a large fallen oak tree. He thought about all of the different abilities he had at his disposal, and began to work on instinctually using them without thinking. He found the task difficult without a live opponent. He instead tried to think of different dangers and scenarios he could find himself in, when he actually did have an opponent.

*I feel like I have used projectiles too much and may have lost my skill with a bow.*

He summoned his bow and practiced his accuracy on a nearby tree. After he was satisfied, he decided to increase the difficulty by shooting the same target from laying flat on his back. He found it extremely difficult to prop his head up, while simultaneously aiming for the small target he had etched into a tree. After a little less than an hour, he was able to hit a bulls eye on the target.

*Dad had said to keep a weapon in hand and a projectile ability at the ready, just in case I had to switch from a close range to a long-ranged assault.*

He thought about the arrow barrage ability Dominic had used in his battle with Sia. It seemed like a handy ability to have in his arsenal if he could learn to summon as many arrows as Dominic. After a few hours he became irritated with the results. He could summon no more than ten arrows at a time. He remembered Dominic had at least twenty or more arrows when he used the same ability.

*No wonder Fox was able to get around my attack so easily the other night. Ten arrows is nothing! It's easier for me to counter, or use my opponents' arrows against them, than it is for me to summon them myself. I should have trained harder.*

After spending another hour on trying to increase the number of projectiles he could summon, he gave up.

*Ten arrows are better than none at all, and it is still a strong projectile attack.*

He took out his bow and practiced shooting multiple arrows at once while sprinting. After thirty minutes of the exercise, he was completely out of breath.

*Gosh I am out of shape and I only have an hour before I have to start heading back.*

Eli summoned an Épée blade that he had practiced summoning with his dad. After using the actual sword in a few training sessions in the weapons room, Eli found the sword more of an asset than a normal sword in certain situations. The Épée sword—that Marius had let Eli train with—had the tip of it altered to be more precise and sharp. Thanks to Eli's bloodline, every time he summoned a Épée blade, it was summoned with the alterations made. The three-sided blade was lighter in Eli's hand than a normal sword. This allowed Eli to be quicker and more precise with his attacks. He also liked how the skinny blade made it more difficult for an opponent to follow his movements. As he practiced with the Épée on a nearby tree, he grew a little more confident in his abilities. He was still irritated by the fact that he could not perfect his arrow barrage ability, but he was satisfied with his close combat skills.

*As long as I don't run into anyone with attacks like Fox's, I'll be okay.*

When Eli thought about his encounter with Fox, he became more and more uncomfortable with the idea that Fox could have followed him on more than one occasion.

*He knows where I live too.*

As the sun began to show itself over the horizon, Eli realized his training session was over. He headed back for the city, wondering if Sia was awake or still sleeping. When Eli passed through the main gates, he noticed a sign posted on a stone column close by:

Funeral Ceremonies Postponed

Until Tomorrow Morning.


-The Council


Jude's face flashed across Eli's vision, when he finished reading the notice. He quickly shook off the image, and then continued the walk home. As Eli walked up his doorstep, he smelled the scent of steak and omelets radiating from behind the door.

*Dad you're awesome.*

When he opened the door and closed it behind him, he saw his dad's silhouette dancing across the kitchen wall in the archway. He walked into the kitchen and stopped when he got there.

"Eli! You are back so soon," said Aileen placing a plate of freshly made flapjacks on the table.

"I just went to train for a couple of hours," said Eli completely confused as to what was going on. "Where's my dad?"

"I think he is just getting out of the shower. He should be down shortly. Jed will be here shortly too."

Eli felt his stomach riot. The thought of the immortal in his house—after all of the disagreements that had been going on with Jude—sent chills down his spine.

*He will straight murder me, resurrect me and then murder me again!*

"That's nice of you guys, what's the occasion?"

"Well your match today in the Trials of course. I know you haven't forgotten have you?" Her smile made him feel both comfortable and uncomfortable at the same time.

"Hey son! Glad you are back," said Marius walking up from behind Eli. He took his usual spot at the table.

Eli sat in his chair still perplexed as to what was going on. Aileen set a large plate of omelets down on the table, followed by a large stack of steak and eggs, and a pitcher of orange juice. Aileen took a seat to Eli's left—in between him and Marius—which left the seat across from her empty.

"Thank you for cooking us breakfast Ms. Bray," said Eli.

"You are very welcome Eli. You can dig in since we are all here now," said Aileen grabbing her knife and fork.

"Aren't we still waiting for Jed? Or is he not coming anymore?"

"Jed is right there," said Aileen with a giggle.

Eli turned back towards the seat on his right to find Jed sitting right next to him with his arms crossed.

"Oh dear Aegis!"

"Good morning to you too," said Jed extending his fangs.

*That really doesn't help right now.*

"I just did not see you, sitting there. Steak please," said Eli averting his gaze.

When Marius passed Eli the steak, a silence enveloped the table. The only audible noise was the sound of forks and knives; and the occasional noise of Jed licking his fangs, which made Eli uncomfortable.

Aileen decided to be the brave soul to start the conversation. "So Eli! Are you excited for today?"

"Yeah kind of. I'm more nervous though, because I know my opponents will be very skilled."

"You'll do fine son," said Marius tearing into an omelet.

"More eggs Eli?"

"Yes please Ms. Bray," said Eli while grabbing a large platter from Aileen.

When Eli was done with the platter, he passed it to Jed. "More eggs—."

Jed turned to him with a look that said, *I will kill you.*

"I am not here to partake in the consumption of your human food. I am here for what you humans call, emotional support. Thanks for the offer though," said Jed retracting his fangs.

Aileen and Marius erupted into laughter at the conversation between Jed and Eli. Eli didn't find it amusing at all. He didn't know why he felt so uncomfortable around Jed all of a sudden. It was true that he had not seen him in a while, but still he used to love being around Jed, and he was not sure what had changed. Aileen and Marius had been talking about something that Eli had missed. When they were finished, Eli found himself asking the question that would perhaps address the dragon in the room.

"Ms. Bray, how is Jude doing?"

Aileen's fork dropped from her hand and wobbled on the floor. She bent down to pick it up. Her shoulder knocked over her glass of orange juice.

"Let me get that for you," said Marius getting a towel. Marius helped Aileen clean up the spill, while Eli and Jed just stared at their frantic behavior.

"Vance has done everything in his power to help Jude the best he could. Four o' clock this morning he decided to stop administering care. He informed me that there is nothing more he can do, and that everything is in Jude's hands now. He said that if any part of Jude's body were to give out, we would know before the morning is over," said Jed in a matter-of-fact tone.

Eli looked to Marius and then to Aileen, who sat frozen staring at Jed. Realizing that it would be impossible to get any information out of anyone else, Eli returned his attention back to the nightmare that sat next to him.

"What did they say the likelihood of him recovering was?"

"Twenty percent. His condition worsened over the night," said Jed unclasping his arms.

Something heavy hit the table. Eli looked up to see Aileen leaping up from her chair and running out of the kitchen, the sound of cries heavy in the air. Marius quickly followed her.

*Great, I clearly have a hit out on my own self. Left alone with a Vampire. This morning couldn't be better.*

"I can tell when you are afraid you know," said Jed.

"What?"

"I said, I can tell when you are afraid," he repeated.

"But I'm not afraid."

"Your fear excites me," said Jed licking his lips erratically. "I can feel your jugular pulsing with warm, fresh, adrenaline-fueled blood."

As Jed sat up slowly from his chair, Eli felt his heart stop, and every other part of his body run for cover. Something about the situation told Eli to run. He stared at the sink afraid to move.

Marius and Aileen soon returned to the room. Eli snuck a glance over towards Jed's direction to find him playing with one of his fingernails. As Marius and Aileen took their seats, Eli could tell a private conversation had taken place during their absence.

"Sorry about that," began Aileen while cutting her steak. "Don't know what is going on with me lately. I'm usually more together."

"It is quite alright," said Marius staring at Eli and nodding towards Aileen.

Eli instantly took the hint. It was his father's way of saying, *fix this.*

"Yeah it's okay Ms. Bray. Again I really appreciate you making all of this for us," said Eli searching for anything to cheer her up.

"You are most welcome. I can't have one of my boys going into battle on an empty stomach. It is a mother's duty to make sure they have their fuel," said Aileen holding up a glass of orange juice.

Once Eli, Aileen and Marius were done eating, Marius cleared the table. Eli went upstairs and washed his face. He stared at his reflection in the mirror and noticed the bags under his eyes.

"Admiring ourselves are we?"

The voice came from behind him. Eli flipped around in a panic to find Jed standing in front of him. His translucent white eyes looked even scarier in the washroom light that spilled out into Eli's bedroom.

"You scared the Pith out of me!"

"My apologies. I just came to wish you good luck today," said Jed.

"You couldn't have said that downstairs, a few moments ago?" Eli was having a difficult time catching his breath.

Jed smiled exposing his fangs. "According to Jude, it is more *personable* when you exchange compliments and kind gestures in private. He is helping me—excuse me—*was* helping me, with my people skills."

"Well thank you for that. Yep. Thanks, and I'm sorry about Jude. I know he will pull through," said Eli finally catching his breath.

"I am sure he sends his regards."

Eli instantly found himself staring at the wall on the other side of his room.

*Can't believe I used to think that guy was cool. Maybe it was because I felt safer around him when Jude was with us.*

Eli took one last look in his washroom mirror, before hearing his dad calling to him from downstairs. "Ready to go Eli?"

"Yeah coming down!"

Marius locked the door behind them. Looking up towards the direction of the Coliseum, Eli noticed the majority of the cloudbank hovered over the top of the building. It made the Coliseum look darker and uninviting, compared to the rest of the city, which was bathed in sunlight and warmth. The three of them began their walk towards the Coliseum.

*This is what I've been waiting for all my life. I'm ready!*

# PLAN Z

There was no crowd of people, no urn, and above all, no support—except for Zane—when Eli entered the holding area. Eli was both happy and relieved when he saw Zane. It had been a while since he had seen his friend, and he felt embarrassed when he caught himself hugging Zane in a tight embrace.

"Whoa! Glad to see you too buddy," said Zane.

"Sorry, it's just been crazy since the last time I saw you. It's nice to see a normal face."

"Crazy training I assume—me too. I barely got any sleep last night," said Zane rubbing his eyes.

*Not what I meant but okay.*

"It's kind of scary isn't it?" said Zane.

"What, the match?"

"No, the emptiness. The quiet. Last time I was here, there was a cluster of talking heads," said Zane shaking his head.

Eli looked over to where the urn normally glistened on the western wall, and found nothing. The only signs of life in the room, besides the other challengers, were the lights that dimly radiated from the Medicinal Quarters, as well as the presence of the three mentors that stood waiting when he entered. Memories of the first time he walked through the large double doors and into the holding area flooded his mind. Faces of fallen peers, acquaintances and friends, one by one flashed across his mind: Tillius, Bree and even Jude. Eli didn't notice when or how it happened, but as Ivor ushered the five challengers into the passage that would lead them to the briefing room, Eli realized his appearance had changed. His blonde hair had somehow been neatly brushed to the side, his favorite belted tunic and combat pants had been replaced with plated armor pants with red detail, and a matching scaled armor vest with the Weapons Master insignia in red on the front. Zane was dressed in nearly the same except for his armor appeared to be more sturdy and covered more of his upper torso than Eli's. Also, for some reason Zane's hair still laid in a tangled mess atop his head.

*Why does his armor look more protective than mine?*

"Hey so I heard your weird friend apparently did so well last round," said Zane with a smirk on his face.

"Yeah I heard the same thing."

"Eh, we will make his match look like child's play," said Zane brushing a hand passed his face. "When we get in the briefing room, we need to chat. However, don't approach me too quickly. We don't want to draw any unwanted attention, if you know what I'm saying."

Eli was confused as to what Zane was trying to say, but he nodded his head anyways. When the stone passage closed behind him, all light became absent from view. While he followed the other challengers in front of him, Ivor's cold and stern voice radiated around him. The more he focused on where his footsteps were taking him, the more he became unnerved by the entire situation.

*I won't lose. I have too much riding on this match. I can't let Sia go into battle alone, and I can't miss this chance to prove to The Council that I am ready for missions.*

A few small lights hung from the walls, when the holding area branched out in front of him. The first thing that Eli noticed, was a small statue that stood dead center in the middle of the room. As he approached it, he found it difficult to breathe. When he finally reached the statue, he realized two things. One, the statue was more like a shrine. Two, the overwhelming difficulty to breathe was gone. Depictions of the Three Brothers stood staring down at him when he looked up.

*How creepy!*

While he made sure his body was nowhere close to touching the shrine, he found something on the base of the shrine. There appeared to be an inscription:

"A path is a path. But yours is not mine,

and mine is not yours."

Eli felt a cold wind whip the back of his neck. When he turned around and realized there were no windows present in the room, he began to lose his nerve.

*This place is weird. I hate when the city goes overboard with putting these crazy-looking statues of the gods everywhere. It's like some kind of addiction for them.*

After everyone had gotten settled, he decided to take a look around for Zane. After a few moments, he found his messy and tangled hair lying against one of the walls that separated what appeared to be a large door. Eli took a look around and found two more doors that were identical. After finding nothing particularly special about them, or eerie like the shrine, he slowly approached Zane.

"Yo!"

"Yo?" A scowl was plastered across Zane's face. "Who uses the word 'Yo?"

"A badass does."

"Clearly I'm not a badass. Sit next to me so we can have full view of the room."

Eli took a seat on the floor next to Zane. He found the floor of the briefing room cold and rough to sit on. The first few seconds sitting there, sent his back into a temper tantrum.

"So I was thinking," started Zane as he lowered his voice to a whisper. "Do you know what you and I have that the challengers from the other rounds didn't?"

"Awesome hair?"

For the first time since Eli had met Zane, he received an annoyed look. He was just trying to lighten up the mood since everyone seemed to be so on edge, including himself.

"Hey, you're my buddy and everything, but this is the only day I am asking you to take things serious for a change, okay? Or at least act like this is important to you."

"It *is* important to me and I *am* serious about it," said Eli feeling insulted.

"Okay well you're not acting like it, so let's get to business shall we?"

Eli felt a bit of hostility from Zane and didn't like it.

*What does he mean I'm not taking things seriously?*

"So like I was saying, the thing that we have that the others didn't—is an ally," said Zane.

When Eli didn't respond, he noticed Zane pass him a look before shaking his head. After a few idle seconds, Zane continued. "So yeah if you're still listening, I was thinking that if you and I should pair up, we can take down the others quicker and easier."

Eli thought about Zane's plan for a while. It would be nice to have someone out there watching his back. Plus it would be reassuring to have his buddy out there at his side taking down enemies.

"So what happens when everyone is dead and it's just you and me?"

"A-Ha! That's when 'Plan Z' comes into play," said Zane.

"Plan Z?"

"Plan Zane. We can call it 'Plan E' if you like, but I think 'Plan Z' sounds better," said Zane with a smirk.

"Whatever. So go on."

"So I talked to a friend of mine. He told me that a couple of years back, two challengers, who were the last ones standing, accidentally knocked each other out in a squabble. The Council ended up stepping in and ending the match since no one was moving. It was deemed a draw, and a draw in the Lord's book isn't a loss. It isn't a win, but it isn't a loss either."

"So what happened to the two who were unconscious?" Eli found himself getting more curious by the second.

"They woke up ten or so minutes after arriving to the Medicinal Quarters. Neither one was deemed a winner, but they both got to move on to advanced classes. So basically, they found another way to move one step closer to being an Agent," said Zane lowering his voice even lower when he noticed someone walk by.

Eli followed Zane's gaze until his eyes fell on the familiar jagged scars he had seen before. Pang's short black hair appeared even darker against the metallic silver tunic, which hung over what appeared to be some kind of steel plate armor. He wore scaled armor pants with metallic silver detail. Eli could see no visible insignia anywhere on Pang's armor.

"That is strange," said Zane.

"What is?"

"The fact that he is wearing silver."

"Looks like someone has been hanging out with the girls too much," teased Eli with a snap of his fingers.

Zane didn't respond to Eli's comment. He just stared at Pang, following his every move. Pang appeared not to notice. He walked over to the shrine, mumbled to himself, and then found a corner to sit in.

"So anyways, what you were saying earlier is we should team up. Then when it is just you and me, we just put on some sort of show that ends with us knocking each other out. Is that right?"

"Exactly," said Zane returning his attention back to Eli.

"But how do we do that—knock each other out at the same time?"

"I was thinking about that. The only options I found were either to engage in a fast-paced sword battle and happen to slip and bash each other in the head with the pommel of our swords, or a projectile attack that smashes our heads against the Coliseum walls," said Zane rubbing the back of his head.

Eli realized his head hurt as well. He found himself rubbing it for comfort. "I would say the first one, but only if you promise not to break my nose. I don't think Sia would like me anymore if you did."

Zane's eyes widened while the biggest smile slowly crept over his face. "So it finally happened!"

Eli couldn't help it. He instantly began to smile so hard, that his face hurt. "Not a word!"

"I can't believe you didn't tell me! I'm the one that fixed you guys up and you don't tell me? Me? Your best friend!"

"Man it literally just happened like one or two days ago, you got to give me a break. And who says you fixed us up? I think I did a pretty good job myself," said Eli.

"I don't know—you almost blew it at the Forgotten Forest. Just saying."

"That's because you and your sister drugged me!"

"Shh! Shh! You're drawing attention. Okay. Can we agree I was at least fifty percent responsible for you guys getting together?"

Eli thought about it for a second. If Zane had never invited Eli to hang out with him and Meara, who knows if he would have had ever gotten the chance to become more acquainted with Sia.

"Forty-five percent."

"Deal," said Zane shaking Eli's hand. "So what do you think? Are we a go on Plan Z?"

A dark shadow crept over Eli's feet—and soon crawled up his legs—until he was completely cloaked in darkness. He looked up to find Pang standing over them.

"Whoa! Man what's your problem sneaking up on us like that!" yelled Zane.

"Your deception will not work," said Pang.

"What are you talking about?"

"Don't say I didn't warn you," said Pang as he slowly turned around before walking away.

"Man you're a creeper!" yelled Zane.

Pang stopped in midstride. His head slowly turned slightly around until his left eye was visible. Its red-orange color seemed to grow more red the longer it looked at them. Eli felt a shutter ripple down his spine, as he found himself jerking his neck around to fight off a chill.

"And you are dead," said Pang. He slowly returned to the corner that he had previously been sitting in.

Eli watched Zane continue to stare at Pang long after he had left. His eyes never flinched, and his nostrils remained flared up for a while.

"Is it me, or does he always sound like he has a very bad cold and sore throat?" said Eli.

"Man, he should be number one on our list. I hate that guy," said Zane punching his fist into his other hand a couple of times.

"On your feet juveniles!" yelled Ivor.

Eli and Zane climbed to their feet, along with Pang and another girl.

"Take your spots at your respective doors. We will begin in five minutes. May the gods have mercy on your weak and frivolous souls," said Ivor. He exited through a door that appeared before him.

Eli and Zane stared at the wooden door before them. Tiny splinters and cracks radiated outward from the top of the door. Eli counted seven of them.

"I'm Zane. What's your name?"

Eli looked over to find Zane talking to a blonde girl next to him. Her hair was almost done the same way as Bree's, but shorter. She wore short black shorts with plated armor around her calves, and plated bracers around her forearms. Her torso was dressed in a tight black battle tunic with silver platted shoulder armor.

"Francesca. Who's your friend?"

Eli felt a kick from Zane. "I'm Eli. It's nice to meet you."

Zane placed his hand against the wall next to Francesca. His feet crossed each other when he began to lean comfortably. "You've met my friend. Now who's your special friend right there?"

A towering brunette with hazel eyes and pale skin, turned around as if in response to Zane's words. She wore tight-fitting black combat pants with the same plated armor around her calves as Francesca. However, her torso was absent of armor and instead she wore a short black shirt that hung above her small naval. Eli could not get over how tall she was. She easily towered over both him and Zane. Her hair was pulled back in a knot that screamed *I'm the type of badass that will cut you.*

"This is Serena, we go way back," said Francesca.

"Who are they?" asked Serena with a jerk of her head.

"This is Zane and Eli," said Francesca.

"Pleasure," said Serena turning back around.

Zane appeared confused. "Did I say something wrong? Wait I didn't say anything!"

Eli found himself laughing under his breath.

"She is probably just a little nervous. Good luck to you both," said Francesca returning to her door.

"Francesca is hot! Smoking hot! Like scorching acid hot." Zane rubbed his hands together as if to warm them up.

"I don't know man. Her bodyguard looks like she would use you to floss with. Maybe you should back off."

"Well that's when you come in. You will be my wingman," said Zane putting his arm around Eli.

"What! Are you kidding me?" Eli pushed Zane's arm off of him. "In five freaking minutes they will be trying to kill us! You must be insane!"

"No, I just forgot—scratch that last thought then. But Francesca is still hot though. Just saying."

Eli could hear the cheering and stomping of the crowd above them. The small lights that hung from the walls shook slightly at the sound of every stomp that came from overhead. As a bright light entered the room, Eli looked to his right to find the large wooden door in front of Francesca and Serena open. When Serena stepped into the light and out of view, Francesca gave one last look at Zane and winked, before passing through. The door closed behind them as another uproar from the crowd erupted through the walls.

"Did you see that?"

"Man focus," said Eli feeling the presence of his nerves getting the best of him. He was blinded as his door creaked open exposing a light so bright, that he had to shield his eyes for a few seconds.

"Remember stick together, and at the end, a pommel to the face, but not the nose," said Zane stepping through the light.

Eli watched his friend disappear from view. He waited a few seconds, took a deep breath and entered.

# FINAL ROUND

The voice told him to let go. It told him he would find peace and comfort in his submission. It promised him peace of mind and stability. However, Jude refused its proposition. He felt like he had been fighting off the omniscient voice for weeks. As his eyes opened, a bright light blinded his vision. The smell of fire and herbs shrouded wherever he was.

"Professor! Professor! He's awake," screamed a voice.

Jude felt like he had the worse headache imaginable. Slowly making himself rise, his hand quickly searched for something to prop himself up. He found what felt like a pillow, and placed it behind his neck against the wall. When his vision cleared, he realized he was in one of the beds in the Medicinal Quarters.

*How long have I been out?*

He instantly had a flashback of Jed's voice searching throughout the darkness. Jed had been there talking to him. Jude remembered hearing his brother's voice every time the omniscient voice stopped. It was the only thing that he had to hold on to, and to help him fight off the urge to let go. Jude remembered himself grow weary of fighting the darkness a couple of times. He told the voice it was right and he was ready. Just before he followed the voice, he remembered Jed's voice break through, shattering everything around him.

*He told me not to give up, and if I did, he would follow me.*

Jude found himself laughing as another flashback came across his mind.

*He said he would move back in if I woke up.*

Jude figured that Jed had to have visited often, because he remembered multiple isolated occasions where Jed's voice penetrated his conscience.

"Thank you Pith! Thank you Rune! Thank you Aegis!" screamed a voice.

Jude looked up to see Professor Lynn standing over him. She was dressed in burgundy pants and a black shirt, with a burgundy jacket. Both grief and joy looked present on her face, while Jude focused on the figure that stood before him. "Professor?"

"Yes Hun, how are you feeling?"

"Better. How long have I been out?"

"Not too long. We brought you in here right after your match. You went unconscious after I specifically told you to keep your eyes open," said Lynn with a scolding finger.

"Sorry," said Jude feeling himself chuckle just before coughing.

*Oh no! What time is it? Has it started?*

"Professor! Has the third round of the Trials started yet?"

"The challengers were just brought into the briefing room. I was on my way to the Coliseum, but I wanted to check in on you before I left. Perfect timing on my part," she said clapping her hands together.

"I need to go," he said pulling the covers off.

"Wait just a second there mister! You are not going anywhere. You have some serious injuries. You are lucky to even be here! It took every healer at our disposal, including Vance, to even give you a shot at recovery. I'm surprised you aren't in a two year coma," said Lynn.

Jude took in all what she was saying. Had it really been that bad? All he remembered was feeling happy to see his Mom, Marius and Jed there at the end of his match. The next thing he knew, he was waking up in the bed he was in. If round three of the Trials was about to start, then Eli would definitely be a challenger. Jude had to be there.

"I know Professor, and thank you so much to all of you. However, my best friend is about to go out there. Out into that mayhem. I have to be there for him. Please..."

"I don't think its neither appropriate nor safe Hun— I'm sorry," said Lynn patting him on the shoulder.

Jude thought of the breakfast he and Eli had at his house on their very first day at the Academy. They were in this together, and he would not let him down. Jude swung his legs over the side of the bed.

"Either you can help me to my seat in the spectators area, or you can force me to climb all of those stairs by myself," said Jude. He had no desire to make Lynn feel guilty. However, if she chose to be an obstacle in his way, he would find a way around her.

Lynn and another healer exchanged glances. The healer was a small woman dressed in all white with short brunette hair. She clearly opposed it, since Jude saw her swing her head back and forth so hard, that only hair was visible on her face.

"If I do this for you, you owe me one hour after class once the Trials and Necrosis threat are over. Are we clear?" said Lynn.

"Deal."

Lynn had found Jude some crutches that made him feel awkward when he moved. She accompanied him up a secret Council entrance in the holding area, which appeared after pushing a small button next to one of the small lights that hung on the walls.

"If you tell anyone about this, I will turn into a bobcat and eat you alive," warned Lynn.

As they made their way over the last step and through the light that appeared, Jude found himself looking at the familiar white and red seats that circled the spectators area. He looked around and saw no one on the black sands down below.

*Great! I made it!*

"Where did you want to sit?"

Jude searched around and instantly found Jed's snow-white hair. He then found his mother and Marius right next to him.

*I'm glad to finally see mom and Jed working things out.*

"My family is right over there," said Jude pointing.

Lynn helped Jude walk down the stairs towards the front row. As Jude walked passed a group of guys on his right, he noticed their eyes widened before screams surrounded him.

"It's the Prodigy of Pith!"

"He's awake!"

*Prodigy of Pith? What are they talking about?*

"Alright alright, everyone settle down," said Lynn helping him down the last step.

"Jude..." said Marius when Jude sat down.

Jude found himself extremely happy to see Marius. He appreciated him coming to his match, even though Eli hadn't. He wanted to call him dad. "Hey Marius. How's it going?"

Aileen jumped up from her seat and came crashing down on top of him. "Oh my baby!"

*Ouch! Not the leg!*

"Oh baby I am so happy that you are okay. Oh my Aegis! I prayed every hour on the hour, and they answered my prayers," said Aileen showering him with kisses.

*Oh gosh I hope people aren't watching.*

"Okay mother, before you break him in half," said Jed.

Aileen returned to her seat, but quickly grabbed Jude's hand tightly over Jed's lap. He could tell it would be a while before she let go.

"Well I see you're in good hands, so I will leave you to your family," said Lynn.

"Wait," said Jude grabbing her hand. "I want you to meet my family."

Lynn turned around with a small smile on her face.

"Professor this is my brother Jed and my mom Aileen," said Jude pointing to Jed and then Aileen. "Mom, Jed, this is my mentor Professor Lynn. She is the best Professor at the Academy. She teaches my Combat Specialist classes—and makes a mean troll."

Jude noticed that Lynn looked embarrassed as her shoulders rose to her face, when she shook Jed's hand and then Aileen's hand. "This is Marius. He is my—well he is basically my dad." Jude saw that Marius looked taken back, since his eyes widened before a smile crossed his face.

"Well it is very nice to meet all of you. Jude is an excellent apprentice and makes a mean swamp snake! I shouldn't tell you this but—he is one of my favorites; and trust me when I say that the word 'favorite' is rarely used in my vocabulary," said Lynn smiling.

"Thank you very much. I am glad to hear that he is doing well," said Aileen looking from Lynn to Jude.

"He is! And after his last match, I know we will be seeing great things from him," said Lynn.

Now Jude felt like he was embarrassed, and sunk down into his seat. Lynn waved a goodbye at everyone before leaving. Shortly thereafter, he saw her appear in the roped area next to the throne, where he saw Bishop sit during round one of the Trials. She waved at him once she sat down.

"Nice to see you're doing okay little brother," said Jed.

"All because of you."

"Me? I really can't take credit for you pulling through such a severe condition," said Jed shaking his head.

"I don't know how often you visited, but it must have been a lot. For the record, I heard you every time you spoke to me. It saved me."

Jed stared at him for a while. His translucent white eyes gave no hint of what he was thinking or feeling. His eyes returned their attention ahead of him.

Aileen's hand began to squeeze Jude's hand tightly. "Why are you even out of bed?"

"It's the last round, I had to be here."

"Had to be here," started Aileen as she looked at Marius. "Do you hear that Marius, my nearly comatose son risked his life to get out of bed to see five children try and kill each other!"

"That is not why I came. What I should have said is, it is Eli's round. I just wanted to be here for support. We have both been looking forward to this our whole lives after all."

Aileen and Marius just stared at Jude. He didn't expect them to understand. He felt like parents always thought what their kids did was reckless and immature. He knew it meant something to him to be there, and he hoped that if Eli spotted him in the audience, it would mean something to him too. Bishop, accompanied by Professor Ivor and Professor Vance, appeared between a row of seats, before walking to his throne. A few guards trailed shortly behind the trio. Bishop was dressed in the most luxurious gold and red dress robes that Jude had ever seen. It was hard to make out the detail from the distance, but jewels sparkled from his shoulder pads, as he took his seat in the bishop-themed throne. The throne looked complete and regal with Bishop sitting there. The two white bishops that rose up on either side of his shoulders gave him added height and superiority, while his face looked humble and calm.

"Honey you were amazing down there," said Aileen finally letting go of his hand.

"Yes Jude, you blew me away. Those were some difficult opponents. You made us all very proud," said Marius with a smile.

"That means a lot. Thank you."

"It seems like our training has finally paid off," said Jed nudging Jude with his shoulder. "While you were on recess, I have been practicing my people skills."

Jude instantly felt his body shutter while worry crept over him. "Uh oh. What happened?"

"Nothing—yet. It is difficult, but coming along. I will keep you posted," said Jed rustling Jude's hair with his hand.

Jude watched as Anya strolled out onto the black sands of the arena. She was dressed in full red and brown leather armor. Red gloves covered her hands as she held them up to silence the crowd. Jude happened to look up, and soon realized that there was still was no roof on the Coliseum. The sides looked smoothed out, but a giant opening was still present from Jude's last match.

"May I have your attention please!" Anya's voice echoed throughout the Coliseum. "We will now begin the final round of the Trials of Magic, Might and Lineage. Presenting the challengers of the Combat Specialist bloodline." Anya pointed to the door underneath the Pith statue. The door swung open displaying two girls, both dressed in black. "Francesca Lita and Serena Piera!" The two girls took their place in the center of the arena next to Anya.

"I know them! They are in my class," said Jude.

"That's a large one," said Marius pointing to Serena.

"Presenting the challengers of the Weapons Master bloodline," began Anya.

"Oh! Oh! Oh! Here we go," yelled Aileen hitting Marius on the shoulder.

The door underneath the Aegis statue swung open, and soon Zane and Eli walked out onto the sands. "Zane Humphrey and Eli Brassie!" announced Anya.

A high-pitched scream, followed by thunderous applause, erupted next to Jude, as Aileen went into a cheering frenzy. Marius soon joined her.

"Go Eli! Storm the field!" screamed Jude through his hands. Eli and Zane had been walking to the center of the arena to join the others when Eli froze. Jude stared down at him as he stared back.

*Does he see me?*

Jude raised his hand slowly. Eli raised his hand slowly.

*He sees me.*

"You can do it Eli! Storm the field buddy," screamed Jude.

Eli soon broke out of what appeared to be shock, and joined Zane and the others in the middle of the arena. Jude noticed that Eli's eyes continued to stare.

*Either he doesn't want me here, or he is surprised to see me. I'll assume it's the latter one.*

"Presenting the challenger of the Magi bloodline," began Anya. The last door underneath the Rune statue slowly opened, as a lone figure stepped out onto the sands. An instant flashback combined with a headache hit Jude. It was of Bree independently walking out onto the same black sands. Her blonde hair blew in the wind as the sun kissed her big blue eyes. "Pang Quarrels!"

Pang walked slower than any of the other challengers. He took his time while taking short but powerful steps across the sands. When he finally got to the others—he folded his arms in front of him—and stared at a spot in the sands. Jude decided to take the opportunity to show support for his new friend.

"Go Pang!"

Pang's head jerked up and instantly found him. Jude waved back so he would see him. A confident grin and an arched eyebrow appeared on Pang's face. He waved slowly back at Jude before refolding his arms and turning his attention back to the sands beneath him.

"Last one standing is the victor," announced Anya. Blue sparks erupted around the General as she disappeared. Jude looked straight up to Bishop to catch her appearing by his side. Bishop rose to his feet and walked out onto his private balcony in front of him before he began.

"The final round of the Trials of Magic, Might and Lineage will now begin. The final round will be: Eli Brassie versus Serena Piera versus Zane Humphrey versus Francesca Lita versus Pang Quarrels!"

*Come on Eli. Time to show them what you can do!*

"Begin!"

# A FRONT
# ROW EXECUTION

"Now Eli!" screamed Zane as he wrapped his arms around Pang and apprehended him from behind. A dagger appeared in Eli's hand, before he charged straight for Pang. Pang tossed Zane over his shoulder and hurled the brunette at Eli.

"My word he's strong," said Aileen.

Zane and Eli tumbled one on top of the other in a tangle.

"Heads up Zane," said Pang. He was soon thrown against the wall behind him.

Serena back flipped up in the air and came crashing down on Pang's back—as his body laid motionless on the floor. "Francesca you're on!" Serena quickly placed Pang in a headlock, while her captive made no attempts to break free.

Pang just stood there trapped in Serena's grip, while an enormous wolf chomped its jaws and licked its teeth before closing in.

"Smart! An alliance eh," said Pang.

"That's right genius! Rune be with you," said Serena.

The wolf leaped into the air, and as it came chomping down, a large hand grabbed its throat. The wolf chomped and growled as it tried to break free from Pang's grip. Serena picked Pang up and tossed him. His grip loosened, and soon his body slid across the sands until it came crashing into an adjacent wall.

"Take care of him! I'll get the other two," said Serena as she took off towards Zane and Eli.

Jude watched the wolf close in on Pang as Serena closed in on Eli and Zane. Jude felt torn not knowing which to watch, but in the end his eyes fell on Eli and Zane.

"Come on Eli on your feet!" yelled Jude. He hoped that Eli could hear him.

Both boys returned to their feet while Serena slowly approached. Zane whispered something to Eli. A sword and shield appeared in Zane's hand while a bow appeared in Eli's. A battle cry erupted from Zane as he charged Serena. He sliced at her head while she front flipped landing behind him, kicking him in the back. An arrow hit home digging into her shoulder and knocking her back. Eli readied another arrow and fired just as she rolled to the side avoiding it. Zane charged her again while Eli ran in a circle around her firing arrow after arrow. She dove to avoid one of Eli's arrows and instantly went into a backbend all the way to the ground to avoid an arc slice from Zane. Two arrows buried themselves in her thigh before she let out a scream. She kicked both feet at Zane, which sent him a few feet off of the ground. Serena's hand grabbed his armor and face-planted him into the ground.

Eli ran in for a direct attack with his sword and shield in hand. "You're mine!" He sliced at Serena's left leg, but she spun backwards to her right to avoid the attack. Her body came to a halt when Eli's arm did a backswing bashing his shield into her face.

"Yes!" screamed Jude clenching his fists.

"Smart move. He anticipated her dodge," said Jed.

Serena skid to the floor while Eli threw his shield to the side, and leaped into the air over her body. He came down with both hands on the pommel of his sword. His voice echoed throughout the Coliseum. "You're done!"

A dark object soared through the air and intercepted Eli. The large wolf and Eli tumbled over each other. The wolf ended up on top of the blonde boy pinning him down. Eli dug his fingers into the sands trying to get from underneath the unconscious wolf.

*Come on Eli there's your chance! What are you doing? She is right there. Stab her! Do something!*

Eli dug and dug but was unable to break free. The wolf soon started moving when one of its massive eyes found Eli. Jude looked over to Zane, who was executing a frenzy of swings and slices with Pang, who successfully dodged every hit—while dodging strikes from a giant cobra that loomed over him from behind.

Jude became enraged. "What the heck is he doing? He can't take on Pang and Serena at the same time while his so called 'partner' is about to get devoured!"

"Isn't it obvious? He has hostility towards Pang, and since he is fighting emotionally instead of logically, he's being crippled by his over-confidence," said Jed.

"Well my boy could use some help!" yelled Marius. He eventually rose to his feet as if hoping to get a better angle of the battle.

"Zane! A hand please," said Eli.

Jude jerked his attention back over to Eli, who had both his hands on either side of the wolf's jaws trying to hold it off, while it chomped and snarled at his face. Drool from the wolf's mouth cascaded down on one of Eli's eyes and his chest as it began to overpower him. Jude looked back over to Zane, who had apparently struck a blunt blow on Pang with the pommel of his sword. Before he could follow up with another attack, a black coil started from his feet, and wrapped around his ankles, knees and eventually his torso. The large hood of the cobra towered over Zane, while the snake tightened its hold on him. Jude went into a panic.

*He can't help him.*

Jude grabbed his crutches and forced himself to his feet. "Eli! Zane is in trouble. He can't help you! Get out of there!"

Eli's head jerked his direction and then back to the wolf, before his fist came barreling into the side of the wolf's jaw. The wolf rolled off of him letting loose a series of deep sobs. Eli jumped to his feet and took off running towards Zane, who was jerking his head left and right in an attempt to dodge the bites from the cobra. The wolf quickly trailed after Eli, covering more ground than the blonde boy could.

*The wolf is too fast. He won't get to Zane in time, let alone be able to dodge the wolf.*

A bow appeared in Eli's hand, before he fired multiple arrows at an alarming rate towards the gargantuan snake. A line of five arrows dug into the hood of the cobra in a straight vertical line. A loud hiss erupted throughout the Coliseum as the snake rocked back and forth, loosening its hold on Zane. Eli stopped and turned around, and instantly was bitten and then tossed into the wall next to him. The impact of his body hitting the wall rocked the Coliseum while his limp body made no effort to move. A series of gasps filled the spectator area.

Marius appeared to recoil in place. "Oh no! Not my boy! Get up son! Get up!"

The wolf charged Pang, who had just picked up the entire cobra and punched it to the other side of the Coliseum. His arm came up in an uppercut when the wolf closed in, which sent the wolf tumbling across the sands, and smack into the cobra. Serena and Francesca returned to their normal form, but Serena was the only one that returned to her feet. Francesca laid at her feet motionless, while Serena nudged her with the bottom of her foot.

"Get up!" yelled Serena down at Francesca.

There was no movement. The wind blew gently threw the hair of her lifeless body. A bobcat took Serena's place and soon she charged after Pang, who had his back towards her while fighting off swings from Zane's blade.

*Oh no. Pang doesn't see her.*

"Pang! Behind you!" screamed Jude as he saw Serena's paws leave the ground.

Pang casually and slowly stepped aside—missing Serena's pounce. She instantly came clawing down on Zane. A frenzy of claw swipes sent blood splattering on the sands and wall behind them, while Zane tried to hold her off. Pang turned his attention back towards Francesca and broke into a sprint towards her lifeless body. A small hiss let loose throughout the Coliseum, as the bobcat was pinned by its shoulder to the wall next to it. The arrow pinning it, shined in the presence of the sun's rays. Jude turned towards the direction it came from, and saw Eli on his feet bow in hand.

"Yeah! That's my boy! Shut em' down!" yelled Marius clapping his hands.

"Oh no he's injured," said Aileen. She closed a hand over her mouth.

Jude watched Eli limp across the sands towards Zane, who was struggling to rise up. When he got to the boy, Eli tried to help him up. Zane's face rose up, causing Jude's hands to come up over the sides of his face, as he saw the painful-looking lacerations on Zane's. A small dust cloud flew their direction, as Serena in her normal form fell to the ground. She pulled an arrow out of both shoulders, before she returned to her feet. She turned to Eli and Zane, who were still having a hard time getting off of the floor. Eli's eyes caught her instantly. When she took a step towards them, Francesca's scream stopped her.

"Serena help!" Francesca's feet dangled above the ground, while she remained trapped in Pang's grip.

Pang held her by her neck higher, as he whispered something into her ear. Jude saw that whatever he had said to her, made her shake her head violently back and forth until tears streamed down her face. Jude turned back to Serena, who apparently had forfeited her attack on Eli and Zane, and had taken on her bobcat form once again. Her claws sunk deep into

Pang's back after she pounced. Pang screamed for the first time since the match had begun. He twirled in circles trying to detach Serena's claws from his back.

*This would be the perfect time for an attack.*

Jude looked back over to Eli and Zane who just stood there watching.

"He's done for," echoed Zane's voice against the arena walls. A grin quickly took control of his face.

Jude not only became angry, but thought for a split second that he was ready to leave. "Are you kidding me?"

"Told you, emotional and over-confident," said Jed shaking his head.

Eli left Zane behind after sprinting towards Francesca. Zane soon followed, moving a little slower. When Eli got to Francesca, she had already used a vial and had taken on the form of a giant hawk, evading Eli's sword attack as she took flight. A vibrant screech from the hawk filled the Coliseum, as it came diving down at Pang, who had just released himself from Serena's claws. Francesca scooped him up by his shoulders and circled him around the Coliseum. Serena took the form of a giant wasp, and soon became level with Francesca—who just held Pang in place. The wasp's stinger drew circles in the air as if taunting him.

"Oh my goodness! What a horrible way to die," said Aileen. She buried her face in Marius' shoulder.

The stinger attacked, and as it did, Pang caught hold of it causing a *crack* when the stinger detached. As it hit the ground in a loud *crash*, a tremor vibrated the battle arena. Erratic foreign buzzes let loose from the wasp, until it suddenly lost altitude and crashed into the ground. The hawk screeched, while it circled the Coliseum and then tossed Pang directly into Eli and Zane—who were too busy looking at Serena return to her normal form. The three boys tumbled and rolled across each other, until all three of them crashed on top of each other into the wall next to them. Pang was the first to his feet and then Eli, who tried to attack with a new dagger, but was caught by the wrist and thrown back at Serena by Pang. Francesca instantly took advantage, and went into a series of dive attacks down at Eli, who continued to dodge.

When Zane returned to his feet, Jude became confused—due to the motionless stare that Zane gave Pang. He mumbled something and then two swords appeared, just before Zane attacked Pang's shoulders and then legs. Pang dove to the side and kept running at the wall, while Zane followed in hot pursuit with a fury of dual slices. When Pang finally met the wall, he turned and backhanded Zane instantly. His attack hit straight into Zane's chest, sending him tumbling back across the sands.

Jed began to rustle in his seat. "Wait a minute. What's going on?"

Jude looked to Eli, who was firing countless arrows at Francesca while Serena was still motionless. Confused he turned back to Pang and Zane, and just saw Pang standing there while Zane struggled to his feet.

"What do you mean?"

"That Pang kid's vitals are off the charts," said Jed.

Marius' head darted towards the Vampire. "What? How do you know that?"

"I can sense it."

Jude looked back over to Pang, who now stood with one arm folded behind his back. His other arm was outstretched in front of him, while his finger pointed down at the sands in front of him. Drops of blood dripped from Pang's finger, as he appeared to be drawing something. Jude was horrified when Pang was finished. What looked like a circled 'P,' was formed on the sands by the blood that dripped from the boy's finger. He flicked his finger and folded the hand across his chest. Pang's eyes fixated on Zane, who had the look of horror plastered across his face.

"You freak!" yelled Zane.

Pang just stared back motionless. Jude saw a plan in his red-orange eyes.

Zane appeared to be growing restless. "What, nothing to say? No witty remark?"

Jude looked down and noticed Pang's drawing had disappeared. Pang shoulder-charged Zane, sending him tumbling to the ground. Zane quickly rolled and returned to his feet, as Pang tried to stomp him with his heel. Jude was sure Zane would summon some sort of weapon, since Pang was somewhat open to an attack on the side, but he didn't. Instead, he tackled Pang to the sands punching him in the face repeatedly. A thunderous laugh engulfed the Coliseum as Pang laughed hysterically while enduring Zane's attacks. Zane's consecutive punches to the side of Pang's face grew louder as time passed.

*It's like Pang is enjoying it.*

Both Pang's legs came up behind Zane, wrapping around his neck, and tossing Zane backwards. Both boys returned to their feet and engaged in hand-to-hand combat. Zane swung at Pang who dodged and sliced him on his neck with the side of his hand. Zane fell to his knees but quickly recovered. A backhand sent blood flying out of Pang's nose. Zane just stood there with the biggest grin Jude had ever seen.

*He's so arrogant.*

Pang stood motionless with one hand on his face. As he turned his attention back to Zane, who was still standing there, Jude felt his body shutter when he the saw the rage in Pang's eyes. Zane went into a back kick but Pang was faster and intercepted Zane's attack, sending him tumbling to the floor. As Pang slowly followed Zane's tumbling body, he stood over Zane when the brunette ceased movement. Zane sat up and tried to swing up at Pang, who easily caught his wrist. Zane screamed as Pang tightened his grip. This time it was Pang who had the smile.

"It's time for your punishment!"

Zane's screams stopped as he looked up into Pang's eyes. A grunt came from Pang as the hand holding Zane's wrist came jerking away in the opposite direction holding something. Horrific painful screams radiated throughout the Coliseum. Screams mixed with cries echoed off the walls. The mood of the Coliseum around Jude quickly switched to horror. More and more loud painful screams from Zane continued to bounce off the arena walls. Pang held something above his head. Marius was the one to break the horrific silence.

"Dear gods! He severed his arm!"

Screams from the spectators sounded everywhere. Jude looked at Pang's hand—and to his horror—saw a completely severed arm hanging there. Blood and gore dropped from the shoulder of Zane's severed arm. Loud *thuds* began to sound around Zane, as Pang raised the boys severed arm and began to beat him with it. The bloodied arm came down harder and harder as it clubbed Zane like a blunt weapon. Cries for help came from Zane, while he was struck repeatedly by the arm that he had lost. Jude saw many people next to him look away at the sight, while others continued to scream. When Pang raised the arm once more, he was snatched up causing the severed arm to fall from his hand.

"Thought you had enough," said Pang up at the hawk that carried him.

The hawk carried Pang up through the opening in the roof and out of the Coliseum, until they were both out of view. A series of grunts radiated from Jude's left, and as he turned his head, he caught Serena pinning Eli down. Eli head-butted her in the face, and when she let up, he pushed her off of him and took off running towards Zane. Once Eli got moderately close to Zane, he stopped dead in his tracks. One of his hands covered his mouth and soon Jude saw the horror in his eyes. After a few seconds, he began to move again, helping Zane sit up. He whispered something to Zane, who shook his head back and forth.

"No! I'm not doing it without you! Now get up now!" echoed Eli.

When Zane and Eli both returned to their feet, a loud buzzing sounded in the Coliseum. The buzzing was so loud, that Jude had to cover his ears for a few seconds. The wasp was back, looking brand new and equipped with a new stinger. It flew towards Eli and Zane, while the two boys whispered something to each other. A thin but sharp-looking sword appeared in Eli's hand, as Zane began to try and run towards the wasp ahead of them. Eli quickly trailed Zane, covering more ground than him. Once Zane was a few feet from the wasp, he got down on his hand and knees while Eli continued to sprint towards Zane. The wasp striked.

Eli stepped on Zane's back and launched himself up over the wasp. "Like I said before, you're done!" His blade came down clean, and soon the two halves of the wasp hit the black sands with a *thud*. When Eli hit the ground rolling, the two halves began to turn back to their human form.

Zane returned to his feet and found the upper half of Serena's body. A blade appeared in Zane's only hand, before it came crashing down decapitating her. The crowd around Jude went wild with cheers.

*Barbaric. That's someone's child or friend.*

The sound of wings came back to the Coliseum, as a large bird carrying a body, came back into view above the Coliseum. The hawk flung the body down at the arena, sending it tumbling across the sands. As Pang hit the closest wall to him, he quickly returned to his feet. The bird landed on the sands in front of him, easily towering over him by a couple of stories. Jude saw a smile appear on Pang's face.

"There's no hope for you!" yelled Pang.

Loud erratic screeches came from the hawk while it slowly turned back into Francesca. Jude looked down and went into shock when he saw the circled 'P' insignia glowing beneath

Francesca's feet. The girl screamed and struggled, while her body slowly rose up a few feet from the ground, before stopping.

Pang closed in on Francesca. "You've activated my trap!" Pang's hands clapped together, as a crimson essence coiled around his arms, his torso, and eventually his legs.

"Blood Magic!"

Francesca screamed while struggling to break free. She remained imprisoned off of the ground, while the insignia underneath her continued to glow. Her screams echoed.

"Serena help me!"

A smile came across Pang's face while he stared into her eyes. "Blood execution!"

Pang's barbaric gesture made Jude tense. A quick and loud *crack* became audible, as Francesca's body dropped a couple of feet, before coming to a violent halt. Her lifeless body hung from her neck by an invisible force, rocking back and forth. To Jude, the sight resembled a lynching, and sent chills down his spine. When Pang turned away from Francesca, the insignia disappeared, and her body collapsed to the ground. No one in the entire Coliseum said a word or moved a muscle. Jude looked around, and even his mom and Marius were speechless. Jude found himself afraid to move. He saw Pang in a different light, after witnessing him administer such a brutal death.

Pang began his slow walk back towards Eli and Zane, who just stood staring at him. When Pang was only a few feet away from them he stopped. "Funny thing about the human neck. It is extremely fragile and can easily render a man paralyzed if injured. Or even in some cases," said Pang turning his head back to Francesca. "Death." Pang looked back to Eli and Zane who still stood where they were standing. "How's the arm Zane?"

A sword appeared in Zane's hand as he took off in a charge towards Pang. A series of arrows missed Zane while they darted towards Pang—who dove backwards on his back to dodge both attacks. He rolled to the side and quickly returned to his feet.

"You are a puppet in a puppet show. You know that right," said Pang to Zane while he continued to evade his attacks.

Jude was baffled at how easily Pang ducked and sidestepped under and over each attack that Zane threw at him.

Eli appeared behind Pang with two swords of his own. Pang screamed. He shoulder-charged Zane, sending him tumbling to the floor, before he took off in a sprint away from Eli. Pang quickly turned back towards Eli and Zane. A dagger appeared in Pang's hand. Eli and Zane appeared to ready themselves. However, just when Jude thought Pang was going on the offensive, he sliced his own forearm. A stream of blood ran down his arm and between his fingers before hitting the ground.

"Your time is up! Control is no longer yours!" yelled Pang. He wiped the blood with one of his hands, and then held the palm of it at his opponents. "Blood Magic!"

*Oh no!*

A red glow appeared on the outstretched hand Pang was holding. It covered his whole hand until it ran up his arm. Eli and Zane sprinted towards Pang with their swords in hand.

"Blood domination!"

Jude saw Eli keep running but Zane stopped cold in his tracks. His body went into violent convulsions and his eyes widened. Pang grabbed Eli by the neck when he finally got to him. After he swung Eli around, he tossed him over his shoulder, sending his body tumbling across the sands, and right into Zane. After Eli quickly returned to his feet, he screamed.

Marius leaped to his feet. "Wait a minute! What's going on? What's he doing?"

Eli turned around to find Zane executing a back slice at Eli's legs. Eli jumped back just in time to dodge, but dropped his sword, which caused it to dissolve. "Zane what are you doing?"

Eli circled Zane slowly, anticipating and dodging the attacks his friend was throwing at him.

Zane continued to swing repeatedly, until Eli grabbed his wrist. While the two boys stood locked trying to overpower one another, Eli finally tossed Zane over his shoulder and climbed on top of him.

"What's wrong with you? I'm still on your team—remember? We kill him first," said Eli.

When Pang appeared behind Eli, he picked him up and tossed him across the arena. Zane soon returned to his feet and walked slowly next to Pang, as if he didn't even notice his presence.

"Zane snap out of it!" yelled Jude finally realizing what was going on.

Eli quickly came to his feet and fired a few arrows at Pang. Just when Jude was ready to cheer, Zane's body jumped in front of Pang taking the damage from all three arrows.

"No! No," said Eli collapsing to his knees.

As if not even noticing the arrows, Zane closed the distance between him and Eli, before bringing his sword up and over Eli's head.

*No!*

"Get up son! Please!" yelled Marius.

Zane's head began to jerk around violently while his sword still hung in the air. Eli continued staring up at Zane never moving from his spot.

"Eli! You have to do it!" said Zane.

"Zane! Zane it's you buddy. Whoa I—."

"No! I can't—hold on. You have to kill me!"

"Are you crazy? I'm not going to—," started Eli before Pang appeared behind him, twirling Eli around once, before letting him go. Eli's body became eye level with the spectators briefly, before slamming back down into the arena sands. He returned to his feet with a sword in both hands. When he turned around, he caught the sight of Pang and Zane both charging him. They both crisscrossed paths a few times, as if they were trying to confuse Eli.

Zane took the lead, crossing in front of Pang and bringing his sword up. When it came down it stopped, and soon a large object hit the ground with a *thud*. The sword dropped from Zane's hand and soon his headless body joined it. Eli's swords stayed frozen outstretched in the air, while his eyes stared down at Zane's body. Pang took advantage of the opportunity and charged Eli, before landing on top of him. Jude was confused when Eli didn't even fight back, while Pang unleashed a series of punches. Blood gushed from Eli's nose and ears while Pang continued to pommel him.

"Son, what are you doing? Fight back!" screamed Marius.

"Honey get up!" yelled Aileen.

"I don't get it," said Jed.

Pang got up, grabbing Eli by the neck and holding him up off of his feet.

"He had to kill a friend. He's lost the will to fight," said Jude.

Marius, Aileen and Jed all looked at Jude in unison. He felt their eyes on him, but he never acknowledged them. He felt Eli's pain. He wanted to go down there and fight the rest of the battle for him.

When Pang's fist smashed into Eli's face, Eli's body darted down at the sands, causing a dust storm.

Pang gripped his dagger and sliced his shoulder.

"Blood Magic!"

"No!" screamed Jude. He jumped to his feet briefly, and soon he came crashing down. His crutches lay next to him. Ignoring them, he clawed his way up. Jed and Marius tried to lend him a hand but he declined. He didn't want anyone to touch him or get in his way. He just wanted everyone to leave him alone. Jude hoisted himself over the rail that over-looked the battle arena. "Eli no! Don't do this! Fight back! Please!"

Pang extended his hand as a smile crept across his face. "Blood domination!"

Jude saw Eli's body finally move. It slowly returned to its feet and soon a dagger appeared in his hand.

*Yes! He's back in the fight!*

But something was off. Something was different. Eli slowly walked with his dagger in hand towards Pang. The Coliseum was silent, except for Eli's footsteps across the sands. When he got to Pang, he blankly stared up into his eyes, before dropping to his knees. Eli brought the blade up to his own neck and just stared up at Pang.

*Pith no—don't let this happen.*

The urge to cry out to Eli, and stop him, washed over Jude. His mouth continued to open, but no words came out. Anxiety, fear and sorrow controlled him. Jude felt some movement next to him. He looked over to see Marius with one foot over the railing of the battle arena, as Jed tried desperately to pull him back.

"Let go of me! That's my boy! That's my son!"

Blood ran from Eli's neck as the blade slid a few inches. The sight made Jude lose all comprehension of time. He saw his friend cutting his throat in front of him. To his left he saw his brother trying to stop Marius from interrupting the battle. He saw his mother crying hysterically. For a second, he thought he saw himself, absent of emotion or thoughts. Everyone moved in slow motion. When Jude turned back towards the battle, time began to flow once again.

Pang held his hand up and Eli's hand stopped, but blood continued to drop from his neck. Pang turned his attention towards the area Bishop was sitting and walked over to him. Neither Eli nor the dagger moved.

When Pang finally arrived in front of Bishop, he stopped and looked up at him. "The battle is clearly mine. I do not wish to finish participating in this battle you all find so entertaining. You all have the audacity to find entertainment in forcing your own people to kill one another when war is on your doorstep. You claim you are desperate for men, but you still engage in such barbaric activities. If you refuse to claim me the victor of this match, I will carry out your will and end this boy's life; and prove to you how barbaric your land's traditions truly are—in the most savage way possible. The choice is yours."

Commotion broke out throughout the spectators area, as people talked amongst themselves. Jude stared at Bishop; hoping he would submit to Pang's request and save Eli.

*Why would he do what Pang says? He's the Lord of our city and this is our tradition. Our people dream of competing here and to better themselves so they are prepared for battle. There is honor, respect, experience and rewards for competitors of the Trials. I guess it depends on what is more important to Bishop.*

The three mentors huddled around Bishop's throne. Jude could tell not only that the spectators were getting restless, but also his mom and Marius as well—who had abandoned their seats so they could pace in front of them.

"I'm all for our traditions and what they stand for," started Marius. "But please! This is my son! I can't lose him."

The crowd around Bishop dissipated when the mentors took their seats. Anya approached Bishop's private balcony that over looked the battle arena.

"If I may have your attention please," announced Anya with outstretched arms. "By order from your Lord and leader Bishop, I give you the winner of the final round of the Trials of Magic, Might and Lineage. Pang Quarrels!"

Applause and whistles erupted throughout the crowds, as people rose to their feet at the decision. Boos and protests soon followed, as spectators threw garbage and miscellaneous objects down onto the sands.

"You dishonor the traditions of our ancestors," yelled someone behind Jude.

Soldiers soon intervened in an attempt to counteract the uproar. Jude watched Marius collapse to the floor in tears, while Aileen comforted him. Jed appeared uninterested in the decision, as he picked his fangs with one of his nails. Jude on the other hand felt like he was dreaming. He was waiting for Anya to say that she was kidding, and have to watch his best friend cut his own throat. When he saw Pang exit the arena and Eli drop the dagger while shaking his head, he knew it was safe to breathe. While Jude watched Eli take in his surroundings, he could see the confusion plastered across his friend's face. Pang did not stay for the audience applause. As soon as the door underneath the Rune statue had opened, he quickly exited from view. Anya appeared shortly after, helping Eli to his feet. When Eli took a look around, his eyes met Jude's. Jude's stare quickly turned from Eli down to his neck that was still streaming blood.

"Catch him!" screamed someone behind Jude as Eli's body hit the ground.

# Part Two
# Mate in Two Moves

◆◆◆

"FATE IS LIFE'S WAY OF REMINDING US
THAT THERE IS NO ESCAPE."

ΑΩ

# OUTNUMBERED

Bishop felt even more eager than usual, as he made his through the outer chamber of Council Hall. This meeting was long overdue and he knew that the answers he would receive today, would decide the next step for his people. Hero portraits and long silk banners of every color, fell from the walls on both sides of him. The homage and memories they immortalized of the rulers before him, gave him a sense of confidence but also humbleness. It was an honor to walk the very halls that his predecessors had. When he opened the large wooden doors in front of him, the eyes of his loyal council members shifted his direction.

"Sorry I'm late my friends, it appears that in these troubled times, even I have to struggle to keep myself together," said Bishop.

After the Trials had come to an end, Bishop had called for an emergency council meeting. Before making his way to Council Hall, he had met up with Marius to talk briefly, and lost track of time.

"No apology needed," said Vance standing up to honor Bishop along with the others.

As Bishop took his seat at the head of the large stone roundtable, he looked around at the members of The Council that he had grown to call friends. He first looked to his left and saw Anya, the beautiful but fierce General that he had come to look at as a daughter. Her short black hair appeared lighter today against the black shoulder armor and black tunic she was wearing. He could see the worry in her eyes, even though her training aided her in perfectly masking her emotion. Next to her was Conall, Anya's new Lieutenant, who sat poised and just as void of emotion as Anya. He was adorned in a silver version of Anya's shoulder armor, and wore a sleeveless silver chainmail layer over his bright red long-sleeve tunic. His hands sat bandaged and clasped together in front of him, as he studied the others around him. Next to Conall was Fox, who had apparently received Bishop's message loud and clear, that if he were late to the next meeting, he would be put on watch duty at the main gates for the next couple of months. As usual he was cloaked in all black down to his shoes. His plain black combat shirt and black pants matched his hair and eyes in almost unnerving perfection. His eyes and expression differed greatly from Anya's and Conall's, since there appeared to be nothing behind Fox's eyes. Studying Fox closely, Bishop didn't see any presence of any emotions or soul behind them. Fox had served as his Tactical Emissary ever sense he had to flee his village—after Lord Egon's forces destroyed it long ago.

*It has been a while since I have met an outsider so dedicated and loyal to our people.*

Next to Fox were three empty seats. Normally there would be an Agent of each bloodline present, however, Bishop felt like it would be more fitting to just have the members that had been with him from the very beginning. Next to the three empty seats were Ivor, Lynn and Vance, who he had known for longer than he could remember. Except for Vance, Bishop had been on missions with all of them in his younger years. He was comforted to see that his friendships had lasted throughout the years.

"So let's begin shall we," started Bishop. He draped his royal blue cloak over the back of his seat before turning to Ivor. "Professor Ivor, have we heard any news from any of our allies?"

"I am afraid not my Lord. I have sent countless messages to all three of them, but so far our plea for aid has gone unanswered."

"None of them," said Bishop shocked.

"None sir. Not even our allies in Geminate," said Ivor.

"But they have been our allies for over a decade now," said Vance.

Anya stirred in her seat. "Are you sure that we have received nothing from them?"

Ivor turned his head slowly towards Anya and stared. All eyes in the room fell on the two of them. "If you are implying that I am too inadequate to handle the communication between our land's allies, then I will have to stop you right there, and inform you that what you are implying is fallacious and ludicrous."

Bishop could feel the tension instantly weighing down in front of him. He felt it was a necessity for him to keep everyone on the same side. "I do not believe that the General was implying any of the sort Ivor," started Bishop quickly. "I believe she was just as shocked as the rest of us in regards to the decision of all three of our allies to not respond to our call for aid."

"Apologies sir," said Ivor as he turned his attention back to Bishop. "I will continue to send for aid and will inform you of any responses."

"Much appreciated Professor," said Bishop turning to Anya. "Next would be our offensive and defensive forces. General, how goes the assembly and training of our Agents?"

Anya rose to her feet with her hands clasped in front of her. "Sir! Everything is going according to plan except for the problem with our lack of men. I have gathered further details from Fox, and he has informed me that he estimates around four hundred Necrosis closing in on our lands. I have decided a buffer of at least two hundred Agents, for a total of six hundred men, would be sufficient to ensure that every last Necrosis is neutralized before they reach our city, villages and farms. The only issue is, we do not have that many fully trained and ready men sir."

"How many soldiers do we have General?"

"Three hundred sir."

Bishop saw a mirror reflection around the table of the worry on his face. He knew that Kismet was low on Agents. He had been problem-solving ways to train and raise more men. This Necrosis threat could not have come at a worse time. His backup plan had been for their allies to make up for the numbers they didn't have. However, with the news that their allies were failing to respond, he worried that he would have to make some rash decisions.

"Well we will also need soldiers here guarding our city and villages, just in case this unknown enemy decides to send a covert team here during the battle, just like they did after Caleb's battle," said Bishop. He felt himself recoil at his words. He looked to Anya, but saw no signs of any ill effects by his words.

"I agree sir," started Vance. "I believe it would be reckless and foolish to leave any of our land unguarded with anything less than one hundred men. Not to mention we will of course primarily use Erudite soldiers here in the city—but we should also mix in some Agents as well. "

Ivor's head immediately jerked towards Vance, as a scowl appeared on his face. "One hundred men! You have to got to be facetious! You heard the General; we only have three hundred men. If you were to have one hundred here, that would leave two hundred of our men to fight four hundred of those undead abominations!"

"And with all do respect Vance, the Erudites *are* Agents," said Lynn.

"Well I do not believe that now is the time to get into a debate over whether their lack of abilities make them any less of a Agent or not. All I am saying is that they have less of a chance of taking down as many enemies as a *real* Agent—that's all," said Vance in a matter of fact tone.

"Well I believe that will definitely be a discussion that we will be having in the near future, because I beg to differ with you. If you believe that Agents without abilities cannot stand against mindless Necrosis, then why do we need such a large number of Bloodline Agents for battle, when one Bloodline

Agent carries the destructive power of nearly ten warriors? To be honest, if we are sending our best Bloodline Agents into battle, I believe that one hundred Bloodline Agents should be able to completely neutralize the four hundred Necrosis with ease," said Lynn crossing her arms.

"And with all do respect Ivor, I am skilled enough in elementary mathematics to be able to comprehend what I am proposing. You know that I am man of practicality, and I only suggest what I believe will be a guaranteed success," said Vance.

"And for that I thank you Vance," said Bishop quickly. "So does anyone have any suggestions on how we can increase our numbers in the next two days?"

Silence descended upon them as each of them brainstormed possible options.

"Even though they have given us difficulty in the past, the Amorphous have not necessarily been opposed to an alliance with our lands. Perhaps this is a sign and a chance for a new alliance," said Lynn.

"Not a bad idea. This may be the answer we have been praying for," said Bishop weighing the probability. "Does anyone else have anymore ideas?"

Bishop's eyes fell to Fox, just as the Emissary opened his mouth.

"Why not use the Academy Agents-in-training?"

A gasp came from Lynn as she stirred in her seat.

"The students?"

"Whatever you want to call them. I mean they are being taught directly by *you* mentors. So they should be adequate, shouldn't they," said Fox with a grin on his face.

"I beg your pardon you degenerate," said Ivor with a snarl on his face. "I'll have you know that I have been responsible for molding some of the most proficient Agents and Operatives in history. All of this before you were old enough to wear your first dress," said Ivor smirking.

"Yeah right. Is that why you were the only mentor that only chose four contenders for the Trials of Magic, Might and Lineage? Must I remind you that not *one* Weapons Master won any rounds of the Trials? How weak! Anyways, I'll have you know that I was born wearing the prettiest dress in the world gramps," said Fox with a wink.

"Fox the disrespect of our fallen comrades will not be tolerated. Now if you have a serious proposition for what you are suggesting, I would like to hear it," said Bishop.

"Wanna get some food after this," asked Fox over Conall to Anya, who ignored him. "Gosh what's your problem, I was going to pay. Well for mine at least," said Fox laughing to himself.

Bishop, along with all of the others, stared at Fox awaiting his strategy. Fox's careless disregard for authority and respect, along with his lack of sense of urgency, were the only qualities that Bishop could do without when it came to Fox. However, Fox had been responsible for coming up with more than a couple of ingenious strategies and suggestions in the past, and Bishop respected his opinion just the same.

"Alright alright, since everyone decided to look like a mean raisin. I don't think it's fair that it's six versus one. Like I said before, you are training students in the art of combat. Why not just have those in the advanced classes, as well as the Erudites, guard the city while our armed forces engage the Necrosis in battle. Unlike Vance, I *do* believe that the Erudites are *real* Agents," said Fox winking at Lynn, who sighed at the gesture.

Bishop noticed the eyes in the room turn to him, awaiting his response to Fox's suggestion. "I don't know if I feel comfortable sending our youth into battle against these creatures. While it is true that they have been trained, they have never been in real battle outside of the Trials," said Bishop.

"Oh that's fine," started Fox. "We can always just use the thousands and thousands of Agents we have at our disposal. Oh and not to mention the millions we have on backorder."

"I find your disrespect of our Lord both dishonorable and distasteful," said Conall crossing his arms.

"Oh get a sense of humor Anya junior," said Fox.

"Fox may be right sir. With no allies and no guarantee the Amorphous will aid us in battle, hard decisions may be unavoidable," said Vance putting his hand on Bishop's shoulder.

Bishop felt backed into a corner. The safety of his people was number one on his list of priorities. However, how far would he go to protect them? Thinking of the young fresh faces of the sons and daughters of his people dressed in armor, and ready to lay down their lives, was hard to take in.

"Sir," said someone in the room.

"I won't be the one to make our sons and daughters lay down their lives for us. Our first priority is to send a small team immediately, not tomorrow, not in a couple of hours, but immediately to the Relinquished Isles to see if the Amorphous will send us aid. Lynn, I believe that since you have the better rapport with the Amorphous, you would be the best candidate to lead this small team. You would have a half an hour after the meeting to ready yourself, before your team departs," said Bishop.

"You don't even have to ask my Lord," said Lynn with a smile.

"Now as for you Anya," started Bishop as he turned his attention towards the General. "I will have you continue to train the three hundred Agents we have. In addition, I want you to send word to the three winners of the Trials of Magic, Might and Lineage; that there will be an exclusive mandatory training session for them tomorrow at six o'clock in the morning sharp. Since they will be directly under you on your team, I want them fully trained, briefed and ready to go."

"Yes sir!"

"Now Vance, I would like for you to get the word around by any means necessary, that any advanced students in our

Academy that are willing to join our armed forces, contact you directly. Let me be clear, we are not forcing them. This will be a decision for them to make. I want all of those who have elected to fight, to meet tomorrow morning at six o' clock to begin their training. It will not be absolute that these individuals will be enlisted. This will be our backup plan if the Amorphous refuse our request for aid. Do I make myself clear?"

"Yes sir!" said everyone in unison. The only exception was Fox, who was playing with a thread on his shirt.

"Anya, I do believe that Jude, Sia and Pang will be great assets to you on the battlefield. They may be young, but I believe they are some of our best; and I hope you will utilize them completely," said Bishop.

"Agreed! Will do sir," said Anya rising to her feet along with Conall.

"May fate be your ally."

# DESCENDIT
# CUM ROACHES

Jude had stopped by the Medicinal Quarters to check on Eli directly after the match. The hut was empty, except for Eli and the few healers that walked its aisles. Eli was still unconscious when Jude had arrived, but the healers assured him that it was temporary. They informed him that Eli should be conscience and approved for release later on in the afternoon, after his last treatment from Vance. The news brought light to a darkness that had manifested in Jude's mind. On his way out, he ran into Aileen and Marius, who had also stopped by to check in on Eli. Jude reiterated what the healer had told him, which resulted in a series of "Thank the gods!" Jude had asked Marius if it would be okay for him to come by his house later on to check in on Eli, after he was released from the Medicinal Quarters. Jude was relieved when Marius told him that his door was always open when it came to Jude and his mother. Before Jude left the Medicinal Quarters, the healers performed one last healing session on his lower body. Jude was relieved to be leaving his crutches behind.

After leaving the Coliseum completely, Jude took a walk around the city to clear his head, beginning in the Eastern Hold. So much had happened in the last few days, and he was having difficulty processing it all. He had won his first Trials of Magic, Might and Lineage, and had almost died in the process. He also saw the emotional destruction of his best friend after Eli had to kill Zane.

*That was painful to watch.*

Last but not least, he believed that he and Eli had finally put all of the petty disagreements behind them. Before leaving the Eastern Hold, Jude had found a curious bouquet of purple flowers that were carelessly thrown to the side of one of the houses. The color reminded him of a battling Magi, except it was more of a piercing purple. He set the flowers on the first step of the closest house, in hopes that whomever lived there, would appreciate their return. When he entered the Market District, he became overwhelmed with the amount of people that inhabited it. Citizens, shopkeepers, farmers and small children, littered the streets of the district, while they shopped, socialized and mingled.

As Jude passed a small shop, something in the window caught his eye. When he walked up to the tall glass window, he peered in at a black armband that sat isolated on display. The armband had a square peace of thin metal attached to it, and on the metal, was an etched drawing of two small figures. The figures resembled the silhouette of two small warriors side-by-side. The first silhouette had a warrior holding a sword in his left hand and a black circle in his right. The second figure was identical, except it was shaded a little darker and the sword was in its right hand and a white circle in its left. Jude looked up to see the name of the shop.

*Zebediah's Misappropriated Oddities. Hmm sounds interesting.*

The scent of wood and old books filled the room, when Jude entered Zebediah's Misappropriated Oddities. Tall and large bookcases covered every inch of the four walls of the small shop. In the center of the shop, were five or six small tables, with stray and unorganized trinkets, and miscellaneous items. Behind them furthest from Jude, was a short wooden counter. After briefly examining the layout of the shop, he approached the counter.

"Hello?"

Silence.

He turned around and headed back towards the window, to the armband he had seen earlier. As he picked it up and examined it, he noticed the metal plate that carried the carving was lighter than he had expected, and that the armband did not slip on, but was meant to be tied around the arm.

" Non possum adiuvare vos?"

Jude jumped, dropping the armband and hitting his head on the top of the display. Quickly turning around, he found an older gentleman standing over him.

"I'm sorry?"

"Ah facitis latine loqui," said the man laughing. "I asked you if I couldn't help you."

"Wait, you asked me if you could not help me? Why?"

"Because you weren't looking at that armband that's not sitting right there."

It took a while for Jude to understand what was going on, after checking for the scent of alcohol in the air. "It is a really nice armband. Where is it from?"

"Well it wasn't given to me from a man in Geminate," he said.

Jude thought about what the man had said for a second. "So you stole it?"

"Stole? Who stole? Not I! Then you? Who are you?"

"Wait what?" Jude became irritated by the conversation, and for a second, pondered leaving.

"Mutum mutum ego numquam dicere," he said laughing hysterically.

Jude picked up the armband and examined it. "Okay, so you got it from someone from Geminate. What does it mean?"

"Ah! Well I won't tell you what it doesn't mean! The balance! Yes the balance! Light and dark! Good and evil! Drunk and boring! All for the balance," he said clapping his hands to no audible tune.

"Okay, but why depict it in the form of two warriors?"

"Quia matris tuae caput est quoque magnus!"

"I don't understand," said Jude feeling ready to give up.

"Don't tell! I'll tell! Only because you can't tell! The world was not always balanced! No it wasn't! But two warriors overcame trials! They overcame tribulations! All for what? To protect their people from the grandest threat."

"What was the threat?"

"Phobophobia!"

*This guy is impossible.*

"Well how much is it?"

"Five hundred gold," he said.

"I can buy a house for five hundred gold."

"Then two silvers," he said with a glare.

"Alright I'll take it," said Jude eager to leave as soon as possible. He reached into his pocket and gave the man two silvers before tucking the armband into his pocket. "I didn't get your name."

"Don't get it? I don't get you! You know what I don't get? Cockroaches! Why are they here? Who sent them? What's their purpose? Where do they come from? Why are they ugly? Why do they walk funny? And above all," said the man curling his hands into fists. "Why do they keeping taking my keys!"

"I will just assume that you are Zebediah," started Jude as he turned towards the door. "Thanks for the armband. Have a good night!"

"Descendit cum roaches!"

Jude was so eager to leave the shop that he didn't even see the little boy when he crashed into him, and knocked him to the ground.

"Ouch!"

"I am so sorry," said Jude extending a hand down to the boy.

The boy knocked his hand away and returned to his feet. "Wait! I know you."

Jude examined whom he was talking to. The boy could not be any older than eight or nine. He wore a royal blue sweater and beige shorts with many pockets. "You do?"

"Yeah! The Prodigy of Pith storms the field once again," said the boy punching the air in front of him.

"Mik! What are you doing?"

Jude looked up to find Eli's friend standing in front of him. He instantly recognized her purple eyes when she stopped in front of him. She wore tight-fitting black pants and a matching shirt. A long bright red scarf hung from her neck and passed her waist.

"I am so sorry. Wait, I know you," she said.

"No you don't! I know him! The Prodigy of Pith is *my* friend," said the boy.

"Jude right?"

"Yes. Wyatt right? Sia Wyatt?"

"Yes, and this is my little brother Mik," said Sia.

"Who's little?" said Mik with a scowl.

"I am sorry if he caused you any trouble," said Sia.

"No it was my fault. I was not watching where I was going."

"Hey! Hey! Down here!" said Mik.

Jude looked down to see his eager face staring back up at him.

"I saw your battle. Well I only saw the first few minutes because I had to get home, but you were awesome."

"Thank you Mik. I really appreciate it."

"So when are you going to teach me to be a badass like you?" asked Mik.

A gasp erupted from Sia's direction, causing Jude to look up. "Mik! Where did you learn that word from?"

"Um school?" Mik appeared to be nervous for the first time since Jude had met him.

"I doubt that, and now that you are lying to me, you are in big trouble when we get back," said Sia.

"Ah man!"

"We really should be going," she said.

"Hey wait," said Jude trying to catch up. "Eli gets out of the Medicinal Quarters later on today. I was going to go over his place and check on him, and if he was well enough, I was thinking we could all go out to the Forgotten Forest to celebrate his recovery." Jude felt unnerved when Sia simply stared back at him with no response.

"Sure. I will see if our friend Meara can come as well. She really needs to get out of the house. Should we just meet at his house around seven tonight?"

"Seven is great. See you then," said Jude.

After leaving the Market District, Jude decided to head to the library instead of home. He wanted to research the armband he had just purchased. He didn't doubt that the old man that sold it to him had been telling the truth—to an extent. He just wanted to do his own research to make sure that all what he knew about it was true. When he entered the Academy, a memory of his first time passing through its doors flashed in front of him. Making his way into the library, he was not surprised to see that there was no one, except for Ms. Lowell, working there.

"Jude! How are you?"

"I am well Ms. Lowell. How are you?"

"Couldn't be better," she said returning something to a non-visible area beneath her. "I set aside these two books for you, that we just got in today. I thought you might want to be the first to read them."

"Wow! Thank you Ms. Lowell," said Jude taking the books.

Ms. Lowell was one of the three librarians that worked in the Academy library. The other two were his mom Aileen and another lady that Jude had not met yet, due to her strict no talking policy. Ms. Lowell and Aileen had been friends for as long as Jude could remember. He liked Ms. Lowell. She was one of the sweetest people he knew. She always set aside any books she thought he might be interested in, and always let him check out as many books as he liked. What he liked most about her, was the fact that she always had a huge smile on her face no matter who came in.

As Jude made his way to his normal table, he noticed someone was already sitting in his usual chair. When he took a seat in the chair right next to it, he recognized who was sitting next to him.

"You are the only person I know, who after getting out of a heated battle like that, goes to the library."

"You are the only person I know, that after coming out of a near death coma, walks around as if nothing happened," said Pang with a smirk.

"You were awesome."

"Awesome but what?"

"Where did you get abilities like that?"

It was the one thing that Jude had wanted to ask Pang, ever since Eli's battle. He had never seen or even read about abilities like the ones Pang had displayed in his battle. Pang got really close, as if he was going to tell Jude a secret. Jude leaned closer so he could hear better.

"Magic," said Pang with a small laugh.

"Very funny."

"I am serious!" Pang closed the book he was reading and rose from his seat.

"Leaving already?"

"Well, I mean I did just get out of what you call a 'heated battle,' a few hours ago," said Pang packing his belongings.

"So you aren't going to tell me how you got your abilities?"

Pang stared down at him, void of all evidence of emotion. The orange and red in his eyes seemed to separate and circle one another in an infinite cycle. "If you want to know that badly, I will tell you—but not here."

"Okay then where?"

# THE MEMOIRS
# OF PANG

After finding a book on Geminate artifacts, Jude left the Academy with Pang. He tried to start up idle conversation with Pang on the way through the Market District, but Pang's short answers gave Jude the impression that he was not up for conversation.

*He is so up and down, that I never know when he is in the mood to socialize.*

Pang led Jude out the main gates, and north of the city. After a little under a couple of miles, a small settlement of dark wooden houses came into view. Dozens of villagers socialized and scurried in and out of houses—under the moon's crescent embrace. As they walked to the right of the settlement, Jude noticed a lone house that was slightly smaller than the rest. A small wooden sparring dummy stood behind a small garden, exclusively full of the same white chrysanthemums that Jude had seen on Dominic's coffin.

After Pang unlocked the door, the two of them entered. The first thing that Jude noticed upon entering, was that the house was primarily one large room. He could barely make out a small room around the corner on his right, but he couldn't be sure. Four or five bookcases, filled with assorted books, were evenly spread out among the four walls in the room. Jude was confused when he noticed the décor that surrounded him. A large quantity of paintings that appeared to be more expensive than the house, clung to the walls around him. Two of the paintings Jude recognized from a book he had read on historical art.

*That one painting is worth more than my house and everything in it.*

A small full bed dressed in sheets, but no blankets, sat next to a small wooden nightstand holding a single book. Pang's voice caught him off guard.

"Thirsty?"

"Sure what do you have?"

"Alcohol, water or cider basically," said Pang.

"Um, cider will be fine."

Pang disappeared around the corner, to a room different from the one that Jude thought he saw earlier. Jude took a look around, examining some of the books in the bookcase that stood next to him. Most of the books were on different combat strategies as well as a few books on body conservation, Praxis history and historical art. A small chest served as a bookend on the last shelf. It appeared both foreign and old, and drew Jude's attention. When he reached down to touch it, Pang returned.

"Here you go," said Pang handing him a cup.

"Oh thanks."

"What do you think you are doing?"

Jude felt caught off guard by the question, and examined Pang for a few seconds before responding. "Excuse me?"

"Don't you ever—and I mean ever—touch that chest again!" Pang slammed his cup on the table and brought his curled hands up to his chest. Before Jude could open his mouth to apologize, Pang silenced him. "You brought this on yourself! The flesh I will take, the bones I will shatter, and your eyes I will have—you filth!"

"I'm sorry!" yelled Jude.

The rage that had been present in Pang's eyes, slowly dissipated. Time hung thick and stationary for what felt like minutes. When Pang took his seat and clasped his cup, Jude took it as a sign that danger had been averted.

"Do not take this the wrong way, but please do not ever touch that chest—ever!" said Pang.

The urge to look over his shoulder at the chest he had just examined, wore at every corner of Jude's mind. He took a deep breath and concentrated on why he was there, before nodding. The chair Jude sat in stood around a small table holding an old candle. "I apologize. It's just I have never seen a chest like that and—nonetheless I get it, and I apologize."

The awkward silence of sitting across from a stranger, soon paralyzed Jude in place.

"So, I have noticed that you have many luxurious artifacts. How long have you had them?"

"Probably five or six years. Art is something very important back home. Mostly everyone has at least a few pieces of ancient and valuable artifacts from their ancestors. Our people are extremely proud of their heritage," said Pang.

"Isn't that the painting of the Crystal Legion?"

"Yes, a couple of my ancestors were apart of the legion," said Pang.

"That painting is supposed to be worth like nine hundred gold—more than my house."

"What does money have to do with it?"

"Oh nothing—I am just saying," said Jude feeling awkward.

"No matter the value, the artifacts hold sentimental value. Why is it that the first thing that comes to someone's mind is—how much—when they set eyes on something? It's infuriating."

"I didn't mean any disrespect. It's just my family has been struggling for sometime since my father died. My mom works non-stop in order to maintain somewhat of a normal life for us—well for me. I rarely see her. It is just a bad habit I have developed over the years of appraising something the minute I see it."

When Pang failed to respond, Jude realized there was a cup in his hand that warmed his hands while soothing his nose. After realizing that he had made Pang angry after Pang had already given him the cup, he decided it was most likely free of any poison or harmful substances. He took a sip.

"Wow! This cider is better than the cider we have at home."

"It's because it's from back home. Not here," said Pang sipping his cup.

"Where is back home?"

"What is now known as Praxis."

Jude took a sip of his cider while he studied Pang. He was hard to read and figure out. He never appeared happy or sad, except for the few times he cracked a smile or showed a smirk.

"If you are to understand how and why I have the abilities I do, you must agree to two rules. One, you do not say a word while I am talking. Two, you do not tell anyone *anything* about what I am about tell you. Agreed?"

Jude nodded, afraid if he spoke, that it would break Pang's first rule.

"Before Praxis was what it is today, I grew up in a city called Bestir. It was a moderately-sized city surrounded by mountains and small villages. The winters were brutal and the summers were winters. Our king was Erasmus Tiziano. He was a merciful king. However, he was also strong, intelligent, patient and skilled in almost every combat technique. He was the heir to his father's throne, and rose to power after his father had passed away. The people of the land were overjoyed when he became king. His father had spread peace, and the land prospered during his rein; and Erasmus reminded them of him. I was about eight years old when Erasmus rose to power. My mother was pregnant with my little brother Isaac, and my father was a builder. We had a nice sized house around the corner from the palace. I remember crime was always really low, everyone had work, and for the most part, life was easy and peaceful."

Pang finished his cider and placed his cup to the side before continuing.

"Erasmus was a unique King. He cared deeply for his people. I remember one time he came by the house to visit us when my mother was a few weeks away from giving birth to Isaac. He told us that if there was anything that we needed, to just ask. He was like that with everyone. Erasmus made everyone feel like they were apart of his immediate family. Then one day everything changed. Everyone knew that Donat was both envious and furious when Erasmus took the throne. Even though Erasmus was next in line, Donat had tried to convince his father to make him king instead before he died; but his father refused. One day our city had a huge festival. Everyone was there, including the royal family. The king mingled with everyone like he usually did. Erasmus and Donat had gotten into a huge disagreement. Not wanting to argue in front of his people, Erasmus asked Donat to come by the castle later on, to talk about their disagreement. That night he was murdered. They found him three stories beneath his balcony on the castle lawn. His neck was broken."

Pang left the room and returned with more cider. He filled Jude's cup and then his own, before sitting back down and continuing.

"You see, Erasmus was positive, non-judgmental and understanding. Our city was one of the most diverse lands that existed. People from all over lived there peacefully. Erasmus welcomed the diversity. He believed that being different was a gift to everyone, because then everyone could learn about different ways of life. Donat on the other hand, was the opposite of Erasmus. He was cruel, greedy, cunning and intolerant. He hated Vampires, Amorphous, or even anyone with abilities that he deemed different than his own people's. He hated a large group of the people that lived in our lands. He felt like they were inferior and unworthy to live behind our walls. Shortly after Erasmus' death, Donat immediately rose to power, and that is when everything changed. The whole city was destroyed, and a new one was built in its place. Cold black-stone walls that were intentionally built high enough to block out most of the sun, stood atop the ashes of our fallen city. Donat said that most of the people that lived in our city were not worthy enough to experience the sun's rays on their skin. So he took the sun away from us. A system of ridiculous and manipulative rules were set forth by Donat, before the decree was instated. Donat called it the Chasten Decree. He ordered that everyone that was not of a preordained bloodline, culture or race, to either leave the city immediately, or be executed."

Pang stopped when he heard Jude choke on his cider. Jude was blown away by Pang's story. He almost didn't believe that someone could be so cruel as to threaten the execution of people who were not born the way the king had wanted.

"Before Donat rose to power, a unique old man lived next door to us. His name was Mr. Amdis. When I was younger, I always noticed how different he was. I was fourteen when my little sister Nola was born. I was playing outside of Mr. Amdis' house, when I noticed something in the window. When I peered in, I noticed furniture flying around the room in his house. Mr. Amdis suddenly peered into the window with blood leaking down his face. The sight scared me and I ran. I spent the next couple of days avoiding him, until one day I bumped into him on my way back from school. He asked me to come to his house. He was a trusted family friend, so I went with him. When we got to his house, he explained to me that I could not tell anyone about what I had saw. I asked him why, and he just simply told me, 'people always make an enemy out of those who are different from them.' I asked him more questions than I care to remember. What I do remember is that he told me that what he was using was called Blood Magic, and that he learned it from an ancient Vampire that he met a long time ago. I asked him how it worked, and he explained to me that the blood in his veins fuels his abilities. He had to either be injured, or injure himself, in order to use his abilities. I was only fourteen, so I did not understand why anyone would hurt themselves in order to move some furniture around the house. He told me that there was a whole world of other abilities that I was unaware of, and that they were only attainable through Blood Magic. I remember coming back day-after-day with more and more questions. The most memorable one was a night that I came over. He explained to me that he had lost the abilities he was born with, when he received his Blood Magic abilities. I told him that I didn't understand why anyone would go through so much to give up the abilities they were born with, for an ability they could only use by hurting themselves."

A knock sounded at the door. Pang froze in place along with Jude. "You tell anyone you were coming here?"

"You would know since I have been with you ever since we made the decision to come here at the library."

"Dearly noted. I am not expecting any visitors either," said Pang quietly walking to the door. He looked out the small window above the door, and then the larger window next to it, before taking his seat. "No one is there. Stay alert."

"Got ya. So you asked him why he would give up so much—for his abilities," said Jude eager for the rest of the story.

"Right. So yes I asked him, and all he said was, 'how far would you go to protect the ones you loved?' I didn't understand the meaning of his words, because I was so young. However, I was seventeen when Donat ordered the Chasten Decree, and I quickly came to understand what Mr. Amdis meant. My family was native to our city. Our ancestors had been born there. However, Donat did not like our loyalty to his brother Erasmus when he was king, along with a few other families. He ordered us to leave the city as well, or risk being executed. Donat ordered that my father be fired from his job so we had no income coming in. My mother and father were in denial about Donat moving forward with the execution. They didn't believe that he could get away with it. One night I was walking home with my little brother Issac. We were almost home when a group of soldiers ambushed us. They knocked us both unconscious, and when we woke up, we were in the torture chamber beneath the castle."

"The smell of vomit and decomposing bodies hung in the air. Blood decorated the walls and floor of the chamber. Torture tools unlike any you could imagine littered the room. My brother Isaac and I hung nude by our hands from a chain that hung from the ceiling. Donat was the first person I saw, along with the soldiers that had jumped us. He told me that my family was scum and that we were not worthy enough to live in his city. I told him that my family had lived there for generations, and that we had every right to live there. That was a huge mistake. The soldiers whipped us for longer than I can remember. I blacked out after the first ten minutes. When I woke up, I was covered in blood and my body burned and throbbed from the pain. I then had to watch my little brother go through what I had just went through. The cries and screams that barreled from his mouth, were more painful than the lashings I had just went through. Pieces of skin from his back were flung in every direction as the glass dug into his back before ripping away. I begged them over and over to stop, but they wouldn't. They whipped him repeatedly for an hour before stopping. I prayed to the gods that they would at least let my little brother survive, and that they would let him go. They took Isaac down from the chains he had been hanging from, and laid him on the table in front of me. Donat told my brother 'your family is dishonorable and defiant, and suffering will be your punishment.' They tortured him Jude. They tortured my little brother. They started with small things like torching sensitive parts of his body—like the bottom of his feet and his lower back. The removal of his fingernails was definitely one of the toughest forms of torture he had to endure. I kicked and screamed trying to break free. I told them that I would do whatever they wanted, if they let him go. After the nails, every torture tool on the walls was utilized on Issac. Every time he was seconds from death, one of the soldiers would heal enough of his wounds to keep him alive. Cuts, lacerations and burns pillaged my little brother's body. The one I remember the most was when they strapped him face-down, and took a handsaw to both of his Achilles Tendons. I remember that was when I broke my wrist from trying to break free. Isaac passed out afterwards. When he woke up, they had tied him to a post that stood in the middle of the room. They dowsed him with oil and lit him on fire. I stared into my little brother's eyes as his burned. He cried out to me over and over again begging me to make it stop. 'Pang please make it stop! Please big brother! It hurts,' was what he cried out to me, but I couldn't do anything. All I could do, was watch helplessly as my little brother—that I was supposed to protect—burn to death. Isaac was nine years old."

"I welcomed the death I thought was coming. Life lost all meaning after I lost Issac. However, Donat didn't kill me. He told me that he was keeping me alive just so I could run back and tell my parents about what had happened to Issac. He wanted me to tell them that our deaths would be worse, if we refused to leave. After they threw me out onto the streets, Mr. Amdis found me. I was too injured and lost too much blood to walk. He took me back to his house, and used his Blood Magic to heal my injuries. It was then I told him that I understood, and that I wanted to learn how to use Blood Magic. That night he did the ritual to make me like him. I will save the details of the ritual for another time, but afterwards I felt like half of my identity had been taken away, but I didn't care. I went to each of my family and told them about what had had happened to Isaac and I. All I remember was my dad catching my mother, as she collapsed to the floor in tears. My little sister Nola was only three years old, so she didn't understand the gravity of the situation."

"I hugged each of my family and told them that I loved them. I also told them that this would be the last time that they would see me, and that I wasn't coming back. They pillaged me with countless questions asking me what was going on, and where I was going, but I didn't tell them anything about what I had planned—or the ritual that had just taken place at Mr. Amdis' house. All I told them was that they did not need to leave the city, and that they didn't need to live in fear anymore. I snuck into the palace, passed the guards and into Donat's quarters. His face when he saw me behind him in the mirror he was looking into, was a lifetime supply of bliss to my heart. I will never forget the sheer panic and fear in his eyes, as I controlled his every move. I made him follow me down a secret corridor that led from his bedroom to the torture chamber, and I subjected him to the same torture techniques as he did to us. Every torture tool on that wall, I used on him countless times. Only this time, when he was most weary, I controlled his hands and made him administer his own torture. I have to say, the handsaw to his Achilles Tendons and the flames to his back and feet, were my favorites. There was no escape for him. It took an hour or so for him to come back to consciousness after that. That was when he begged. Oh yes he begged for his wretched life. However, unlike him I am more merciful. So before his execution, I found a bottle of acid that sat on a nearby table. He of course refused to drink it himself, so I had to lend him a hand. His body convulsed a lot, causing an overflow of blood and acid shot from his nose, ears and mouth. When I saw the life start to leave his body, I decided to end his misery. So I set him aflame in the same spot he murdered Issac. That was when I learned the Blood Execution ability. A voice in my head, during his torture, thirsted for his blood. After his death, I just knew the spell. It's hard to explain—but I knew it the way my eyes knew to blink. It was instinctual."

"Afterwards I fled the city of course. It would not be long before his body was found. I camped out every day for two months until they named a new king. The royal bloodline was broken, so they had to elect another. They chose Erasmus' political advisor William Gallows. The choice could have been worse. Once I saw that Gallows had retracted the Chasten Decree, and that my family was safe, I fled. I had stayed too long anyways, and could not risk being discovered on the outskirts of the city."

Jude took in all of Pang's crazy story. He felt more overwhelmed than he felt like he had ever been. His story was filled with so much pain and loss, with no clear happy ending anywhere to be seen. "Do you ever see or talk to your family?"

"Not since I left. They don't even know where I am. I do sneak back to Praxis from time to time, to ensure that they are still okay—that and leave money. My little sister Nola looks about twelve now, and is as beautiful as she wants to be. However, no matter how great the land of Kismet is, it's excruciating to live this far from my family. Every day is a struggle for me," said Pang.

"What did you tell Bishop when you came here?"

"That my village was destroyed, and that I was hoping to find refuge here. He is a kind and trusting man, almost to a fault, if I do say so myself," said Pang.

"Sorry about Isaac. He didn't deserve what happened to him. Neither of you did."

"Gratitude."

Jude noticed that for the first time since he had met Pang, he could finally sense emotion. He saw the pain behind his eyes. However, with that pain was also courage. "It took a lot of courage to do what you did. I am not sure anyone could make the sacrifices you have made."

"And that is what gets me," started Pang. "That is why during my match, I chose not to kill your friend Eli. Leaders are so careless with the lives of their people sometimes. They look at them as expendable or a needed sacrifice. They never stop to think about the magnitude of the pain they cause in the process. The fact that they had us participate in such an event, that calls for the massacre of its own people, is disgusting."

"You are not from our lands. So you know nothing of our culture. You insult both my people and myself by insulting our traditions. We have the Trials of Magic, Might and Lineage because it is a tradition passed down by the gods themselves to our ancestors. People are not forced to participate. If you are elected, you can decline without any consequences. However, no one does. The Trials represent a coming together of all three of the bloodlines respectfully in combat. It is an honor to make it to the Trials. I have been hoping to participate in the Trials all of my life, and have been lucky to do so," said Jude finding himself angry.

"I apologize to you. You are right, I do not know of your people's customs and traditions. I learn a little more as time passes," said Pang.

Jude felt no more anger. Pang's apology felt genuine and heartfelt. "Apology accepted."

"All I was saying is that many people believe they know what a real sacrifice is, but they don't. A lover in a relationship may think he is making a big sacrifice by giving something up so the two of them can be together, or even changing a part of himself to make the relationship work. Or a king may sacrifice a large number of his soldiers, just to keep his people safe. People like that don't know the true meaning of sacrifice. Someone who knows what a real sacrifice is, knows that they themselves will most likely not benefit at all from the outcome. I do not believe anyone in this world knows the true meaning of sacrifice, except for a handful of individuals and parents in this world," said Pang.

"Parents?"

"Yes mothers, and sometimes fathers as well. Some families every day go without food, water or even clothes on their backs. I have seen mothers who have slaved away to find food, only to give every morsel of it to their children, and keep none for them. I have seen mothers buy their child a gift knowing that the expense will result in countless brutal hours of labor, in order to earn the money back to put food on the table. Those are the people who know what true sacrifice is. But don't get me wrong; there are mothers and fathers who should have never been gifted with children. Parents who think of no one but themselves. They lie, deceive, manipulate and so much more, just to make sure they come out on top, keep a certain lifestyle or even appear a certain way to their peers," said Pang.

"There are times when I wonder why the people in this world lie to one another. I wonder why people are so brainwashed with the animalistic instinct to do whatever it takes, including hurting or destroying the lives of others, in order to come out on top. It leaves me baffled when I see how people in this world spend more time hating and hurting one another, than helping each other. I just don't get it. I mean there are strengths in numbers, and last time I checked, there are millions and millions of us here. Don't people realize that with the vast number of people that exists, if we all worked towards the same goal, we would all come out on top," said Jude.

"You will come to realize that every last person in this world is at least a tiny bit selfish. We are wired that way. Whenever things do not go exactly the way we want, our brain goes into selfish overdrive, and makes us sacrifice every positive and negative thing around us, until we come out on top," said Pang in a matter-of-fact tone.

"I have never been like that," started Jude. "I will admit that I may have had some small selfish moments here and there. But I have never hurt someone else or destroyed their life in order to make mine better. I always think of how my actions affect others first, and me second."

Pang left and returned with some more cider. After filling up both of their cups, he returned to their conversation. "The advice I am about to give you, you can take it or leave it. Bad things happen to good people, while good things happen to bad people. Why? I could tell you why, but it isn't important. What is important, is how a good person deals with the bad things that happen to them."

"Meaning what? Like ignoring them?"

"No, that would be your first mistake," said Pang.

"Okay then what?"

"Realize that you are a good person, acknowledge the bad things that are happening, and make a decision that you will not let the bad things take away what makes you a good person," said Pang glaring.

Silence hung in the air for what seemed like minutes, before Jude found his voice.

"Why are you telling me this?"

"Sometimes, bad things do not happen to good people. Instead, bad people happen to good people. The reasons for this is not important—what is important—is realizing when someone is a lost cause, and will do more harm than good to you in the end."

Jude became enraged, when Pang intentionally kept ignoring his question. "Answer me! Why are you telling me this?"

"For someone so smart, you can be really dumb sometimes, you know that," said Pang laughing.

"I did not ask you to insult me, I asked you to answer me. Now I will ask you again. Why are you telling me this?"

Pang ignored Jude's questions. He rose from his seat, went into the other room, and came back with a pitcher. After filling both of their cups with fresh hot cider, he took his seat. "Let's just say that Blood Magic has its advantages."

As Jude drunk his warm cider, he thought about Pang's words. After a few failed attempts at deciphering their meaning, he gave up. However, for the first time since Jude had known Pang, he felt like he saw the real Pang Quarrels for the first time.

After leaving Pang's village, Jude saw his new friend in a new light. The mystery that once shrouded him, as well as the question marks that surrounded every one of their conversations, seemed to slowly slip away like a light dream. Jude took one last glance back at Pang's village, and felt the humble calmness that came from the soft lights that spilled out of the small windows. Thousands of stars gave the village an intimate feeling of warmth and comfort. As Jude walked through the main gates, he noticed two extra soldiers stood guard at its doors.

The Western Hold's familiar sight would have been comforting, if it was not for the covert activity displaying in front of him. Marius' head whipped back and forth, appearing to be looking for something. A tall, cloaked and hooded figure stood straight up next to him. After a few seconds, the two entered the house slowly. Jude checked all of the surrounding corners and buildings. When he was satisfied that no one else was nearby, he sprinted quietly to the side of Marius' house. He opened the tattered wooden door that led him through the house's side gate. Three windows laid on the side of the house.

*Okay. What did Jed say about tracking someone?*

Jude took a look around at the floor in front of him. He took note of anything that he could step on that would make noise. He then looked around at every corner and shadow, which he could used to conceal his presence. After identifying only one useable corner, he slowed his breathing. He pictured himself meditating on an open field, and soon heard and felt nothing but silence all around him.

*Okay now to anticipate my target.*

He closed his eyes and pictured Marius and Bishop walking in the front door a couple of minutes ago. He realized that the first room they would come into, would be the living room with a couch, a few chairs and a table. It seemed like a plausible location to socialize. However, Jude figured that the living room was too close to Eli's bedroom; and if Marius and the lone figure wanted to have a private conversation, the living room would not suffice.

*Marius has a tendency to entertain in the kitchen. He will probably offer his guest hot cider and—.*

A rough sound emanated from the last window next to Jude.

*The kitchen!*

He knelt down and slowly crept underneath the window lights next to him. He was careful to walk around the patch of leaves, stray pebbles and lone twigs that littered the floor around him. As he crept up towards the last window, he noticed that it was slightly cracked open. Jude quickly identified the lone figure, when his eyes became level with the stranger's. The Magi's dark purple eyes glared towards the middle window to Jude's right. Their essence was filled with both power and mystery. He wore a long baggy navy robe with a matching hood, which laid at his back. Marius stood at the stove with his back to both Bishop and Jude. As Bishop turned his attention back towards Marius, Jude repositioned himself in the dark corner next to the window.

"We have to be quiet, my son is still upstairs sleeping in his room," said Marius.

"How is he doing?"

"He will be fine thanks to Vance."

"Great. I am glad to hear it."

"I am just happy it's over," said Marius handing Bishop a small cup.

The two of them took a place at the kitchen table. Bishop's back was facing Jude's sight, but after a couple of sips from his cup, Bishop rose from his seat.

"Mind if I switch you chairs?"

"Um. Sure my friend," said Marius.

Marius and Bishop switched seats, and soon Bishop's dark purple eyes glared at the window Jude peered through. Jude's heart quickened and his stomach did more flips than he could count. He was trapped in between wondering if Bishop had discovered him, or if he was just daydreaming. Marius broke the silence.

"Everything okay?"

"Yes. Yes, I'm sorry. I just thought I felt something."

"Well we have to make this quick, my son's friends will be here soon."

"Very well," said Bishop sipping his cup. "The prisoner refuses to talk. We have not been able to uncover anything."

"Are you sure? Maybe your men just aren't asking the right questions."

"Trust me, he won't talk," said Bishop shaking his head.

"How do you know?"

Bishop took a long sip from his cup. "Because after questioning, he bashed his forehead into the side of his cell. He's dead."

"By the name of Pith."

"I am afraid we will have to go through with the plan, or all will be lost," said Bishop.

Marius' head tipped down towards the table, but Jude heard nothing for what felt like minutes.

"I know it is difficult, but it is the—."

"No! I won't do it!"

"Marius."

"I refuse to put my son in that kind of danger," said Marius.

"Marius you know that if there was another way, we would not be here. Plus your son has talents. You were at his match, you saw him."

"He still has a lot to learn."

"You know the consequences if we do not go through with it my friend."

"I said no!" said Marius slamming his fist on the table.

"Very well."

"I am sorry."

"As am I my friend—as am I." Bishop stood slowly from his chair. He took one last sip from his cup, before placing it on the table. He raised his hood over his head, and started for the living room.

"Wait," said Marius extending his hand towards Bishop.

Bishop stopped in place, but did not move or turn around. "They have done it you know."

"Done what?" Marius stood slowly from his seat. His eyes appeared both wide and worried.

"The enemy has infiltrated our city's walls, and has made contact with your son," said Bishop turning to face Marius.

"When did this happen? Who has made contact? Tell me!"

"Both are wise but unanswered questions. The gods refuse to shed light in the darkness that creeps over our borders. Rune has went against their will, and has haunted me the last couple of nights, with vague dreams and nightmares of what will soon come to pass."

Silence.

"If I do what you ask, if I give it to him, he will become their next target. They will never stop hunting him," said Marius.

"Not before he has had time to become as strong as the gods have destined him to be."

"But what of the curse? I do not believe any parent could bestow such a thing on their own child," said Marius cradling his face in his hands.

"Which do you fear more, losing your power or losing your son? Because for the first time since I have known you, I am uncertain," said Bishop.

Marius' face sprang from the comfort of his hands. His eyes widened, bringing with them both shock and anger. "How could you? How could you ask me such a question? Eli is my life. I would give up anything for him."

"You may not have to if you trust the gods—and trust me," said Bishop.

"Will you protect him?"

Bishop finally turned around and faced Marius.

"What?"

"If I should fall, and I am not able to be there for him, will you protect him?"

"With all my power."

Footsteps on an old surface sounded far away.

"Dad," said a voice from the direction of the living room.

Jude returned his attention back towards the kitchen, and saw Marius cleaning the stove. Jude looked around and saw no sign of Bishop. He hugged the shadows in the corner, knowing that it would not be long before Bishop exposed himself, and discovered Jude's presence. After a few seconds, he decided he would rather be discovered at the front of the house instead of the back. He walked slowly and carefully around to the front door. He knocked twice, waiting for Bishop to reveal himself from an unknown area. After a few seconds the door opened.

"Ah Jude my boy! Come in!"

# DRUNK WORDS, SOBER THOUGHTS

The clouds clung to the moon's embrace while the wind turned its will against the two boys, as they made their way to the Forgotten Forest. Eli was ecstatic to find his friends Jude and Sia waiting for him at his house, once he was released from the Medicinal Quarters. Thanks to Vance, Eli felt nearly brand new, except for a few bruises and body aches that came and went at their own accord. Sia had told Eli that she was going to swing by Meara's house, and the two of them would meet him and Jude at the Forgotten Forest. Eli could barely wait to see Sia again. She was all that he thought about, during his short stay at the Medicinal Quarters. Even though Eli was meeting Meara and Sia soon, he realized that it had been a while since him and Jude had hung out, just the two of them.

"Wait, so what was my dad telling you and Sia before we all left?" Eli stepped over a large root that erupted from the ground.

"He was telling us that Anya has organized a mandatory training session tomorrow at six o'clock in the morning."

"For everyone?"

"No, it is only for Sia, Pang and I," started Jude as he examined their surroundings. "However, I heard that Vance is taking volunteers from the Academy, to help defend the castle while we are at war with the Necrosis."

"That Vance is amazing I tell you! I was feeling like I had been disembodied before my last healing session with him," said Eli feeling good enough to run.

As the two of them reached the beginning of the fog, Eli recognized the familiar melody that entranced him the last time he was in the Forgotten Forest. A mixture of water, drums, wind and chimes filled the air. Eli was relieved to remember that this meant they were close.

A gasp came from Jude's direction. "Whoa! Do you hear that?"

"That catchy melody? Yes," said Eli laughing.

"It is incredible. I have never heard anything like it. Do you know where it comes from or how it was created?"

"Not a clue."

Jude had asked Eli countless times if he knew where they were going, which Eli took no offense, because he had asked Zane the same questions before. That is when memories of his night out at the Forgotten Forest with Zane hit him. He was walking through the very fog, and on the very path, he had been on when he was with Zane.

"So Jude."

"So Eli."

The two of them laughed hysterically for a second, while the ground rumbled and the tree that blocked their path submerged.

"Can I ask you a personal question?"

"Sure," said Jude.

"When Bree passed, how did you deal with it?"

The tension grew thick and if it were not for the forest melody, silence would have dominated the forest around them.

"Not well. I am still dealing with it. I just take it one day at a time—as textbook as that sounds."

"But what do you do when past memories of the two of you comes up? See it's been happening to me, and I keep trying to shake them off and ignore them, but it's difficult."

"Well that is the problem," started Jude. "Why ignore good times you have had with someone who has passed? Shouldn't you keep those as close to you as possible so that you can always remember them?"

"I suppose so, but won't that make it harder to deal with it?"

"For me it makes it easier, because then I feel closer to her. But then again, that is just me. I cannot speak for everyone else," said Jude with a shrug.

The small shapeless lanterns and vast number of trees, sparked familiarity in Eli's mind, as the large, open square space appeared before them. Everything was exactly as Eli remembered, except hardly anyone was swimming. Instead, everyone was either at Inzanity, or sparring with the wooden dummies to their left. Long lines snaked around in an arch of eager participants, ready to do battle with the lifelike sparring partners.

"Did you see that?"

"What?"

"That dummy just body-slammed that guy!" said Jude pointing towards the sparring area.

"No way!"

As Eli took a few steps towards the line of participants, Jude grabbed his shoulder.

"Before the night is over, we definitely have to try that out. However, we probably shouldn't keep the girls waiting, if they are already here."

"Good idea," said Eli.

*I have a kiss waiting for me anyways.*

Eli led Jude up the stairs to Inzanity, and found himself hopping two steps at a time. He became more and more excited to see Sia, as they got closer to the top.

"This place is awesome," said Jude when they made it over the last step of the large tree trunk.

"Man! All the tables are full!"

The entire tree trunk, which served as Inzanity's floor, was covered with a wide variety of partygoers. It was Jude who spotted Sia and Meara at a table next to the bar, in the very back corner of Inzanity. As Eli and Jude made their way through the tables, Eli noticed many abrupt and obvious stares from the people around them.

"The Prodigy of Pith is here! He's my man just so everyone knows," yelled a female voice from no clear direction.

"I hate when people yell that title at me," said Jude.

Eli felt like he was nearly going to fall over. He would love it if people acknowledged him everywhere he went, and called him by an awesome title like Jude's.

"Are you serious? Come on, it's kind of badass if you ask me."

"I don't know."

"Well from what I heard, you earned it. So why not be proud of it?"

"I *was* proud of it. You are right, I earned it, and I was happy I did. However, when people started yelling it at me everywhere I went, it lost its meaning. Plus I do not feel right that the people of our city choose to remember my one accomplishment, and ignore the countless people who died in the process. I guess what I mean is, I would think it was badass too if people did not make such a big deal out of it."

"Yeah I hear ya. I mean if you want, I could always start a rumor that your middle name is something ridiculous. That way people will stop calling you by that title," said Eli.

"What about 'The Plague?' That way people will leave me the Pith alone."

"No no it has to be something cool. What about 'Big J'? You know 'Big Jude.' You could make it an acronym for short if you wanted," said Eli.

"No I am afraid that one freaks me out."

"You're right. Too weird."

As the two of them finally made it to the table, Eli noticed that Meara and Sia were already sitting next to each other.

"Ah you didn't save me a seat," said Eli leaning down to kiss Sia. He was both mortified and confused when she turned away. "Okay. Well Meara, do you mind sitting next to Jude so I can sit next to Sia?"

"Yeah I do mind. So lets keep it moving," said Meara rolling her eyes.

"Eli, you and Jude just sit together okay," said Sia pointing to the seats in front of her.

Eli turned to Jude as they sat down. "Wanna be my date?"

"I don't know. I have a three drink minimum," said Jude.

"Wow you're high maintenance."

"So Meara, I finally finished the design of the back of the dress," said Sia smiling.

"Good for you," said Meara as she stared out over Inzanity.

"What dress is that?" asked Eli.

"So Jude, six o'clock tomorrow?" asked Sia.

"Yes, six. Sounds like we are in for quite the day too."

*Hmm, maybe she didn't hear me.*

"Do you know what the training will be on, or what we will be doing?"

"Not a clue. But if I had to guess, I would say team combat tactics, since we will be working directly under Anya," said Jude.

"I'm getting a drink," said Meara getting up from the table and heading to the bar.

Eli watched Meara talk to a guy at the bar while she ordered a drink.

*I wonder what is wrong with her. She is not her usual loud and playful self. She was so much more talkative last time we were here.*

"So did you see how great Eli was at his match?" asked Jude.

"No I am afraid I missed it," said Sia.

Eli felt like he had just hit his head, and was sure he must have overheard her. "Wait what?"

"I missed the match. Sorry E'," said Sia.

"You didn't go?"

"No, and I—am—sorry. Are you mad?"

Eli felt her and Jude's eyes on him. "No, I just didn't know that you weren't there— that's all."

"Well you missed an amazing fight. I have never seen Eli so agile and skilled before. I was blown away," said Jude giving Eli a punch on the shoulder.

Meara plopped down in her seat sipping a drink. Sia asked the obvious question that everyone else appeared to have.

"No drinks for us?"

"Since when am I a server," barked Meara.

"Ew. Well what are you drinking anyways?" said Sia.

"That Mors in Speculo drink," said Meara chugging it down.

"Meara!" yelled Sia snatching Meara's cup away from her mouth.

"You have three seconds to hand that back before you catch my fade."

Eli was completely confused as to what was happening in front of him—and what exactly a "fade" was. As far as he knew, Meara and Sia were best friends, and always had been, since he had known them both. When Eli looked over to Jude, he saw the same awkward expression on Jude's face that he was sure was showing on his own.

"One," said Meara.

"Meara you should not be drinking this and you know it. Besides, you are a lady, and a lady does not over-drink," said Sia shaking her head.

"Two."

"Fine take it!" said Sia slamming the cup down on the table in front of Meara. "I need some air. Excuse me." Sia abandoned her seat and headed towards the stairs.

"Look around! You're outside honey! Air is all around ya!" yelled Meara across the bar with her cup in her hand.

"I'm going to see if she's okay," said Eli following Sia.

*Jude is going to kill me for leaving him alone with that lunatic.*

Eli made his way through the dozens and dozens of people that blocked his way. When he made it to the stairs, he saw no sign of Sia. As he made his way down the stairs, he took advantage of the view to scan the area for her. When he made his way down the last few steps, he stopped and looked around, realizing there were way too many people.

*It will take hours to find her.*

Turning around to make his way back up the stairs, a thought crossed his mind.

*I'll just try one spot, and if she isn't there, I give up.*

He turned back around and headed to his left. He followed the small river for a few steps. When the lake's familiar calm and dark surface came into view, the next thing he saw was her reflection. He walked through the muddy grass around the lake's shore, until he found her. Without any words he took a seat next to her.

"Wanna talk about it?"

"Not really," she said staying fixated on the lake.

"What's wrong? Talk to me."

"What is the point of me telling you 'no' to you asking me if I want to talk, if you are still going to ask me to talk?"

For the first time, Eli felt himself genuinely angry with Sia. He understood that something was going on that he was unaware of, but that didn't give her the right to be completely hostile towards him. He reached in to give her a small kiss on the cheek. She quickly pulled away.

"Will you stop!" yelled Sia.

"What is you're problem?"

"Your immature pay attention to me clingy act. I find it irritating," she snapped.

Eli felt confused, angry and hostile all at once. He had not done anything to her that he knew of.

"I'm sorry if I bothered you. All I wanted to do was help," he said getting up from his spot and heading back towards Inzanity. He covertly looked over his shoulder a couple of times while he walked away, to see if she was looking or following him, but she wasn't. The climb back up the stairs of Inzanity felt longer than usual. A cascade of assorted leaves rained down upon him, as he covered the last few steps. Quickly getting back to the table, he noticed an unusual sight.

"Wait, so what did the crazy shopkeeper say again?" Meara was laughing hysterically at her and Jude's conversation.

"Descendit cum roaches, or something like that. I do not even know what that means," said Jude shrugging.

"It means 'down with the roaches," said Meara nearly falling over.

Eli took his seat next to Jude, happy to be back with his best friend. "What's so funny?"

"I was telling her about this crazy shop I visited in the Market District earlier today," said Jude.

"What happened?"

"You're not really going to make him tell the story all over again are you?" said Meara.

Jude and Eli looked at each other in unison.

"Alright I am back," said Sia taking her seat.

Eli made no effort and had no desire to look her way.

*Sorry Jude, I think the nickname 'The Plague' has already been taken.*

"I will buy us some drinks. First round is on me. Well second round for Meara," said Jude with a smile.

Eli felt like the real Meara had been abducted in the short twenty minutes he was gone when he saw her smile. Once Jude had left the table, Eli felt like he was in hell. The two girls stared back at him as if he was two seconds away from being interrogated. Sia's gaze however, had nothing on Meara's, which looked like she was going to poison his drink once he turned around.

*If the Three Brothers really do exist, someone please tell them to take me now.*

"So Meara, you look nice today," said Eli trying to lighten the mood.

"I look like crap. Thanks for reminding me."

"Your hair looks effortless. Don't worry, I don't think you look like crap. He doesn't know what he is talking about," said Sia.

"Wait what? I just told her that she looked nice," said Eli angrily confused.

"Yea, but she was serious, you clearly weren't," said Meara with a glare.

"How do you know if I was serious or not. For the record I was. But clearly you know me better than I know myself," said Eli looking around to see if anyone was listening.

"Don't yell at her Eli!" snapped Sia.

"Back with the drinks," said Jude sitting down with four cups.

"Thank the gods," said Meara.

"I got us all some drink called 'Anti-gravitatis.' I don't have a clue about what it does, but the person at the counter said we will thank him later," said Jude passing everyone a drink.

After a few sips of his drink, Eli felt like he was floating away. He found himself constantly looking down at the floor and the table, to make sure that he was still sitting in his seat.

"Man that rocks out loud," said Meara dancing in her seat.

"Yes, it is pretty good," said Sia.

Eli looked over to Jude, who was doing what looked like dancing in his seat. Unsure on whether or not Jude was aware of what he was doing, Eli leaned in closely. "Doing alright buddy? I know you don't usually drink."

"Oh I'm good my brotha!" yelled Jude.

"Shh buddy you're loud," said Eli trying hard not to laugh.

"Have you ever realized how catchy this music is? It is like some soothing hypnotizing melody an evil witch plays to lure young children into the forest before she eats them," said Jude still moving.

Eli decided to go ahead and laugh right along with his friend. He downed the last bit of his drink, and after feeling like he floated into space, found himself laughing uncontrollably with Jude for no reason. Eli barely noticed when Sia and Meara rose from their seats.

"Next round is on us. Want to come?"

Eli and Jude both looked at each other, and then erupted into uncontrollable laughter. As the two girls left the table, the mood at the table seemed to turn completely opposite from what it was earlier. Inzanity felt more merry and enjoyable. Jude and Eli made idle conversation about topics that Eli forgot about three seconds after talking about them. He didn't care what they talked about; he was having fun.

"Man I am so glad we went out tonight buddy," said Eli wrapping his arm around Jude.

"Whoa whoa whoa! You better not be throwing in the towel, we still have two things on our list! Dummy fighting and fish nighting! I mean night fish. Wait it's coming to me. Night fishing!" yelled Jude.

Both Eli and Jude erupted into laughter. Some guys at a table behind them said "cheers" to Jude and Eli, after telling them a joke that made both tables laugh hysterically.

"Alright we are back," said Sia holding two cups.

Meara came back shortly with two cups as well. Sia kept a cup and handed Jude the other, just as Eli had stuck his hand out to receive it. His hand stayed frozen in the air, as he remained shocked by the cold shoulder Sia was giving him. He slowly extended his hand to Meara for his drink instead.

"Nope. Both these babies are mine—sorry!"

*This is freaking ridiculous. What are we five and telling each other that 'you can't play with my toy?'*

"Meara you obviously are mad at me about something. Why not spit it out already?"

"I don't know what you are talking about."

"Meara we are friends, the least you can do is tell me why you're mad at me," said Eli trying to be as respectful as possible.

"Friends? Is that what you think? We are not friends, because I have seen how you treat your friends," said Meara

"And how do I treat them?"

Meara downed her first drink, burped into her arm, and then downed her second drink before continuing. "You stab your friends in the back! That's how you treat them!"

"I've never done that to any of my friends!"

"You liar!" yelled Meara grabbing Sia's drink, and throwing it in Eli's face.

Everything had happened so fast, that Eli wondered how it all happened. One minute him and Meara were arguing, the next she had thrown a drink in his face, and jumped over the table, grabbing him by the collar of his shirt. It took Jude and Sia to tear her off of him. Sia held Meara's arms behind her back in an attempt to restrain her.

"You are disgusting Eli Brassie! You are filth! You murdered my brother! You murdered Zane! He was your friend!" yelled Meara as she kicked to break free.

"We should go," said Sia dragging Meara towards the stairs.

"He trusted you!" yelled Meara while Sia dragged her down the stairs.

So many eyes stared at Eli after Meara and Sia had disappeared from view, that Eli felt like he was dreaming. As he turned back towards Jude, who had taken Sia's seat across from him, he saw the shock on his friend's face.

"What the Pith!"

"She blames me for Zane's death and she's right," said Eli.

"Stop right there. Don't even start thinking for a second that you need to feel guilty for what happened in the Trials. You both went into that match knowing that one of you would eventually die, no matter if you were on a team or not. Plus you had no choice, since Pang controlled Zane. Do you remember what happened? Do you remember when Zane came to and told you that you had to kill him because he had no control? Or are you blocking everything out so you won't have to deal with it?"

"I'm not blocking it out. I'm just still coming to terms with it."

"Come on," said Jude getting up from the table and walking towards the stairs.

Eli followed his friend out of Inzanity. He made sure to keep his head down, so he would not have to see the stares he knew were posted around him. Jude led Eli down the stairs and back to the sparring area they had passed earlier. The lines had significantly diminished when they got there. A smirk appeared on Jude's face.

"How about some aggression training?"

Eli felt himself start to feel better. As one of the sparring dummies returned to its stationary position after defeating a shorter boy, Eli took his place in front of it. The limbs of the dummy turned softer as they came alive, while eye and nose sockets materialized on its face.

"I accept your challenge," it said.

As Eli prepared himself, two wooden swords appeared in the dummy's hands.

"Defend yourself!" it said in a rough muffled tone.

Eli had summoned a war blade, just in time to block both attacks. As the dummy overpowered him, Eli heard the chants and cheers of the others behind him. He canceled holding off the attack and rolled around to the back of the dummy. He turned around just in time to catch the dummy executing a spin attack. With both swords out at its sides, the dummy spun around vigorously in a repetitive full turn, as it closed in on Eli. Eli parried one sword attack and then dodged the next, for a few cycles into the dummy's attack until it hit home—sending him face first into a dirt pile.

A muffled battle cry emanated from the artificial opponent. "Victory is mine!"

Eli looked up to see a hand waiting for him. He grabbed it knowing it was Jude's. As he turned back towards the dummy he had been sparring with, he saw the face he never thought he would see again on its shoulders.

"You have to do it," said Zane.

"No!"

Eli darted towards Zane, hoping to reach him before he disappeared. Before he could get to him, an arm had a tight grip on Eli's wrist. He turned around and found Jude staring at him with a confused expression plastered across his face.

"Eli what are you doing?"

Eli looked at his friend and then looked back at Zane. The dummy stood stationary void of any life. Eli came to terms with the fact that there was no other explanation, other than the fact that he had imagined Zane a few seconds ago.

"Can we go?"

# COVERT AFFAIRS

Jude knew somewhat of where he was going on the way back from the Forgotten Forest. He could tell that Eli had a lot on his mind, and that Jude would need to be the one, for the most part, to be doing the navigating.

"I think I know what happened to you back there. If it makes you feel any better, it has happened to me as well," said Jude.

Eli looked up for the first time since they had left.

"It has?"

"Yes. I see Bree every now and then as well. My only advice for you, is to come to peace with Zane's death, and don't run from any thoughts of him."

"Got ya," said Eli.

"If it makes you feel any better, I know they are having the funeral ceremony in the morning. I can go with you, if you were thinking of attending."

"Why?"

"I don't know. Maybe for one last goodbye or something."

"No I mean, why would you go with me to pay respects to Zane? He hated you, and I'm pretty sure you hated him too," said Eli.

"I will let you think about that one for yourself. The point is, I will go with you if you need someone to go with. I went to Bree's with Jed, and he filled me in on all the proper attire and all of the customs."

"What time does it start?"

"Five o' clock in the morning."

"How long is it?"

"A little over an hour," said Jude.

"What about your mandatory training session? It starts at six o' clock in the morning. You will be late, and I'm pretty sure Anya will not be happy if you are."

"Well Anya is not my best bud now is she," said Jude with a smile.

"Alright. But only if you're sure."

After exiting the forest, Jude noticed that Eli became more talkative than he had been. Jude wanted to ask his friend if he knew why there was so much animosity from Sia earlier, but he did not want to bring up any ill feelings. Jude filled Eli in on proper attire for the funeral ceremony in the morning. Since Zane was of the Weapons Masters bloodline, red ceremonial attire would be the only appropriate clothes to wear. Neither Eli nor Jude had any red attire, so Jude volunteered to ask his mother and Jed if they had any that they could fit. If they didn't, Jude decided that he would just go ahead and buy some from the Market District tonight, without Eli knowing.

The Western Hold was quiet when Jude turned the corner from the main gates. Eli continued to talk about his visit to Erudite Hall with his dad.

"I just didn't realize how unfair The Council can be sometimes," said Eli.

"It may sound unfair, but at least the Erudites have not given up. The day that the Erudites give up on their dreams, that is the day that someone needs to step up and take the lead."

A hand grabbed Jude by his wrist from behind, causing him to jump. Eli noticed Jude's recoil and instantly turned towards his direction. The scent of urine and garbage doused the air around him. His chest was bare and his pants were tattered.

Both the hair on his head and face appeared to be untamed and unclean. For every one tooth he had, there were three missing.

"Please, anything you have would mean so much," said the man.

"Whoa get your hands off of him," said Eli.

Jude stared deep into the man's eyes. He saw nothing but pain and hunger. The man released Jude's wrist at Eli's request, and slowly turned the opposite direction.

"Wait," said Jude.

The hunger was even more prevalent in the man's eyes, when his gaze returned to Jude's.

"What is your name?"

Curled eyebrows and a tilted head, told Jude that the man was not expecting the question.

"Tedric—Tedric Gregory," he said approaching Jude.

"You better back off corpse."

"Eli shut up," whispered Jude. "My name is Jude Bray. It is a pleasure to meet you Tedric." Jude reached into his pocket, and returned with two silvers. When he held the silvers out to Tedric, the man just stared motionlessly.

"Jude what are you doing? He's probably swindling you," said Eli.

"Shut up it's my money." Jude returned his gaze to Tedric. "Go on—take it."

Tedric took the two silvers from Jude and instantly released two tears. The tears ran slowly through the many wrinkles and crevices that clung to the man's gaunt face.

"Thank you. You are too kind. I have not eaten in days," said Tedric.

"Can I ask what happened to you?"

Tedric's eyes widened and his lips parted slowly before he responded. "No one ever cares enough to ask me my name or how I came to be—this."

Jude could tell that Eli was getting both bored and uncomfortable. The constant shifting of his posture and his heavy breathing, did nothing short but divulge every ounce of his dwindling patience. When neither Jude nor Eli responded, Tedric continued.

"Like I said my name is Tedric Gregory. I inherited the Weapons Master bloodline. Over the years I worked extremely hard mastering all of my abilities. I even advanced through the Academy at a rapid pace. I was an Operative by the age of twenty-two—."

"Yeah okay," said Eli shaking his head repeatedly. "Only the best become Operatives. They are paid well for their missions as well. Operatives go on to be legends—not homeless."

Jude was both shocked and insulted by Eli's comment. He quickly elbowed his friend in an attempt to silence any pending insults.

"Well you are right. Operatives *usually* do go on to be the stuff of legends. That probably would have been my fate if I was not betrayed," said Tedric.

Tedric's comment had immediately grabbed Jude's attention. "Betrayed?"

A tear ran from Tedric's eye, as he stared at the silvers that laid in the palm of his hand.

"It is okay. You do not have to tell us," said Jude.

"You are a kind young man."

Jude smiled before turning towards Eli's house. Eli quickly followed with an eagerness that showed that he was ready to go.

"It will be the end of you!" yelled Tedric.

A shutter ran through Jude's body. He felt anxious and nauseous. He felt like he had just got caught doing something wrong. When he turned around and laid eyes on Tedric, who was now a few blocks away, he found himself speechless.

"What did you say?"

Tedric remained just as silent and still as Jude for a few seconds, before responding. "You are a kind young man—and it will be the end of you."

Countless thoughts rushed through Jude's conscience. As they came and went, they were forgotten almost instantly.

"Come on J, let's go."

Jude followed Eli back towards his house. The air seemed colder and heavier when they came across the Lin Kitz corner.

"Why did you even give him money? He was creepy looking to begin with," said Eli shaking his head.

"Because I know how it feels to be hungry."

"Well so do I, I have gone without breakfast and lunch before in the same day."

"Sorry E but you don't. You have never went days without food—I have, and so has he. When I looked into his eyes, I saw the hunger. I could have given him a leaf off of one of my mom's garden vegetables, and I am sure that he would have been equally grateful."

"Whatever. I don't think he looked that hungry."

"I know because I am a survivor of the beast of hunger and starvation. I am forever scarred," said Jude.

Jude was not surprised that Eli did not understand. Aileen always told Jude that Marius was blessed to always have an honorable job that was able to more than provide for his family. After Jude's dad had died, Jude remembered that his family had always struggled to keep everything they had. Getting a job at the Academy library was the biggest blessing for Aileen, because they allowed her to work as many hours as she desired.

Even though they have been stable for the past year, Jude will never forget the sleepless nights fueled by empty stomachs and rivers of tears. There were times that Jude had wished that he had anything in his stomach, just to keep the stomach pains at bay, long enough for him to succumb to his dreams.

*I never want to have to go back to filling up on water from my washroom sink, just so I can go to sleep at night.*

As Jude walked Eli up to his door, he could smell the aroma of Marius' hot cider in the air.

"Want to come in?"

"I do, but we have to be up really early tomorrow for the funeral ceremony, plus I have that training from the abyss to worry about. That reminds me, we never went night fishing," said Jude.

"Oh yeah that's right."

"How about if I am not too exhausted after training tomorrow, we go after that? It will probably be day still, but we can always go regular fishing."

"Sounds like a plan!"

"Hey, if you are not doing anything tomorrow after the funeral ceremony, I would check out Vance's recruitment. We could really use someone smart guarding the city."

"Alright, I'll think about it," said Eli opening the door.

"Feel better buddy."

◆ ◆ ◆

Fox used the walls around him to help guide himself down the dark and wet corridor that seemed to go on for miles ahead of him. As his eyes submitted to the shrouding darkness, his right hand finally ran across something that caught his attention. A small crevice dug deep into the stone that housed it. Fox reached his hand inside, and was not surprised by the small rough lever that sat erected from the bottom of the crevice. He retracted his hand and looked up at the ceiling above. Darkness cloaked every inch of the area above him. He glanced back at the adjacent wall, and then the floor beneath him. He saw nothing but darkness around him, so he re-examined the wall holding the lever.

*I'm getting bored with this.*

He grabbed two small rocks that he found on the floor, and placed a scrap of paper from his pocket at his feet. After two hits from the rocks, a spark lit a small flame on the edge of the paper. While Fox twisted the paper to keep the flame from burning too fast, he held the flame above his head. Large sharp spikes hung upside down, caked with clutter and broken skulls. After a few minutes of thought, he hugged his back to the wall alongside the crevice and away from the spikes; and quickly pulled the lever before pulling his hand back. The spikes above him shot down so fast, that the momentum made Fox lose his balance, before he dashed away. Light poured down in front of him, erasing the darkness as it continued.

"Not too difficult," said Fox as he began to walk towards the light. His ear twitched as he began to debate on whether or not he heard something behind him.

*Clever.*

When he launched himself into a sprint, he could hear the piercing behind him growing louder. As the doorway filled with light ahead of him grew closer, the floor in front of Fox instantly dropped into a trench. Jumping on to the wall next to him, he ran along its rumbling rough surface, barely avoiding the trench. Barreling into the doorway of the new room, he darted to the side of the doorway and clung to the wall. A countless barrage of daggers and swords whizzed through the doorway. A few seconds later, the sound of metal on stone sounded throughout the room. When Fox gazed around the chamber he was in, he noticed fifty or more long stone steps, cascading down from a large stone table, that was drowned in a ray of light—which shot down from the ceiling. An assortment of large leaves and plants grew out from the corners and walls of the room. The aroma of freshwater and fresh cut grass filled the air.

The sound of Fox's knuckles cracking on both hands, echoed while Fox ascended the stairs. When the last five steps leading up to the stone table came into view, Fox stopped.

"Shall we introduce ourselves?"

When he turned around towards the door he had entered through, a large figure inhabited the doorway. At first glance it appeared to be a large man. However, as Fox sized him up, he came to the conclusion that his abnormally large stature and broad muscle capacity, were too enormous for him to be human. The stranger had to be over eight feet tall, and had arms larger than many of the trees Fox had seen around his city. While Fox descended back down the stairs, the figure slowly approached Fox, as he matched his steps in unison. As Fox came to a halt in front of the mute stranger, he confirmed that no one else had followed him.

"So what do they call you?"

A patch of spikes surrounded the gloves on each hand of the stranger. His bare large chest rose and fell simultaneously, along with the grunts that vibrated through his gritting teeth.

"Let me guess, your name is Eugene right?"

The room echoed the sound of a small rockslide, as Fox barely sidestepped the creatures charge. Coming to a halt, the creature slowly turned back towards Fox, and brought both its enormous fists up to its face. The spikes on both hands shined like a fresh blade.

"Hand-to-hand combat huh? Sure! Why not?"

Fox mimicked the creature's fighting stance. As the creature brought its powerful fists down, Fox leaped over his head, slamming the bottom of his heel into the creature's neck, before rolling to the ground and up to his feet. Fox was so pleased with his own speed, that he didn't see the creature's attack when his fist came back for a second attack. The stranger backhanded Fox, sending him flying across both stone and leaves. The taste of metal and blood filled his mouth, while he forced himself back to his feet. Charging the creature, Fox ducked under its first swing and let loose a few consecutive punches to the creature's abdomen and sides, before ducking under the next attack. Grunts emanated from the creature, as it staggered from Fox's attacks. When it regained its composure, it clasped both hands together before smashing them into one of Fox's shoulders. Fox felt his body slam violently flat on its back, as his vision went hazy. Fox shook off the particles that floated in his vision. When his vision finally cleared, he was able to barely dodge a stomp from one of the creature's large hooves.

The room echoed with pursuit, as Fox sprinted away from the creature. The creature's large stature and footsteps, made the ground beneath Fox rumble, which eventually made him lose his balance. Air whipped at Fox's neck when his body hit the ground face first. He looked up to see dozens of spikes, resembling the ones on the creature's hands, projecting from the wall in front of him. He looked back at the stranger to see both his fists straight out preparing for another attack.

"I see you don't play fair. That's okay, because neither do I," said Fox jumping to his feet.

When Fox ran to the wall, he heard the small sound of the piercing spikes soaring through the air. He kicked both feet up on the wall and ran along its smooth but sturdy surface. Dozens and dozens of spikes followed closely behind him, burying themselves into the wall he ran on, as Fox continued to flee. The creature kept its stance, while its projectile attack followed Fox's movements.

*Come on you may be big, but they have to be there somewhere.*

Pain both cold and hot shot through Fox's side just before he fell from the wall, and tumbled to the ground. He chose to ignore the obvious blood that he knew coated his hand after pulling the spike out. Fox's stomach sank when he watched the creature leap high above his head, higher than any man could ever jump. The creature's head almost touched the top of the chamber before its large feet began hammering down over Fox's body. Fox rolled to the side and evaded the attack, but was thrown by the impact of the creature hitting the ground. The room seemed to spin around him, as he felt his feet leave the ground. He felt his head wobble around in a circle once the creature held him at eye level by his black tunic. The three red diamonds glowed on the creature's body.

*Ah there you are. Now which one?*

When the creature let loose a roar, Fox's hair blew as if a strong wind had blown passed him.

"You know, you really should do something about your miniscule vocabulary; and also that breath," said Fox watching the creature's other hand prepare for a final attack.

*Got ya!*

Fox's punch into a small crevice of the creature's neck was not as strong as he would have hoped, but it was still all he needed to be released from the creature's grasp. When Fox fell to the ground, he rolled and returned to his feet. He found himself coughing from the lack of air, which made the pain in his side feel worse.

The creature fell to its knees and sat there motionless, except for its eyes, which moved around savagely.

"Trying to move is pointless," said Fox with a smirk as he wiped some stray blood from his face. He unleashed a fury of punches at the creature's face, which flung in all directions, as it took in Fox's consecutive attacks in their entirety. Time seemed to escape Fox until he lost the feeling in his right hand. He looked down to see swelling, tissue and blood.

"Now look at that. You made me break my hand."

The creature's body slammed into the floor after Fox's roundhouse kick. Fox picked the creature up by its neck and glared into its eyes. "You will not get in the way of my mission."

Forcing his injured hand into a fist, he fought through the pain and anxiety that came with the movement. He punched a targeted area under the creature's arm, and watched the eyes roll back in the creature's head, as blood fell from its nose and mouth.

"The ladies don't call me a knockout for nothing."

Studying the corpse of his fallen enemy, Fox kept an eye out for any idle movements. Even though he knew the creature's heart had ruptured, and that there was no way it could still be alive, years of combat had taught him that carelessness is a sign of weakness. As Fox made his way back up the cascading stone stairs he had climbed earlier, he applied pressure to his injured torso. When his body stood completely in the ray of light that permeated from the ceiling, anger caused him to grit his teeth. He stared down at a bare stone table that betrayed him. Looking up into the light above him, he cursed.

"Where are you?"

# A PLAN REVEALED

Jude had woken up early in the morning, after going to the Forgotten Forest with Eli. After bathing, grooming and getting dressed, he had gone to Eli's house. Jude was able to borrow two Weapons Master ceremonial robes from Jed. Once Eli had changed into the fiery red robe, the two of them headed for the southern gates. Eli was able to see Zane one last time, before the shepherds carried his body down the pilgrim's path. Zane's detached arm had been carefully placed next to his body, so it appeared as if it was still attached. Aside from a few scratches and bruises, his body had been restored to look almost new. Eli had told Jude that he didn't need to attend the rest of the ceremony down the pilgrim's path, but Jude persuaded him to reconsider. After Zane's baby cherry blossom tree had been planted on his grave, and the sunrise hit its petals, Jude and Eli turned back for the city.

"I'm glad I stayed for the whole ceremony. I feel a little better about everything," said Eli.

"Good, I am glad to hear that. I felt the same way after coming here for Bree's."

"I must admit that I had expected the ceremony to be longer. Didn't you say that it was usually an hour to an hour and a half?"

"Yes, I guess I was wrong," said Jude.

*Bree's felt like over an hour to me.*

"So that means you won't be late to your training session."

"I am *not* looking forward to that," said Jude.

"I hear you. She is pretty hardcore I hear."

"And that is an understatement from what *I* hear."

Both boys erupted into simultaneous laughter.

"I still have to admit that I wish I was going with you. I mean both you and Sia are there. I understand that Pang clearly won, but I still feel like that spot was reserved for me," said Eli.

"Don't worry, it won't be long before you and I are side-by-side storming the field," said Jude hoping he was saying the right words.

"Yeah I guess."

The city was livelier than ever when Jude and Eli passed through the southern gates. Merchants, small children and students joined the people returning from the funeral ceremony, on the streets of the city. Dogs barking, small conversation and muffled footsteps filled the air.

"Hey can I ask you a favor?"

"No."

Jude found it difficult to hold back laughter when he saw the shock on Eli's face. After a few seconds, he found himself laughing uncontrollably.

"I was kidding," said Jude nudging Eli with his elbow.

"You slug in a ditch," said Eli laughing along with Jude. "I was wondering if you would mind if I went with you today—you know, to your training session."

Jude studied his friend for a few seconds. He did not mind Eli going with him. On the contrary, having his best friend there to support him would be just what he needed after the past week. However, as he looked into Eli's unyielding blue eyes, he began to wonder if there was an ulterior motive behind his request, since showing support had not been one of Eli's strong points in the past.

*I know I should not doubt you. You are my friend. I just don't know.*

"You sure you don't want to enlist in Vance's recruitment? You will get to fight with us."

"I won't be fighting *with* you guys. I will be stuck back here in the city, counting the passing clouds and picking my nose."

"The fact that you admit that you pick your nose, reinforces my decision to never shake your hand again, or let you touch me again."

"Jude I'm serious."

"Well you are free to go wherever you like. If you would like to go with me to the training session today, I will definitely enjoy having you. However, just remember that your 'spot' you feel like was taken from you, is still there. If it were me and I really wanted to help Kismet and help myself advance, I would enlist with Vance, because then I would at least be fighting. If you go with me, you will just be sitting at home while the rest of us are at war. The decision is of course yours."

The running water from the fountain in the middle of the Market District, vaguely muffled the commotion that was present by the surrounding townspeople. As the Academy stairs rose up in front of him, Jude felt a new sense of confidence. The Academy gave him support and hope. He knew that behind those walls, were people and mentors that would help him get stronger and better himself, so no one could stand in his way. The mentors of the Academy were his second support team that would help make sure that no one ever hurt his friends or family.

"I want to go with you."

The outer area behind the Coliseum was completely opposite of what Jude had expected. After following the directions that Marius had given him, Jude exited through a set of hidden back doors. Jude and Eli found themselves on what looked like a large flat plain. The soil was dried to the point of cracking, and there were no signs of vegetation or life, except for the small patch of trees that rose in front of a small group of tall mountains, far off in the distance. The air was filled with the scent of fresh pottery and burned wood. Jude was surprised to see that Sia and Pang had beaten him there. The two of them stood a significant distance apart, in the center of the plain. There was no sight of Anya, which eased his anxiety. A set of large boulders tucked to the side a few yards from Sia and Pang, caught Jude's attention.

"So maybe you should watch from here," said Jude.

"What, afraid I'm going to embarrass you?"

*No, just afraid that you will forget that no one here is against you. We are all on the same team.*

Eli was staring at Jude, which made Jude realize he had missed what Eli had said.

"Huh?"

"I was just saying that I wanted to say hi to Sia, then I will come back and watch from here. Cool?"

"Sure."

The two of them joined Sia and Pang in the center of the plain. Pang was dressed in a light gray battle tunic with black combat pants. A lone ring hung from a silver chain on his neck. Sia was dressed in tight-fitting black leather pants, with a short red long sleeve shirt, which exposed her naval.

"Hey guys," said Jude looking from Pang to Sia.

"Hey Jude," said Sia showing a small smile.

"It is about time you made an appearance," said Pang with a smirk.

Eli quickly approached Sia with a grin on his face.

"Hey Sia."

Jude nearly laughed at the child-like grin on Eli's face. Jude was surprised to see Eli so excited to see Sia, after the awkwardness of the previous night.

*I probably won't get it until I meet a girl that I like as much as he likes her.*

"Hey Eli. How are you?" she said.

"Pretty good," said Eli grabbing her hand.

The tension filled the air as Jude watched Sia snatch her hand away. Jude had to give Eli some credit for keeping his composure after her resistance. Jude hoped to avert any further awkward moments, so he decided to change the subject.

"So, has Anya showed up yet?"

"No. If I had to guess, she plans to arrive right at six," said Pang with a smirk. He played with a scar on his hand.

"Because you know everything right," said Eli.

Jude jerked his head to Eli surprised by the outburst.

*Oh no, not today.*

Pang looked as if he did not even hear Eli's comment. He began to fiddle with a different scar on his arm. When he realized that everyone was staring at him, he turned his attention to Eli.

"I am sorry did you say something?"

"I said you think you know everything," said Eli.

"No I believe you said 'because you know everything right,' or something to that extent," said Pang.

"Don't think our match means that you're better than me, because you would be surprised at what I can do."

"Really? I did not know you could do anything other than cower in fear at the sight of true power. My apologies for my error," said Pang bowing to Eli.

Jude had anticipated Eli's next move, and was relieved he was able to catch Eli's wrist as he swung at Pang.

"What is your problem?" asked Jude furiously.

"What's my problem? I think you should ask him what his problem is," said Eli snatching his wrist from Jude's grasp.

"You verbally attack me and then claim I am the one with the problem. I should have killed you when I had the chance. I won't make that mistake again—I promise you," said Pang.

"I will drop you!" yelled Eli.

"Like the way I dropped you and your big mouthed friend in the Trials?"

This time Jude had to hold Eli back by his waist to keep him from attacking Pang. The sight of his best friend fighting over petty issues that were from the past, embarrassed him.

*I knew you would make me regret this.*

"Alright that is enough!"

Eli stopped his attack on Pang at the sound of Jude's voice.

"You are my best friend, but honestly I do not know what is wrong with you. You are not supposed to even be here. You did not earn the right to be here, we did. I let you come as a favor and instead of appreciating the courtesy; you pick a fight with my friend who has earned his spot here. Why don't you see that we are all on the same team here? We all fight for the same purpose."

"No we don't. Not yet, but we will. I plan on asking Anya to allow me on the squad," said Eli in a matter-of-fact tone.

"Eli don't. You are only hurting yourself," said Sia.

"What? You don't want me on your squad Sia?"

"It is not that 'E', it is just that there is no honor in being given a reward that you didn't earn. There is only shame."

"What? I don't understand. Out of all the people here, I would expect you to be the first one to be on my side."

"I am on your side. I just don't agree with what you are saying. Anyways, Anya will never go for it," she said.

"She will if most of the team votes with me. I know I can't expect Pang to be on my side," said Eli glaring at Pang.

"You've got that right. I did not sign up for babysitting," said Pang turning his attention away from the conversation.

"But if you and Jude vote in my favor, she will have to," said Eli.

"I am sorry E', but I won't support it."

Jude saw hints of the pain and disappointment in Eli's eyes. He hated to see his friend hurt, but he agreed with everything that Sia had said. He did not understand why Eli would want to be on a squad that he did not earn the right to be on. It felt embarrassing and dishonorable, and Jude felt embarrassed for his friend. When he saw Eli's eyes fall on him, he knew what was coming next.

"What about you Jude? You're the current big shot of the Trials. Clearly your vote holds a little more weight than the others. Will you stand with me?"

Jude became more aware of the scent of the burning wood around him, as he stared into the blue of Eli's eyes. The soft breeze that blew across the plains carried the scent gently passed Jude's face. The chirping of the birds far away, broke upon his back, as he saw the strands of Eli's hair hide his face.

"It would not be right. I am sorry I can't," said Jude.

As Eli stared back at Jude, Jude could tell that his friend felt betrayed. Before Jude could say anything else to soften the already given blow, Eli turned his back towards all of them, and retreated back towards the Coliseum's back doors.

"Eli wait," said Jude.

When Eli reached his hand out to open the Coliseum doors, they opened. A tall figure stood in the doorway accompanied by another figure, slightly shorter than the first. As Jude watched Eli walk through them and into the Coliseum, he wondered if he had made the right decision.

# COMBAT 101

Jude felt his nerves grow more and more present, as he stared into Anya's eyes. Her short black hair blew lightly in the wind, as her unyielding gaze seemed to analyze everyone. Anya was dressed in black leather combat pants similar to Sia's, except for a few small tears on the legs. A large black utility belt held a small dagger that hung from her waist. The top of her body was covered with thin but sturdy metal plate armor with matching shoulder armor. Anya was soon accompanied by a younger man, that Jude was sure was around Pang's age. He was dressed in beige combat pants and a thin sleeveless piece of silver chainmail armor, that hung over a black long sleeve tunic. His short brown hair sat perfectly groomed and controlled on his head. His arms hung crossed behind his back, as his gaze matched the stern and unyielding posture as the General. Jude recognized him as Lieutenant Conall Titus.

"I am General Anya Briars. You will refer to me as General. It is my job to properly train you in the art of combat. First and foremost, when I am talking there is no talking, no shuffling and no sneezing. When I point to you, you will report in!"

Anya's gaze washed over Jude, Sia and then Pang. Silence enveloped them for a few seconds, before Anya's eyes locked with Jude's, as her finger pointed towards his direction.

"General! Jude Bray, Combat Specialist, reporting in!"

Anya's gaze fell right next to him, which Jude assumed that Sia would be next.

"General! Sia Wyatt, Magi, reporting in!"

398

"General! Pang Quarrels—assailment specialist, reporting in!"

Jude could not see any change in Anya's expression. Even the young man that accompanied her, kept the same expression as hers.

*I would at least like to know if I completely blew it at my introduction.*

"Rule number one of combat. You are all a team. *We* are all a team. When you are all on a mission you will work together, you will eat together and you will sleep together—well figuratively speaking. You will fight together, and for some of you, you will die together. You three stand before me, because you have proven your skill in battle far exceeds that of your peers. Individually you can accomplish greatness. Together, you could be legendary. Any questions?"

"Yeah I have a question," said a familiar voice behind Jude.

*Oh please oh please, don't tell me that you are that stupid.*

Eli soon appeared next to Jude. The scent of sweat permeated from his direction, and heavy breathing accompanied the scent.

"Who are you? Report in," said Anya.

"Um I'm Eli. Eli Brassie. I was in round three of the Trials."

The silence returned as Anya stared motionlessly at Eli. Jude began to think that he had been wrong in telling Eli he could come to the training session. He had already tried to attack Pang a couple of times, and as far as Jude was concerned, had made everyone including Sia uncomfortable.

"No you are ignorant, oblivious, dishonorable and disrespectful," said Anya moving her folded arms to the front, and finally displaying a hint of emotion.

"What? I haven't done anything. How am I dishonorable, disrespectful and all of those other things?"

"Exactly! You have not done anything except disrespect me, your peers and embarrass yourself. Lieutenant Titus, please escort our unwanted guest out of my sight. Effective immediately!"

For the first time since he had arrived, Conall moved from behind Anya and clasped Eli by the arm.

"Get off of me!"

"General! Permission to use force," said Conall.

*Wait what? Force?*

"Permission granted Lieutenant!"

Both a yell and a groan came from beside Jude, as he heard Eli fall to his knees. The sound of his friend struggling filled the air while Conall apprehended him.

"Wait! General," said Eli.

"Cease and desist Lieutenant," said Anya.

Jude wanted to turn around and see what was going on, however he was afraid if he did, that Anya would punish him for breaking rank.

"So the uncivilized and dishonorable child finally learns respect. Speak!"

Jude heard the fast footsteps behind him, and soon Eli stood back at his side, along with Conall.

"General! I request a spot under your command!"

Jude felt so angry with his friend. He knew Eli had some kind of undercover plan for coming to his training session today. Jude wanted so badly to think that Eli was just coming to show some support finally, since he had not normally shown him any support since they had started at the Academy.

*Can you just be normal for once?*

"You *request* a spot?" said Anya.

"Yes General sir, I mean mam."

"While my first instinct is to laugh at you, I must ask, why do you believe that you deserve a spot on this squad?"

"I've waited my whole life to become an Agent. To be the best is my life's mission," said Eli

*No, you just do not like to lose. Do you ever stop lying?*

"Your life's mission eh? So you are telling me that every day you were training for excruciating hours, relinquishing all distractions and only living to better yourself. Am I right?" said Anya.

Jude knew the answer to this question. While he cared about his best friend more than anything, he knew that Eli had not been disciplined with his training. Jude had noticed that Eli had become so caught up with his social and love life, that training had taken a backseat to everything else. Even Marius had talked to Jude, asking him to motivate Eli to get back on track, but Jude knew there was nothing he could say to break Eli out of whatever world he had been living in. Jude just wondered if Eli would be honest about it.

"No mam I haven't."

"No what?"

"No General—I haven't," said Eli.

"My apologies but I am confused. We have hundreds and hundreds of students that dedicate their entire lives every day to training and bettering themselves, in hopes of receiving the opportunity to be under my command. What makes you so special that you can slack off and act foolhardy, but still be able to gain such an honor?"

"I know General. I just got sidetracked that's all. I am hoping that if the team—*squad* would have me, you would reconsider," said Eli.

"So the team supports your admission do they?"

"Well I hope so," said Eli lowering his head.

Jude kicked himself for it, but he closed his eyes. He could not believe what was going on around him.

"Quarrels!"

"General!"

"Do you vote in favor for the admission of this individual amongst your ranks?"

"No General!"

"And why not?"

"General! I have fought hard and sacrificed a lot, in order to get where I am standing. I deem it unfair to have an individual receive the same opportunity, when they have displayed zero acts of honor, discipline and above all—skill," said Pang.

Jude saw a ghost of a smile pass across Anya's face as she turned her gaze to Sia.

"Wyatt!"

"General!"

"Do you vote in favor for the admission of this individual amongst your ranks?"

Jude's eyes opened wider at this conversation. The tension became so thick in the air, that he found it too difficult to breathe through his nose, so he began breathing deeply through his mouth.

"No General!"

"And why not?"

"General! I do not believe that there is any honor in being given something that others have had to work for. Anyone that receives anything that they did not earn, dishonors themselves and their name. It is a disgrace," said Sia.

Jude knew that Eli was feeling even more betrayed than ever now, and would feel even more more betrayed, once Jude agreed with his fellow comrades.

"Bray!"

"General!"

"Do you vote in favor for the admission for this individual amongst your ranks?"

*No mam I do not.*

Jude felt like Eli had brought all of this on himself. Jude had completely supported Eli enlisting in Vance's recruitment, which would give him the exact same opportunity to fight in the war, just in a different way. The fact that Eli had abandoned the opportunity and tainted Jude's reward for his hard work, training and studying for the Trials, upset him.

"General! I vote in favor to admit him!"

Jude felt Sia and Pang break rank and turn their heads his direction.

"And explain to me why you go against the unanimous decision of your fellow comrades to admit an individual who has no honor or respect for his people, his land or his comrades."

"General! I have known this individual for many years. I believe that even though he can be reckless and undisciplined at times, his courage and love for our land and people, will prove him to be an asset to the cause," said Jude. He found himself fidgeting in place as Anya's glare sent chills down his spine.

"You know Bray, I was impressed by your match. You show much promise and skill. When I look at you Bray, I see an aspiring Operative that was born to make the right decisions, and does not know the meaning of giving up. However, you do know that if I take your word and admit this individual, and he fails to live up to your words, I can no longer have either of you present on this team. Such failure would be completely dishonorable and would warrant both of your dishonorable discharges. I cannot risk the safety of your fellow comrades, my men or myself, just because of your childhood loyalty. Are you really willing to put your future and reputation on the line for him?"

*I promised I would protect him, in any way I can.*

"General! I understand, and I will take full responsibility for him."

Anya's gaze turned to Eli, and as it did, Jude felt half of himself regret his decision, and the other half support it.

"Last name?" asked Anya.

"Brassie!"

"Brassie fall in line!"

Anya soon returned to her previous position she had been standing in earlier. Conall soon joined her, taking up a spot behind her on her right. His arms returned to a folded position behind him.

"Rule number two! You may live, fight and die as a group, but never put the safety of your comrades ahead of your mission. Your mission is always, and will always, be your number one objective. You can ask me how many of my fellow comrades I have seen slain in battle so I could accomplish my mission, and I would tell you around five hundred. However, I would be lying because I lost count at around five hundred. As harsh as it sounds, every last one of you are expendable and replaceable. Our city, land and families are not!"

Jude watched as Anya and Conall retreated a few yards back, before turning around and regaining their previous posture.

"Each and every one of you has a role on this team. I want all of you to look to your left and then to your right. These people hold your lives in their hands. Roles are important, because they ensure not only the safety of the mission, but also the safety of your fellow comrades. Respect your roles and you increase the success rate of your mission. Travel outside of your roles, and some of you may pay with your very lives. Due to the fact that you are all inexperienced in real combat, your roles will be whatever I tell you they are—for now. If you can all display the skill needed to become true Agents, I believe even you will be surprised at what you are capable of after a little training. Exercise number one, I will need a volunteer. Fresh meat has always been my fancy, Brassie front and center!"

Jude watched Eli scurry in front of them until he was standing in front of Anya.

"Face your comrades Brassie!"

Eli turned around and immediately locked eyes with Jude, who returned his gaze. Pain washed over Eli's face and a scream became audible, as Anya kicked him in the back of his leg and twisted both his arms behind his back in one quick movement.

"Bray!"

"General!"

"Front and center!"

Jude took his spot a yard or so in front of Eli and Anya.

"You are in the midst of battle. In a split second you notice your comrade is seconds away from death. You have ten seconds before he becomes a casualty. Save him!"

# CASUALTIES
# OF WAR

Eli felt the feeling in both of his arms go in and out, while he remained pinned under Anya's grasp. Jude had looked taken back when Anya had told Jude to save him. Eli had wondered at this point, if Jude even cared to, judging by the expression on his face.

Jude took off in a sprint towards them. Eli was shocked at his quickness. While Jude did not move as fast as he heard Vampires did, he still ran faster than anyone Eli had ever seen. Spinning daggers formed in front of Eli.

*What? I didn't do that!*

The spinning daggers launched at Jude, who did a single front flip that hoisted him high in the air, before hurling a small object down at Eli. Darkness shrouded Eli when he saw a large shield materialize above him and Anya. He heard a small ding and soon saw a small vial shatter immediately as it hit the floor. A cloud of black smoke erupted around Eli. He coughed and coughed but could not hold his hand to his mouth because of Anya's tight grip. The grip on his arms suddenly loosened as something rough slid against his arm. When he tore away from her grip, he ran out of the smoke and looked back. The large cloud of black smoke shrouded everything leaving everyone blind to what was going on inside of it. A light breeze blew across the plains, pushing the smoke away. A large black snake stood coiled around Anya gripping her tight. Its long tongue licked the air next to her. Suddenly the coils disappeared, and

Jude's arms replaced the grip around the General's neck. After Jude was completely himself, he retracted his grip.

"Anticipating your opponents defense. Nice work Bray. You pass," said Anya.

Jude, saying nothing, saluted the General and then returned to his post in line.

*I must have a lot to learn, because not responding to the General seems rude and disrespectful to me.*

Anya went through the same exercise with the remaining comrades. Sia successfully rescued Jude with a combination of an earth prison and a sleeping spell. Pang had no trouble rescuing Eli from Anya's grip. Eli didn't know why Pang didn't just go ahead and use some of the Blood Magic abilities that he had used on him and Zane in the Trials. Instead, he allowed a few of the daggers to hit him in order to get in close to Anya. Once he had a hold of Eli, he ripped him so forcefully out of Anya's grasp, that Eli found himself double-checking to make sure that he did not leave any of his limbs behind. Eli unfortunately was the only one that did not pass the first exercise. He had tried to save Jude from Anya, by matching Anya's projectiles with his own. He didn't know why he failed to realize that the General's attacks would be stronger than his own. After a minute of failed attempts and bleeding wounds, Anya held Jude up and slit his throat with her finger, and told everyone that Jude was a casualty.

Eli had felt ashamed when he fell back in line. He refused to look up to see the expressions of his fellow comrades. He decided that there was nothing that he could do about it now.

"Exercise number two!" Anya threw the dagger that hung from her belt to the floor in front of her. "Lieutenant Titus and I are the enemy. This dagger in front of me is a piece of vital information that is a threat to Kismet security. Retrieve this information by any means necessary! Brassie and Wyatt! You're up!"

Eli walked alongside Sia to the middle of the plains in front of Anya and Conall. He was both happy and upset at their collaboration. Fighting next to Sia was a dream come true to him. However, after the way Sia had been acting the past couple of days, he was not sure how he was feeling about her anymore. Anya's voice broke him out of his thoughts.

"Begin!"

Eli took a direct approach, trailing the barrage of daggers that he had fired at both Anya and Conall. Just when he thought that he had done something right, Conall jumped in front of the attack, holding up his forearms in front of his chest and clenching his fists.

"Total defense perimeter!"

A circle of several shields appeared around him and the General, spinning in a revolving motion at high velocity. The attack blocked all of the daggers. Eli noticed that the shields also blocked both Anya's and Conall's vision, so he kept up his speed in hopes of securing the dagger. Suddenly the shields branched out further, slamming into Eli's face and sending him flying back.

"Arrow barrage!" yelled Anya.

Eli shook off his daze, and looked up to see Anya's attack closing in. The back of Sia's long brown hair cut off his vision when she leaped in front of him.

"Speculum!"

Eli jumped to his feet just in time to see Anya's arrow barrage fire back towards her. Conall's shields had disappeared, and just as they did, Anya and Conall saw the impending attack and both leaped out of the way to avoid it. Sia took the opportunity to close the distance between her and the dagger, and left Eli behind as she went into a sprint. Anya and Conall both returned to their feet in unison. Conall summoned two swords as Anya met Sia in battle with a series of throwing daggers that materialized above her head, before launching. A haze formed in front of Sia, causing the throwing daggers to dissolve before getting too close, but she was helpless to Conall who bashed her across the face with the pommel of his sword. While Sia rolled across the dry ground, Anya summoned a sword and shield in her hand, and with Conall, surrounded Sia. Sia let out a scream as she fired flames at the two of them while rolling to avoid their combined attacks.

*Sia!*

Eli ran to the brawl and charged Conall in the back, who rolled to his feet. A second scream drew Eli's attention, who found Sia trapped in Anya's grasp with a dagger to her throat. A voice sounded from behind him.

"Forceful constriction!"

Eli felt something at his feet, and as he looked down, he discovered a long chain coiling up his legs. When the chain finally covered his body all the way up to his shoulders, he knew he was helpless. The dagger at Sia's neck disappeared and was replaced by Anya's finger that ran across it. Eli felt a finger run across his neck as well, before the chains around him disappeared.

"Failed! Both of you are casualties," said Anya with an irritated expression on her face. "Fall back in line!"

Eli followed behind Sia. When he caught up to her, he checked for any signs as to what she was thinking. When no signs were visible, he decided for a more direct approach.

"Why didn't you try harder?" he asked.

"*Me* try harder? You must be certified crazy."

"Because of *you*, we lost and it's making me look bad!"

He did not understand why Sia didn't try as hard as she had in the Trials.

"You do not need my help when it comes to looking bad," said Sia glaring.

"The one, and I mean one, thing that I hate worse than losing, is a snake. Are you doing this to get back at me for joining the squad? Are you mad that you lost that little debate?"

"Get your hands off of me!" said Sia.

"Get my hands off of you? I'm not even—," started Eli as he looked down at his hand. Her wrist was flushed at the spot where his hand firmly grabbed it. He instantly let go.

"I'm sorry I—."

"Why didn't you go after the dagger? It was like two feet away from you!" she yelled.

"It was? But you were in trouble."

"Yes it was! And even if I was in trouble, the mission was to retrieve the dagger, and my danger was creating the best diversion. You made me look like a fool in front of the General," said Sia quickening her pace.

Eli was left feeling both hurt and confused as he contemplated Sia's words. He didn't understand how she could be mad at him. He didn't even realize that the dagger was next to him. All he knew was that she screamed and she was in trouble. He thought that she would like that he at least tried to come to her rescue.

"Quarrels! Bray! You're up!"

Anya and Conall returned to their original positions.

Eli watched as Jude and Pang walked to the center of the plains in front of Anya and Conall. Anya again threw the dagger in front of her.

*Humph. I bet Jude is happy that he gets to be paired up with his new best friend.*

"Begin!"

Jude whispered something to Pang and then broke out in a sprint. Anya leaped forward, and just as her mouth opened, Jude flipped high in the air and Pang soon ran from underneath him, shoulder-charging Anya. Conall charged Pang with his sword and shield in hand. Pang sidestepped in all directions to avoid Conall's attacks. However, Conall was extremely quick with a blade and soon nailed a direct hit at Pang's leg. Pang collapsed to one knee as Conall charged in with his sword in hand. Eli saw Jude leap high in the air behind Conall, before tossing something down at him and Pang.

"Bombs away!" yelled Jude.

The large black smoke, which Eli had seen from earlier, shrouded Pang and Conall. When the smoke dissipated, Conall was trapped with both his hands tangled behind his back by Jude. Blood ran down Pang's leg, as he forced himself into a sprint at the dagger. Anya had returned to her feet and was standing ready with her bow in hand. When Pang closed in on the dagger, Eli thought it was over. However, Pang dove out of the way as an arrow whizzed past him. Jude let go of Conall just in time to dodge the arrow.

"The intelligence is jeopardized!" yelled Anya.

Conall quickly returned to his feet. Ignoring Jude, he charged for Pang. Jude pursued Conall, and after executing a front flip that sent him towering above everyone, Jude came crashing down as an enormous arachnid.

"Whoa!" said Eli as the ground made him stagger.

The spider was so enormous, that it crushed Conall and Anya as it hit the ground. The two of them rolled out from underneath the spider. Conall took to a frontal assault with a sword in each hand, while Anya took a long-range approach after summoning her quiver of throwing daggers. The spider snapped at Conall when he swung his sword at one of the spider's colossal legs. The spider snatched Conall with its two front legs and began spinning him. White string cocooned Conall until he was unidentifiable. After dropping Conall's immobilized body on the floor, the spider stampeded towards Anya, who summoned a sword and shield, and met the spider in battle. The spider matched Anya's swings with bites of its own.

"Intelligence retrieved," said Pang.

Anya's sword and shield dissolved when she turned towards Pang. Jude returned to his normal form while Anya began to free Conall from the webbing he was ensnared in. Once the Lieutenant was free, the two of them met Pang and Jude in the middle of the plain.

"Objective complete," said Anya.

The General and Lieutenant saluted both Pang and Jude, before taking their original place. Jude and Pang fell back in line while nudging each other along the way. Eli hated to see Jude so friendly with Pang. He failed to understand why his best friend could even stand Pang. Pang was conceded, dishonorable, weird and just a bad guy as far as Eli was concerned. When the two of them returned to their spots, Eli took a look back down at Pang, who was looking straight ahead.

*You have no idea how much I would like to sucker punch you right now.*

Pang turned his head slightly to Eli's direction, as if hearing his thoughts. He smirked at Eli before blowing him a handless kiss.

*Okay now I just want to beat you with shovel.*

"Never! I mean never! Put the safety of a comrade before your mission. That is cardinal rule number two. We saw the end result of this by Wyatt and Brassie. Their mission had two casualties and a failed mission, as a result of their ignorance. With a failure like that, you mind as well exile yourself from that shame," said Anya.

Eli heard a small grunt from Sia's direction and found himself taking a half step away from her. He did not intend to make them fail their exercise. He thought he was doing the right thing by wanting to protect her.

The remainder of the training session was spent running and other various physical exercises. Eli had tried to find excuses to venture next to Sia to try and talk to her, however every time he did, she would end up running faster or striking up conversation with Jude or Pang. He took the hint as she was still mad at him, and decided to give her space.

When the sun began to set, Anya called everyone, except for Conall, to the center of the plains. Conall headed towards the Coliseum saying nothing to anyone in the process.

"It is my job to fully prepare you for what lies ahead. That is why I will take it upon myself to fully brief you on the mission tomorrow."

Eli followed Anya and the others into the same double doors that he had seen Conall enter a few seconds ago. Anya ushered them down a long corridor that Eli had not seen when he had first arrived to the training session. After several minutes, a large arch leading into an enormous dark-stoned chamber, came into view. In the middle of the chamber was a large round black table, accompanied by matching chairs that surrounded it. Eli took a seat in between Sia and Jude. Anya took a seat at the head of the table with her hands firmly clasped in front of her. Eli noticed that the three bloodlines insignias were etched into the table's surface.

"Welcome to one of three briefing rooms in the city. Since none of you have ever been on an official mission, I do not expect any of you to really have anything constructive to add to this briefing," said Anya.

Conall soon entered through the arc Eli had entered through. He did not take a seat, but took a firm stance at Anya's side with both hands behind his back. After a nod from Anya, a stack of white paper folders appeared in his hands. He laid one folder flat on the table in front of Pang, before proceeding to Jude.

"As I speak, Lieutenant Titus is passing around your mission intelligence. In these folders contains nearly all of the information that we have on our enemy, and any supporting targets."

A snow-white folder was placed flat in front of Eli. His hand came up to open it, but then recoiled, afraid that he was breaking some unknown rule. Conall handed a folder to Anya before taking a seat next to her. When Anya opened her folder, Eli noticed Jude mirror her action, followed by Sia and Pang. Eli opened up his folder, and his eyes instantly fell on an image of a grotesque and vile creature. The site was so unsettling, that he found himself turning his head. After taking a deep breath, he returned his attention back towards the parchment in front of him. His site then fell on a large block of words and information. Anya cleared her throat as if confirming the room's attention still laid on her.

"Your enemy target is the undead creature known as a Necrosis. Their origin is—classified. Their exact numbers are—unknown. Their leader is—unknown. Their strengths include immunity to pain, increased speed, abnormal strength, accelerated healing and regeneration of body parts. Their fighting style is limited to scratches, bites and removal of enemy limbs. Please note, while their brains are not capable of utilizing any type of weapons or magic, one bite from these creatures will result in immediate fatality. Their weaknesses include the inability to coordinate with others, as well as the absence of problem-solving skills. Elimination of this target can be achieved by the following: One, is a direct and efficient attack to the heart. Second, is the complete removal of the heart from the target's body. There have been reports of some failing to regenerate after decapitation, however this method has not been tested nor confirmed. Your mission is the complete elimination of every last enemy target. Are there any questions?"

Silence hung in the room as Anya's gaze went from Conall to Pang, and eventually around to Eli. Jude's hand rose up next to him.

"General! How is their weakness to poison?"

"Their weakness to poison has not been tested, so therefore, their weakness to poison is unknown."

"General! Have there been any other sightings of enemy targets?" asked Conall.

"Negative Lieutenant. As of this morning, our sources indicate that they hail from the western region only. Any other questions?"

Eli looked around the table at the people who would be his first real comrades. While he always looked at Jude as his comrade, it was nice for them to be officially on the same squad. He always knew that Jude would have his back. That was something that he never doubted for a second.

When his gaze fell on Pang, Eli felt his face scowl. There was something about Pang that Eli did not trust. He looked suspicious and didn't seem to be the trustworthy type. Eli did not understand why Jude thought Pang was worth hanging out with. When Sia's beautiful light purple eyes met his, Eli felt himself blush. The moment was short lived since the minute Sia's eyes met Eli's, they looked away.

"Great progress today. I apologize for this next part. Tomorrow, we all leave for the border of Kismet. We will all meet at the main gate at four in the afternoon. We should arrive at our campsite a little after sunset. I suggest that all of you go home, get some rest, and prepare yourselves for your first real mission. It is uncommon to send new Agents out on a mission as dangerous and imperative as this, especially after only one day of training—and basic training at that. However, time is not on our side. I shall pray that the Three Brothers watch over all of you, and that we will all meet at this very spot after the battle. Dismissed!"

When Eli rose from his chair, he instantly looked towards Sia, who met his gaze briefly before quickly exiting.

*This ends now.*

# SURRENDER

$E$li bid farewell to Jude quickly after the group's departure. He wanted to make sure that he didn't miss Sia. When he exited the Coliseum, he caught the familiar sight of her bouncing curls, proceeding down the stairs. After some minor resistance, Sia had agreed to go to their secret spot, so Eli could talk to her about a few things. The two of them had no issues opening the statue door of the woman that led into the meadow. The second they had approached it, it instantly swung open. Sia had declined when Eli had proposed them going for a swim in the hot spring. So the two of them had decided to sit in the midst of the smooth green meadow, with the hot pink, purple and blue flowers that laid spread out throughout the blades of grass. Eli felt as if he was sitting across from a stranger whenever he looked at her. She sat fumbling with a pink flower while her gaze stayed down as his stayed up.

"Hey," he said touching her hand.

She paused looking down at his hand on hers.

"I'm sorry for earlier today—if I hurt you. I don't know what came over me. I just hate to lose. It doesn't make it okay—what I did to you. I'm *really* sorry I guess is what I am trying to say."

She remained silent, turning her attention back towards the flower she was playing with earlier.

"Can you look at me? I want to see your face," he said.

Her light purple eyes gazed into his, as a small weight was lifted from his shoulders.

"What are you thinking right now?"

"I have missed this place," she said.

"Me too. But I've missed you more."

She cracked a small smile for a few seconds before it left. When he realized that words were far from her lips, he continued.

"What has happened to us?"

"What do you mean?"

"I feel like we took a step forward the last time we were here. But recently, I feel like we have taken a million steps back. I feel like the sight of me makes you angry, and you hate being around me. I'm embarrassed to say it—but it hurts," he said.

"I am sorry if I hurt you, that was never my intention. I understand completely if you don't want to see me again."

"See like that! Why do you do that? It's like you don't even care. It's like you have already given up on us when we have just started!"

She looked away from his gaze.

"Look at me!"

Her face turned quickly back at his. Her eyes were wide and filled with shock.

"I'm sorry for yelling, I just can't take it anymore. I need some answers."

"I don't know what to say," she said.

"I just need the truth—right now."

"I am just in a dark place right now," she said looking down slowly.

He put a curled finger under her chin and gently lifted it up until her eyes met his.

"Talk to me."

"I have always tried to fight the way my father treats Mik and I, from changing me or having an influence on my life. I have just come to the conclusion that it is impossible. I am angry and hurt all of the time. Sometimes I want to just run away from here and never come back. But I cannot do that to Mik. I am just in a dark place right now. I do not expect you to understand or want to deal with it, because I know it is my problem and my fault."

"Why do you think you have to do everything by yourself?"

"Because I have always had to since my mother left. If I didn't, then I do not know where Mik and I would be. My father never cooked for us or took care of us. We would have starved or been homeless. I am just accustomed to taking care of us," she said.

"Well you don't have to do it alone anymore. That's what I've been trying to get you to realize."

"I cannot ask you to take on that responsibility. It isn't fair."

"You're not. I'm offering it."

Silence passed over them as the furry creature with the big blue eyes scurried up and sat between them. For the first time, it let Eli pet him.

"Look, I'm not saying that I can take care of everything. But what I *am* saying, is that I want to help in any way I can. Even if it's something as small as walking Mik to school—or anything, just tell me. If I can do it, I will,"

"Eli it isn't that easy. I am just afraid that the dark place I am in will affect you, and that is not fair. I will never forgive myself if I was the one responsible for taking away what I love about you so much."

"And what do you love about me so much?" asked Eli with a smile.

He caught her blushing while she fumbled with both the flower next to her, as well as her words. "I don't know." She placed a strand of hair behind her ear. "I like how when I look at you, you see me as how I was before my father's cruelty took over my life. I feel like you don't judge me and that I can be myself around you."

"Then why don't you?"

"Honestly, I am waiting for you to leave," she said staring back at him softly.

"Why would I leave?"

"I don't know. I am just used to people never really staying around. My mom left, a lot of my friends stopped coming around, and the first boy I liked could only handle my dad for two weeks before he left too. I just don't like getting my hopes up anymore."

"Listen to me when I say this," he said staring directly into the center of her eyes. "I'm not going anywhere. I will always be right here—at your side—no matter what.

"You promise?"

"If you let me—then yes."

"How much have I hurt you?"

He felt like her question could be a loaded question, and wondered if he was walking into a trap. He felt like it was only fair that he be completely honest, since he was asking her to do the same.

"Since we are being honest, it hurt when you didn't come to my match at the Trials, the other night at the Forgotten Forest was kind of infuriating and most recently—today."

"And you are still here?"

He sighed, feeling exhausted after reliving all of the hurt feelings he had been carrying around with him the past few days. "I'm still here."

"Why? I have been horrible to you," she said.

"Because I care about you, a lot. I don't understand how I could care about someone so much but I do. I have always had feelings for you ever since we met. But when I saw you on the floor of your room the night of the incident with your dad, I realized how much you mean to me."

"I have kind of pushed you away because I care for you too, a lot. I just felt like you would eventually leave, and I wanted to hurry up and start the healing process of getting over you," she said looking down at the furry creature that stared back at her. "You are just not what I have pictured for myself—you know—in life," she said.

"Like I said I'm not going anywhere. I just need you to be with me. I mean truly be with me. There can't be any fear of who knows about us, no secrets, no more shutting me out, okay?"

She looked back up into his eyes. The purple in her eyes tore down his defenses while they seemed to dig up all of his insecurities. Her eyes rested down. She lightly grabbed his hand and placed it on the side of her face as her eyes rested on his. "I surrender."

"Surrender?" He studied her in hopes that her face would reveal any clue to the meaning of her words.

"Surrender to what?"

"My feelings for you. It hurts to fight them and I am done—done being in pain," she said. "You are kind, understanding and honest. It is rare to find those qualities in someone."

*"Anyways how was the party?" asked Jude.*

*"What party?" Eli could feel his heart beginning to beat faster than normal. As he began to attempt to quiet it, his hands became moist as he fidgeted under Jude's gaze.*

*"The party in the Forgotten Forest," said Jude.*

*"Oh yeah I was invited by my friend Zane but I didn't go," replied Eli. His stomach felt nauseous as he tried to determine whether Jude believed him.*

A loud splash of running water broke Eli out of his daze.

*I'm sure everyone tells a little lie every once in a while. Besides, my lie didn't hurt anybody. As long as I am not hurting anybody, I'm really not doing anything wrong.*

He studied his surroundings, and immediately reestablished the connection he was once feeling.

"I care for you," said Sia.

Her eyes never flinched—and he never blinked—afraid that the moment would vanish before his very eyes. His lips lightly touched her's. Even though it was not the first time he had kissed her, he felt as if it was. A rapid light squeaking jumped from under them. As the kissing slowly stopped, Eli and Sia laughed at the small furry creature that hopped up and down beneath them.

"You know, we still don't know his name," said Sia.

"What if he doesn't have one?"

The creature's small ears dropped down, as the squeaking sobs escaped from its non-visible mouth.

"Maybe we should name it," she said.

"Hmm what about Tobi?"

The creature's small tongue stuck out as it shook its head back and forth. Sia laughed at the sight.

"Either he is not a boy or he doesn't like Tobi," she said lifting it up over her head. "Definitely a boy."

"He sure likes to squeak a lot, what about Jabberjaws," said Eli giggling to himself.

For the first time the creature's baby blue eyes turned dark purple as its' squeaks screamed anger.

"Okay okay—no to Jabberjaws. Well whatever your name is, you're pretty spiffy when it comes to understanding me."

The small creature's baby blue eyes returned as it hopped up and down squeaking vibrantly.

"I think he likes that one," said Sia picking him up in one of her hands. "Am I right? Do you like Spiffy?"

The small creature's large eyes closed tight as it hopped up and down squeaking simultaneously.

"Alright Spiffy it is," said Eli holding up an open hand. To his surprise, the little creature snuggled its face next to the palm of his hand. "Hope your cat doesn't find out. He might get jealous."

The sound of the waterfall, the geyser and the light wind shrouded the air once silence halted the conversation.

"I do not have a cat."

"I know," he said.

"I am sorry. I—."

"You don't have to explain. I get it," he said meeting her gaze.

"No. I lied to you and I was wrong to do so. I owe you an explanation. I did not want anyone to know about my father—no one. I tried my best to conceal the bruises, scratches and injuries. But I should have never lied to you, and for that I am sorry."

Their eyes locked momentarily before their lips touched. Eli could not tell who had initiated the kiss, but he didn't care. After its' naming, Spiffy took off running after a firefly that had buzzed by. Eli and Sia spent time talking about the training they had undergone earlier. To Eli's surprise, Sia said she was happy when he was chosen as her partner, regardless of the outcome. She explained that even though she stood by what she had said about earning something instead of being given it, she was still happy that Anya allowed him on their squad. She also said that if he ever yelled at her again, she would "end him," which sent chills down his spine—even though he knew that he would never act that way again. After a few quiet minutes, Sia met his gaze.

"May I ask you a question?"

"Anything," he said.

"How long have you known Jude?"

"Jude? Forever it feels like. We grew up together." A montage of memories poured into Eli's vision. They were memories of Eli and Jude, the self-proclaimed unstoppable Operatives, saving the world from the forces of evil that lived in their backyard.

"He is nice. I like him," she said.

"Yeah he is a good guy. I'm glad you like him."

"You guys must be really close. I mean, he put a lot on the line today vouching for you," she said.

"I know. Even though I am grateful he did, I still don't understand why—I mean I feel bad."

"Why do you feel bad?"

"Because honestly I'm not entirely sure I would have done the same for him if the situation was reversed."

"I think you would have," said Sia kissing him on the cheek. "You have a good heart."

"Thanks." Eli could feel his body temperature rise and his face flush. Taking in a few deep breaths, he tried to regain his composure.

"May I ask you another question?"

"Sure," he said growing more curious by the second.

"At Inzanity, you told me that you didn't believe in the gods, why is that?"

"Oh—that. I don't know, I guess I have never really seen anything to make me believe that they exist—that's all."

"But our homes and the very land we sit on now, were created by them—and are infused with their magic. I mean look at where we are now, every inch of this place glows with Rune's aura—his magic," she said.

"And why does a place glowing purple mean that it came from Rune or any of the Three Brothers? Why can't the world just naturally be magical?"

"I am so confused, because everything about our people's way of life derives from the gods. Where do you believe our abilities come from? Do not tell me that you believe those did not come from the Three Brothers either."

"Look, don't get me wrong. I'm not saying that it isn't possible; I just do not think we have any evidence of their existence. Unless the Three Brothers walk up to my house and knock on my door—or find some indisputable way of proving their existence—I cannot decide to blindly believe in their existence just because our people do," he said.

"So then you do not believe in Anim either," she said with a sigh.

"Same thing, if the fallen brother shows himself, I'll believe."

Silence hung between them as the soft grass tickled Eli's fingertips. "How is Mik doing?"

"Mik? He is doing well. Well his grades could be a little better. I have been trying to get on him about it without being too overbearing. I want him to always look at me as his sister and not his mother. That way he feels like he can tell me anything," she said.

"I'll talk to him, I think I know a way to get him more motivated about school."

Sia stopped in place for the first time since they had began walking around the meadow. "Thank you."

"You're welcome," said Eli grabbing hold of her hand.

"You know Mik really likes you. You are all he ever talks about to both me and his little friends," she said.

"The feeling is mutual. I really like him too. He is probably the coolest little kid I have ever met, and he loves the bow just like me." Eli was both surprised and happy by the abrupt kiss that Sia gave him.

"Sorry," she said.

He took her in a tight embrace before their lips touched. "For what?"

Eli and Sia had said goodbye to Spiffy before leaving the meadow. After a rough start, Eli had grown fond of the little creature. The conversation was minimal on the way back to the city. Eli spent most of the time teasing Sia softly and picking a flower for her every time a new one came into view. By the time they had reached the forest edge, Sia had a bouquet of flowers in her hands.

"You know, people might think that I just got married with all of these flowers."

"As long as they think I'm the groom, who cares."

After setting the flowers aside, Eli had grabbed Sia's hand as they made their way to the main gates. When the soldiers standing guard there came into view, Eli let go of her hand. Once they were within a few feet of the soldiers, Eli felt her hand grab his as they walked passed the guards. He looked down to make sure he felt what he thought he did, and then looked up at her face. She kissed him gently on the lips as they continued towards the Market District. When Eli walked Sia up to Ms. Lowell's door, the flickering porch light washed over her.

"You know the offer still stands. You know, to stay with me. Both of you."

"I will keep it in mind," she said.

The two of them stood staring at each other with both their hands clasped together.

"What if I, you know, do it again?"

"Do what?" He kissed her lightly on her forehead, chin and then cheek.

"If I am mean to you," she said looking down at their hands.

"Hmm, how about we have a special word."

"A special word?"

"You know, if one of us is being mean to the other. The other can say the word to lightly let them know. That way no one is offended."

She began to laugh while she lightly swung their hands. He was feeling embarrassed and began to join her laughter.

"What? Dumb idea?" he asked.

"No no it is a great idea. What is the word?"

He took a minute to think about a word that would mean something to both of them. He wanted a word that reminded her of him, but something that was also neutral.

"Hmm, something not offensive, but positive. What about spiffy?"

"Spiffy? You mean our little friend's name?"

"Yeah! That way I can say 'Sia you're being spiffy.' I mean, thinking of his weird little face makes me laugh," said Eli.

"Deal!"

He gazed at her, analyzing every inch of her face. Her mouth opened slowly and paused before she spoke.

"Where did you come from?"

"That's a good question."

"Seriously," she said giggling. "You are different, but in a good way. I never pictured myself being where I am now. I mean, I always pictured myself being with a different kind of guy."

He felt as if she just punched him in the stomach with both fists. The feeling was such a heavy blow, that he wished she would have just slapped him instead.

"Oh, I'm sorry," he said.

"No no! I am sorry. I didn't mean it like that. I just pictured someone different—that's all. I am happy we met.

"Good, because so am I. I mean, as long as you were not picturing being with Pang," said Eli pretending to vomit.

"He is actually not *that* bad."

"He makes me feel like one of my arms fell asleep, and no matter how hard I swing it and beat on it, it won't wake up. He is a nuisance," said Eli feeling his temper rise.

Sia giggled for a few seconds before returning his gaze. The sight lightened his heart and made him smile. Before their lips touched, the door behind them opened. He instantly let Sia go in fear of disrespecting Ms. Lowell if she was behind the door. Mik's smooth short brown hair bounced in front of him.

"Eli!" Mik wrapped his arms around Eli's legs.

"How are you my friend?"

"I'm good, but you are still supposed to teach me some awesome bow techniques," said Mik making a pretend bow with his small hands.

"I haven't forgotten. But what's this I hear about your grades not being so good?"

"I don't know," said Mik crossing his arms and sticking out his bottom lip.

"I'll make you a deal. If you get your grades up, I will not only teach you some bow techniques, but I will teach you how to dual wield two swords."

Mik's arms dropped as his face lit up. "Really? You promise?"

"Promise," said Eli extending his hand.

Mik shook Eli's hand vigorously, while his grin grew wider.

"We really have to get to bed, it is late," said Sia ushering Mik inside.

"Okay," said Eli watching the two of them enter the doorway.

"Goodbye Eli! Bye!" said Mik waving back.

"Bye Mik."

When the young boy was out of sight, Sia's eyes returned to Eli. "I will see you tomorrow?"

"And every day after that," he said.

When Eli walked back to the Western Hold from the Market District, he could not help it that he was smiling along the way. A massive feeling of content and positive energy swelled inside of him.

*I never thought I could ever feel this good.*

A woman on the opposite side of the street dropped a bag she was carrying. Eli wasted no time running over there to help.

"Thank you young man," she had said with the biggest smile.

When the Lin Kitz statue came into view, he felt a presence closeby. He stopped to analyze his surroundings. Except for a mother and daughter going into a house, no one else inhabited the Lin Kitz block.

*I am probably just tired. I have had a long day—a long and wonderful day that is.*

When he opened the front door, he smelled the scent of warm bread and hot metal. He closed and locked the door behind him.

"Is that you son?" Marius' voice came from the direction of the kitchen.

"Yeah it's me dad. I had the best day today like you wouldn't believe!"

"I am taking a break from work right now, so I decided to make some croissants. I will be in there in a couple of minutes," said Marius.

Eli took his shoes off and set them next to the living room table. He reorganized some falling books in the living room bookcase. He looked over and noticed that the table was slightly off-center, so he fixed that as well. He took a few deep breaths as a smile ran across his face.

*The house smells amazing!*

His ears rang as his body smashed into the wall—on the opposite side of the room. A creaking above his head drew his attention. He noticed the falling cabinet just in time to dive to the side.

"Activating tactical optics," said a woman's voice.

"Son what is going on in there?" yelled Marius.

"Zero traps or explosives. Both targets detected," said the same voice.

A large cloud of gray smoke erupted throughout the room, shrouding everything around it. Many footsteps sounded nearby. Eli coughed repeatedly as he tried to return to his feet.

"Target acquired," said a voice.

"Who are you?" asked Eli towards the direction of the voice.

The smoke soon subsided as four figures dressed in all black light armor with black straps everywhere stood before him. Black cloths were tied snuggly around their mouths while black hoods helped to conceal their identities.

"Subject's name is Eli Brassie. His bloodline is Weapons Master—twenty years old. Common attack methods are the longbow and projectile assault. We want this one alive. Engage," said a woman's voice.

A bow appeared in one of the stranger's hands before he fired multiple arrows simultaneously. Eli dove to evade the attack.

"What is going on in here?" Marius entered the room from an unknown direction.

"Second target acquired. Second subject's name is Marius Brassie. Widower. Bloodline—Weapons Master, forty-four years old. Common attack methods—dual wielding and projectile assault," said the woman.

"Occult Operatives. Eli run!" yelled Marius.

Eli returned to his feet and sprang for the front door. One of the Operatives appeared in front of him instantly. Eli dove backwards summoning his bow. When he landed on his back he fired countless arrows at the Operative—who blocked each arrow with his blade.

"Subject one is on the offensive. Implementing force," said the Operative.

Eli jumped to his feet and summoned his Epee blade just in time to block an arc attack from the Operative's blade. Small explosions sounded behind Eli, but he kept his attention glued to the Operative in front of him, who was matching every one of Eli's attacks with ease. An excruciating burning pierced his back as he found himself pinned to the wall behind the Operative. He looked over his shoulder to see an arrow—unlike any he had ever seen— digging into his back.

Someone tore the arrow out of Eli's back before kicking the back of his legs, restraining his arms behind his back, and holding him down by his neck. He looked down at the floor behind him to see a pair of black leather boots, and knew it was one of the Operatives. Marius' voice soon rang throughout the room.

"Seismic Force!" yelled Marius.

Eli felt himself blown back to the wall behind him.

"Eli move!"

Eli quickly returned to his feet and ran towards Marius' voice. When he turned around, he discovered that the four Operatives had returned to their feet as well.

"Debilitate!" yelled an Operative as he leaped in front of the group.

"Retaliation!" yelled Marius.

*He's a Magi.*

Eli felt himself collapse to the floor as all feeling left his body. He soon heard the same Operative, who attacked, cry in pain. When the feeling returned, Eli quickly jumped to his feet. The sounds of a sword match sounded next to him, as Marius took on two of the Operatives in a rapid direct assault. Marius ducked under both Operatives' attacks just in time to trip one of them. The Operative hit the ground with a *thud*. The other took the opportunity and shoulder-charged Marius. As Marius soared through the air, daggers formed around him and fired back at the Operative that bashed him. The Operative dove out of the way and fired back a barrage of his own arrows.

*No dad!*

Eli found himself leaping in front of the Operative's attack. "Threat replication!"

Eli's attack mirrored the Operatives, and soon Eli found himself staring at the Operative's body while it hung motionlessly pinned to the wall behind the other Operatives. The sound of blades sounded behind Eli.

"Kai is down," said the women Operative. She stood next to the Magi from earlier. "Tristan is engaging subject two. Focus fire on subject one." She sprinted at Eli, before running into a kick that dug deep into Eli's chest, knocking him over the fallen cabinet.

He found himself winded and searched frantically for which direction was up and which was down. His arm pulled as his body was lifted from the ground and tossed into the air. The ceiling became his view until it was covered by a foreign body—who climbed on top of him—and hammered him to the floor. Pain shot everywhere when Eli tried to move his arms and legs. He opened his eyes and saw the Magi Operative standing over him.

"Amaurosis," he said holding his open palm over Eli.

Eli fought through the pain and blurriness of his vision, while he raised his hand to meet the Operative's.

"Retaliation," he said. All the energy in Eli's body instantly drained, as he found himself gasping for air. His chest and head burned while his eyes fought against him to stay open. Darkness caved in from every corner of his vision.

"Eli!" yelled Marius before Eli heard his dad's grunt and then a crash. "What have you done to my son!"

*Dad I'm here. Help me.*

"Mission complete!"

◆◆◆

Eli fought against the nausea as he tried to decipher the voices around him. When his eyes finally opened, his vision was still cloudy. A mixture of black and white radiated everywhere while he tried to focus on a single object.

"He is awake. Go get the boss," said a voice.

After a few minutes of failed attempts to focus his vision, Eli closed his eyes, and soon found himself submitting to the exhaustion that poured over him.

"Wake up," said a voice in front of him.

When his eyes opened, he realized for the first time that he was gagged, and his arms were tied firmly behind his back. He wiggled his hands in an attempt to break free.

"It is pointless to try and resist," said the voice.

The voice sounded male and sent chills down Eli's spine. Eli titled his head up, and after a few minutes, his vision cleared. An Operative sat a few feet in front of him in the brightest room Eli had ever seen. The stranger's bright hazel eyes were draped with the straight short black hair that fell across the Operative's long face. His arms were buff and he had a handful of small scars that decorated his chin and high cheekbones. The walls, the floor, the ceiling and the table in front of them, were all painted a bright and blinding white. Eli found himself blinking more than usual in response to the brightness of the room before him. He attempted to speak, but was silenced by the cloth that was tied over his mouth.

"Oh, let me get that for you," said the Operative.

When the cloth was removed from his mouth, Eli waited until the Operative took his seat before he responded.

"What's going on? What is this place? Why am I here? Where is my dad?"

"In due time. First, I believe that we should properly introduce ourselves—don't you?"

"Yeah. Okay, sure."

"You can call me Kai," said the Operative.

"Okay—Kai. My name is—."

"Your name is Eli Brassie. You are twenty years old, you are a first year at the Academy, your father's name is Marius Brassie and you are an only child," said Kai.

"How do—."

"Your favored weapon is the longbow, you are only able to cast novice level projectile abilities, you lost miserably in your first Trials of Magic, Might and Lineage, and you are romantically involved with a Ms. Sia Wyatt," said Kai.

*How does he know so much about me?*

"Okay, so you know a lot about me—so what. What do you want?"

"Ah! Now we are getting somewhere," said Kai as he sat up from his chair, walked behind Eli, and returned with a black jar.

"Eli Brassie, what I want from you is really quite simple. Our sources indicate that the Agent we are looking for has been rendezvousing with you at your home twice in the last few days.

This Agent is responsible for releasing a Necrosis amidst our streets and has infiltrated our city's security. I want his name."

"Infiltrated what?"

"I was really hoping that since I was told you were an obedient young man, that it would not have to come to this," said Kai taking the lid off of the jar in front of him.

As Kai's hand reached into the black jar on the table in front of him, a hissing sounded throughout the room. Hundreds of tiny legs moved independently under the long black coil of its thick and scaly body that laid coiled around Kai's wrist. Two long antennas moved freely at one of its ends. The antenna looked like they were as long as one of Eli's fingers.

"Do you know who this is?" asked Kai.

Eli felt himself ready to vomit at the creature.

"No? Well I will tell you then." Kai stood slowly from his seat as a sinister smile formed on his lips. "This is the rare and beautiful lingering ravage bug. They are nearly all but destroyed. I was able to rescue this little guy from a hungry mama bird that tried to feed it to her young. He goes by Agent Slate, but his real name is Ebon. He is in the same family as the centipede if I am not mistaken," said Kai as he stopped behind Eli.

Eli screamed as loud as he could, when he felt the creature's tiny moving feet on the nape of his neck. Soon he felt a heavy and long object slithering around him. He screamed again and felt something thin and soft enter and exit his mouth. He looked over one of his shoulders and saw the two long antenna of the bug wavering back and forth against his cheek.

"Get that crap off of me! Get it off!" Eli struggled in his chair against his binding.

"Shh shh shh! You see, I wouldn't frighten Ebon if I were you. They scare easily. Now where was I?"

Kai took his seat across from Eli as the creature slithered up Eli's neck towards his ear. Its antenna floated in and out of Eli's ear making his body shutter.

"Oh yes I remember. Now they call it the lingering ravage bug for two reasons. Number one, it tends to move much slower than normal centipedes and bugs, due to its hundreds of tiny legs. They say it tends to linger on whatever surface it crawls on. Ebon here has over three hundred legs—I am so proud. The other reason comes from its carnivorous nature. You see, lingering ravage bugs have a tendency to erupt into a feeding frenzy when presented with warm tissue and flesh. But other than that, they are extremely playful creatures."

Hissing radiated all around Eli, making him tremble underneath the legs that marched slowly across his body.

"Now many confuse the lingering ravage bug for the giant centipede, probably because of their many legs and similar body. I guess if we didn't want to be so technical, we could say that the lingering ravage bug is a large black centipede. A large black centipede that has an affinity for warm human tissue," said Kai.

Countless numbers of tiny legs crawled and slithered across the back of Eli's neck, as the bug ventured to his other ear. He found his body shaking non-stop, as he grew more and more aware of the hundreds of legs that marched across his neck. Suddenly Eli felt one of the hairs on the back of his neck pull. He jumped. A sharp hiss radiated from his other ear. Eli bit his bottom lip trying to prevent himself from screaming. A warm tear ran down his face.

"I will give you anything you want—please!" said Eli.

"Now the rare lingering ravage bug primarily lives in warm climates. Cold climates are too troublesome for poor Ebon."

The bug slithered to the front of his neck before dozens of its' tiny legs found his chin. Eli's mind stayed fixated on the legs that now marched up the side of his face.

"Sometimes people find them dwelling inside recently deceased bodies. The human body provides a blissful home of comfort and warmth when it is active. That is where you come in," said Kai getting up from his seat.

The bug's antenna waved in and out of his eyelashes causing him to blink. Right when it found Eli's nose, Kai snatched it away. Eli was unaware of how much air he was deprived of. The air tasted so good. He gasped for more and more air while he felt a river of tears running down his face. Eli's chest rose and fell violently while he tried to shake off the lingering feeling of the bug on his skin.

"Now I am going to ask you one last time," said Kai sitting on the table in front of Eli. The bug coiled itself around Kai's wrist like a thick bracelet. "Give me the name of the Agent you have been rendezvousing with. If you refuse to tell me, or if you lie to me, I will be forced to send Ebon in to get the information for me. I believe we used the mouth for the target a couple of months ago. Poor woman, she nearly choked on Ebon before he killed her. I think we will do the ear this time."

Countless tears fell down Eli's face like stones. He found himself hiccupping with tears every time he tried to say something. His neck felt hot and his lungs could not get enough air. "I'm—telling you—the truth. I swear. I don't know I swear."

Kai sighed heavily as he got up from his seat on the table. He brought Ebon up to his face and kissed it. "Are you ready buddy?" He slowly approached Eli sending shutters down Eli's back.

"No! Please! I swear I don't know anything. I will do whatever you want!"

The antenna dug into his right ear hole causing his entire body to flinch.

"Open wide!" hissed Kai.

Eli threw all of his weight away from the bug causing his chair to hurl him to the ground.

"So you want to take this lying down? Fine with me," said Kai. His shadow shrouded Eli, while the hissing grew louder. When the antenna reentered Eli's ear, Eli gripped his eyes closed and bit his lip.

"Get away from my son!"

Eli heard a mixture of struggles and grunts before the loud crash startled him. His chair shot up and hammered down on its metal legs. When the binding around his wrists was cut, he sprang up instantly from his seat. Kai stood motionless glaring at him from one of the corners of the room. Ebon sat coiled around his wrist as Kai petted him.

"Son are you okay?"

Eli looked over and never felt so happy to see Marius. Tears fell from his eyes as he leaped into his dad's arms. "Dad! Oh dad!"

"Shh it is okay son. I am here, it is all over."

Eli opened his eyes, and from over Marius' shoulder, he could see Bishop standing in the doorway with his arms clasped firmly behind him. Marius let go of their embrace and patted him on the shoulder. Before Eli could tell what was going on, he was swept up into Bishop's embrace. After a few seconds, Bishop pulled him away and met his gaze.

"I am so sorry my friend. I had no knowledge of this and came over here as soon as possible," said Bishop.

"It's okay. I'm fine."

Bishop looked over to Kai who had not said a word since Bishop and Marius had intervened. "I believe Kai here owes you an apology," said Bishop.

Silence hung in the room as the three of them stared at the shocked Operative.

"Well," said Bishop.

After a few sighs, grunts and rustling, Kai's gaze met Eli's. "Kai apologizes."

"Don't let it happen again," said Eli glaring.

# A WHISPER
# IN THE NIGHT

Eli felt liberated when he stepped into the night air. When he set eyes on the moon that watched over him, his heart finally began to beat normally. Eli had been blindfolded by his dad and escorted out of the room he had been held captive in. When asked why, Marius explained that the area was a black site, and that only authorized individuals were allowed to have knowledge of its location. Marius had showered Eli with apologies and random embraces on their way pass the Coliseum. Bishop had accompanied them and told Marius that he needed to have an important conversation with him that could not wait. Marius insisted on walking Eli home and told Bishop that their conversation would have to wait. It was Eli who made the final decision, telling his dad that he would be fine. After much rebellion and hesitation, Marius gave Eli one last embrace before departing with Bishop.

The Market District seemed more peaceful than ever when the fountain came into view. As Eli walked up Ms. Lowell's porch, his hand froze when he went to knock.

*It's late. Everyone has to be sleep already.*

He turned around and sat on the floor beneath him. Even though he could not speak with Sia, knowing he was close to her, gave him a slight bit of comfort. He rested his face in his hands as he brought his knees up close to him.

"Eli," said a voice behind him.

He turned around to see Sia standing in the doorway. Leaping to his feet, he wrapped his arms around her. "I'm so happy to see you!"

"Whoa! Eli what are you doing here? What is going on?"

"Can you come with me—to our spot?" asked Eli.

"Eli it is really late. Everyone is sleep and tomorrow is a big day," said Sia.

He stared back at her, hoping she would see the desperation in his eyes that he could not explain with his lips. After a few seconds, her shoulders dropped and she sighed.

"Okay, hold on I need to get a coat," she said before disappearing inside.

◆◆◆

Eli was comforted by the shock on Sia's face. It was the confirmation he needed that showed that she cared about his wellbeing. He also felt comforted to know that what he had experienced was as horrible as he perceived it to be.

"Eli that is terrible and unacceptable," she said.

"I feel like Ebon, ha, is still crawling on me."

He shuttered under the thought and was surprised when Sia mirrored his movements. Her arms soon wrapped around him and hugged him tight.

"I am so sorry that happened to you. Is there anything I can do?"

He pulled her away and met her stare. The eyes he never stopped dreaming or thinking about stared back at him. As his lips lightly touched hers, she laid back bringing him with her. The smell of fresh grass and assorted flowers filled his nose while his lips ran along her neck. Her chest rose and fell rapidly while her hands never seemed to find the spot on his back they were looking for. He stopped the embrace and looked down at her. She bit her lip and smiled.

"I mean it, if there is anything I can do, please tell me," she said.

He rose up and propped himself up on one hand. After a few seconds she joined him.

"Tell me about your day. How was it?"

She smiled and kissed him lightly on his cheek before responding. "Well besides the training session with Anya and the amazing time I had with you, I mostly stayed home and read a little."

"Really?"

"Yes why?" she asked.

"Nothing, I'm just starting to believe that I'm the only one that hates reading."

"I believe if you find the right book, you will change your mind about reading."

"Hmm I don't know," he said feeling skeptical. "Can I ask you a question?"

"Sure."

"How does one become an Operative?"

"A lot of hard work."

"Really? Well what is the difference between an Operative and an Agent?"

"There is a *big* difference. Agents are like the soldiers and warriors that will be accompanying us into battle tomorrow. They are fighters that have showed exceptional skill in combat with their respective bloodlines. Basically, Agents are soldiers of our armed forces," she said.

"And Operatives?"

"Operatives are on a whole other level. Only the best of the best become an Operative. Operatives do not go on normal missions or participate in battles like the one tomorrow. They are a special type that goes on delicate and imperative missions that are usually high profile and top secret. After the Operatives, comes the Special Operatives," she said.

"What about the Occult Operatives—where do they fit in?"

His heart began to race when he saw the look on her face. Her eyes widened and lips parted as she stared at him like he was from another world.

"Did you say Occult Operatives?"

"Yeah, they were the ones that attacked us," he said.

"Occult Operatives are a phantom Special Operative team. They are on a level of their own. They only deal with one thing—and one thing only."

"What is that?"

"Treason," she said never blinking.

"Treason? But why would they come after my dad and I? We have lived here all of our lives. My dad and Bishop are friends."

"I cannot answer that question. All I know is that once you are a suspect of the Occult Operatives, only one of two things can happen," she said.

"Tell me."

"Either you are proven innocent, either by evidence or the real traitor being captured, or—."

"Or what?"

"They neutralize you—permanently," she said never leaving his gaze.

Silence clung to every inch of the meadow around them. The waterfall and spring filled the air with ambient noise while he thought about her words.

"Well everything is fine because my dad and Bishop stopped everything. Clearly they had the wrong people," he said.

"Eli that is not the point. The point is that even though we know you had nothing to do with this Agent, there is some kind of link between you and the traitor. Occult Operatives do not just lie and say that they have a source if they don't. Some part of what Kai said has to be correct. Someone is either setting you up or—."

"Or what?"

"Or you are their next target. They could be after you and just have not had the opportunity to attack. Maybe they have been spying on you or have broken into your house. The Occult Operative's source could have seen them coming out of your house and thought the Agent had been meeting with you or your dad."

Eli thought about every place he had been, every time he had remembered to lock the door, and if there were any occasions where something did not feel right. "I'm too tired so I can't think of anything."

She kissed him lightly on his cheek. "I am sorry. I did not mean to overwhelm or scare you."

"It's okay. I feel comfort when you are near," he said.

"The feeling is mutual," she said with a smile.

"So what were you reading?"

"Just about ancient weddings and ceremonies my ancestors used to have."

"Do you find that—entertaining?"

"Yes, I mean—why wouldn't I?"

"I don't know. Weddings just seem—boring," he said.

She laughed at his response as she tucked a strand of hair behind her ear. "What, don't you ever want to get married someday when you find the right one?"

"Not really, I mean—I don't know. I know when my mom and dad got married, my dad turned down many missions because he always wanted to be with my mom; and whenever she was on missions, he wanted to go on the ones she was on. I don't want that to happen to me. I don't want anything to stand in the way of me becoming an Operative and becoming the best. I feel like I want to be a Special Operative now," he said laughing.

When no response came from Sia, he looked up at her. Her gaze stood frozen staring at him as her eyes seemed to blink without her noticing.

"What?"

"Oh, nothing—sorry I must have gotten lost in thought," she said.

"It's okay, don't worry about it, it happens to me all the time."

Silence soon returned and an unwarranted tension filled the air. Eli was confused as to where the tension came from and why, but couldn't put his finger on it.

"So—no kids?"

"Kids! No, definitely not," he said laughing. "I mean, how can someone bring kids on missions with them. They just get in the way."

When she returned a stern gaze, he felt alarmed.

*Shoot! Stupid Eli! Stupid!*

"Except for Mik, like I said before, he is the only kid I like."

Sia returned a small smile but soon ended it. "When we get back from the mission, maybe we should go out—you know—to eat somewhere nice," she said.

"Um—sure, I mean, what is wrong with this place—it's amazing."

"No this place *is* amazing it is just—I don't know if we have ever had a real date yet."

"Every time I'm with you I feel like I'm on a date," he said before kissing her on the lips. He waited for a response but only got a stare. "Hey yeah we can definitely do that—if you want. As long as I am with you, it doesn't matter where we go," he said.

She jumped up into his arms kissing him passionately. He smiled between kisses feeling relieved that he had finally said the right thing for once.

"Like I said before, tomorrow is a big day. I really should get some rest," she said.

"K."

They both returned to their feet and headed for the entrance of the meadow.

"Hey Sia."

"Yes E."

"Thanks for listening."

# A CLUE, A LIE,
# A BETRAYAL

Jude spent the rest of the evening training by the watering hole with Jed, after the training session with Anya. Jude went over the various exercises and rules that the General had went over with them. Jed made a few comments here and there, but for the most part, listened quietly. Jude was relieved when Jed told him that he too would be at the border fighting the Necrosis along with the rest of them. The thought of his older brother fighting by his side sent a reassuring comfort and peace of mind throughout Jude. After training, Jude and Jed both retreated back home. Jude was happy that his older brother had "moved back in" to their home. Jed explained that he usually does not leave the house unless he is out hunting while Jude and Aileen are sleeping. He told Jude that he enjoyed the familiarity of being back in his childhood home.

When Jude woke up, he looked out of the window and noticed the sun had just begun to rise. Its minimal golden rays caused the mountains around them to glow with a brilliance that made Jude stare. The smell of bacon and fresh-baked bread filled the air as Jude climbed out of bed. When he opened his door and ran down the stairs, a whiff of air quickly passed him.

"I'll race you!" yelled Jed speeding by.

Jude increased his speed knowing that there was no way he could outrun Jed. As Jude turned the corner into the kitchen, he found his mother at the stove and Jed sitting at the kitchen table with his empty hands open as if he was reading a newspaper.

"Ah! Well look who it is! Grandpa Jude, nice to see you my boy," said Jed.

"Very funny," said Jude hitting his brother on the shoulder before taking his seat.

"Good morning boys!" said Aileen setting a platter of ham and bacon on the table. "Jude did you sleep well?"

"Yes mom. No night terrors what-so-ever."

"Good! What about you Jed, how was the hunt?"

Jude's head whipped from his mother to Jed and back to his mom again.

*What the Pith?*

"Hunt was good. Drank so much blood, I feel like I won't have to hunt for a few days, which is nice since we leave this evening for the border," said Jed.

"Any—people?" asked Aileen.

"Surprisingly no. Not this time. I tried this new thing Lynn had told me about called 'prosimian dieting.' Primates are the closest mammals to us, and since they are, Lynn believes that their blood is closer to ours as well. She proposed that I try feeding off of their blood instead of human blood to see if my thirst is quenched from it."

"And?"

"You know what, it wasn't half bad. Only problem is, flies are usually buzzing around the corpse of the monkey as I feed on it. Gets kind of aggravating at times."

Aileen brought over a pitcher of orange juice as well as a plate of eggs, fruit and fresh bread. Aileen soon took her seat and led a small prayer before reaching for the eggs. After Jude poured himself a glass of orange juice, he committed the scene to memory.

*This is how it should be.*

"So—*mother*, you know Jude and I leave this evening. It will be Jude's first mission."

"I know! I know! Don't remind me. I'm already worried sick over it. But do not get me wrong, I am very proud—of both of you," said Aileen.

"Mom we will be fine," started Jude. "Jed and I together is a recipe for legends."

"I know. But I still worry."

After Jude finished breakfast with his mom and brother, he headed upstairs to his room. He showered and got dressed in the most comfortable clothes he could find. He closed the door behind him as he left the house, and instantly noticed Jed's presence on the side of the house.

"I believe you are getting sloppy," said Jude turning towards the direction he knew Jed was at.

Jed stepped out of the shadow of the house with a grin that exposed the full length of his fangs. "I truly believe my work is done—at least in that area. Where are you headed?"

"To see a friend in one of the villages on the outskirts of the city."

"I see. Well I am off," said Jed.

"Where are you off to?"

"I got a lead on a possible Vampire sighting in the North. I plan on checking it out."

"We leave from the main gates at four today. When will you be back?"

"I'll meet you back at the house at three, sound good?"

"Sounds good," said Jude.

A few stray clouds floated in and out of the sun's path, causing the shadows around the city to come and go. The village appeared slightly different than the last time Jude had visited Pang's house. There were no signs of life or activity amidst the small village. A large tumbleweed blew passed Jude, and down the main street that divided the uninhabited homes. As he made his way passed the other houses and towards the lone wooden house, he saw a figure in the front lawn. Pang sparred fast and savagely with a wooden dummy that moved with impeccable agility. As Jude came to a stop a few feet behind the sparring match, the dummy returned to a motionless stance.

"Funny thing about these dummies, they are less predictable than they seem," said Pang toweling his face as he turned towards Jude.

"Predictability is caused by behavior, which means that you are inferring that the dummy behaves like a person behaves. If that is true, then I believe we have cause to fear them taking over the city at some point in the future."

"Only fools do not fear the inevitable domination of the wooden dummies," said Pang.

Jude just stared back at his friend, questioning the sincerity of his words. Finally Pang erupted into laughter after a few seconds of silence.

"It is called *joking*," said Pang.

"I thought so, but with you, I can never be sure."

The two of them entered Pang's house, and Jude soon found himself sitting at a familiar table.

"Hungry? Thirsty?"

"No I am good. Thank you."

Pang came back around the corner with a cup in his hand. Jude noticed the lone ring that hung from the silver chain around his neck.

"What is it with the necklace?"

Pang turned slowly, holding the ring in his hand. While his fingers fumbled with the ring, Pang's gaze stayed glued to Jude, before taking his seat across the table.

"It was Issac's. He was wearing it the night he was murdered. After justice being served by Donat's death, I retrieved it from his body. It's all I have left of him, this and a couple of pictures," said Pang.

"It is nice to have something to remember him by," said Jude scratching the back of his neck hastily. When he realized his gesture, he quickly dropped his hand back down to his side. "I wish I had something of my dad's to remember him by. However, he did leave me a box of mementos—that I am very grateful for."

Silence.

"Yeah. So good work yesterday during the training."

"Thanks—you too," said Jude.

"I feel like I owe you an apology. When I first met you, I did not think you were as good as you are."

"You are lucky that I am not your enemy then, underestimating me could have been your downfall," said Jude nudging him across the table.

"Correct you are. So what do you think we can expect from the mission tomorrow?"

"I don't know—it is my first."

"If I had to guess, I would say tons of agile enemies and the need for massive combat control. Other than that, I am clueless," said Pang with a shrug.

"Do you have any of that awesome hot cider we had last time?"

Pang retreated to the small kitchen in the back and soon returned with a cup and kettle. After pouring them both a cup, Pang returned to his seat. "I have you hooked. It's over, I will have you coming back for more cider until the maggots have claimed your grave."

"If you keep talking like that, I won't have the stomach to even look at a cup."

"Hey I have a question," said Pang.

"What is it?"

"That Eli guy, what's his deal?"

"What do you mean?" asked Jude feeling worried.

"I have never had a problem with him or his loud mouth friend, but he still seems to have major issues with me."

"I think he let Zane get into his head a little, and I think he has brainwashed himself into believing you stole his spot on the squad. I hate to say it, but I would say ignore him if he is rude. I am hoping that he will come around soon," said Jude sipping his cider.

"I am still confused as to why you put so much on the line for him today. He completely failed at every exercise."

"That is because you don't know him like I do. He is my best friend, and I know what he is capable of. Trust me, once you guys get over your differences, you will see."

"I do not care what you say, any kind of relationship, including friendships, are a two-way path. I mean, he has not showed you that he even deserves the opportunity you gave him, or has even mentioned repaying you for what you did," said Pang.

"I don't do things for my best friend because I am expecting something back. I will admit that it does get infuriating at times always being the one to watch his back and him never returning the favor, but he is my friend."

"A person is only born with so much kindness. If you are always the one to give all the time and never receive anything in return, sooner or later all that will be left inside is darkness," said Pang with a shrug.

After realizing that they were both on opposite ends in regards to Eli being enlisted on the squad, Jude and Pang talked about various attack strategies that they believed might help. Afterwards, Jude planned to leave and offered Pang an invite to meditate with him; but Pang declined claiming mediation wasn't his thing.

After leaving Pang's village, Jude found himself lost in his own mind. A small voice in his head kept telling him that Eli's covert plan from earlier, was not a one-time event. No matter how much he tried to shake the thought that his best friend was becoming more of a competing comrade, rather than his friend, it kept returning.

*It has happened numerous times since we have joined the Academy. While I want to keep overlooking his moments of selfish and dishonest behavior, I can't let our friendship jeopardize our mission or my own personal mission.*

Jude headed towards the watering hole, which he normally visited with Jed. It was the first time that he intentionally went there in the daytime. As he walked through the veil of leaves and branches, the light aquatic world spread out in front of him. The sun's rays shined effortlessly down at the water hole, casting movement along its surface. Bears, deer, squirrels and many other forest animals, gathered along its edges to both bathe and drink from the water. As Jude approached, many of the squirrels looked up and then dispersed. Once his footsteps came to a halt a few feet from the water, the bears and larger animals ceased their activities to examine his movement.

Jude sat cross-legged in the spot where he was standing. He noticed that the animals continued their activities as if ignoring his presence. Both hands sat on their own knee as his breath drew deep before being expelled from his mouth. While his chest lightly rose and fell, Jude found the familiar calm and peace that he had been hungry for.

*Dear Three Brothers,*

*Being gods I know you already know the outcome of whatever events await us. All I ask, is that you give all of us the strength to not only protect our city, families and people; but to give us the wisdom to make the right decisions. And also, if you could let my dad know that I miss him, and I wish he were here. Lastly, please tell Bree I miss her as well.*

Something wet and soft ran across his hand. He opened his left eye to find a baby fox sniffing one of his fingers. Jude moved his hand to pat the fox on the head, but missed as the fox retreated back a few steps. The fox stared straight into Jude's eyes. He could see the fear. He felt his heart sadden from the effect his presence had on the fox. He reached into his pocket slowly and grabbed a piece of the bread that he had gotten from Pang's house. He slowly placed it in front of the fox, which sniffed and licked it once, before gobbling it down. The fox closed the distance between them licking Jude's hand several times. The animal's fur felt smooth and warm as Jude ran his hand across the top of its head repeatedly.

"Sorry if I scared you. I am just lost. I need some answers," said Jude looking into the Fox's eyes.

The fox scurried away behind Jude with its tongue hanging freely. It soon returned carrying something in its mouth. The object was square and tan. When the item fell to Jude's lap, his eyes widened, his heartbeat quickened and his hands moistened, when he recognized the symbol that stared back at him.

# BLIND-SIDED

The table shook fiercely under Bishop's fist, as he attempted to settle the commotion around him.

"Today above all days I have no time for any prideful and petty squabbles between any of you. Now Lynn, are you absolutely positive that there is nothing we can do to get any support from the Relinquished Isles?"

"Unfortunately, I am positive sir. The Amorphous race says that we have not displayed any loyalty to them in the past couple of decades. Also, they are suspicious of what our land could have done to warrant such a threat," said Lynn.

Bishop felt so insulted, that he felt like he needed a couple of days to get over the hurt feelings that he was experiencing. "Warrant such a threat? Are they insane?"

"To many they are," said Vance.

"Those are the best ones," said Fox licking his lips. "A little wine and a shoulder massage and bam! You got yourself a tsunami of a ride. The insane ones do things normal people couldn't even imagine. Ah Penelope."

Bishop felt his anger getting the best of him.

"Enough! This is no time for tomfoolery! Our enemy is at our door. Your families are in danger! Your children are in danger! Your homes are in danger! Our very lives are in danger! Unless it is about remedies for the danger we are in, I don't want to hear another word out of anyone's mouth!"

"I think we have no other choice but to go on with the backup plan," said Lynn.

Silence traveled to Bishop, along with the stares of his fellow council members. Bishop looked into the eyes of those waiting to hear his approval on the idea. Grimness and sorrow ravaged the faces of everyone around him; except for Fox, who sat with his feet up whistling his signature tune.

"Lynn I know, but I cannot bring myself to do it. I cannot bring myself to sacrifice the lives of our students, our children!"

"It is not a sacrifice my Lord. You underestimate them. They are strong, courageous and willing. They will not let you down," said Lynn.

Bishop's throat dried and his heartbeat became audible to his ears. He had to re-grip the glass he was drinking out of, when it nearly slipped out of his grip. As he set the cup down on the table, the memory of the Necrosis that attacked the young woman flashed in front of his eyes.

"Very well. Move forward with the arrangements. I want every Agent that will be defending our city, fully briefed and prepped on their duties, the mission and anything else that will ensure their success."

"Understood," said Vance.

"General, I assume you and your men are completely ready to leave from the main gates in the next couple of hours," said Bishop.

"All of my men, including Lieutenant Titus and the four that will be under my personal command," said Anya.

"Four?" said Ivor.

"Yes four. I have recruited Eli Brassie as well."

"I must admit General, I thought that even someone such as yourself, had the sense to realize when they have recruited such a lost cause," said Ivor folding his arms with a smirk.

"Who I have recruited for my squad is no one's business but Bishop's and my own," said Anya.

"That is where you are wrong General! If your so-called men fail to successfully complete their mission, then you are not only placing their lives in danger, but my own as well. I will not sit idly by and let degenerates defend my safety. My Lord, I vote that Eli Brassie be removed from under the General's command. He did not win in the Trials of Magic, Might and Lineage. On the contrary, he would not even be alive if that Pang brat had the stomach to finish his dirty work," said Ivor.

"I have to say that I have noticed a great deal of dislike on your part in regards to Mr. Brassie," said Bishop. "Are you sure your decision comes from wisdom and not anger?"

"Sir, I am his mentor. I have seen what he can do with my own eyes. He is immature, reckless, undisciplined and would be a liability to everyone around him."

Bishop felt the need to neutralize this argument before it got out of hand. "While I humbly respect your opinion Professor, I believe that we cannot leave such a decision up to just one person. General! How many exercises, during your time with Mr. Brassie, did he pass?"

Bishop saw the drop in Anya's composure, a few seconds after he had asked his question. Before she spoke, he already knew her answer.

"None sir."

"None! Even my blind niece could pass at least one training exercise. I cast a vote for the discharge of Eli Brassie," said Ivor.

"All in favor?" said Bishop.

Everyone's hand, except for Conall and Anya's, went up before Bishop's eyes. It was at that moment, that Bishop wished his vote would have tipped in Eli's favor.

"Then it is decided. General—."

"But sir," said Anya.

"You are to notify Eli Brassie that he has been discharged from the squad on the basis of insufficient skill level. However, he has been charged with the safety of the Western Gates instead."

"Yes sir," said Anya.

"We will get through this," said Bishop looking into the faces of every one of his council members. "When life gives us enemies, we neutralize them."

Everyone's heads nodded in agreement and never left Bishop's gaze. After a few long stares, the worry Bishop had been feeling dissipated; and all that was left was determination and eagerness.

"Meeting adjourned. Fox can you stay for a few minutes please?"

"Sure! Why not," said Fox.

Bishop waited for everyone to exit Council Hall. Lynn came by and gave him a hug and told him that everything was going to be okay. Vance stopped by and told him that he would come by later on to discuss placement of the Agents and students that were to stand guard of the city. Conall was the last to leave, as he trailed quickly after Anya.

"What can I do for you sir?" asked Fox.

"Necrosis are uncoordinated, and I have no reason to believe that we have any reason to fear when it comes to the city's safety. We will have hundreds of skillful Agents keeping the Necrosis at the border before they are destroyed. However, I am always about being prepared, which is why I must ask you a huge favor."

"Sir?"

"Ever since you have lived here—after your city was destroyed by Lord Egon a few years back—we have been through a lot together," said Bishop.

"Yes sir. You gave me a home when everything was taken from me. I could not be more grateful for your kindness. I promise you, the Necrosis will not lay a finger on anyone. These creatures do not know the level of danger they are in when it comes to me," said Fox.

Bishop stared proudly into Fox's eyes as remembrance formed within him. "You know Fox when I first saw you, you reminded me of someone."

"Who sir?"

"My son. His name was Liam. He fought and died beside our previous General. He fought to defend our people from the Necroborns, when they were not our allies. When you first stood in my chambers, when the Agents first brought you to me, I was at a loss for words. Seeing how physically and emotionally damaged you were—along with hearing your story about the loss of your brother—truly hurt my heart. I have thought of you as my son ever since."

Fox just stared into Bishop's eyes. For the first time Bishop saw Fox's face soften. He barely blinked, and there was a sheen to his eyes.

"Thank you sir. Ever since I lost Cur, I have felt like I am alone in this world. But you have made me feel at home, and like I still have a family," said Fox.

"Well back to our previous topic, I would like for you to accompany Anya to the border. I am confident that our current soldiers will be more than enough to eliminate the Necrosis threat. However, I will have better peace of mind if we had you there as well. Your skills in battle are a huge asset, and I believe that Anya will agree with me. Afterwards, I would be honored if you would serve as one of my advisors," said Bishop.

"Advisor sir?"

"Yes my advisor. You would still be my Tactical Emissary in regards to delicate and imperative missions, but you will also serve as one of my advisors. I believe you have been on many different types of difficult missions, and have always come out successful. I would have you be my Tactical Advisor as well. You would help decide our Agents most effective battle formations, ranks, training and really anything having to do with any conflicts or combat."

"That would be an honor sir," said Fox extending his hand.

Bishop shook Fox's hand before he found himself locked in a tight embrace by Fox. It was the first time since Bishop had met Fox, that he had seen his young Emissary show any signs of emotion. As Bishop walked Fox to the door, he wrapped his arm around him.

"I have to say, I expect Ivor's face will look pretty sour when he hears the news, but that is something I am definitely looking forward to seeing," said Bishop with a grin.

"You and I both sir, especially since now I have the power to overrule him on a few things," said Fox with a smirk.

Bishop knew that he shouldn't encourage the bickering between Ivor and Fox. However, he was more pleased to see the livelihood—that once existed behind Fox's eyes—return with such promise.

◆◆◆

Eli had spent most of the morning training in his usual spot in the outskirts of the forest. His endurance had increased dramatically, and his accuracy with a bow had increased as well. He had tried to do the total defense move that Conall had done on him the previous day, but he could not figure it out. He had yelled the exact words Conall had, over and over, but still nothing happened.

*I guess that means I can't just yell the names of abilities I have never used and expect them to work.*

Eli felt both frustrated and defeated at the realization that his Weapons Master skills paled in comparison to Conall's. He had used the retaliation ability on Mr. Wyatt, and he was positive that the ability was a move that he did not even know existed.

*If I had a better mentor, maybe I could figure it out. I could always go to the library like Jude does and read up on it.*

"I can't stand books," said Eli to a tree in front of him.

After returning to the city, Eli had stopped by Ms. Lowell's. After a few long anticipated kisses, Eli made plans with Sia to walk with her to the main gates from Ms. Lowell's, after he had a chance to change his clothes.

"Don't be late," she said kissing him on the cheek.

Eli felt like he could not have burst through his front door any faster. He slammed the door closed behind him, and threw his bag on the floor. He ran up the stairs, slamming his bedroom door behind him. After bathing and brushing his teeth, he ran to his closet.

*In a situation like this, I could not imagine wearing anything other than you.*

Eli grabbed his trusty brown belted combat tunic from his closet, and slipped it on—along with some tan light armor combat pants. As he stared at himself in the mirror, he noticed he saw a difference in his demeanor.

"Twin blades!" he said as a sword materialized in each hand. "Long bow!"

"Eli!" yelled Marius from down the hall.

"Yeah dad?"

"Can you get the door son?"

Eli dissolved his bow and ran down to the front door. The smell of freshly smithed metal and leather greeted his senses when he opened the door.

"Good afternoon," said Anya standing with her hands clasped behind her back.

"Afternoon. I mean General, good afternoon."

"May I come in soldier?"

"Please, come in," said Eli opening the door wider.

As Eli followed Anya to the center of the room, he was surprised when she didn't take the seat next to her.

*Maybe she has to be the last to sit, because of rank or something.*

He took a seat in front of her and waited for her to take the seat in front of him.

"Can I get you anything General? Something to eat or—"

"I am afraid that I am on a bit of a tight schedule. I have come to inform you that you have been discharged from our squad—effective immediately," said Anya.

"What? Discharged? Why?"

Eli found himself rising from his seat in a fighting stance.

"The Council has agreed that since you were not skillfully equipped to successfully complete any of the exercises from the training session yesterday, that you would be a liability on our mission. You have been tasked with being on duty at the Western Gates to defend the city grounds during the mission. Good day," said Anya turning for the door.

"Wait," said Eli grabbing the back of Anya's shoulder.

Eli's ceiling spun quickly and his wrist shot into pain, as he felt himself flipped and thrown to the ground.

"Make sure that does not happen again," said Anya staring down at him.

Eli watched the General's feet as she exited the front door. Anya's pace stopped cold when she saw Eli appear in front of her. His chest rose and fell quickly as he tried to catch his breath.

"Please—whatever I did—I'm sorry. I will do anything to make it up to you. Just please don't take me off the squad."

Anya just stared deep into his eyes. Her unforgiving eyes tilted up and down while she analyzed him. Eli hoped that she would accept his plea, and just let him make up for whatever he had done—after the mission.

"Stand down soldier," said Anya brushing passed Eli. Anya's presence grew more and more distant, until finally, she was out of sight.

"Who was it son?" Marius stood in the doorway behind him.

Eli said nothing. He just stared towards the direction of the main gates.

"Son? What's wrong?"

"I've been discharged," said Eli dropping his head.

"Discharged? What? On what grounds?"

"For being a complete idiot," said Eli retreating passed his dad and into the house.

Eli made his way into the kitchen and sat at his usual spot with his head planted firmly facedown on the table. He heard his dad's footsteps when he entered the kitchen, but he ignored them. A few minutes later, Eli felt a warm dish rub against one of his hands. He looked up to see steam rising from a lone cup. Marius took his seat across from Eli with his own cup.

"Go ahead, tell me. What's going on?" said Marius.

"I didn't pass any of the training exercises yesterday, so Anya decided to cut me. She says I'm a liability."

"Liability? That is rubbish," said Marius pretending to spit to the side.

"I mean she's right. I did fail all of the training exercises. But she is wrong when she says that I'm a liability. That squad needs me!"

"She didn't give you any alternative? She just said you are out—that's it?"

"No, she said I'm in charge of the Western Gates," said Eli.

"Well congratulations son! That is a big job. I had to do it as well when I was your age. It is *a lot* more difficult than it looks."

"Dad I'm not being a worthless gate guard!" He didn't understand how his dad could sit there and congratulate him on being demoted. Eli was furious, and he expected his dad to be furious right along with him.

*I wonder who all knows. I could always just hide in the crowd of Agents until we get to the border. Who cares if they see me because I will already be at the site. They would be crazy to refuse my help if I was already there.*

"Are you listening to me?"

"No—I have to go," said Eli getting up from his seat.

"Son where are you going?"

"To the main gates. I'm a part of that squad no matter what anyone says," said Eli. He grabbed his bag and headed for the front door. He was annoyed when he heard Marius' footsteps behind him.

"Then who is going to watch the Western Gates?"

"Who cares? They can watch themselves as far as I'm concerned," said Eli.

"Son you can't just disobey orders it's dishonorable."

"Dishonorable? Dishonorable? You have the nerve to talk to me about honor? A man who disobeyed direct orders from his superiors and turned his back on his own comrades in the midst of battle. Don't talk to me about honor dad. If anyone is dishonorable it's you!" said Eli as he slammed the door behind him.

# IMMINENT DEATH

Eli was speechless when he saw Sia in her battle gear. She wore a tight-fitting black combat body suit with patches of baby blue detailing. A long cape, matching the body suit, covered her back.

"You look, amazing!"

"Yeah right. This stupid combat suit is too tight along my waist. I think it is too small for me," she said sighing.

"I'm serious Sia," said Eli kissing her on the lips. "You look amazing."

Eli nearly kissed her again when he saw the pink rise in her cheeks. He bid farewell to Ms. Lowell and Mik, telling them to keep all of their windows and doors locked, and to stay inside.

"When you get back, will you teach me those moves?" asked Mik hastily.

"Remember our deal? Grades first," said Eli.

"I got a perfect score on my exam. I can show you if you don't believe me."

"All of your grades need to be good though," said Eli.

Mik folded his arms and poked out his lip. His cheeks filled with color and his eyes watered slightly.

"Perfect score huh?"

"Yes sir!" said Mik with a big smile.

"Alright, one lesson. One lesson is all you get until I see some improvement at school. Anymore bad grades and the deal is off," said Eli.

"Yes! I can hear them now! 'Look out! Here comes Mighty Mik with the unstoppable combos!' Heads will roll!" said Mik punching the air in front of him.

Eli and Sia left the Market District and headed towards the main gates. An assortment of Agents, students and civilians passed by them on the way. As the area in front of the main gates came into view, adrenaline coursed throughout Eli's body. Straight lines of Agents stood single file stretching further back than Eli could see. The soldiers stood in lines organized by bloodline with the Weapons Master soldiers with red armor, standing in ten or so lines between the soldiers in blue armor and the soldiers in black armor.

"This way," said a voice to the left of Eli.

He looked over to see Jude waving him over. Eli and Sia made their way over to a small area to the side of the Magi Agents. Pang and Jed stood idly by, appearing to be unaware of the others' presence.

"I did not think you would show," said Jude.

"What? Why wouldn't I show up?"

"Whoa! Calm down. I was inferring that you would be too nervous to show up, but I was kidding."

"Oh yea," said Eli laughing nervously.

*Okay so Anya hasn't told him yet.*

"Hey Jude," said Sia.

"Good afternoon. You look nice and ready for battle," said Jude.

"I plan on killing those creatures quick and painful. I have a younger brother I am playing hide and seek with later," said Sia with a wink.

Eli noticed that everyone was staring at him. He caught a couple of people whispering about him as well. He knew that everyone knew he was discharged. It would only be a matter of time before the others found out as well. His stomach felt uneasy and made him nauseous. As if hearing him, all of the soldiers lined up turned in unison and stared at him.

"You are discharged!" said all the men simultaneously.

"Eli!" yelled Jude.

"Yo."

"Yo? Man are you okay?" asked Jude.

"Yeah why wouldn't I be?" Eli felt uneasy under Jude's gaze. He didn't say anything, just stared at him.

*Why in the heck is he staring so much?*

"Eli I know something is wrong or at least up. What is going on?" said Jude.

"Nothing."

"Look at me!" yelled Jude.

Eli was alarmed at Jude's outburst. He stared straight into his friend's green eyes. They were different than he remembered. Ever since he knew Jude from when they were kids, Jude's eyes were kind and sincere. Now, Jude's green eyes were still sincere and kind, but they were also unyielding, complex and wise. If anyone would understand what was going on with his situation with Anya, it would be Jude.

*I mean Jude would not only understand, he would probably have a solution to get me back on the squad.*

"Whatever it is, you can tell me. I won't tell anyone I promise. Did something happen?"

Eli casually looked over at Sia. Her beautiful light purple eyes drew attention against her pale skin. Her light pink lips looked soft and warm. Eli looked back at Jude. His unyielding gaze seemed to have never left their position, or even blink.

"Nope. We're good. I promise."

Everyone around the campfire broke into laughter at Garren's story. Jude had to hold his hand over his mouth to keep from laughing too loud.

After meeting up with Anya and the rest of the Agents, Jude, Sia, Eli and Pang followed the General out of the gates and through the northern part of the surrounding forest. To Jude's surprise, no one spoke a word as they traveled. The only noise audible was the sound of the crunching leaves under their feet, as well as the occasional greetings from the nature around them. After the trees and darkness came to an end, the view opened up to a vast and large flat plain similar to the plains in the back of the Coliseum. Anya was quick to divvy up duties to everyone. Jude had been assigned to helping a group of men build a perimeter around their campsite. At first he believed that the task would not be difficult at all, however as he and the other men completed a quarter of the perimeter, he realized it was a lot more tedious than he had anticipated. After four to five hours, the perimeter was completed to Anya's specifications. Afterwards, Jude joined Eli, Jed and a small group of Agents around a large campfire that sat in the middle of the camp. An Agent by the name of Garren had been telling them about an undercover mission he had been on in Praxis. His mission had been to eliminate the king that ruled over that city. Jude listened intently after he realized that the details of the story resembled the one Pang had told him.

"Wait wait I'm not finished yet," said Garren using his hands to try and silence the group of people around him. "So like I said, I grabbed the keys from the unconscious guard, after placing him inside the very cage that he had told me I would spend the rest of my life in. I headed for the king's chambers, which was right after the torture chamber they had 'punished' me in. However, as I approached the door to the torture chamber, the air filled with the scent of fresh gore and rotting flesh. I opened the door to find that someone had already taken care of the king! His eyes were ripped out and his face and body were burned beyond belief. His torso was filled with bruises and scratches. When I kicked his body over, there was a large hole in his throat as if something burned through his neck from the inside out! That's why I always say, just when you think you have gotten away with something, life comes back to show you who's boss!"

A series of nods and signs of agreement displayed around the campfire. Jude found himself trapped in thought as he came to the conclusion that the story was not a coincidence. Garren had been on a mission to assassinate the same king that Pang had killed.

*So Pang did not even have to kill him. If Garren was skilled enough, King Donat would have died anyways. I wonder if he knows that.*

"Hey Bray!" yelled Garren.

Jude instantly broke out of his reverie and looked up in response to the call.

"Oh sorry, not you little Bray. I'm not used to having children on missions with us; especially ones with the same last names as us grown folks," said Garren with a laugh.

Many deep laughs from the other Agents vibrated around the campfire.

*That's right keep laughing. Lets just hope that you do not run into someone one day that is younger and more skilled than you. Your underestimating will be your downfall.*

"Do not let those innocent green eyes fool you. Jude's skills are more deadly than you anticipate," said Jed.

"Uh oh, here comes the big bad older brother to the rescue," said Garren holding his stomach in laughter. "There is no disrespect from me Bray, just fun. Why don't you tell us about some of the missions you have been on."

"Very well. It was night. The clouds hung low covering up most of the night's moonlight. A small cottage precariously sat on a mountainous ledge above a small village. Silence and stillness allied itself at my side. As I peered into one of the small windows of the cottage, my targets were oblivious. A man laid motionless in a wooden bed in the middle of the room. The heaviness of sleep in his conscience had started to weigh down, igniting the rise of his subconscious. The woman sat on a chair in front of a mirror brushing her beautiful long blonde hair. Her smooth pale skin was bare and her jugular began to beat boldly and loudly in response to my presence. After finding an unlocked side door I slipped in, undetected of course. The disgusting smell of meat hung in the air alongside the scent of flowers. After a couple of idle minutes, her heart beat quickened and her ear twitched before she jerked her attention to my position. She saw nothing but the closed side door she had forgot to lock. She was unaware, but I stood a few feet away from her, wedged in the shadows between her bookcase and the wall that housed the door. Her gaze stayed fixated on that door. Her chair creaked as she came to her feet, closing the distance between herself and the door before locking it. When her attention turned back to the contents of her small cottage, she turned towards the corner I once was in. While I peered at her rosy cheeks from beneath the bed, my mouth watered at her ignorance and unawareness that her death was imminent. She sat back down on her creaking chair in front of the mirror. When she grabbed her brush and raised it to her head, a pale hand caught her wrist. She looked at the hand and then looked in the mirror. A pair of colorless eyes and sharp fangs stared back at her. The movement of her larynx signaled a pending scream. My hand felt a crunch when it gripped the warmth of her neck, shattering her larynx. Low raspy noises slipped from between her red lips, while tears ran down her rosy cheeks. Her eyes projected the same familiar words that everyone in her position had: 'Someone help me!' As my fangs shredded through the warm skin of her neck and found her jugular, fresh warm blood gushed across my palate. Her blood tasted warm, sweet, intoxicating and rejuvenating all at the same time. For a human, I guess it would taste like fresh warm honey that is just sweet enough to keep you coming back for more. A change in breathing from the man soon surfaced. When his eyes opened he saw his wife standing before him. 'Honey? What's going on? Couldn't sleep? Or did you change your mind about my offer?' I dropped her body. When his eyes fell on me, they fell down to his wife, and then returned to my gaze. I could tell by his eyes that he knew it was over. There was no one to help him. There was no hope left. There was no escape. His heart rate sped out of control, and before it could take the joy of his death out of my hands, I ripped back the covers and my fangs sank deep into his heart. The taste from his heart was sweeter than the neck of the woman. The heart is always the keeper of the body's most valuable and delectable possessions."

Silence hung over the campsite. Wide eyes stared harshly back at Jed, as his story came to an end. It was definitely not the story that Jude had expected his brother would tell. He expected some heroic and exciting tale of countless enemies, advanced techniques and an epic ending. However, after listening to Jed's story, all he felt was nausea and fear.

"That is not a mission!" yelled Garren. "That is just sick!"

"It is a mission," said Jed glaring. "It is a mission I go on every day, of every week, of every month of every year. It is the mission of the hunt."

"You knew that was not what I meant! I meant real missions. Missions of honor and skill!" yelled Garren.

"That *was* a real mission. It was a mission of vast skill. I would like to see you silence two humans in a village without so much as a single sound rummaging through the night. As for honor, well I believe you and I have different definitions of the word. So how do you humans say? Agree to disagree my friend," said Jed standing from his spot exposing his fangs.

Jude watched his brother stare at Garren for what seemed like minutes before turning his back and returning to his tent. It took what seemed like forever for conversations to return to the campfire.

"Your brother sure knows how to tell a story," said Eli.

His infamous brown belted tunic seemed to hang a little big on his body. Jude began to wonder if his friend had lost weight recently. Jude rose to his feet while keeping his gaze on Eli.

"Come on lets go."

"Where are we going?"

"Follow me," said Jude turning for the southern area of the plains away from the camp.

# PROGRESS

Eli felt like no matter what he did, his lungs would never be able to get enough air. Hunched over with his hands on his knees, he closed his eyes to shield them from the dust cloud that had blown past him.

"Remember you *are* on a team. Everyone has a job. Stop trying to do things by yourself," said Jude.

"I know I know," said Eli straightening back up.

"No you don't, that is why you are not getting it," said Sia.

*Great gang up on me. You know how much I like to be picked apart.*

Eli had followed Jude to a bare and remote part of the plains and away from the camp. The sky was clear and the moon was nearly full. The rough and open terrain had proved to be an excellent spot for the training that Jude had set up for them. Eli was surprised to find Sia and Pang waiting for them when they arrived. Eli was sure that Jude had to have coerced Pang to come somehow, since it was no secret that Pang and Eli didn't get along.

"I have another idea," said Jude taking a spot next to Sia. "Sia you are my ally and will be my defense."

"Right!" She threw a wink towards Eli.

He found himself blushing at Sia's gesture, and soon realized that he had not been paying attention to whatever Jude had said.

"Eli!"

"Huh?" asked Eli.

"Focus buddy focus," said Jude.

"Okay okay I'm ready. What do you want me to do?"

"Pang is your ally. You will be his offense and he will be your defense," said Jude.

*Seriously Jude, what did I do to you for you to make Pang my partner?*

"Can I have you or Sia as an ally instead?"

"Eli!" yelled Sia.

"Look, I'm not particularly fond of you either. However, we are on the same squad. You are my comrade, and as long as you return the same courtesy, I won't let you fall in battle," said Pang.

Eli felt his eyes widen and his stomach drop.

*I must be hearing things. Either that or it's wishful thinking.*

"What did you say?"

"I refuse to repeat myself. Take it or leave it," said Pang.

"Eli!" yelled Jude.

Eli examined Pang for a few seconds. "Alright lets go."

Eli saw Jude take something from his pocket, and soon he saw a sword appear in both of Jude's hands before he took off in a charge. Eli summoned his bow and matched Jude's charge with a sprint, as he fired countless arrows. The arrows stopped in their tracks inches from Jude's face and redirected themselves back at Eli.

*Right Sia is his partner.*

Eli felt his body leave the ground as Pang yanked him out of the path of the arrows.

"You're up!" said Pang. He tossed Eli head first over the barrage of arrows towards Jude.

Panic was the first thing that gripped Eli as he soared through the air. However, after the first couple of seconds, he noticed that he had the advantage over Jude, who looked up in disbelief.

"Blunt force!" yelled Eli.

Jude leaped to the side to avoid the spinning war axes. As Jude returned to his feet, Eli realized that Jude did not anticipate the war axes curving back around for a second attack. Jude ran into a front flip that hoisted him in the air until he was eye level with Eli. Pain shot up Eli's arm as Jude grabbed his wrist and flung him straight down at the ground. Air whizzed passed him, while the ground grew closer. Just when he was sure he was going to smash into the rocky floor, his body stopped in midair, hovering above the ground. Eli looked ahead to see Sia with her fist held out in front of her. Her other hand had the war axes twirling around her fingertips.

*She's going to skewer me!*

"Back at ya!" yelled Sia readying the axes she controlled.

Before she could attack, Pang shoulder-charged her, sending her flying across the plains. Eli's body was let loose by the invisible grip, allowing him to roll to his feet, once his body hit the ground. Pang turned around to look at Eli, but before he could say anything, Jude landed sitting on Pang's shoulders. He did a back flip that sent Pang soaring behind him. Jude turned around and took off in a sprint towards Pang. Eli began to pursue, but realized that he had forgotten about Sia. He laid on his stomach in an attempt to not draw any attention to himself. Sia had returned to her feet and began to pursue Jude while mumbling to herself. Eli sprinted after her. When she came to a stop in front of Pang, as he pinned Jude down, her hands curled into a claw position.

"Debilitate!" yelled Sia.

Jude broke free from Pang's grip, while Pang stood motionless in the same position. Eli realized that this was his opportunity. Jude summoned a sword in his hand and brought it above his head.

"I don't think so," said Eli.

Jude turned around, and to Eli's relief, was surprised to see Eli behind Sia with a dagger to her neck.

"Finally!" said Jude. A smirk passed across his face.

Pang's arms came down as he began to move again. Sia slowly turned around in Eli's grasp. Their chests were touching and the air he breathed was warm. He never took the knife down from Sia's neck, as he stared into her peaceful but piercing eyes. Her lips opened slowly.

"Barbaric tonight aren't we?" she said.

He said nothing, just felt himself melt on the inside. Her lips lightly touched over his. He kissed her back but never let the dagger down.

Sia licked the top of the hand that held the dagger to her throat. "So are you going to kill me?"

Eli found himself dissolving the dagger. He pulled her in by her waist and began to kiss her harder than he ever had. She moaned between kisses. Just as he was about to kiss her neck, his arms were yanked back and pinned behind him.

"What the—?"

"Even I don't blame you for falling for the oldest and most dangerous trap in the world," said Pang behind Sia.

"What trap?" asked Eli confused. Eli curved his head around to find Jude restraining him.

"Sorry E, I could not help myself," said Sia kissing him on the cheek before walking away.

Jude released his grip on Eli's arms before patting him on the shoulder.

"Good job buddy," said Jude.

"Thanks, but why are you congratulating me? I fell for the 'oldest and most dangerous trap in the world," said Eli dusting some newly-found dirt off of his clothes.

"We were just having fun with you there. I am congratulating you because you finally utilized an ally and fought as a team; and with Pang at that."

"Yeah what was up with that, pairing me with Pang?" said Eli. He lightly punched Jude on the shoulder as they both continued to laugh.

"Hey, I knew you were up for the double challenge!"

Pang and Sia soon joined them.

"Alright, now I think that we should work on fighting together—all four of us," said Jude.

# A BEAUTIFUL
# NIGHTMARE

Eli was passed the point of exhaustion after training with the group. Jude had subjected the four of them to a few scenarios that he believed they might come across in battle, and walked them through the best options for success. At the end of the training, Eli realized that he had learned a lot. Now when he pictured himself in battle in his head, he discovered that he had better problem solving skills when it came to combat. A newly-found confidence swelled up inside of him.

After heading back to the campsite, Eli decided that he needed to wash up after such an intense training session. He found his tent and entered. A single bed ran along the back flap. A stack of his favorite armor and clothes he had brought from home, lay scattered on the floor of the tent, next to a table with two chairs. A picture of him, Marius and Mya sat on a small end table. He grabbed the picture and sat on his bed. In the picture, Eli sat between his mom and dad, who stood smiling. Marius had one hand perched on Eli's shoulder. It was the picture that Eli always kept by his bed. It always gave him comfort whenever he missed his mom or just needed to know that his dad was near.

*"Don't talk to me about honor dad. If anyone is dishonorable it's you!"*

"I'm sorry dad. I didn't mean it. You're the most honorable man I know."

He sat the picture back on the end table, grabbed a towel from one of the drawers, and returned to his feet. He exited his tent after taking one final look at the picture, before closing the flap behind him. A smaller group of men still occupied the campfire. Most of them were drinking and still telling stories. Eli set off towards the western part of the plains, where he had seen an isolated watering hole when they had first arrived at the border. There was a larger watering hole that the Agents had been using on the eastern part of the plain that was closer. However, Eli decided that he needed alone time, and sought as much solitude as possible.

The walk took him around ten minutes and gave him some much needed thinking time. He thought about Pang's words and how, even though Pang admitted he did not like Eli very much, he still told him that he would have his back in battle.

*I will definitely need more reassurance than that. But it is still nice to hear him say that he won't let our differences get in the way of us supporting each other. I guess I had him figured out wrong.*

When the watering hole came into view, Eli felt himself relaxing as if he had already got in the water. The watering hole's transparent waters rocked softly and quietly in all directions. The reddish clay of the plain that surrounded the watering hole, made the clarity of the water seem more pronounced. He stripped down to his shorts and slowly treaded in. The water was slightly warm and felt good to his body, as he dunked his head underneath its surface. He swam around a bit, diving and resurfacing a few times. He swam on his back, gazing up at the moon that seemed to watch over him.

*"Stop trying to do things by yourself!"*

"Jude is right. I have to stop thinking I have to do everything alone. I don't understand where this feeling of overly-independent behavior came from. I also don't understand where I learned the phrase 'overly-independent'? I must be hanging around Jude too much."

Eli found himself chuckling at the memory of him and Jude drinking the Anti-gravitatis beverage from Inzanity and laughing hysterically.

"I guess that isn't a bad thing," said Eli laughing to himself. "Regardless, I need to drop the stupid behavior and trust Jude. He is my best friend and we have always trusted each other with our lives. I should have told him about what had happened with Anya and me being discharged. He's my family and I need to remember that."

He dunked his head one more time and then began to rub water along his arms and neck.

"First thing in the morning I'm going to tell him."

"Tell him what?"

Eli turned around to see Sia standing along the edge of the watering hole. She wore small light pink shorts with a long matching—nearly transparent—top. She dipped one of her toes into the water before continuing.

"And who?" she continued.

Eli found himself stumbling for words. She had caught him off guard, and he realized his brain seemed to go on a quick lunch break.

"I'm sorry what happened?"

"That is what I am asking you," said Sia pulling off her top and revealing a pink bra.

"I'm sorry," said Eli closing his eyes with his hand. "Let me know when I can look."

"Ha—okay I will," said Sia.

His body bobbed in the water as he kept his hand over his eyes.

"You can look now," whispered Sia softly. She sounded mere inches from him.

He took his hand off of his eyes to find her staring back at him. He gazed at her starting with her lips, and ending with her neck. His eyes began to slip down to the top of her wet bra that stuck to her skin, so he looked away.

"I'm sorry. I didn't mean to," he said looking away.

Her finger lifted his chin up so his gaze found her smile. Her lips came in closer and lingered in front of his. He waited for her kiss but felt nothing. He slightly opened one eye to see her eyes closed and pink lips floating closer, before stopping. His hand wrapped around her waist slowly and lightly touching her moist skin. Bumps rose from her skin as he lightly ran his fingers up her side before tickling her skin. A moan came from her lips while his other hand grabbed her side.

"Eli."

"Yeah," he replied looking up at her open eyes.

"Kiss me."

When their lips touched, the heaviness in his heart dissipated. He picked her up out of the water, and brought her closer to him. She wrapped her legs around his waist and locked her feet around his back. Her hands ran savagely through his hair as he kissed every inch of her neck.

"Eli."

"Yeah," he said continuing to kiss the nape of her neck.

"I have never done this before."

He stopped kissing her neck and returned his gaze back to her face. "Neither have I."

She stared at him for a while. Her head bobbed up and down in response to the water. "I am scared," she said staring into his eyes.

"Don't be. I won't hurt you. I promise."

Their gaze stayed locked on one another for what seemed like minutes. He realized that she had the courage that he wished he had, when she was the first to break the silence.

"What should we do?" she asked.

Eli grabbed Sia's hand and slowly led her out of the water and up on the plains' rough surface. He dried her legs softly with the towel that he had brought from his tent. He dried her thighs and waist and fought back the urge to stop when he dried her stomach. Finishing with drying her hair and face softly, she spoke for the first time.

"Your turn."

Sia dried Eli in the same manner and order he had dried her off. Her hands would occasionally slip off of the towel and touch his stomach or chest as she dried him, but he made sure to keep his thoughts on other things.

After getting dressed, Eli led Sia back to the camp. Neither one of them said a word but their hands stayed locked the whole way. He was grateful that his tent was on the edge of camp, so they would not draw too much attention. He opened the flap of his tent and waited for Sia to enter. She smiled and entered under his arm. He followed closing the flap behind him. He watched her look around his tent and wondered what she was thinking.

*I hope it's clean enough for her.*

He didn't expect that her tent could be too different from his, since everyone, except for Anya and Conall, had the same type of tent. She slowly approached the end table. Picking up the picture, she sat on his bed. He took a seat next to her.

"Do you miss your mom a lot?" she asked.

"All the time."

"Me too," she said running her fingers along the picture's surface. "Sometimes I dream about her."

"I don't dream about my mom, at least not when I sleep. I only dream about her during the day when I see something that jogs a memory."

"I dream about mine when I am sleep *and* when I am awake. It is always one of two dreams," she said.

"Really? What are they about?"

"The first one is the most frequent one. I dream of the day when she left, but this time I am much older. I cry constantly begging her not to go. She tells me 'princess I have to go but I will be back I promise.' The second one, I bump into her in the Market District, buying fruits and vegetables. I hug her but she doesn't know who I am. Both dreams always end in painful tears."

"I'm sorry," he said.

"It is not your fault."

"I know, but I'm still sorry I can't do anything to make you feel better," he said.

"You always make me feel better. Each and every day I am with you. It is just, there are some pains in life that some people can never heal from."

"I understand."

She sat the picture back on the end table as his arm wrapped around her. He took the small jacket that she was wearing off of her small shoulders, and placed it on one of the chairs that sat closeby. He took off his tunic and set it on the table. As he turned around, he noticed Sia's cheeks blush, at the sight of his bare chest. When he walked back over to her, she laid down on his bed against the tent's back flap. He laid down facing her.

"Mik was sad to see us go," she said.

"He was?"

"Well he was sad to see you go," she said laughing. "You are kind of his idol."

"I'm sure he was more sad to see you go. You're his big sister, you're always number one," he said cupping her face in his hand.

She smiled while returning his gaze. Her lips brushed his cheek. Her eyes blinked slower and slower until finally they closed. He watched her sleep for a couple of minutes, taking in her beauty and perfection. Being close to her made him feel almost entirely complete. As his eyes closed and the darkness behind them surrounded him, he thought of his mother and father, and how much they meant to him.

*I promise I will make you proud mom—you too dad.*

◆◆◆

Jude awoke to a series of knocks on the frame of his tent. After the training session, he figured that it would be wise to get as much sleep as possible, since he was informed that they would be slightly out-numbered.

"Mr. Bray," said the voice outside of his tent.

"One second."

Jude slipped on a black sweater and the combat pants he had on earlier. He ruffled his hair in a mirror that sat against a chair. He opened the flap and was greeted by a younger Agent dressed in silver scaled armor from head to toe.

"Sorry to wake you sir, but General requires your presence immediately," said the soldier.

"Of course."

Jude followed the soldier throughout the camp. The campfire had been extinguished and the campsite was empty of people, except for a few carefully placed Agents that stood watch. As the large black tent rose up ahead of him, Jude looked around at the other tents, and came to the conclusion that Anya's had to be more than twice the size of the other tents. The soldier leading him, opened the flap and ushered him in. Jude expected the soldier to follow him, but instead he stood outside the entrance. The black inner flaps matched the outside. Small white couches, tables, rugs and chairs decorated the large space. As Jude's eyes came to the center of the tent, he saw a familiar tangle of blonde hair and the back of a familiar brown tunic.

"Eli?"

"Ah Bray! Glad to see you made it here so promptly," said Anya.

She sat in a tall black chair that stood behind a long dark wood desk, which was littered with various papers. Two Agents stood on either side of her behind the chair.

"Of course General, I came as soon as I heard you needed me."

"I have to admit that I am very disappointed," she said.

"While I do apologize General, I have to admit that I am confused as to why you are disappointed."

"Who is this boy that stands next to you Bray?"

"General he—," started Eli but was silenced by a quick look from Anya.

"General, this is Eli Brassie," said Jude confused.

"Correct Bray, and I take it by your calm demeanor, that you are not surprised to see him standing by your side."

"Surprised? General, why would I be surprised?"

"It has come to my attention that at nineteen hundred hours, you were spotted around the camp's central fire, partaking in social conversation with this individual, as well as a few other Agents. Is this correct?" said Anya.

"General yes that is correct but—."

"And at twenty-one hundred hours, you were again spotted south of the campsite participating in physical training exercises with this individual along with a Ms. Sia Wyatt and Mr. Pang Quarrels. Is this correct?"

"General yes that is, but I still do not understand why I am being asked about my activities today, and why I have been summoned," said Jude.

"You are an intelligent individual Bray. I am sure that even someone as young as yourself knows that harboring a discharged Agent is grounds for your own discharge."

"A discharged Agent?" Jude's eyes immediately shot to Eli. His friend's gaze sent chills down his spine. Clearly everyone in the room knew what was going on except for Jude. "Eli what is going on? What is she talking about? Who was discharged?"

Eli looked down at his feet ignoring Jude's gaze and question. Worry crept into Jude's mind, as he realized that the silence that came from his best friend, could be nothing more than bad news.

*Wait, did she say my own discharge?*

"General, can you please tell me what is going on?"

"At fourteen hundred hours, Mr. Eli Brassie was approved for discharge by The Council on the grounds of insufficient skills. He was immediately notified of this intelligence, and seeing as how he stands right here before us both, has decided to disobey our orders and infringe Kismet's Warfare Decree," said Anya propping her elbows up on the table and interlacing her fingers.

Jude found himself struggling to absorb all of the information. For one, Anya was telling him that Eli had been discharged, but Jude knew that could not be true. Eli may not be the best Agent according to the General's standards, but Jude knew that his friend would be a huge asset to the team, especially after the successful training session they just had. Besides, even if by some chance Eli was discharged, Jude was sure that his best friend would have told him.

"General, forgive me for my ignorance, but are you sure it was Eli who was discharged?"

"One hundred percent, because I was the one that notified him in person of his discharge," said Anya with a hard unyielding expression on her face.

Jude felt like time stood still at his feet only. He felt as if everything to him ran in slow motion, but the area around Anya and Eli ran normally. His brain struggled for a few minutes to not only absorb everything, but to realize what it all meant. He turned to Eli who was already returning his gaze.

"You lied to me," said Jude feeling a fraction of enlightenment.

"Jude no—I didn't lie to you. I just didn't tell you," said Eli.

"But that *is* lying to me. You knew something that you knew I should have been made aware of, and you chose to not tell me in fear of what I would say."

Eli said nothing to Jude's comment. He just stared back with soft eyes and curled brows.

"Bray do you recall what I told you when I agreed to accept this individual within our ranks?" said Anya.

"Yes General," said Jude.

"Please remind us, if you would be so kind."

"General, you told me that he was my responsibility and that if he did not live up to my promise of being an asset to our team, that we would both be discharged. And I agreed," said Jude.

"Jude Bray! In compliance with section nine and article four of the Warfare Decree instated by Lord Rizal Byrne, you are here and henceforth dishonorably discharged on the grounds of mendacious activity."

Jude simply stared at the desk that the General sat behind. The wood looked smooth and nearly brand new. He figured it had to be expensive. His ears heard what the General had said, but his heart begged and pleaded with his brain to conceal the information. His mom passed in front of his eyes.

*Aileen's frail body sat helpless on the floor of a dark and bare basement. Cobwebs and clutter hung from the corners. A boy walked in the basement. He was dressed in rags and had many cuts across his face.*

*"Jude, how is my big brave warrior?" Her voice was low and raspy. Tears ran from the boy's green eyes as he took a seat next to his mother.*

"Mom, I am so sorry. I was not able to get any work and we have run out of money."

"It is okay, we will be fine," said Aileen holding her hand to her mouth as she began to cough. When her cough subsided, blood ran down the back of the hand she had been holding over her mouth.

"No mom, it is not okay! You are sick and I have no way to help you," said the boy shaking his head.

"Don't cry my son don't..." Aileen's body fell to the basement floor as Jude failed to catch her in time.

"Mom! Mom!" Jude shook his mother violently, but no movement or sound came from her.

"General please, he didn't know. I chose not to tell him because I knew that he would tell you and wouldn't let me stay on this mission," said Eli.

Flames seared from the floor around Jude's feet as his footsteps retreated in response to the heat. Darkness swam around him as the cold air froze him in place.

"May you burn in the flames of your dishonor forever," echoed a voice throughout the darkness. A bellowish laughter erupted from every direction swallowing Jude up into pain and fear.

Eli's voice broke Jude out of his thoughts. The familiar dark wooden table came back into view, and Jude realized there was no going back.

I'm sorry mom. It is all my fault—I failed you.

"Pascal!"

"General!"

One of the soldiers appeared at Anya's side.

"Send word to the perimeter that we will need half a days supply of food and water for two of our men that will be leaving immediately."

"Yes General! And what of their tents?" asked Pascal.

"They can house the armory just in case it rains before morning," she said.

"Yes General!"

As the flap fell behind Pascal's departure, tension no longer inhabited the air—only rage and sorrow were present. Anya turned her attention back towards them. Jude was still speechless and in disbelief of what had just happened. His brain refused to conceal the truth any longer. As the information filled every inch of his conscience, he began to wonder what he could have possibly done to prevent what had just happened.

"You are both dismissed. May the gods watch over you both."

# ACRIMONY

After leaving Anya's tent, Eli had swamped Jude with a series of apologies and explanations. However to Jude, they were all just excuses, and he felt like he had no reason to be angry with Eli. Jude had believed in his friend and put everything he had fought so hard for on the line to support Eli, and his best friend failed him. However, it was not the fact that Eli had failed him that upset Jude. It was the fact that Jude's flawed judgment, in regards to his best friend, had made Jude lose any hope of protecting those he cared about.

Jude passed by many other soldiers on his way out of the camp. He did not understand why, but his head hung low and his presence felt unwarranted. A large open plain opened up in front of him, void of any plants or animals. Off in the distance, he noticed a small rocky mountain covered with various trees and plants. After a little under an hour, he arrived in front of a small rocky and cavernous mountain. The top of the mountain was an easy hike for Jude, even though he felt like cheating and using the raven's blood in his belt to fly to the top. A couple of large orange and grapefruit trees littered the area. Jude took three oranges and a grapefruit, before hiking back down the mountain.

When he looked towards the direction he had originally came from, he realized that this would be a sleepless night if he did not find something to aid his comfort. He hiked back up the mountain and retrieved some large leaves he found from a foreign tree. The tree seemed familiar, and the familiarity was what brought Jude to its secluded location behind the other trees.

Jude breathed a small sigh of relief, once he had finished with his makeshift bed. He sat cross-legged on the leaves and opened his backpack. He took out the small book that the fox had brought him a couple of days prior. Millions of thoughts and explanations ran through Jude's mind, as he stared down at the cover. Two small figures were etched in the book's soft cover. Both figures tickled the back of his mind. He reached into his backpack and took out the armband that he had purchased a few days ago from Zebediah's Misappropriated Oddities. His heart began to race as his slippery hands dropped the armband. He looked in every direction. Wide, open and uninhabited plains went on for miles all around him.

After tying the armband around his right arm, he picked up the book with the similar inscription. He flipped through the first few pages and realized that all of the text was handwritten.

*It is a journal.*

Most of the journal was blank, except for a few handwritten pages at the beginning. Closing the journal, he reached into his backpack and took out a book that he checked out of the library on Geminate artifacts. He opened the book to the folded page he had been reading a couple of days ago. The symbol of the two figurines stared back at him. Under the figurines was a lone sentence:

"Balance is power."

Jude had read everything in the chapter on the symbol of the light and dark figurines. Nothing aided him in understanding their purpose. From the book, Jude had learned that the people of the Geminate land primarily worshipped Pith over the other two gods—Rune and Aegis. He also learned that the Geminate people had learned from Pith how to reach a level of enlightenment that balanced not only their heart and soul, but their bodies as well. This resulted in the people of Geminate inheriting tremendous power. Jude closed the book on Geminate Artifacts and opened the journal to the first page:

*"As hard as it is to admit, life has gone on without me. The white-stone walls brought both agony and peace, when I laid eyes on them today. After concealing my face, I did what they told me I could never do, I entered Kismet. The citizens that ran aimlessly by bring sickness to my stomach. They still lay oblivious to the enemy that they worship."*

Jude shuttered at what he had just read. Whomever the journal belonged to, they had gotten into the city. The person concealed their identity and infiltrated the city's gates.

*I wonder if this is the person that Bishop was telling Marius about that night.*

He peeled an orange and ate a piece. After wiping his hands on his pants he flipped to the second page:

*"The longer I stay, the longer I do not wish to do what must be done. My eyes laid on a few old comrades and friends I used to know. Even though they betray me every day with their prayers to those three demons they call gods, I feel a fraction of compassion for them. The one that truly gives me pause—is her."*

Jude's eyes grew heavy and soon he found himself nodding off. He closed the journal and set it aside. He took the small jacket his mom had made for him out of his backpack. It was a jacket that she had given him when he was nine years old. Whenever he stayed the night anywhere but home, he always brought it with him. He closed his backpack and used it as a pillow atop the leaves. He covered himself with the jacket and smiled at the scent of warm cotton and spices. Thoughts of home swam throughout his conscience. As he looked up into the stars that stood watch over him, he thought about whom the journal could belong to.

*It is hard to believe that a stranger could get across the border without anyone noticing, let alone the city. Maybe whoever it is, killed anyone that discovered them. But then there would be news of killings amongst the villages and cottages that surround the city. Still it is pretty difficult for someone that is not from Kismet, to walk amongst the soldiers and citizens, and not raise any cause for suspicion. Judging by the second page, I can conclude that it most likely is a male.*

He grabbed the grapefruit and started peeling it. The outer peel was challenging and showed some resistance to its removal.

*He would have to be a man of stealth.*

He choked on the grapefruit as his head sprung up from the ground. He hit his chest violently trying to clear the passageway in his throat.

*Or maybe he is not a man. Maybe it's a —.*

A cold wind blew passed Jude making him shiver in response. He decided that sleep was the most important thing since the Necrosis was the top priority right now. They would be at the border in the next ten hours, and Jude needed to be ready.

*It would be dishonorable to disobey orders, and go to war against the General's will. I should just go home like I was ordered to.*

He closed his eyes and slowed his breathing. Right before sleep was ready to take him, Eli flashed before his eyes.

*"I was wondering if you would mind if I go with you today—you know, to your training session." Eli's tangle of blonde hair sat draped across his forehead and one of his eyes, hiding its presence.*

Jude awoke in alarm. He looked around and saw nothing but the night sky hanging peacefully over the plains. He fluffed his backpack in an attempt to make it more comfortable, before lying back down, and closing his eyes.

*"One hundred percent, because I was the one that notified him in person of his discharge," said Anya*

Jude felt the leaves shifting underneath his restless body. He thought of his mother and Jed having breakfast with him a couple of days ago. The sight rewarded him with comfort.

*"I didn't lie to you. I just didn't tell you."*

Eli and Jude having drinks at Inzanity flashed before his eyes. Eli's arm hung loosely across Jude's shoulder.

*"Jude Bray! In compliance with section nine and article four of the Warfare Decree instated by Lord Rizal Byrne, you are here and henceforth dishonorably discharged on the grounds of mendacious activity," said Anya.*

"I am tired of you! Do you hear me? Tired," yelled Jude as he sat up.

Somewhere far away crickets chirped in unison to the night's humble embrace. Cold sweat slowly fell down Jude's warm face, while he studied his surroundings.

"He is supposed to be my friend."

The crickets ceased after a few minutes. The silence became more prevalent.

"You are not my friend. You are a snake!"

The taste of warm metal caught his attention. He reached into his mouth and his finger returned with the faint presence of blood. The smell of a campfire blew in the wind.

*It must be from the camp.*

He looked towards the direction the scent was coming from, and his eyes fell on the cave that he had ventured to earlier. A small active glow shined from the cave's darkness.

*Could be the enemy.*

Jude reached into his backpack and took out his utility belt. He clasped it around his waist. He noticed the Geminate armband was still tied firmly around his arm. Looking down at it, he felt a surge of confidence.

*If the enemy does lie ahead, and I eliminate them, maybe I can earn back my honor.*

He remembered Jed's tracking advice, specifically the ones pertaining to stealth, and set off towards the cave. The plains were absent of leaves or other items that Jude could step on and give away his presence. He was surprised when he quickly and soundly arrived at the cave. A cold air and sinister whisper brushed across his face. The mouth of the cave was void of any clues of what it contained inside, except for the faint glow. He examined every angle of the cave's outer surroundings. No signs of a roof opening or ulterior entrances were visible.

*If I walk in the front, I will certainly be discovered; and I would hate to have to use any vials.*

He quietly hiked up the side of the cave to where he picked his oranges and grapefruits from earlier. A small hole leading down, laid between two grapefruit trees. Looking down the crevice, his eyes fell on a lone figure moving about. No one else seemed to accompany him.

*They could be hiding or sleeping deeper in the cave.*

Jude found a small rock that laid next to him and threw it towards the entrance of the cave. The figure's head jerked towards the direction of the entrance. After a few seconds, the stranger left Jude's view.

*Looks like I'm up.*

He grabbed a vial from his belt, injected himself and dropped down the crevice. His feet flared with pain as he pointed the tips of his feet as vertical as possible. When he landed, he hit the ground with a softness that gave him a confidence boost. The cave was not as deep as Jude anticipated. A few large boulders sat separated along the back of the cave. A small campfire sat a few feet away from Jude with a lone backpack and blanket next to it. Jude looked towards the front of the cave and saw the figure looking around the outskirts of the entrance, so Jude slipped behind one of the boulders. After a few minutes, the sound of footsteps grew louder, as the noise approached Jude's direction. He peered around the boulder just as the figure's face became close enough to identify.

"Is someone there?"

Eli looked up at the crevice that loomed over him. Jude felt his heart begin to beat faster. He knew his breathing would soon want to join it, so he closed his eyes and tried some light meditation. His breathing soon slowed and his heartbeat followed. He looked back over the boulder and found Eli lying down next to the campfire.

*You are a snake.*

The campfire crackled slightly as Eli's breathing began to slow. Light moisture trickled down his forehead as one of his feet began to kick in place. After a minute or two, his movement ceased.

*"I was wondering if you would mind if I go with you today. You know, to your training session."*

Jude's heart began to race.

*"I didn't lie to you. I just didn't tell you."*

His hand twitched as he summoned a dagger in his hand.

*"Jude Bray! In compliance with section nine and article four of the Warfare Decree instated by Lord Rizal Byrne, you are here and henceforth dishonorably discharged on the grounds of mendacious activity."*

He crept around the boulder, avoiding a few small pebbles that laid in his way.

*You have brought this on yourself. You befriend someone as negative and evil as Zane, but then you punished me, even after you knew you lied to me—me, your so called best friend. Why are you horrible to your family and loyal to that degenerate. You take away my honor, my purpose and my family. This is warranted. This is only right. You have lied and betrayed me, so this is fair. I take your life, the way you ruined mine. A life for a life.*

"Do it," said a soft voice next to him.

He nearly jumped, as he looked frantically around the cave. His heart began to race again as he fought to keep his composure. Fresh adrenaline coursed through his veins. There was no one there—just him and Eli.

*I am tired of you ruining my life. I have always been nothing but good to you. I always helped you study when we were younger. I begged Vance to save your pompous girlfriend. I allowed you to accompany me to our squad training even though you were not on the squad. I put my honor, my life, my family's life and protection on the line to help get you on a squad that you did not even deserve. Every nice thing I do for you, you betray me or deceive me at every turn. I am tired of you ruining my life. Do you hear me! I'm tired! You will get what you deserve—in the end.*

"Do it," said the voice again.

Jude tightened his grip on the dagger before bringing it to Eli's neck. As fresh sweat coated the blade, Jude took a deep breath, closed his eyes and exhaled.

"A life for a life..."

# THE FALICHE PLANT

Jude decided not to go back to the city. He had trained so hard; and after everything that had happened, he knew his presence could help give their men the advantage they needed to win against the Necrosis.

*I don't care what the General says. This is my mission, and she will not take it from me!*

When he awoke, he realized it was still somewhat dark outside. He looked towards the horizon and noticed the sun had not yet risen yet. He turned his attention back towards the long winding river that was the Kismet border. The calm river's transparent waters ran quietly and smoothly down its path, and headed towards the small patch of lone trees that he had visited the evening before. He took two oranges and a grapefruit from the trees before heading back to the spot where he had slept. He peeled one of the oranges and the grapefruit, and started eating. It was warm, but the light cool breeze that consistently blew across his face, cooled him down significantly.

After finishing the fruit, he crossed his legs and began to meditate. His hands sat comfortably on his knees, as he breathed in the warm air deeply. He held the air in his lungs for a few seconds, before releasing it through his mouth. As the routine became more and more natural, Jude felt the heaviness that sat melded to his shoulders all night, lighten. During the breathing, Jude focused most of his energy analyzing every aspect of all of the animals he had ever transformed into, as well as the ones on his belt that he had not yet used. Jude opened his eyes and examined the sun's rays that barely peaked over the horizon. He closed his eyes and returned to his deep breathing.

"Hey," said a voice in front of him.

Jude's eyes sprung open and fell on a set of blue eyes that stared back at him. It was Eli.

"Please leave," said Jude closing his eyes.

"Jude please, at least let me—."

"I said now!"

Jude heard rustling across the ground. He assumed that the noise signaled Eli respecting his wishes and leaving. Jude thought about the night before. He knew that any thoughts of harming Eli, in any way, were wrong. After carefully exiting the cave, Jude ran as fast as he could to his backpack and jacket, which he had left behind. He spent hours praying to the Three Brothers for forgiveness before crying himself to sleep.

When he heard no more commotion around him, Jude assumed Eli was gone.

*I wanted to punish him for all of the numerous times he had betrayed and deceived me.*

His stomach tightened and his heart raced when he thought about the gravity of the situation.

"I mean I found a cave closeby, I would think you would rather stay in there than outside smelling that rotten food smell," said Eli.

"For the last time leave me—wait, rotten food?" Jude took a while to focus on the smell in the air around him, and found himself nearly vomiting at the odor. His eyes flung open. "That is not rotten food, that is the smell of decomposition." He leaped to his feet and looked to his left and saw nothing. He looked in front of him and saw nothing. He looked to his right and saw a dark shadow that crept down from the horizon.

Eli approached him with haste. "What is it?"

Jude realized that there was no time to explain, so he grabbed his bag, and took off towards the campsite. He heard Eli's feet in hot pursuit behind him.

"Hey wait!"

Jude refused to slow down. He pushed his body to run faster. When the tents rose up in front of him, he focused all of his energy to his legs. Agents carried logs, weapons and crates across the camp. Jude heard one of the Agents swear as he barreled passed him. Sprinting into Anya's tent, Jude hoped that the General would be dressed, and not be too angry about his interruption.

"Bray!" Anya looked up from a paper on her desk. "Have you lost your—."

"General! Pardon the interruption. Necrosis are closing in from the north," said Jude as clearly as he could.

"Necrosis?" Anya's eyes widened and her lips parted. "Are you sure?"

"General yes! We need to move now!"

Anya appeared to snap out of some sort of trance before she returned to normal. "Copy that! Pascal!"

"General! Already on it!" It took Pascal no time to exit Anya's tent with the news. Eli barreled into Anya's tent shortly after. He bent over gripping his knees as he tried to regain his breath.

"While your presence here is dishonorable and no longer warranted, I appreciate your service. You both are free to head back to the city now," said Anya rising from her seat. She turned to an armoire and opened it.

"General! While I completely respect your orders, I have to decline," said Jude.

"I do not know what sleeping on the plains has done to your brilliant mind, but just in case you have forgotten, you have no authority to decline my orders," said Anya placing a pair of slate-black shoulder armor on her shoulders.

"General! Please excuse the arrogance, but my presence may impact the outcome of this mission significantly. I have been working on something that could tip this battle in our favor."

"I do not have time for this Bray. If you have a point, now is the time to make it!" said Anya.

"I am not leaving. I have trained for this moment and there is nothing you can do to make me leave."

"This strategy you claim you have, are you positive it will work?" asked Anya.

"Yes General!"

"If your strategy proves to be as valuable as you claim, then I will think about formally retracting *your* discharge," said Anya.

"General I understand!"

"So how does this strategy work?"

"Just send word to have Lieutenant Titus, Quarrels and Wyatt join me at my old tent, along with the two of you, as soon as possible," said Jude looking from Anya to Eli.

"Consider it done," said Anya.

Jude hurried out of Anya's tent and headed for his old tent. As he rushed inside, he ran smack into a pile of boxes that stacked high above his head.

*Wow they didn't waste anytime.*

He opened his bag and took out a small silver case. He opened the case and stared at the six vials that sat secured inside. A knock vibrated the frame of the tent.

"Come in!"

Anya was the first to enter, followed by Conall, Pang, Sia and finally Eli. They all sat in a circle around Jude.

"Okay listen closely to what I am about to tell you," began Jude holding up one of the vials. "This vial holds something that I have been working on for a long time. Its primary ingredient comes from the faliche plant."

Pang's eyes widened. "The faliche plant? How did you—."

"Sorry we are pressed for time," said Jude. "I mixed in careful quantities of that plant, a few other ingredients and my blood."

"Explain its purpose," said Anya.

"It will heighten your senses. You will be abnormally faster and stronger than you could imagine. You will be a faster thinker in battle, as well as another ability I am not at liberty to discuss as of now. But trust me, it is invaluable if it works," said Jude.

"Impossible," said Conall folding his arms. A scream radiated from outside of the tent.

"I promise you," said Jude staring into Anya's eyes.

"Inject us—all of us," said Anya holding her arm out.

# NO VICTORY

$J$ude leaped backwards into a flip, projecting himself high above the battle. The three Necrosis did not expect to see Pang charging straight at them at high velocity, after Jude's body had left the ground. A series of snarls sounded before Jude's newly-summoned blade brought the undead's life to an end with a stab to the heart. The vials that the squad had taken, proved to be a bigger advantage than Jude had hoped. While it made the five of them offensively more deadly, its newly added speed gave them an amazing defense. The battle had started organized, with Anya sending Agents into battle in a controlled formation. Jude, Eli, Pang and Sia were instructed to stay close to Anya and Conall, however once the battle had begun, Jude found himself separated from their group most of the time.

"While I was in the air," started Jude as he dodged under a Necrosis' arm with ease before stabbing it in the heart from behind. "While I was in the air, I saw them swarming in on the General and Lieutenant. Go now!"

"Are you sure that you will be okay? I don't want you to get bitten and come back as a dark bringer of death and destruction—because that's my job," said Pang. He grabbed a Necrosis by the neck and slammed its head face first into the ground. The ground splattered with the crimson stain and remains of the shattered head.

"Yes, now go!"

"On it!" said Pang barreling into a crowd of Necrosis and sending them flying.

When the Necrosis returned to their feet, their attention turned towards Jude. A snarl sounded behind him, and when he flipped his head around, he saw an incoming attack from another small group of Necrosis.

"Clearly fate is not your ally today," said Jude.

A large cloud of black smoke exploded shrouding everything in darkness. Out of the smoke came a giant arachnid barreling down on top of a group of Necrosis and crushing them. The spider spun around grabbing five Necrosis, with its' front legs, before cocooning them.

"Creeping inferno!" yelled a voice from behind him.

A large sustaining burst of flames coiled around the captured Necrosis like a snake before engulfing them. The ground shook beneath his weight, as Jude spun around to see Sia in her black and baby blue body suit. Jude returned to his normal form.

"Feel the burn!"

"Well well, aren't you a pleasure to have at my side," said Jude.

"I am afraid that the pleasure is forbidden—unless you are reckless, honorable and go by the name of Eli."

"Got my flank?"

"Always do," she said with a wink.

"Lets go!" Jude summoned a blade in one hand and a shield in the other. The two of them took off running through a crowd of fighting enemies and allies. While running side-by-side with Sia, Jude decapitated a few Necrosis while keeping his speed. A Necrosis had caught him off guard by jumping in front of him, but was instantly trapped in Sia's earth prison, which gave Jude enough time to eliminate it. Everyone around him, except for Sia, seemed to move in slow motion.

"Have you seen the General or Lieutenant?"

"Yes, Pang got to them shortly before I found you. They should be okay for the moment, but I have not been able to find Eli," said Sia keeping up with Jude's pace.

"Lets find him fast."

"Ready when you are."

After an injection from a vial, Jude's enlarged gargoyle form snatched Sia up before taking flight above the crowd. From above the battle, Jude could see countless Necrosis pouring in from all directions. Explosions and flames clung to every inch of the battlefield.

*We are significantly outnumbered.*

"Oh my Aegis! Jude look!" yelled Sia.

Jude looked down to see a dozen or so children, surrounded by a horde of Necrosis on all sides. A variety of assorted combat armor covered their torsos and legs. They all stood huddled together, relinquishing their over-sized weapons and cowering before the gnashing of teeth around them. A young girl screamed.

"Catch me!" yelled Sia. She jumped from Jude's back, barreling down over the surrounded children.

*What is she doing?*

The wind blew violently and the sky darkened, causing Jude to flap his wings harder.

Right as Sia was halfway to the ground, the sky rumbled with the sound of thunder, as a bolt of lightning struck her with a direct hit—halting her fall.

"Rune's Rein!" screamed Sia. Her arms rose towards the storm above her, chaining lightning across the Necrosis beneath her. The children beneath her screamed in unison as lightning bolts rained from the sky in a circle around them, turning the surrounding Necrosis to ash.

Jude's instincts sent worry, when the lightning stopped and the sky calmed. The lightning bolt, which had been holding

Sia suspended in the air, lightly faded causing her body to continue its descent towards the chaos beneath her. Jude dive-bombed towards the crowd. One of the children looked up and screamed.

*I'm not going to make it.*

He amplified his size, and just when Sia was nearly to the ground, he tucked one of his massive wings under her body, and kicked up for the sky. He felt her small body roll across his wing and down to his back.

"Whoa! Close one," said Sia tightening the grip of her legs.

"Nice work. Insanely crazy, but nice work," growled Jude. He looked down to notice the area around the children was scattered with the sizzling ash remains of the Necrosis that once stood there. Dagger barrages fired in all directions amidst the pandemonium, as Weapons Masters drove back countless hordes. A colossal primate leaped in front of the Weapons Masters, burying its fists into the ground in front of it, and causing a trench to open up and swallow the Necrosis that closed in.

"There!" yelled Sia pointing down. "I see him!"

Jude looked down to see Eli being surrounded by five or six Necrosis. As Jude circled around the battle to aid Eli, he saw his friend eliminate two of the Necrosis at incredible speed. Soon a Necrosis jumped on his back from behind, sending him tumbling to the ground. The other Necrosis soon joined the first as they all piled on top of him.

"Debilitate!" yelled Sia.

The Necrosis went flying in all directions, as Eli emerged from the cluster. Jude set Sia down before returning to his normal form at her side. He front flipped on top of the shoulders of one of the Necrosis, cracking its neck, before leaping to the next. When he was done with his third, he saw that Sia and Eli had dispatched the others that had surrounded them.

A stray Necrosis, faster than the others, sped at the three of them, but was soon cut down by an ally Weapons Master.

"Thanks for that," said Eli.

Panic overtook the Weapons Master, as he looked passed them and off into the distance. His bottom lip quivered and his teeth chattered, as he slowly brought his finger up.

Sia was quick to ask the question that Jude was too afraid to ask. "What is it?"

"Nyctimene!" yelled the Agent.

Jude flipped around to see three enormous bat-like gargoyles flying in from the east. Their shrieking battle cries rang throughout the battlefield, sending chills down his spine.

"Look out!" screamed Sia pushing Jude out of the way with remarkable speed. He tumbled to the ground and returned to his feet. A fourth nyctimene gained altitude after its failed attack on Jude.

*What do we do?*

Jude looked around for any fellow Combat Specialists. "We need to find the—."

"Pascal! Bray! Wyatt! Anyone," yelled a voice from behind them.

Jude ran through the crowd of Necrosis. He offered quick assistance to any fellow Agents that he passed along the way. A small group of Weapons Masters and Magi laid injured at the feet of some incoming Necrosis. Knowing he could not afford to stop and help, he tossed a vial at the injured allies. Black smoke erupted around them, concealing them all.

*I hope that at least gives them time to get away.*

When he had finally got through the crowd, he saw Anya laying on the ground clenching her arm with one hand, and holding a throwing dagger in the other. Pang and Conall stood in front of her, fending off incoming Necrosis. One grabbed a hold of Pang's neck, but Pang grabbed its wrist and broke it off, leaving a decomposed hand around his neck. It was then that he noticed Jude's presence.

"Bray! Good thing you are here. The General is injured and needs assistance," said Conall.

"But I am not a healer," said Jude.

"I have some herbs that may help," said Sia as her and Eli joined the group.

"I don't care who does what. Just do it! We will buy you time," said Conall.

Sia joined Anya on the floor, while the rest of them returned to the incoming swarm. Screams radiated throughout the crowd, as the four nyctimene swooped down snatching up large groups of Agents, and sending them hurtling towards the ground. One of the nyctimene swallowed a Weapons Master whole, who was trying to summon a weapon, but to no avail. A large group of Necrosis caved in around Jude and his group. Jude reached for his python vial and injected it. His enormous body coiled around Pang, Conall and Eli blocking their backs and sides, in an attempt to provide defense. From his eyes, his comrades looked like small pets. Jude's large head reared up from behind the three Agents, tasting the air in front of it. The air reeked of death, rotting flesh and vomit. The scent made Jude's python form giddy with anticipation.

"Bray has got our defenses, you two on the assault," said Conall.  He leaped in front of the group, throwing one of his hands up at the hundreds of incoming Necrosis.

"Cannonade!"

Conall's voice triggered a deafening explosion that detonated in front of him. The sky rained with the arms, legs and heads of the Necrosis that once stood there. A large, open and uninhabited area laid before the Lieutenant.

Jude watched Eli and Pang join Conall in battle. A group of Necrosis all fell in unison, as Conall lopped off their heads with a quick slash of his sword. Pang picked Conall up and hurled him forward at an incoming group of enemies, which were skewered together, as Conall's blade plunged through the three of them. A couple of Necrosis came in sprinting behind the three of them but were swallowed whole, as Jude attacked one, and then the other.

Someone screamed. The four of them turned around to see a Necrosis dragging Sia into a horde.

"Get off of me!" she cried. She kicked and screamed in an attempt to get free.

Jude heard Eli scream behind him.

"Take this!" said a voice next to Jude.

The Necrosis dragging Sia collapsed to the floor on top of her—the tip of a blade projecting firmly out of the back of its head. A light wind blew passed Jude before he saw Conall at Sia's side, pulling the fallen Necrosis off of her, and helping Sia to her feet. The two of them stared at each other for a while. Conall said something to Sia that Jude could not quite make out.

"Lieutenant! Behind you both!" yelled Anya.

Jude had lost focus and failed to see the dozens of Necrosis that were mere feet from Sia and Conall. He ran after them in hopes that he would get there in time. Jude saw Conall's hand wrap firmly around Sia's waist, pulling her close to him.

"Total defense perimeter!" yelled Conall.

The familiar shields materialized around both Conall and Sia, before the two of them began to spin at high velocity—and soon the shields joined them. The heavy impact of the shields sent Necrosis flying in all directions. Jude found himself diving out of the way to prevent himself from being mangled by bodies that flew his way. When he looked up, he found Eli lying right next to him. His face was scorched with what appeared to be rage and hostility. He quickly returned to his feet without even noticing Jude's presence a few feet away.

When the attack stopped, so did Conall and Sia. Dozens of Necrosis laid motionless in a circle around Conall and Sia's feet—which were still in close proximity to one another. A small smile seemed to appear on her face, before she returned to Anya's side. Conall returned to Pang's side, while Eli and Jude returned to their feet.

"Quarrels and I will hang back and defend them. Bray, you and Brassie buy us some time," said Conall taking a stance next to Pang, who was now in front of Anya and Sia.

"Why don't *I* hang back and you and Jude buy us some time," said Eli.

The glare from Conall was foreign to Jude. Instead of the emotionless and collected demeanor he always displayed, the look of a savage killer now took its place.

"We are on it Lieutenant," said Jude as he pulled Eli back towards the battle. "That was a dumb move, even for you." Jude took off running into the crowd. He summoned a blade in each hand, and as Eli matched his pace, Jude noticed that Eli had summoned the same.

"Crisscross assault. If you don't know it, then just follow my lead," said Jude never losing speed.

"Okay."

A line of Necrosis closed in. Jude ran diagonal in front of Eli's path, who went the opposite direction in response. The two of them closed in quickly on the Necrosis, crisscrossing their paths in an attempt to confuse their enemies, and slow their response time. The Necrosis in front slowed down looking from Jude, who crisscrossed to the left, then to Eli, who had went the opposite direction. Jude closed in stabbing both swords through the first Necrosis heart, which sent it tumbling to the ground. Two Necrosis closed in too fast for him to react. Jude felt a foot on his shoulder and looked up to see Eli jumping over his head, crashing down with both of his swords outstretched. He sat kneeled on the ground between the Necrosis who stood motionless. A few seconds later, their heads slowly fell to the floor, followed by their bodies.

"Oops—sorry," said Eli towards the fallen corpses.

Shrieks sounded from all sides of them, as the Nyctimene quickly picked through squadrons of allies. Jude counted three and could not locate the fourth.

"Jude! Help!"

Jude looked up to the fourth nyctimene soaring away with Eli trapped in its claws. Its speed was fast and it quickly put distance between Eli and Jude.

"Not gonna happen!" Jude executed a front flip above the crowd. His feet came down on top of the shoulders of an Agent. He leaped from the Agent's shoulder onto the head of one Necrosis, and then another. Soon Jude found himself running at full speed atop the heads of both enemies and allies. He kept pushing for more speed, knowing that if he slowed down too much, he would lose momentum and fall. A series of snarls and curse words rang out from underneath him, as he stepped on the head of a Necrosis and then a Magi, who were doing battle. As he got closer to the nyctimene holding Eli, he threw both of his hands down on the head of a Necrosis, breaking its neck, and propelling himself higher into the air until he was above the battle. After concentration, his blade appeared in his hand before he brought it directly down above the Nyctimene's back. A shriek so loud, that it made Jude let go of his sword, rang out from the creature. Jude found himself tumbling towards the ground at high speeds, as he fell from the Nyctimene's back. Then suddenly he noticed that he was still falling at the same speed, but it felt slower to him at the same time.

*Thank you faliche vial!*

He easily forced his feet smoothly down beneath him, so that when he finally landed, he landed on both feet with ease. Eli was not so lucky, who tried to land on his feet but ended up tumbling forward and smashing his face into the ground.

"Are you alright?"

"Never better. Thanks. I thought no means no, even when a guy says it," said Eli dusting off his shoulders.

"On your right!"

"Blunt force!" Eli threw his hand out without looking. Two incoming Necrosis fell headless, as the spinning axes slit passed their throats and continued on through the crowd—ignoring ally Agents but decapitating other Necrosis in the process.

"How do they know to avoid the other Agents?"

"Because I pictured only Necrosis in my mind when I summoned them. They will continue to attack until they are stopped," said Eli with a smirk.

Jude did not feel like returning any smirk or smile in response to Eli's gesture.

"We need to get back to the group. Follow me. If there are any Necrosis that get in our way, crisscross formation again," said Jude.

"Right."

The two of them headed back into battle. They came in contact with many Necrosis on the way back to the group, but all of them fell to Eli and Jude's tag-team assault. Jude had to admit that they made a good team on the battlefield. However, that was the only place they made a good team. When they returned to the group, they found Anya on her feet alongside the others.

"Bray," said Anya sticking a sword into one Necrosis, and then turning her gaze to a group of incoming enemies, who fell to her dagger barrage as she blinked.

"General! I managed to kill one of the Nyctimene, but the other three are devastating our already low numbers. I estimate a loss of over a hundred men from their attacks."

"A hundred men!"

"Yes General! Permission to engage the hostiles and eliminate them," said Jude.

Before Anya could respond, a Nyctimene swooped down, snatching her up and taking off to the sky.

"Unhand me foul beast!" yelled Anya struggling.

"Permission granted! Starting with that one!" yelled Conall as he pointed to the Nyctimene that had just captured Anya.

"Copy!" Jude injected himself with a vial, and took off after Anya.

◆◆◆

Eli became pinned down under two Necrosis that snapped down at his face and neck. He struggled to summon a weapon, but realized his concentration was too distracted by not only the snaps from the creatures' jaws, but the odor as well. The rank odor smelled far worse than any rotten meat Eli could imagine. It was sour and hot at the same time, with the scent of vomit mixed in with it. He swayed and grunted trying to push them off of him, while footsteps sounded close by.

"Get off of him now!"

The creatures continued to snap at Eli, as one of their hands grabbed a hold of his neck, cutting off his airflow.

"Implosion!"

Eli finally identified the voice just as shreds of foul smelling flesh, sprayed across his face. As he wiped a mixture of grime, gore, blood and flesh from his face, he looked up to see a pair of light purple eyes staring down at him. They were her eyes. Sia extended a hand towards him, and helped him to his feet when he accepted it. An image of Conall holding her close passed in front of his eyes. His eyes squinted while he felt his jaw clench. Taking a deep breath, he disregarded the image.

"Hey babe," he said.

Sia ran passed him as if unaware that he had said anything. "Creeping inferno!"

Eli turned around to see two Necrosis in spasms underneath the flames of Sia's attack. After a few seconds, the flames dissipated, and all that was left of their bodies, was two small piles of ash.

"I would be lying if I said nice try," she said while glaring at the ash piles. She turned back towards Eli as if seeing him for the first time. "Did you just call me babe?"

Eli grabbed a throwing dagger that appeared above his shoulder, and tossed it at a Necrosis that ran up behind Sia. The dagger buried itself dead-center into the Necrosis' forehead, before the creature collapsed to the floor.

"I guess I did. Sorry."

She looked back at the fallen Necrosis, and then returned his gaze. "I like it when you're deadly." She bit the side of her lip while her chest rose and fell heavily.

Eli felt his body temperature rise, causing his face to feel warm and his forehead moist. His hands clawed around her waist as his breath met hers. He felt her moans between their lips, and soon noticed that his thirst for her taste grew by the second. Snarls sounded from all around them. Just when Eli had planned to cease the moment and eliminate them, Sia mumbled something and soon Eli felt small explosions all around them. She pulled him tighter into a kiss whenever he loosened their embrace. After a few minutes, their lips detached. She wiped his lips and cheeks with her hand, before running off towards a group of incoming enemies.

*Oh my Aegis, I think I'm going to have a stroke.*

Eli heard footsteps behind him and soon smelled a foul odor in the air. A volley of arrows formed in front of him, before shooting back over his shoulder. He turned around and saw four Necrosis falling to the ground. Arrows sat buried in their chests. A scream erupted from behind him.

"Eli help! Help me!"

"Sia!" Eli ran in the direction of her voice. So many Necrosis ran at him from all angles, clouding his view. "Where are you?"

Her scream erupted a few feet in front of him. Dozens of Necrosis blocked his way scratching and chomping as they closed in around him.

"Get off of me!" yelled Eli hurling arrow barrages in all directions.

Dozens of Necrosis fell at his feet, but were soon replaced by others. Eli looked around at the hunger on their faces and panicked. A Necrosis apprehended him from behind, while another leaped on top of him, before pinning him to the ground.

"Help! Please someone—help—me!" screamed Sia. Her cry for help drove him insane with rage.

Eli rebelled against the feeling of helplessness that began to neutralize him. "I said get off of me!" he yelled, as more Necrosis piled on top of him. The scent of rotten meat and vomit filled every inch of the air around him. The itch in his brain returned with a faint presence.

"Cataclysm!"

The word was both foreign and forgettable to him. When he looked up, he noticed the Necrosis were gone. Returning to his feet, he didn't look for an answer to their whereabouts. As he came upon the nightmare in front of him, he felt something inside of him shatter. Daggers materialized all around him—and rained down in every direction—as he directed them towards every Necrosis that laid on top of her.

"Die! Just die! All of you!"

Masses of Necrosis lay at his feet when he saw the last one crawling on top of her. His sword batted its' head into the sky, while its body toppled over with ease. Tangles of matted brown hair caked with blood, laid before him. Grotesque lacerations covered her neck, shoulders and arms. The scent of death covered her. He knelt down next to her, cupping her face in his hand.

"No! Please—say something!"

Her eyes slowly opened. The purple brilliance that always shined effortlessly, was replaced with a shiny veil that shrouded a ghost of the brilliance that once existed there.

"You are here," she said before her body began to lightly shake.

"I'm sorry! I'm so sorry! I tried, I really did."

A light smile touched her lips briefly, before hollow coughs took its place.

"What do I do?" He heard the desperation in his own voice.

Her body was still. For a moment, he thought that he was alone amidst the battle. She blinked slowly once—twice.

"Please, tell me what to do," he said.

"My pouch."

He looked around her waist and set eyes on a gruesome gash on her thigh. His eyes met hers. A ghost of a smile passed her lips. On her waist he found a small black pouch. Inside he found two identical bottles. He held one at eye level to her. Her lips slowly opened as a small stream of black liquid fell from the corner of her mouth. His tear matched what he saw. He opened the bottle and poured the contents into her mouth. While she slowly swallowed, he looked for any signs of any immediate effects. He saw nothing.

"Now what?"

"All my... All my physical wounds should begin to heal and the pain should subside," she said.

"So you're fine. You will be okay—right?"

She did not answer, just met his gaze. The briefing flashed before him.

*"One bite from these creatures will result in immediate fatality."*

He raised her head closer to his and hugged her, as tears fell from his eyes. "Please, what do I do?"

Her hand cupped his face while more tears ran from both his eyes. "Don't leave me," she said softly.

"Never."

He leaned down and kissed her. As she slowly began to kiss him back, a hand wrapped around his waist and took him from her. Two Necrosis had him pinned as they dragged him away.

"No! Get off of me! Damn it! I said get off!"

Sia grew more distant as the Necrosis dragged him further away. She smiled faintly before her eyelids came down over all of the life that he could see. A Necrosis loomed over him. Before he could react, another Necrosis buried its teeth into his neck. He screamed. The pain was excruciating as he whipped his head back and forth in response. The wound burned and ached simultaneously. Another Necrosis climbed on top of him before Eli felt its teeth on his shoulder. His eyelids instantly grew heavy when his body grew numb. The taste of grass filled his taste buds, and then darkness closed in.

◆ ◆ ◆

Jude's body failed to respond when he ordered it to move. He felt his neck stiffen and his back cramp when he tried to force it to get up. As he rolled himself over onto his stomach, pain shot throughout his back and neck. The Nyctimene lay motionless in front of him. Jude breathed a sigh of relief.

*At least I don't have to deal with that anymore.*

The Nyctimene's large head stirred, and soon its eye shot open. Jude quickly reached for a vial, covered his mouth, and tossed it at the creature. A large cloud of dark green smoke, sprang loose from the vial, and shrouded the Nyctimene. The creature shrieked in all directions while it slammed its head violently into the ground. Jude buried his face into the ground to shield himself. When the smoke cleared, he looked up to see the creature's face pillaged with various-sized lesions and raw patches.

*Like I said, at least I don't have to deal with that anymore.*

He bit his bottom lip in anticipation, and forced his body to stand. The pain seemed to vibrate his spine when he came to one knee. His breathing quickened and his heart raced. He pushed up from the ground and immediately his body began to hunch.

*It is moments like these, that make me wish that pain was pleasure.*

"You have a small fracture that pinched a nerve on your lower back," said a familiar voice from behind him.

Jude was slow to turn around, but soon found himself staring into a pair of white translucent eyes.

"One second," said Jed before vanishing. A few seconds later, he appeared in front of Jude holding a snarling Necrosis by the neck.

"You had a visitor." The Vampire drove his hand into the Necrosis he was holding, and returned with a beating heart. "There is no killing these creatures unless they take a direct attack to the heart or a severing of their spinal cord, either directly or by decapitation. I personally like a more entertaining method." The heart turned to dust as Jed's pale hand tightened its grip. He dropped the creature's body to the floor, and soon the dust followed. "As for your fracture and pinched nerve, I can temporarily fix it. However, there's a catch."

"What's the catch?"

"Hold on," said Jed disappearing once again and then reappearing with the stray head of a Necrosis, before tossing it down at his feet. "It's painful."

"How painful?"

"Very," said Jed extending his fangs.

"Do it."

Jed turned Jude around and gripped the sides of Jude's waist with both hands. "Now breathe in."

Jude closed his eyes and did as he was told.

"Perfect and—."

Jude screamed as both hot and cold pain smashed around his insides, originating from his neck. The pain continued to travel in what felt like an infinite loop, while it grew more intense. Jude screamed repeatedly with each scream growing rougher. Soon darkness caved in from all angles, before he felt himself drift off into the comforts of the safe haven behind his eyes.

*A hooded figure dressed in a royal blue robe, walked slowly towards a large stone door. The door depicted an unclear picture along its smooth but rough surface. The figure kneeled to its feet before the door. After a few seconds, the stonewall slid open, revealing a large inner chamber. Once the figure returned to its feet, it entered the chamber and the door slid closed.*

Long extended fangs pierced his vision. Jude shook off his nausea and opened one of his eyes a little more, to find Jed staring down at him.

"You know, rescuing feinting princesses really isn't my thing," said Jed.

"I didn't know that you knew how to tell a joke," said Jude forcing his eyes open.

"Who says I was joking?"

Jude laughed at his brother's words. He forced himself out of Jed's hands and up to his feet. "You have been practicing your social skills."

"Perhaps."

"There is still one Nyctimene left. Can you watch my flank as I try to get to it?"

"May the crows feast on its flesh," said Jed.

Jude started in a slow jog, in fear of the pending pain. However, he was surprised to realize that no pain came at all, even when he quickened his jog.

"How did you do that? I don't feel any pain anymore," said Jude running at full force.

"It's complicated. Lets just say I temporarily fixed your injury, with emphasis on temporarily. You will need to see a healer as soon as you get back to the city, or else the pain will return."

Jude made a mental note and then flipped himself over two Necrosis that had jumped in front of him. He heard snarls behind him and knew that Jed had taken care of them. Soon the immortal was back at Jude's side.

"How are you able to keep up with me?"

"A little concoction I have been working on. Heightens my speed, thinking capabilities and strength temporarily. However, I am running at my max and I am sure you are still significantly faster than me."

"Clearly, since I am only jogging," said Jed with a small curl of his lips.

A Necrosis tackled Jude to the floor. Its' yellow teeth were caked with blood and fragments of flesh when it snapped at his face. Jude rolled on top of the Necrosis, summoning a dagger, before stabbing it in the heart. Jude looked up to find Jed surrounded by three Necrosis. One took a step forward and then collapsed to the floor. Jed stood idle with another black heart in his hand. Both Necrosis charged him and soon Jed was behind them as the creatures kept running. They soon stopped, looked around for a few seconds, and then charged back towards Jed.

"I don't know if anyone told you, but these are the last two seconds of your life," said Jed.

After a blur of movement, the two Necrosis fell to Jed's feet, with their heads turned completely around. Jed jerked his head in small acute angles like a small bird. Jude assumed he was scanning for enemies. When Jude surveyed the area behind Jed, he saw slow movement out of the corner of his eye. He jerked his head to the right to see a fallen Necrosis returning to its feet. Jude back-flipped on top of the Necrosis' shoulders. He locked his legs around the creature's neck before jerking them violently to the side. A loud *crack* sounded from the creature's neck.

"Be smart," said Jude slamming the creature down with his legs at Jed's feet.

Jed jabbed his hand savagely into the creature's chest and returned with a heart. "Stay down!"

Jude sprinted towards the last place he had seen the General, in hopes that she was somewhere closeby. When he looked around, he noticed that for every one Necrosis, there were two to three comrades.

*I don't believe it. We were out-numbered and now our enemy is out-numbered. Our Agents really are legends.*

One of the Agents ran by Jed and Jude, as if unaware of their presence. He stopped a few feet after passing them, and turned around slowly. The ground rumbled under Jude's feet. *Thud. Thud.* Small pebbles leaped shortly off of the ground repeatedly. *Thud. Thud.*

The comrade's finger slowly rose. "Necroborns!"

Jude and Jed turned around to see an army of soldiers led by an extremely large figure closing in on them. When the large figure grew closer, Jude was finally able to fully see him. He appeared to be a man who was taller than anyone Jude had ever seen. His arms screamed power and the large war axe he carried was taller than Jude, and screamed thirst. A mask, made out of what looked like bone, shielded his face while his axe sliced two Magi in half, staining the air with their blood.

"I do not believe it," said Jed turning to face the tall man.

"Who are they?"

"General Rorik. The creatures under his command are Necroborns. They were supposed to be our allies. We are in for a tough fight."

A loud bellow echoed down the battlefield from the direction of General Rorik. He closed in on Jude and Jed, exposing a smile that sent chills down Jude's spine. With a quick swing of his axe, he knocked Jed through the air, sending him tumbling across the plains. Jude stared into the General's mask as he turned his attention back to Jude.

A loud roar emerged from General Rorik. "Bring me their heads! I want to see the skies cry with the blood of their suffering, as the maggots feast on their flesh!"

Light purple was the first thing that Eli saw when he opened his eyes. When he took a few seconds to make out her face, a smile came to it.

"Thank the gods! I thought I was too late," said Sia.

"What's going on?"

"I had one last bottle of cheriye extract left. I gave it to you as soon as I could move again."

He took a few minutes to focus. "This can't be real. You were bitten—by a Necrosis. You died."

"This *is* real. I am here—with you," she said.

"You are alive?" he said cupping her face in his hand.

Her hand touched his as her eyes closed, releasing a tear. "I am."

"How?"

"I do not know. The extract heals physical injuries, but a bite from a Necrosis is—supposed to stop your heart. We both should be dead," she said with a flicker of enlightenment.

"Is this a dream?"

"No, this is not a dream. I am here with you, and you are here with me," she said.

Surprise was clear on her face as he mashed his lips into hers. She kissed him back with the same intensity. A few times she tried to pull away, but he tightened his grip. After a couple of minutes she pulled away.

"We need to get back to the rendezvous point. I heard a horn when you were unconscious. It was—foreign. Something is wrong."

"Let's go," he said quickly returning to his feet.

"You go, there is something I have to do."

"What? No! I'm not leaving you! Not ever!"

"I promise, I will be quick," she said.

Eli followed a few other men back towards the rendezvous point, and after a few short minutes, he met up with Sia and Pang just as Conall met up with Anya. Eli found himself wrecking his brain in an attempt to try and figure out what was so important that Sia had to leave him, after what they had just went through. Conall met his gaze for a few seconds before turning back towards Anya.

*You're dead!*

One of the Agents stepped forward. "What are your orders General?"

Anya surveyed the remaining Agents, as if waiting for all eyes to be on her. "The Necrosis were never the real threat. Their purpose was to dwindle down our forces. I have heard news that the General of the Necroborns, General Rorik, along with an army of Necroborns, have been spotted in section seven. They were supposed to be our allies, but have killed over fifty of our men," said Anya.

Commotion broke out amongst the men.

"Section seven? That is where I last saw Jude," said Sia. Her outburst drew Anya's attention, who regarded her with a slight display of worry.

"Our enemy's strengths and weaknesses have changed. Necroborns are different than the Necrosis. If you cut off their arm, it will grow back. If you cut them in half, they will reassemble. Even if you chop off their head, they will sprout a new one. Unlike the Necrosis, they act and think like you and I. They can wield weapons and formulate strategies like you and I. They will ambush you. They will trap you. They will out-think you. But they won't over-estimate you. The only way to kill them, is a direct stab in the heart, or its extraction," said Conall.

"Wyatt!"

"General!"

522

"I want you and Brassie to head to section seven to find Bray. Perhaps the three of you can come up with a plan to weaken our enemy's numbers," said Anya.

"Copy that!"

"Lieutenant Titus!"

"General!"

"I want you to take all but five men and engage the Necroborns directly. In the next hour, I want to see this floor littered with their corpses. Do I make myself clear?"

"Yes General!" said Conall.

"Quarrels!"

"General!"

"I want you and the rest to come with me. We are burying a General today," said Anya.

After everyone was dismissed, Eli and Sia set off towards section seven. Thanks to Jude's substance, Eli found himself running faster than he had ever run before. As he glanced at Sia while they ran side-by-side, he saw nothing but determination and confidence in her eyes.

*She doesn't even know that I've been discharged and that I am responsible for Jude getting discharged.*

He decided that sooner or later she would find out. So Eli decided that he would tell her after the battle, but make sure to leave the word "dishonorable" out of it, when he told her that he was discharged.

"I'll protect you."

"What?"

"I said I'll protect you. I won't let anything happen to you again," said Eli.

A vast horizontal line of Necroborns charged towards them. Sia and Eli sped to a stop, realizing that they would never be able to get through the swarm.

"Need a lift?"

They both turned around to see a short dark-haired man standing before them. His brown eyes matched his hair, but his light skin paled in comparison to his shiny white teeth that sparkled. He was dressed in black plated armor from head to toe. A necklace of small containers hung from his neck.

"Agent William Morgan, Combat Specialist, at *your* service," he said.

"Nice to meet you," said Sia.

"I'm afraid we don't have time for introductions," said Eli. "Can you get us around those Necroborns?"

"Sure can!" said William detaching one of the containers from his necklace. After drinking the contents of the small container, William sprouted feathers, and eventually transformed into an enormous bird. The hawk let loose a loud shrieking cry as he extended his massive wings.

"Get on," said Sia climbing up the side of William.

Eli followed, finding a spot behind her. He wrapped his hands around her waist when the hawk kicked up from the ground, leaving a large dust cloud in its wake. The sky was peaceful and calm compared to being on the ground. Dozens of clouds floated smoothly and silently by, greeting the three of them softly as they flew by.

*If heaven is real, I expect it to feel like flying amongst the clouds—quiet and peaceful.*

Eli absorbed the sun's rays and the wind's embrace while William flew them high above the line of Necroborns. A few arrows had shot passed them, but William smoothly dodged with ease.

"A little lower please," said Sia.

The hawk descended just in time for Eli to spot Jude lying at the feet of an enormous giant.

"There!" yelled Eli.

"That must be General Rorik," said Sia.

"More like Giant Rorik," said Eli.

"William down there!"

The hawk went into a dive towards the giant. Jude's body left the ground when the giant picked Jude up by his neck. The hawk dropped Sia and Eli off at the closest spot away from the Necroborns. The two of them took off towards Jude and the General.

Dozens of Necroborns piled in front of them in an attempt to block their path. They looked just like regular soldiers, except they moved like savage animals, and smelled of rotten meat and vomit just like the Necrosis. Eli summoned his bow and fired an arrow directly at the Necroborns' hearts, remembering what Anya had said. Two Necroborns collapsed to the floor. Eli looked next to him to see purple projectiles impaling three Necroborns through the chest, before they fell at Sia's feet. Eli found himself a few feet from General Rorik, who appeared to be mumbling something to Jude.

"Jude!" yelled Eli.

There was no response from Jude or the General. Jude just hung lifeless in the General's grip.

"Sia I can't get to him. Help him!"

Sia flew to the ground in front of him, as a Necroborn leaped on top of her. She kicked him off and punched a flame through the creature's chest. "I can't! There are too many!"

Eli tried to ignore the Necroborns and run around them. He was close to Jude, but no matter how much he tried, he could not get to him. He tried to summon a blade and felt his blood energy drop. His vision blurred and his body automatically gagged. A Necroborn leaped in front of Eli and bashed him in the face with its shield. Blood coated his tongue when he tumbled across the terrain. He leaped to his feet only to be pelted with two arrows that knocked him back to the floor.

"Sia! Help!" yelled Eli.

Explosions rose from all sides of him causing the tremors to force him to the floor. A hand grabbed the back of his tunic and pulled him to his feet. It was Sia.

"Go help him—please!" said Sia kissing him on the cheek before shoving him towards Jude's direction. "I got your flank."

Eli ran as fast as he could towards Jude and the General. Dozens of arrows fell to his feet, after coming into contact with a purple haze that formed around him. Necroborns abandoned their bows and took to a direct assault, after realizing that projectiles were useless against the magic that Sia surrounded him with. Any Necroborns that got too close immediately toppled over, as their paralyzed bodies fell to the ground beneath him.

"Would you like to pray to your worthless gods maggot?" growled Rorik. He laughed with tremendous bass.

"I have disappointed them. They won't help me now," said Jude in a faint voice. His body shook violently when he coughed.

One Necroborn grabbed Eli's arm. He summoned a blade with his other hand, but before he could use it, another Necroborn grabbed his hand. Even with his increased strength, the two Necroborns' still over-powered him.

"I tire of playing with you. Die now!" snarled the General as he held Jude higher above the battle.

Eli's eyes burned when the cloud of dark green smoke cloaked the battlefield. He grabbed Sia, who was battling a Necroborn next to her, and ran to evade the burning smoke. Cries and snarls sounded throughout the battlefield, as Necroborns and Agents, fell to the cloud of burning smoke. Eli threw Sia down to the ground in front of him, and soon jumped to her side. He covered his mouth and waited for the smoke to blow over. Once it did, the two of them returned to their feet. Hundreds of Necroborns laid lifeless on the floor at the General's feet. The General stood on one knee while his lungs rose and fell quickly between his grunts.

"Where's Jude?" asked Sia.

Eli looked around but saw nothing but a hundred or so incoming Necroborns from the east. "I don't know. But we have another problem."

◆◆◆

Jude's body was worn down from the battle with General Rorik. The General's brute force proved to be a formidable weapon against him. Seeing how the General had cut a Combat Specialist—in the form of a massive jackal—in half with one swing of his axe, made Jude forfeit his plan of using his blood vials. After the release of the poison, Jude was sure he would die by his own attack. However, when he looked up, he found himself looking into a familiar pair of white eyes.

"Like I said before, rescuing feinting princesses really is not my thing," said Jed.

"If you call me princess one more time, you are the one that will need rescuing," said Jude returning to his feet.

A Nyctimene shrieked from behind them.

"You take the ground and I take the air?"

"Sure! If you think you can handle it," said Jude with a smirk.

"Watch this." Jed laid down on the floor and grabbed his side. He squirmed around in place letting loose a series of moans and cries for help. A shriek came down from the Nyctimene as it changed direction and headed back towards Jed.

"You sure you know what you're doing?" asked Jude.

"Trust me. I have been a predator for a few years now. I know what looks appetizing and what doesn't," said Jed before returning to his moans.

The Nyctimene closed in and its claws came down on Jed. Jude looked in the creature's grasp while it kicked up for the sky, and saw nothing.

"Catch you later little brother," said Jed from high above Jude's view. A lone figure stood arms crossed on the nyctimene's back while it soared through the air.

"Show off."

A group of Necroborns bashed their blades against their shields as they closed in on Jude.

*Only fools taunt before their death.*

Jude charged the Necroborns, who snapped and screeched, in what sounded like enjoyment at his presence. He injected a vial and fired a barrage of arrows. He missed all but two Necroborns, who fell instantly.

*This weapons thing is not my thing.*

He dissolved the bow and threw his hands in front of him. His acrobatics sent him soaring into the air. He threw a vial down casting a black cloud of smoke atop the Necroborns. Grunts and coughs radiated from their position. Their weapons dropped and the shrieks grew louder as a large black snake fell on two of them, crushing them instantly. The anaconda quickly coiled around the remaining Necroborns, going around them multiple times, before its large head towered over them. Jude tightened his coils around all six of their bodies. A series of crunches swam through Jude's scales when the Necroborns heads dropped. Jude loosened his coil and began to swallow each Necroborn. When the feet of the last one slipped down the back of his throat, he noticed a group of Agents engaging General Rorik.

*Payback.*

The anaconda slithered swiftly towards the General, and soon Jude returned to his normal form while still sprinting. The General swung his mighty war axe, sending three Agents tumbling across the plains' rough terrain. The General and Anya circled each other as if in a dance. The General held his axe while Anya's hands were bare of any weapons that Jude could see. The General swung just as Anya jumped flat to the ground dodging the attack. She rolled to the side just in time to evade a stomp. A blade appeared in Anya's hand before she used both hands to stab the ground in front of her.

"Execution style!"

A crack radiated from the sword in the ground and circled the General. Hundreds of daggers formed in midair all around Rorik, before they all skewered him. A thunderous bellow vibrated from Rorik's throat, while he squirmed against the attack. Blood poured from his wounds while his massive contorted hands pulled blades out of his body.

"I'll take it from here General," said a voice from above Jude.

A loud shriek filled the air as Jed flew in standing on the Nyctimene's back. The creature had three or four Necroborns in its mouth that it spit to the ground while it circled the General. Anya looked up at Jed and turned around, heading towards Jude.

"Jude!" said a voice behind him.

Jude turned around to see Sia and Eli running to meet him. Sia threw her arms around him when she finally got to him.

"I thought we lost you," she said.

"Almost but not quite," he said with a small smile.

Jude felt Eli's eyes on him, but he ignored them.

Anya soon joined them. "Bray! Glad to see that you are still in one piece. I take it the Nyctimene was no match for you."

"I don't know, they put up quite a fight General. But I promise you it was their last."

"Good work."

A shriek caught Jude's attention. The General was pulling out a blade that protruded from his neck, just as the Nyctimene smashed into him in a direct hit. Jed's body leaped from the creature's back and landed perfectly on his feet. The Nyctimene and Rorik tumbled tangled in one another across the plains. Jude looked on to see that the creature showed no signs of movement. The same could not be said for General Rorik, who quickly returned to his feet. Leaving the remaining blades and daggers buried in his body, he walked back towards his fallen war axe. When his arm bent down to retrieve it, blood fell from every inch of his body.

Rorik's laugh charged across the battlefield. "Is that all you have?"

Jude snatched a vial from his utility belt.

"No!" said Anya. She held her hand in front of Jude. "I will take care of him. I need the three of you to join Quarrels and Lieutenant Titus at the river. Last time I checked, there were only five of them left. They desperately need your help. There appears to be one last wave of Necroborns, and I am hoping that the eight of you can eliminate them."

"But General Rorik is—."

"That's an order!"

"Yes General!" said Jude.

The three of them kept their distance while they ran passed General Rorik towards the river. Jude's vision swayed and he soon felt dizzy. The floor was unforgiving when his body collapsed.

*"My devotion and faith in you has never been stronger,"* said the hooded figure in the royal blue robe. His knees lay perfectly still at an altar of three male statues. His hands clasped in front of him, as his head remained tilted down. *"I come to you in great distress. Please aid me in my time of need so I can bring the peace you teach is attainable,"* said the man.

*The sound of an opening door behind him caught the man's attention. His kneeling body returned to its feet. When the figure turned towards the sound, Bishop's face peered from behind the hood.*

"Jude," said a voice continuously.

The image faded and was replaced by nausea and a light purple haze. Jude opened his eyes to see Sia staring down at him.

"Jude are you okay?" she asked.

"Bishop."

"Bishop? No that's Sia," said Eli next to her.

"Bishop! He is in trouble," yelled Jude forcing himself out of Sia's arms. He ran back towards Anya who was closing in on Rorik.

"General! General!" yelled Jude at the top of his lungs.

Jude noticed movement from Rorik, and had just enough time to roll under the swing of his axe. He quickly returned to his feet and met Anya on the other side.

"I tire of your medaling mortal," growled Rorik as he started to charge Jude.

"Debilitate!" yelled Sia.

"Bray! I gave you a direct—."

"General! There is no time! Bishop, he is in trouble," said Jude.

"I assure you Bray, he is perfectly safe. We have fifteen highly skilled Agents surrounding the castle, as well as thirty Agents and fifty high-level Academy students, guarding the city gates. Plus we took a few classified measures in order to assure his safety. There is nothing to worry about."

"No General I saw—."

"Bray I gave you an order! Now you will—."

"Shut up and listen to me! I don't know what happened, but I felt some kind of connection with Bishop. It caused me to lose consciousness temporarily. During that time I saw Bishop.

He looked like he was praying in some sort of stone chamber that had a statue resembling the Three Brothers. He was praying to the gods for help from something. At the end someone came in the room. I think the person that opened the door is who he feared. We have to leave now," said Jude.

"You expect me to abandon a mission that holds the safety of our people at stake? All because you had a dream that Bishop was in danger. Do I have that right Bray?"

"It was not a dream, it was a vision!" said Jude.

"Have you had these before?"

"No General, well maybe one other."

"Do you have evidence supporting this vision you had?" asked Anya.

"Evidence? It was a vision!"

"I gave you an order soldier. You and the others join Lieutenant Titus and the other men down by the river. Refusal on your part will mean you have refused orders from your superior which means you are against us. And if you are against us then you are with the enemy," said Anya summoning a dagger that she held in a ready stance. "And if you are with the enemy, I have no choice but to take you down!"

Jude backed away slowly while Anya steadily approached him. Fear coursed throughout Jude's body, along with confusion and panic. He did not know what had gotten into Anya. Why didn't she believe him? Seeing the sincerity in her eyes, he no longer knew who she was. Her eyes looked at him as an enemy. She never took her eyes off of him and she studied him as if anticipating his attack. Jude raised both hands up freely showing open palms. Anya quickly countered with a swipe from her dagger. A cold sensation filled Jude's left cheek as blood ran down his face.

"I was just holding up my hands to show you that I was not a threat," said Jude.

"Make another move and it will be your last!"

"General I apologize for my outburst and my disobedience. I will do whatever it takes to regain my honor, starting with aiding our men down by the river," said Jude walking backwards slowly.

Anya's eyes never flinched. She watched him closely as he turned around towards General Rorik, who still was ensnared in Sia's paralysis. Jude reconvened with Sia and Eli. When Sia dropped her arms, sweat fell from her face.

"I don't know if I could have held that any longer," she said.

Eli walked over to Jude with worry plastered across his face. "What happened? What did she say? Did you tell her about Bishop being in trouble?"

"I did," said Jude walking in the direction of the river.

Sia and Eli soon caught up with him. He looked down to find Sia's flushed hand, grabbing his shoulder.

"Well what did she say?" asked Sia.

"Blood Magic!" The voice echoed far off in the distance, catching Jude's attention, before he immediately identified whom it was.

"We have orders. Come on, Lieutenant Titus and Pang need us," said Jude.

♦ ♦ ♦

Anya never took her eyes off of General Rorik as they circled each other. The Necroborn General had regenerated his head twice, after Anya had decapitated him. She knew that only an attack to the heart would suffice, however, she figured that Rorik's decapitation would give her enough time to eliminate him—permanently. After he had regenerated his third head, Rorik simply laughed at Anya hysterically. She refused to admit it or show it, but the sight unnerved her. Rorik proved to be a formidable opponent, and Anya refused to underestimate him again.

"I do not believe that we have had the chance to formally introduce ourselves," growled Rorik.

"Why waste time with names? Are you stalling because you know your end is here?"

"Ha! Because respect is something that our people hold dear, which is why your barbaric race can never hope to achieve our level," said Rorik.

Anya expected treachery and never lost sight of the General.

"Very well, I will go first. I am General Rorik Gonzaga of The Immortal Lands," said Rorik bowing with his axe over his chest, but never taking his eyes off of Anya.

"Fine! I will play your sick and twisted game. General Anya Briars of Kismet," said Anya returning the bow, but never taking her eyes off of Rorik.

"Briars? General Briars?" said Rorik with a flicker of surprise.

"That's right you sniveling pig!"

A thunderous roar penetrated the plains as Rorik laughed uncontrollably. Blood spilled all over his body from the blades and daggers that still protruded from his body, from Anya's previous attack.

"What is so funny?"

"You! This! Us," said Rorik calming down.

Rorik stared back at Anya, and when he realized that she was not going to respond, he continued.

"About five or more years ago—time is of little importance—I stood on this very plain. Your insignificant race paled in comparison to my men. We slaughtered your kind like the filth you are. Hundreds fell by my hand. However, out of all those maggots, there is one piece of filth I will never forget. He put up quite a fight he did. But just when hope blinded him to the fact that he could not win, I smashed it. He graveled as this very axe brought him face to face with his brutal death," said Rorik erupting into laughter.

"What does that got to do with me?"

"Everything! Caleb Briars was his name, and excruciating death was his fate!" snarled Rorik.

*Caleb wrapped a blanket around Anya's small shoulders. Their treehouse was cold and breezy, causing Anya's baby teeth to chatter.*

*"Don't worry I will protect you. I am your big brother and you are my little sister, and I love you," said Caleb.*

Rorik's laugh brought Anya back to the battle. Nausea and sorrow filled every crevice of her body. Her knees trembled and the hand holding her dagger shook. Warm tears ran down her face but she welcomed them. They were a nice contrast against the icy cold that her heart had been radiating throughout her body, causing her skin and emotions to feel like stone.

"It was you? You killed my Caleb?"

"That would be an understatement General," yelled Rorik as blood continued to run from the weapons that hung from his body. "I destroyed him!"

"Consider yourself eliminated," said Anya as she sprinted towards Rorik.

Rorik met her in battle being the first to attack with the pommel of his axe. Anya sidestepped and countered with two quick stabs to Rorik's neck and back, while daggers rained from the sky piercing him. The back of his elbow slammed into the side of her face, sending her tumbling to her feet. She rolled, and quickly recovered, just in time to evade an attack from Rorik's axe. His axe came down with tremendous force, as it missed Anya, and wedged itself into the ground. Returning to her feet, Anya noticed Rorik having a hard time retrieving his axe from the ground. She took the opportunity and summoned a quiver of throwing daggers on her back. Running in a circular radius around Rorik, Anya tossed multiple daggers that buried into Rorik's neck, chest and back.

*I can't get to his heart. He guards it well.*

She summoned a shield and sword and took to a direct attack. Charging at Rorik with her sword above her head, she panicked when Rorik's axe jerked up from the ground and slammed into her. Dirt stung her cuts while she felt her body glide across the ground. Her body went into immediate shock when she came to a halt. She choked and breathed in dirt, which caused more coughing. She rose up and saw blood falling from her mouth, before slowly sitting up on one knee, and coming face-to-face with the burning pain that imprisoned her body. She looked down at herself to see severely grotesque cuts and bruises across her torso and arms—where her armor used to be. Piles of her armor lye scattered around her, while she fought back the urge to scream. Blood flowed from her stomach too fast for her to stop. Anya placed both hands on her stomach trying her best to force the bleeding to stop. *Thud. Thud.*

Anya willed herself to her feet but her body would not respond. Instead it collapsed backwards, landing her flat on her back. *Thud. Thud.* Her vision swam with dizziness until all light emptied from her vision when the shadow loomed over her.

"Ah! I believe I am experiencing what my uncle's mother's third cousin twice removed calls, déjà vu," snarled Rorik before erupting into laughter. "I never really cared for him. Talked way too much. Don't even remember his name, which is probably the same way no one will remember yours!"

Anya's left eyed closed on its own. Her right eye observed while Rorik's mighty axe came crashing down. She rolled to the side, barely missing the attack. The contact of the axe hitting the ground, projected her body off of the ground briefly, before it came crashing back down. Anya forced herself to her feet, trying to run, but finding herself limping away. She looked down to see blood trailing every step she took.

"Caleb..."she said staring at the continuous bleeding from her torso.

A massive force smashed into her back, sending her body flailing through the air. Her arms were too slow to cover her face and body when she slammed back into the plain's rough surface.

*The world melted away while the floor turned white, opening up as she fell. She fell for what seemed like minutes, before her body smashed into the ground beneath her. The falling had ceased, and everything around her was void of anything and anyone, at least until he came. A soldier dressed in silver plated armor slowly approached her. She screamed when his face came into view. The soldier's face was void of anything. It was as flat as a blank piece of parchment, white and void of any physical characteristics. Massive light gray wings sprung out from its back.*

*"Who—who are you?"*

*One of the soldier's wings covered his blank face. When the wing fell, Anya felt something for the first time at the sight of his face.*

*"Caleb," she said.*

*His face had not changed since the last time she had seen him—when he was leaving for battle the night he died. She began to move into hug him but his hand quickly stood up.*

*"Anya, little sister, I do not exist in your world anymore. That portion of my life is over. Attempting to hug me will only end in your sorrow."*

*She stared into his eyes, and willed herself not to blink, afraid he would disappear. "Take me with you."*

*His soft face smiled and his wings seemed to brighten from light gray to white. "I cannot and you are running out of time. He is coming—and you must be ready," he said.*

*"Please don't leave me," she replied.*

*"I never have, and I never will. Take care little sis. Until the day—we meet—in another life,"* he said as he kissed her on the forehead.

Her eyes awoke to the rumbling of the ground beneath her. *Thud. Thud.* She sprang up and noticed her pain was not as severe, and the blood that had ran from her torso, had ceased.

"Ah! General Briars! Hope you were high enough to see the stars on your last escapade! Wait the sun is still out, so see the star," said Rorik with a snarl. His pace soon quickened, and soon he was sprinting towards her.

The space in between them trembled when the countless swords erected from the surface beneath them. Blades pierced Rorik's legs—locking him in place. Anya approached the General slowly, never taking her eyes off of him. When she was a few feet away, she stopped. The General grunted and struggled in an attempt to break free, but to no avail.

"I am sorry, but I cannot let you win," said Anya as she held out open palms. The sensation of both blades in her hands felt both natural and comforting. Anya looked deep into Rorik's eyes and felt herself smile—when fear radiated from them.

Anya lost all sense of time, when the air filled with the bellows and roars of Rorik's pain. A few times the sight of the severe and grotesque injuries Anya had inflicted, filled her stomach with nausea. When she raised both swords over her head in unison, her brain refused to bring them down for one final assault. General Rorik's body was far passed disfigured. One of his arms barely hung on by a single strand of flesh, while the large open crevice in his stomach, exposed the inner tissue within. When her eyes came to his face, she thought she was staring at a Necrosis.

"Done yet—maggot?" snarled Rorik.

Blood sprayed Anya's face after the back of her hand came down across Rorik's face.

"Impacto!" said Anya.

Rorik's body shot up and then straight back, when an enormous spear shot through the center of his torso and impaled him in place.

"You have lost General," said Anya with a smirk. "We have won! And yes—I am done."

Thunderous laughter rang from between Rorik's jaws. The more blood that spilled from his mouth, the louder he laughed. "There is no victory for you today General!" laughed Rorik between his bloodstained teeth.

"I have my victory! Your men have fallen. You have fallen. We have won!"

Another thunderous laugh emanated from Rorik while his lungs made a noise as if they were gasping for air. His eyes slowly closed and his arms went limp. Anya grabbed his chin and jerked it up.

"What is so funny maggot?" demanded Anya.

"In chess, what is the best way to take the king?"

Anya was confused and baffled by Rorik's question. She became annoyed when she found herself actually thinking about the meaning of his words.

"Draw out his men," hissed Rorik.

# A CLASH OF LORDS

Bishop held the locket tight between his hands as he prayed in front of the Three Brothers statue; which stood against the back wall of Council Hall. When his eyes came up from the ground, they connected with the statue of Rune, the god of magic and wisdom. The sound of a door creaking open, broke his train of thought. He rose to his feet and turned towards the Council Hall doors. A lone figure stood in its doorway.

"Who is there? Show yourself," demanded Bishop.

The figure slowly stepped up and out of the shadows that concealed him. "Jumpy today aren't we?"

"Fox? Is that you?"

"The one and only," said Fox.

"But what are you doing here? You are supposed to be at the border with General Briars," said Bishop confused.

"What am *I* doing here? I think you mean what are *we* doing here," said Fox.

"We? What do you mean we?"

A lone figure stepped through the doorway and into the shadows, concealing his face.

"We—as in him, as in I, as in we," said the figure. His voice was chilling, malevolent and piercing.

Bishop stared sternly at the stranger, trying his hardest to identify him. "And who are you?"

The figure stepped forward out of the shadows peering straight into Bishop's eyes. "Do you ask because you seek answers or do you ask because you seek time?"

"Lord Egon! What in the name of Pith are you doing here?" asked Bishop.

The Lord of The Immortal Lands had eyes as hard as coal but as green as the greenest of emeralds. He wore a long black dress robe with silver detailing. His hair was neatly pulled back in a tight slate-black ponytail, which hung over the back of a long black cloak. Lord Egon slowly walked around the large stone table that Bishop sat at, placing a hand on the backs of the seats as he passed them. Bishop darted up from his seat looking from Egon to Fox and back to the Lord.

"Bishop my Lord, my friend, my um ally—I suppose," said Lord Egon.

He walked towards the statue of the Three Brothers. Fox chuckled under his breath while he took a seat at his usual spot at the roundtable. Bishop broke the silence that was eating him alive.

"What's on your mind my friend?"

"Revolution. Life, death and everything in between," said Lord Egon.

"Care to elaborate your Lordship?"

Bishop turned his attention so he could see both Egon and Fox.

"Baffled is what I have been at how a 'ruler', such as yourself, can be preyed upon as victim to the predators you ignorantly call your gods," said Lord Egon.

"The Three Brothers *are* our gods. They watch over us with love, patience, compassion and understanding. They are in no way 'predators' as you call them," said Bishop.

"Brainwashed you are, and brainwashed you will stay, under the tyranny of your despicable gods."

"Answer me this," started Bishop. "Why does someone as intelligent as yourself, hate the gods so ferociously? Please, help me to understand."

Lord Egon had been staring at the statue of Rune ever since he approached it. He lifted one finger and tapped it on its nose, before turning around. "Ask and you shall receive. Pray and your gods shall answer. Is that not what they lie—I mean, promise you and your followers? Why not ask them? Or do you fear that they are not as mighty as you have hoped?"

"I am asking for your opinion, not theirs," said Bishop.

"Just when wise has claimed divorce, you show me wise is still utterly under your control. Very well, at a price of minimal consequence."

"And what price is that?"

"Take your seat," said Lord Egon.

"Very well," said Bishop sitting in the seat closest to him.

"Bishop my friend, I had no knowledge of the level of disobedience that runs in your weak veins. I said *your* seat," said Lord Egon.

Bishop got up and took a seat in his normal chair. His glare instantly went to Fox, who responded with puckered lips.

"Brilliant!" Lord Egon walked the perimeter of the table slowly. "Fox, would you be so kind?"

Bishop looked to Fox and only saw his chair. A massive blow to the back of his chair made all feeling leave his body. Bishop felt his head slouch to the side, as his neck went limp.

Fox loomed over Bishop's vision. "First time is always a good time isn't it?"

Bishop tried to respond, but found no connection to his mouth or any other part of his body, except his lungs and eyes. Fox retook his seat, placing his feet crossed on the table;

something Fox knew Bishop prohibited, insisting it was disrespectful and rude. Bishop jerked his eyes back towards Lord Egon, who had never stopped circling the table in an infinite cycle.

"While some secrets are best kept for future dates, some steaks are better flaunted in the company of starving dogs," said Lord Egon as he licked his lips slowly.

"One day a voice came to me in the darkest night at the darkest hour. It led me from my prison and to the exact spot where the three merciless gods imprisoned Anim. When my feet stepped onto its exact spot, time stood still for me. That is when Anim showed himself to me. He told me that he knew of the curse—the prison—which the Three Brothers had bestowed upon me. He told me that he could help, if I only listened. He showed me what it is like in that so-called 'heaven' the gods promise is a safe haven. Anim showed me their intolerance and how they create life before punishing life for becoming what it was created to be. I saw murderers, thieves, and abominations given wings, while loyal followers and good people were cast into the darkness for all eternity. Many try to claim that Anim is the evil one and that the Three Brothers are what the world needs. I beg to differ. Anim promises peace and compassion while your gods lie to shield you from one simple fact—it will be a fifty-fifty coin toss on whether or not heaven or hell will be your eternal resting place when your time comes. That is why action needs to be taken. That is why action *will* be taken, and savored and preserved. I plan on aiding Anim in a mission that he has been planning since his imprisonment. I plan on eliminating the Three Brothers once and for all, removing their wretched curse and sparing the world the vicious judgment of the fiends they pray to."

Sheer panic and terror gripped Bishop at Egon's words. The Three Brothers were too strong and too powerful. These were the gods that helped to create life itself. If by some farfetched chance that Lord Egon and Anim did destroy the gods, life as everyone knows it, would cease to exist; and chaos and darkness would enslave the world forever.

When Bishop looked into the Lord's eyes, all he saw was darkness and pain. Lord Egon's eyes showed no signs of the mercy, peace or compassion that he had just preached about.

"We both know very well what hides beneath the very earth of this city. It is only a matter of time before I find it. When I do, I will consume it, along with the others, and extinguish the existence of your pathetic gods— forever."

Nausea tightened its hold on Bishop's stomach, and fear was its ally. Bishop tried to calm himself to analyze all of the possible options he had to either escape or persuade Lord Egon into letting him leave. His mind went erratic as Lord Egon's glare hardened.

"What tomfoolery clouds your judgment?" said Egon.

"I have seen the error of my ways my Lord, my ruler, my everything," said Fox in a high-pitched voice while smirking at Bishop.

"Ah! That is right. Fox did a number on you I see. Fox, if you would be so kind."

All the feeling of his body returned in an instance, after Fox's elbow smashed into Bishop's chest. The force sent him flailing backwards in his chair, causing it to tip backwards. As Bishop laid on the floor gasping for air, Lord Egon loomed over his body. Bishop looked up into the Lord's unforgiving eyes.

"On your feet ingrate!" snarled Egon.

Bishop returned to his feet and was quickly grabbed by Fox, and lead over to the empty space in front of the statue. Bishop's arms stayed trapped behind his back by Fox's grip. Lord Egon joined them, stepping toe-to-toe with Bishop.

"The moment of truth now raises its curtain to the main event," said Lord Egon staring back at Bishop.

"He means you pumpkin," whispered Fox.

"While your faith, beliefs and ignorance shroud you in a veil of unforgiving dishonor; I still believe with proper persuasion, you can be shown the light. All that Anim, the world and I ask of you, is your fealty to Anim and myself; as well as your resignation that will crown me as your successor. We even brought Anim's chalice for the blood ceremony," said Egon with a dark smile.

"You are sick and twisted beyond repair," said Bishop.

"Wrong answer," whispered Fox before kicking Bishop in the back of his knee. Bishop collapsed to his knees as Fox reaffirmed his grip.

Lord Egon bent over until his eyes were level with Bishop's. "Let me clarify something for you. I will go to *any* and *all* lengths to exterminate the tyrants you call gods. I will use your people, this city and all of mankind, to bring the Three Brothers to their knees."

"Kind of like how you are now," whispered Fox.

"But what of your family? You would risk their safety?" said Bishop. The pain paled in comparison to the shock when Bishop face's whipped to the side, in response to the back of Lord Egon's hand.

"Don't—you—dare even speak a word about my family! Time is up—and fate is here!"

"Very well," said Bishop.

◆◆◆

Bishop had stalled Lord Egon and Fox long enough for his antidotal spell to counter the effects of Fox's paralysis. As Lord Egon became more impatient with his failure to respond, Bishop realized that he could no longer prolong the battle that stood in front of him.

"Polaris," said Bishop as his head bashed into Fox's face.

Council Hall rumbled as the stone roundtable detached from its surface and charged into Lord Egon. When Bishop's hand spun around to grasp Fox's throat, Bishop saw emotion in Fox's eyes for the first time. The table slid across the room, slamming into the chairs it was once surrounded by. Bishop hurled Fox over his shoulder, causing Lord Egon to curse at the impact with his ally. The table rose, spinning around the room like a disc, until its hard edges hammered into both enemies, before swooping by to elevate Bishop.

When Fox and Lord Egon returned to their feet, smirks came across their faces while they observed Bishop's position above them. Bishop found his footing and readied himself to go on the defensive.

"Fate is a force no one can run from, not even one as powerful as you," said Lord Egon.

"Fox, whatever he has promised you, he is deceiving you," said Bishop.

Fox just stared back as if he did not hear a word. His eyes stayed cold and his body stayed still. A rumbling sounded throughout the hall, as the chairs that once surrounded the roundtable, detached and began to circle the room at high velocity.

"If that is your answer then I have no choice," said Bishop.

He analyzed the hall while he saw Lord Egon and Fox continue to leap and dive in an attempt to evade the chairs that circled the room. While his subconscious rattled against the chains that once held it, an itch signaled their release.

"Episcope Custos, ego dimittam vos," said Bishop as he welcomed the light blue hue that now coated his vision.

Egon and Fox continued to evade the many projectiles and debris that now circled the room. The ceiling soon collapsed, causing boulders and debris to rain down upon Council Hall. The falling debris eventually joined the already circling projectiles, and soon Bishop heard them hit home, as two bodies tumbled across the floor of the hall. The sky rumbled and the winds screamed while lightning rained from the sky.

Fox leaped to one of the walls and ran along its surface, but a bolt of lightning cascaded down and changed directions, just in time to intercept him. The young Emissary was pinned against an opposing wall before rolling to the floor. Smoke rose from his back, as tranquility seemed to surround it.

The table beneath Bishop rocked violently as a bolt cascaded down towards Egon, before redirecting itself at the hovering table that Bishop stood on. A large crack branched out from the center of the table while bits of its surface began to chip away. The table glided back down towards Lord Egon. Bishop stepped onto the familiar stone floor of Council Hall, just as the table completely shattered.

Lord Egon closed the distance between them and soon Bishop found himself staring into the eyes of the man that he had once called ally.

"I want to see you fall by my hand. Fall as in pain, as in death, as in die die die!" said Lord Egon.

Egon brought forth a blade unlike any Bishop had ever seen. While its pommel was silver, the blade itself was blacker than any shadow or darkness that Bishop had ever seen. The sword stuck in place as Lord Egon stabbed the area in front of him. Bishop's eyes blinked violently when he tried to shake off the illusion that he thought he saw before him. Dozens of copies of Lord Egon seemed to materialize in front of Bishop, until an army of copies stood before Bishop. Blades—matching the one that still sat stuck in the ground in Egon's grasp—shined in the hands of every copy.

The copies walked slowly in a circle until they completely surrounded Bishop. "Fate is life's way of reminding us that there is no escape," said the circle of clones in complete unison.

"Guardian tribute!" yelled Bishop.

The trio of gargantuan inferno pillars twisted and screeched, as they rose from the ground and pierced the sky. While the towering infernos waved back and forth around Bishop, countless clones were pulled in before the burning magic destroyed them. Bishop's eyes met Lord Egon's just in time to catch hundreds of copies form rows in front of Egon. While the towering infernos closed in on the army ahead of Bishop, he saw something stir at the corner of his eye.

"Heads up," said Fox as he appeared from behind one of the blazing pillars and knocked Bishop to the floor.

Bishop rose to his feet while Fox sprang into a direct assault. He glided and swayed vigorously to avoid Fox's attacks. Bishop was well acquainted with Fox's hand-to-hand bloodline abilities, and he had no intentions on allowing any of his attacks to connect. While Bishop danced around Fox's attacks, he noticed the blazing towers were still swallowing countless clones as more and more appeared. A look of annoyance displayed on Egon's face when Bishop commanded the blazing pillars to surround the Lord on all sides.

"The sky shall rain with the severed heads of your people!" yelled Lord Egon over the screeching commotion.

Bishop's concentration on Lord Egon proved hazardous when he felt the feeling leave one of his legs. Bishop felt himself drop to his knees as soon as Fox landed a quick jab to his neck, and one to his abdomen.

"Where is it," Fox mumbled to himself.

"Where is what?"

"The spot in your body that would prove fatal if I attacked it, everyone has one. Yours is just difficult to find," said Fox as he kicked Bishop's legs from underneath him. "Looks like we will have to do this the old fashion way."

Fox's hands descended on Bishop's throat. Bishop found it difficult for his antidotal spell to resist the paralysis that bound him. His heart raced and his vision blurred, while he felt his body gasping for air.

"So you are going to kill me now—is that it?"

"That's the idea handsome," said Fox tightening his grip.

The feeling returned as Bishop's magic grabbed hold of Fox and tossed him towards an opposing wall. Violent coughs and dizziness overwhelmed Bishop when he gasped for the air that he was once deprived of.

"Help me to help you save your land, by handing over what I want—all of them," said Lord Egon as he closed the distance between him and Bishop. Fox matched his steps.

That was when Bishop had realized that Fox's restraint had caused him to lose concentration and lose control of his spell. The pillars, that once scorched anything in their path, were now a distant memory. Bishop quickly returned to his feet and studied the enemies ahead of him. Hundreds of copies appeared behind Lord Egon and Fox, as the familiar blade hit the floor in front of them.

"You know I would not call upon you unless I truly needed your help," said Bishop clasping his hands in front of him. "Custos tuus Vocat te. I summon thee—Rune, the ancient god of magic and wisdom," said Bishop.

Time immediately halted, while the air appeared to stop with it. Bishop's eyes studied the particles that floated in front of him, just as a blinding light forced his eyes to look away.

"From the heavens I was born, from the earth I shall rise," said an omnipresent voice.

When time unfroze, a trench opened up in front of Bishop. Light poured down from an unknown location and a wind current swept throughout the chamber. Lord Egon and his forces braced themselves as the essence of Rune materialized between the opposing sides.

"Rune, my adversary, your fate is sealed!" yelled Lord Egon from across the room.

Darkness erupted from Lord Egon's direction until it covered the entire chamber. Before Bishop could respond, he found himself tumbling through darkness until his feet came crashing down on a hard hot surface. The heat was unbearable and the fissures in the surface glowed with the molten rock that was begging to creep through. Geysers of molten rock rose and fell on all sides of the stone they stood on. As Bishop took his place alongside Rune, Fox took his alongside Lord Egon.

"Your extinction is now Guardian!"

# HOMECOMING

The night was dark and the wind was cold, when the secluded shack came into view. The marshlands were caked with fog and thick clouds that shrouded the marsh with a veil of uncertainty and mystery. The air was silent and the conversation was minimal. The water in the marsh was nearly up to Jude's knees as he trudged behind Pang, who helped guide his steps.

After the battle, Anya joined Jude, Pang, Conall, Eli and Sia—along with four other Agents—and scavenged the battlefield for survivors. Even though Jude wanted to celebrate victory, the sight before him screamed pain and loss. The second half of the battle with the Necroborns, proved to be devastating to their forces. Seeing comrades—that once stood smiling and battling beside him—scattered along the rough terrain beneath him, plunged sorrow deep into his heart.

*I knew that being an Agent meant that I would be around death all the time. But I never thought it would be this devastating.*

After checking for survivors, Anya instructed a Magi Agent by the name of Laia, to heal as much of the surviving soldiers as possible. She was able to significantly heal mostly everyone, except for Pang, who declined any treatments. Afterwards, Anya quickly hurried the ten of them that remained, back towards the direction of the city. She led their group into a foreign and desolate marshland a few hours away.

A lone un-lit lantern hung over the door of the shack. Pascal, one of the Agents, ignited a match and lit the lantern. Soft light sprung from the darkness that surrounded them. Placing an un-visible key in the door, Conall quickly opened the shack and ushered everyone in.

"Pascal! Gerron!"

"General!" said both Agents in unison.

"Surveillance the area. Make sure there is no one—and I mean no one—within the next five miles of here," said Anya.

"Copy that!"

Jude watched as both Pascal and Gerron ventured out into the night until they were shrouded from view. The inside of the shack contained more than Jude had expected. Upon entering, Jude noticed a large dark-wood roundtable, surrounded by many chairs. Many bookcases, paintings and parchment decorated the walls. There appeared to be a few backrooms along the center hallway that stretched from the opposite side of the room. A lone couch sat in front of a long table filled with un-lit candles.

"Everyone but Val and Laia to the roundtable," said Anya pulling the Agents to the side.

After taking a seat between Pang and Conall at the roundtable, Jude studied the conversation between Anya and the two Agents on the other side of the room. Anya was good at whispering, because even though she was only a few feet away, Jude could not even hear a fraction of what she was saying. After a few idle minutes, Val and Laia nodded their heads and exited the shack. When Anya took a seat on the other side of Conall, he rose from his seat and exited the room. The night seemed surreal and uncertain. Jude thought long and hard about his vision of Bishop. He began to wonder if Anya had been right, and that it was just some sort of fictitious joke, manifested by his subconscious. When Jude's eyes sat on Eli and Sia, an image of the night in the cave flashed before his eyes. He quickly shook off the guilt and observed as Sia rested her head on Eli's shoulder. When Jude turned his gaze towards Pang, he felt himself shutter.

When Jude, Eli and Sia had reconvened with Pang and Conall, they were significantly outnumbered. Pang's Blood Magic had caused a large number of the Necroborns to turn on their own comrades, which eliminated half of the Necroborns forces, but left Pang significantly weak and exhausted. He now sat with bloodstained bandages around his arms, wrists and neck. His eyes occasionally closed and opened as if on their own accord.

A few minutes later, Conall returned with cups and a kettle. He sat a cup in front of Anya and then everyone else, before pouring everyone hot tea. When everyone's cup was full, he took his seat at Anya's side—who was fondling a piece of her armor.

"We have a few things on our agenda that need to be addressed before further steps can be taken," said Anya clasping her hands in front of her. Jude noticed Conall mimic the gesture a few seconds later.

Everyone's attention seemed to instantly dart towards Anya. The only sound audible was the sound of a heavy wind that assaulted the shack from the other side.

"First and foremost, the area we are at now is a classified safe house that a handful of our Operatives use. You will not tell anyone, besides those of you here now, about its location. I will kill you myself if I discover that any of you have disobeyed my orders. Second, good work out there today. Even though we lost all of our men except for the ones outside and the ones you see here, the mission was a success—and that is all that matters. Third..." said Anya as her gaze moved directly to Jude.

He nearly jumped out of his seat at the hostile gaze she gave him.

"Bray!"

"General!"

"Will you please tell us again about this—'vision' you had," said Anya.

All the eyes at the table switched to Jude. The tension in the air hung thick and the wind seemed to calm, aiding the silence in its mission.

"Um, certainly. Well it was a vision of a hooded figure praying before a statue that seemed like the one depicting the Three Brothers. The figure seemed desperate and afraid—*very* afraid. He was asking the Three Brothers to help him with something. The sound of a door opening sounded behind the figure. He got up and turned around, and that is when I realized it was Bishop. Then the vision ended."

Silence soon returned, which made Jude feel slightly self-conscious.

"How many of these have you had before this one?" asked Conall.

"None Lieutenant—well, maybe one earlier on the battlefield. I am still a little hazy about it."

"Then why is this relevant? People see things all the time, it doesn't mean that what they see holds any truth or value," said Conall turning to Anya.

"I too did not believe that this 'vision' was of any value, or held any relevance Lieutenant—until him," said Anya.

"Him—General?"

"General Rorik of The Immortal Lands. After he was defeated, he inferred that the point of our battle was to draw our men away from the city, so some unknown force could eliminate Lord Bishop," said Anya.

Wide eyes and clenched jaws circled the table. It was one thing seeing a vision that he was not sure was even true, but hearing his General physically saying the words, made Jude feel both worried and anxious.

"I did not believe that there was any truth when Jude first approached me with his vision. However, after Rorik's words, only a fool would think it would be a mere coincidence," said Anya.

"Then why are we still here! We should be heading back to the city at once to aid him!" said Eli.

"Because if we do return, and what we suspect is true..." started Anya.

"We would be walking right into a trap, and would be eliminated as well," finished Conall.

"If someone is after Bishop, they would be sending enough men to gain access to the castle. We will just have to hope that the Agents and Operatives we have stationed there, are able to neutralize the threat before it reaches the castle," said Anya.

It was a lot to take in. Jude took a few sips from his cup and tensed at the heat. After another sip, his mouth adjusted to the heat and the liquid felt soothing to his body. Sia's voice caught his attention.

"General what are our next steps?"

Anya and Conall stared at each other for a few seconds before nodding collectively.

"We have to assume that the entire city is both precarious and hazardous, as well as controlled by the enemy. So returning there is not authorized," said Anya.

The first thing Jude thought of was his mother and Marius. They were both still in the city and would be in danger. He found himself worrying about Jed as well. Jed had run off in the middle of battle saying something about a Vampire. Jude had not seen his brother since, and the thought of the city being in danger, amplified Jude's worry.

*What if Jed came back to the battlefield and saw I was gone, so he headed back to the city. He would be walking right into a trap.*

"Not authorized? But my family is still there," said Eli.

"All of our families are. However, that does not excuse the fact that walking into a now uncontrolled location without any knowledge, is both reckless and unwise," said Anya.

"It's flawless," said Jude finally understanding. Everyone's gaze sprung to his position. Looks of confusion spread out around him.

"What was that Bray?" asked Anya with curled brows. "What's flawless?"

Jude realized that their enemy's plan was perfectly played. Kismet was led to believe that a threat at the border was the only danger. The enemy must have known that their numbers were low after their battle in the north, so Kismet would have no other choice but to deploy most of their Agents. The city and castle would be left lightly guarded and vulnerable. Jude was sure that the army of Necroborns was meant to eliminate any remaining stragglers that the Necrosis failed to destroy. With Bishop out of the way, Kismet would inevitably fall.

"Their plan. Our enemy. Everything was well-played. It's flawless," said Jude. No one moved or said anything in response to Jude's words. While he did not expect any replies, he hoped that someone would say something soon, to cleanse the air of the sorrow and tension that settled around them.

"Furthermore, it is best if one to two Agents infiltrate the city walls, surveillance the area and report any enemies or suspicious activity," said Conall as he took a sip from his cup.

"I would like to go," said Eli. He quickly stood up from his seat as if ready to leave immediately.

"None of you here have been trained with the proper infiltration techniques. Battle is one thing, but stealth is a beast of its' own. That is why I have no other choice but for Lieutenant Conall and myself to go on this mission—alone."

"I am really in the mood for a massacre as of now—I mean, look at what those demons did to me," said Pang as he squeezed the blood out of a wound. "I demand retribution! An arm, a leg—something! Just give me five—."

"No, it has already been decided," said Conall hitting the table lightly.

Anya's decision to only send Conall and herself, somewhat disappointed Jude. He became fidgety and even more worried about his family as more time passed. He had hoped that somehow he would be able to at least go back to the city in order to grab his family and leave. Sia appeared unaffected by the decision, and was the first to talk about Conall's finality.

"Is there anything we can do to help General?"

"Yes, you can lay low and stay as far from the city as possible. If there is a raid happening, I cannot risk all of our men becoming casualties. I would recommend that all of you stay here, but seeing as how I am not sure how long this covert mission will take, I can understand if a more comfortable location is preferred. Just make sure it is safe, secluded and away from the city."

"Anya and I plan on spending a day—two tops—on this mission. We will be reconvening back at this exact location in the next two days. All of you are expected to be here at sunset. If for any reason both of us are not here by midnight when you return, you have no other choice but to assume the worse. If that happens, I have left special instructions with Agents Val and Laia on how you will proceed from there," said Conall.

Jude did not realize that he had been holding his breath until after Conall had finished. Everything seemed uncontrolled and out of his hands. The current situation was new to him, and in turn heightened his anxiety.

Anya cleared her throat. "Any questions?"

When no one said anything, Anya and Conall immediately stood from their seats. Worry seemed to grow more and more at each passing second. For the first time, Jude began to feel worried for both Conall and Anya. He was afraid that if they left, he would not see them again—ever.

"May fate be your ally," said Anya.

Jude noticed an eye roll from Eli at Anya's comment. Both Conall and Anya left immediately for their mission. When only the four of them still sat at the roundtable, tension and anxiety seemed to dominate the table.

"This is crap! My dad is there, and neither one of those idiots care anything about him!" said Eli crossing his arms.

"That is not true Eli, they are just thinking logically. You are thinking with you heart instead of your head," said Sia.

*At least she keeps him in line.*

"So where do you guys think we should wait? Here?" asked Jude. He watched as Eli's eyes drifted to his spot.

"Sia and I have a place that should be safe. It is in the forest outside the city. No one should find us," said Eli.

*We should all stay together, but your recklessness would probably get us all killed.*

"I do not know these lands very well since I am not from here. I only know the city and my house, which is too close to the city. However, I do not mind running into a few enemies," said Pang.

"No, we have orders to stay far away from enemy forces. We can just stay here. If this place becomes too unbearable, I have a spot where we could go," said Jude.

"That is a good idea. If we aren't together, we should at least have one person with us just in case we run into trouble," said Sia.

"Alright so then it's settled. We will all meet back here at sunset in two days," said Eli.

Sia gave both Pang and Jude a hug before leaving. She actually seemed worried to leave them. Eli on the other hand seemed as distant as ever. He said nothing to both Jude and Pang on his way out except for, "See you in a couple of days."

Jude was surprised when he found himself unaffected by the coldness. He guessed that he had grown used to Eli's lack of dependability as a friend. As the door closed behind them, Jude found himself lost to his thoughts. He wondered if his vision was true, and if it was, if Bishop was okay. He also thought of Jed, Marius and his mother, and if they were okay. When Pang decided to go on a tour of the rest of the shack, Jude took out the tan journal from his backpack.

*Maybe if I keep my mind occupied, I won't worry so much.*

He flipped to the creased page he had marked:

*It pains me to hear the edge in his voice and the coldness in his heart. He talks to me as if I am a stranger—as if I am no one. I have been meeting with him for the past few months but he still refuses to show me any kind of respect or compassion. Those cold white eyes and deathly white hair. His soul really did die that day.*

A long strand of white hair laid stuck in the spine between pages. Jude read the next few pages, and lost total track of time as adrenaline filled his veins. The next few pages were all signed with the same symbol as his armband. Two small warriors stood side-by-side with either a black or white orb in their hands. His heart raced and his eyes fluttered at the sight before him. He looked up to see Pang standing over him. The boy's mouth moved but Jude could not hear a word of what he was saying. Jude read the pages he had just read again, in hopes that he had misread. He looked at the symbol of the two warriors, and after looking repeatedly at the armband that clung to his arm; he concluded that it was unmistakably the same symbol.

"Jude! What is the matter? What's wrong?" asked Pang.

Jude finished the last written page of the journal.

"We have to go."

# REUNION

Eli found himself giddy with anticipation, as he stared up at Sia atop the purple waterfall that fell in the hot spring that he swam in. The warm water brought comfort to every sore muscle in his body.

"I am kind of scared. It has been a while," said Sia from above.

"Just jump. I'm here, I won't let anything happen to you."

She jumped. Warm water rose like pillars. He dunked his head underwater to meet her. As they glided throughout the purple underwater world that dwelled beneath them, Eli felt the worry that he had been feeling, lightly lift from his shoulders. His face was greeted with both warm and cold when he broke the hot spring's surface for air.

"It feels so good that I almost want to fall asleep," said Sia brushing her hair back with her hands.

A small splash rose behind her, causing commotion amongst the lily pads that floated by. Eli instinctually grabbed Sia and pulled her next to him.

"What was that?"

"I don't know," he said.

A few seconds later, a pair of baby blue eyes poked out from the water's surface.

"It's Spiffy!" yelled Sia.

Spiffy swam to Sia's open hands and climbed on top. Using her hands for support, he dove back into the water.

Shortly afterwards, Spiffy came floating by on a lily pad that housed a blue flower.

"Ready to get out?"

"Yes please," said Sia.

Eli quickly climbed over the edge of the hot spring and extended a hand down to Sia. He helped her out of the water and onto the soft grass that laid beneath them. Taking a seat in the middle of the meadow, she reached into her backpack and took out a thin paper tablet.

"If I don't finish the shoulders, I am going to lose it," she said.

Eli watched as Sia flipped to a sketch and took out a pencil. Her gaze turned stern and her presence withdrew into the sketch in front of her. Eli slowly inched over behind her. His lips hung a few inches above her shoulder feeling the warmth radiate from her body.

"What are you drawing?"

She sighed before burying her face into her hands. After a few seconds she returned her gaze to the drawing in front of her.

"Nothing, I mean—just a silly project I have been working on," she said outlining what appeared to be a woman in a long dress.

Eli was surprised at how detailed the drawing was. He felt like it was something you would buy at a shop or see hanging in a house. The details of the woman in the drawing made Eli feel like he was face-to-face with a living person.

"Is this—you?"

He noticed the edge of her eye turn towards his direction quickly, before returning to the sketch. The quiet that came as time passed, made Eli feel on edge. He decided to take a quick nap in hopes of resting his sore muscles and giving Sia the time alone she appeared to need.

He awoke to a tingling sensation across the bottom of his nose. As his eyes gently opened, he instantly discovered the culprit. One of Sia's soft brown strands of hair lightly glided across the side of his nose. A smile crept over his face as he went to kiss her on the back of her head—but stopped.

"Dad," he whispered from behind Sia.

Marius stood staring down at him from the center of the meadow. Black armor layered on top of a fiery red long sleeve sweater, fitting his body in complete perfection. The tip of what appeared to be a bow loomed up from behind him, while a small dagger hung from his waist. The dagger looked very old and not of this time. The pommel and shape of the blade went against every way blades were forged in Kismet. While his eyes were stern and formal, Eli could sense a fraction of worry within his dad's blue eyes.

"Dad, how did you—when did you get here? How did you find us?"

"There is not much time," said Marius as he extended his hand towards Eli. "Come with me son."

Eli felt confused and wondered if he was dreaming. He went to get up, but caught the slow rise and fall of Sia's shoulder under her breath. Her sketch clung to the protection of her small hand. A pleasant smile was present on her lips and her face was absent of any pain or any worry. She looked beautifully peaceful. Eli looked back up towards Marius. His dad's hand still stood extended. Lightly untucking his arm from underneath Sia, he slowly and quietly crossed over her until nothing stood between him and Marius. When he looked up into Marius' unyielding eyes, he felt as if he was face-to-face with a stranger. While everything about the man in front of him said it was his dad, there was a presence that was foreign yet familiar to him.

"There is not much time," said Marius.

As soon as Eli took Marius' hand, he was dizzy with the violent turns and abrupt drops, as he tumbled through the swirls of total darkness and blinding light. His shoulder collided with a hard and unyielding surface that sent pain shooting up his arm. After shaking off the nausea and dizziness that still consumed him, he felt a hand picking him up by the waist.

Marius stood by his side atop the dark cascading stone stairs they stood on. The cold air brushed across the nape of Eli's neck causing him to shiver. When he looked around him, he found himself surrounded by hundreds of large trees that pierced the night sky and covered the purple full moon.

"Come on son, it is time," said Marius. He slowly ascended the stairs without so much as a glance to see if Eli was following. El regained his footing, and followed.

"Dad, what is going on? Where are we?"

"I love you son, more than you will ever know," said Marius without breaking stride.

Eli thought about the last words he had said to his dad before leaving the city, and instantly felt the guilt rise up from every inch of his body.

"I love you too dad, and I am so sorry about what I said to you—about the dishonorable thing. You are the most honorable person I know. I just said what I said because I was angry. I'm sorry dad."

When they both reached the top of the cascading stairs, Eli realized that they now stood on a large flat stone surface. A stone altar sat in the middle of the surface they stood on. Eli's eyes widened and he instantly assumed a fighting stance, when he saw the dozens of robed and hooded figures that circled around the altar in front of him. Tall goblets of amethyst flames stood between each figure, casting a glow on the navy robes that masked their identities.

"Dad!"

When Eli returned his gaze back to Marius, he was hit with a heavy force that caused his vision to spin and his head to hurt. When his eyes opened and his vision cleared, he realized he was now laying on a cold and hard surface. However, what scared him the most, was the fact that his hands and legs were bound to the altar that he now laid on.

"Dad help me!"

The circle of hooded figures parted as another stepped up to the altar. His hood fell and his face rose, and soon the familiar blue eyes brought both comfort and fear to Eli.

"Dad why are my hands and feet bound? Why am I here, and who are these people?"

"Eli, my dear son. I love you so much and always will. You are the greatest accomplishment of my life. You make me proud every day, and please never forget that. What comes now is out of my hands and out of desperation. I do what must be done, will be done and cannot be undone," said Marius as he reached for his waist. The familiar dagger, with its' curved blade, rose in Marius' hand.

Eli heard himself scream as the lanterns casted a shine across the tip of the dagger. Marius' hand quickly covered his mouth. A warm tear fell down the side of Eli's face.

Marius' eyes closed. "In the name of faith and duty, I lay my son atop your sacred altar."

A series of undecipherable chants rose around him. Eli's head whipped back and forth at the hooded figures that finally showed some signs of life. He felt his heart threatening to tear open his chest and flee. He tried to yell to Marius, but was silenced by his dad's tight grip that still imprisoned his lips. The chanting rose and fell in a continuous loop in perfect unison amongst the strangers, which never moved from their positions.

Eli's anxiety and fear rose dramatically when foreign and sinister words fell rapidly from Marius' lips. Eli slowly calmed himself, and then focused his concentration on the chains that now bound him.

*Maybe I can manipulate them like the forceful constriction move Conall did on me during training.*

When his senses felt the chains and willed them to loosen, a purple haze stabbed his mind causing his head to hammer itself into the altar he laid on. Heavy pain spread across the back of his head. He tried again and was met with the same end. Dizziness swam over him as the chanting around him continued. His daggers formed faster than he had anticipated, and shot down at the shackles around him. The same purple haze returned, but this time, sent excruciating pain up his legs and arms. When Eli finally shook off the pain, he noticed the chanting and commotion had ceased.

Looking up at Marius, he felt his dad's hand release the prison they had once bestowed on Eli's voice.

"Dad, why are you—," started Eli before Marius' finger shot up. Eli's lips instantly slammed closed and ignored any of his commands to open them.

Marius' finger drew a picture in the air in front of him; and as he was finished, a foreign but eerie rune glowed before him. The rune hovered for a few seconds before burying itself into the center of Eli's savagely rising and falling chest. A silent scream ripped through Eli's body when Marius' eyes closed and then opened with a blaze of untamed fury. While the blue flames consumed and danced throughout his father's eyes, Eli's brain told him that he did not know the person that stood before him.

Both of Marius' hands clasped around the dagger as it pierced the cold night sky. The chanting grew louder and more rigorous. A drumming coursed throughout the altar and the air around Eli, causing his heart to hurt from the speed it raced.

"As you are bound, so is he. His fate is yours and yours is his. Chained through time, magic and faith, you shall be ever be tasked with what I bestow upon you. No magic shall break this seal. No evil shall weaken its hold. Only through your will, and yours alone, shall the seal be broken, the secret unleashed and the balance restored."

Eli did not see the dagger come down. The first thing that he had noticed was not the pommel that stood from his stomach, or the pain that came with it. It was the absence of the once violent flames and the presence of the endless rivers that danced down his father's face. Eli's lips became unhinged as the pain dominated him. His eyes fluttered from the heaviness and his chest grew cold. Anger, fear and pain all demanded retribution. Angry words begged to be released from Eli's prison.

"I love you dad."

Spiffy growled at his abrupt movement when Eli sprang from the soft grass. The familiar light blue eyes brought confusion and uncertainty.

"I give up. I cannot figure out how the shoulders should look," she said.

"You're here," he said.

"Huh?"

"It was a dream."

"What was a dream? Are you okay E?"

The sound of the waterfall converging with the anticipating hot spring, filled his senses. Blue and purple petals floated aimlessly down from the trees that housed them. He caught Sia's stare as her surreal amethyst eyes brought up recollections of the dream that was slowly slipping through his fingertips.

"E, are you okay?" asked Sia.

"Yeah. Yeah I'm fine—sorry. What were you saying again?"

The alarm left her face and was replaced with disappointment. "Nothing. I was saying I give up. I cannot figure out how the shoulders should look," she said.

"Shouldn't you just—know?"

Her face turned to him displaying both confusion and hostility.

"I mean, won't it just come to you eventually—won't you just—know?"

"I guess there is no rush anyways, it is not like this has to be done anytime soon," she said putting the sketch away in her backpack.

Eli lightly placed his hand over the hand she used to prop herself up. She rested her head on his shoulder while a small sigh left her lips.

Sia's hand began to play with one of the belts that made up his tunic. "E."

"Yeah."

"I am really worried about Mik," she said.

"Don't worry, everything will be okay."

"E."

"Yeah."

"Can you tell me how you really feel instead of giving me the boyfriend answer?"

He laughed at her question before kissing her on the top of her head. "I am worried about everyone back home. I am worried about Mik, my dad, Bishop—everyone," said Eli.

Silence shrouded them while Sia played with each of his fingers individually.

"So—Conall is pretty cool," he said.

"Yes, he is."

"So—what's his story?"

"I don't know—do you?" she asked finally returning his gaze.

"Nope," he said feeling foolish.

"So if everything is okay, and life goes on—then what?"

"What do you mean?"

"You know," she started as she raised her head from his shoulder. "With us. Where do we go from here?"

"Where do you want to go from here?"

"I asked you first," she said with a small smile.

"I don't know. I guess take it one day at a time," he said with a shrug.

When she said nothing, he was afraid that he had said something wrong. He quickly attempted to recover.

"Is that okay?"

"Well of course it is not okay," said a familiar voice.

Eli turned around and instantly went into shock. The tightly kept brown hair, broad shoulders and large muscles laid perfectly contained inside the navy dress robes he wore. He stood stern in front of a small army of twenty or more unidentifiable Agents.

"To think, my daughter—sleeping with dogs now. How revolting," said Mr. Wyatt.

"Daddy?"

"Bring the harlot to me. Kill the boy!"

Jude had examined every inch of his surroundings when the watering hole drew near. When he pushed the brush aside and set eyes on the still water that mirrored the clouded moon that loomed overhead, he readied himself. After noting the watering hole's location, Pang had decided to retreat back to his home in order to get a few things he felt were too valuable to risk losing. Jude tried to persuade him to stay, in fear that Pang would be walking into a trap, but Pang refused to listen. He reassured Jude that he would be back in an hour and took off towards home.

The urge to meditate swam within Jude. He needed some way of reducing the anxiety that swelled within, however, rage soon overtook him. He injected himself with a vial, and after assuming his raven form, sat perched on a nearby tree. It was not long before the trees swayed, wind ceased and the animals fled; and then Jude knew that he had arrived.

He carried a motionless body in his arms. While his eyes surveillanced his surroundings like the most vicious of predators, the body came tumbling from his arms as his fangs soon followed it. Grunts, gnawing and agitation manifested in front of Jude. The air filled with the scent of death. Jude flew down to the base of the tree he had sat perched on, and immediately returned to his normal form. When his hand went for his backpack, the feeding stopped.

"What insect has gotten trapped in my web," said Jed rising from the body.

When Jude's eyes locked with the whites of his brother's, time froze once again while blood fell from Jed's mouth.

"You know better than to sneak up on a Vampire," said Jed.

"You know better than to lie to me—or at least I thought you did," said Jude throwing the journal at Jed's feet.

Jed's eyes never looked down at the journal. They stood fixated on Jude's gaze. A small smile exposed a bloodstained fang.

"What is this?" asked Jed.

"You tell me."

"I do not know which is why the question falls to you."

"You are a snake."

"No, I am a Vampire—a hungry Vampire I might add," said Jed.

"Since you plan on continuing to play coy, I guess I have to be the one to make the first move. When I asked you if there was anything else that you were not telling me, and you said no, you were lying," said Jude.

"About?"

"Probably everything. That journal documents the journey of a stranger that has been visiting our city for the past few months. At first I thought it was some lone spy that had infiltrated our city for security information. However, when I got to the last written page, I figured out who it really was."

Jed reached down slowly to pick up the journal. He flipped through a couple of pages, and cracked a smile before reading its contents aloud:

"I met with my son for the last time. I know now that there is nothing left of the son that I once fathered. His eyes are left with an unfulfilled hunger and his heart is filled with shadows and deceit. As far as I can tell, there is no soul left to be saved. He assures me that my other son curses my existence and my once true love denies it.

However, I cannot be sure if this broken shell of the son I once knew can be trusted. As I bid farewell to the home I once knew, I know that they have truly won."

"A strand of your hair was tucked inside the last page so I know that you have at least opened this journal before—or have even read it. Also, the symbol etched into the inside of the back cover, is the same symbol that dad had used to sign classified documents when he was an Operative," said Jude twisting his armband so it was visible. "Also, the last few pages are signed with the Geminate symbol that is on my armband. I assume that means this armband is dad's, and either you or mom tried to get rid of it. Luckily for me, I stumbled across it in a shop in the Market District a few days ago."

"Where did you get this?"

"That is irrelevant. What *is* relevant is the fact that you and mom have both been continuing to lie to me after all of this time. Dad is alive, and was in our city," said Jude.

"Yes, no, maybe, I don't know," said Jed smiling.

"Why are you and mom trying so hard to keep dad away from me?"

The only sound that came to Jude's ears was the sound of the water next to him. No birds sang, no crickets chirped and no wind blew.

"Oh my, my, my, what do we have here? Does the thirst deceive the eyes, or does the mind betray the senses? If I taste, will I hear? If I hear, will I touch? If I touch, will I feel? If I feel, will I see? If I see, will I taste? Does the heart corrupt the mind? Does the mind deceive the thirst? Or does the thirst control the senses?"

The alien behavior sent chills throughout Jude's body causing him to ready himself.

"If you refuse to tell me, then I will just have to go look for dad myself," said Jude never leaving Jed's hostile gaze.

Jed's movement was quick, but Jude turned around just in time to counter Jed's direct assault.

# EPILOGUE

Mik awoke to an empty stomach and something soft rubbing against his face. As his eyes peered open, they laid upon the yellow eyes of a tiny black kitten. When he sprang up from his bed, the cat retreated the opposite direction.

"I'm sorry Mr. Cujo," said Mik.

The cat hissed before running through the crack in the door. It took Mik a few minutes to stretch and fully awake. He threw his legs over the side of his bed and hoped that the bottoms of his feet would finally touch the floor. When they still hung a little higher than the wood floor, his lip poked out.

"Man I'm tired of being small," he said as he crossed his arms.

He lifted his nose high in the air and was surprised when he did not smell the dinner that he had anticipated. Mik had taken a small nap when he had got back to Ms. Lowell's. The woman promised him that she would have his favorite dinner ready for him when he awoke. Jumping to his feet, he swung open the door and exited. He looked out over the railing of the staircase and into the living room that sat underneath him. The kitchen, couch and dining room table were all bare.

*I wonder when Sia is coming back. I miss her.*

Mik descended the stairs and burst into Ms. Lowell's room. Her bed laid perfectly made and her room was just as tidy as it always was. Closing the door behind him, Mik ran into the kitchen. Nothing was left out or set aside for him. He noticed a bright red plate next to the stove. A smile came to his face when he saw a stray blueberry cheesecake cookie that sat on the plate's shiny surface staring back at him.

*Ms. Lowell will be mad at me if I spoil my appetite. She might even tell Sia and then I will really be in trouble.*

He turned away from the cookie as quickly as possible. He looked back over his shoulder at the plate. The blueberries in the cookie seemed even bluer than normal and the cheesecake chunks looked soft enough to melt in his mouth. He ran for the plate, grabbed the cookie, and ran back upstairs to his room—closing the door behind him. The cookie lasted only a few seconds before Mik realized it was gone. Opening his door, he descended the stairs once again. When he got to the last step, he stopped and looked around.

*Hmm, maybe Ms. Lowell went to buy some food for dinner. Ah! I hope she makes cheesy baked potatoes tonight! That would be awesome!*

He made his way to the front door in hopes of catching her as she came in. He went to open the door, but realized it was already cracked open. He opened it a little more before he felt something at his feet. When he looked down he heard the meow of a cat sound closeby. Mr. Cujo stood staring up at him with his straight black tail waving slowly from side-to-side.

"Mr. Cujo you're going to get in trouble if Ms. Lowell finds out that you went outside," said Mik bending down to pick up the cat.

The cat purred in response to his touch, which made Mik smile. As he began to rub the cat, his hand ran across something wet and gooey. He raised his hand to find a sticky and thick crimson substance matted throughout the cat's fur.

"Ewe Mr. Cujo, what is this?"

A hiss erupted from Mr. Cujo causing Mik to drop him in alarm. Wiping both of his hands on the beige shorts he was wearing, he finishing opening the front door. A long object laid atop the porch steps beneath his feet. As he walked over to it, he noticed a shredded bag alongside stray potatoes, tomatoes and other vegetables. He looked down at the object he had seen earlier, and finally recognized her.

"Ms. Lowell, are you okay?"

Her body laid face-down on the porch steps. Her white sweater was stained with red and the light pink dress she wore was nearly shredded to pieces. His hand slowly poked her shoulder.

"Did you fall? It's okay I fall all the time. My sister has some medicine she uses to clean me up. It works I promise."

Silence was prevalent. Mik squinted in response to a foul odor that blew throughout the air. He covered his mouth with the back of his hand and used his other hand to shake her a little more the second time.

"Ms. Lowell did you fall asleep? Why aren't you answering me?"

Mik's hand finally flipped her body over. A large gash bisected her face, which matched the gash that circled her throat. Blood dried at the corner of her mouth while moist blood still slowly fell from the crimson circle in her stomach. Ms. Lowell's eyes were wide as they met his gaze. Mik sprung to his feet when he heard himself scream. He stumbled backwards away from Ms. Lowell and fell flat on his back. He turned to the side and locked eyes with a second pair of motionless eyes. He screamed and scraped his knee while trying to get to his feet. He looked down at the pair of eyes and found a soldier dressed in steel armor. Crimson liquid littered every inch of his body. The handle of a metal object protruded from his mouth. After a few seconds Mik realized it was a dagger like the ones painted on his wall at his old home.

He took a step back and his foot hit something. He looked down and locked eyes with another familiar face.

"Mrs. Cunningham?"

Tears ran down his face as he ran away from the house and further into the Market District. Bodies laid scattered around the large fountain that stood in the center of the district. The once pure and refreshing water that poured from all three statues, was replaced with the dark crimson substance that now caked the bodies of the familiar faces Mik once knew.

Mik looked around at the part of the city that had become his new home ever since he had left his old home. Dozens of lifeless eyes stared back at him. A continuous stream of warm tears fell down both his cheeks while his gaze circled the area where he was standing.

"Where are you big sister?"

"Oh do not cry young man," said a voice behind him.

Mik turned around to see a large man that he had never seen. He was an older man wearing a red robe, which layered on top of silver armor that shined from beneath. He held his hands firmly behind his back.

"Who—who are you?"

"I am a friend, a friend that can help you find your sister. Isn't that what you desire?" said the man.

Mik began to wipe away his tears with the sleeve of his shirt. "You can help me find Sia?"

"Yes—I can. Come with me," said the man extending his hand.

"My sister always told me not to go with people I don't know. I think I will just go look for my sister on my own, thank you mister," said Mik as he began to grow suspicious of the stranger.

"I am afraid you do not have any other options," said the man grabbing Mik's collar.

Mik struggled beneath the stranger's grasp.

"Let me go!"

Mik heard the sound of his shirt tearing, and soon fell backwards against the rough stone beneath him. He turned around and instantly started running as fast as he could. When the footsteps behind him ceased, he continued to run towards a lone house with a soft light in the window. Suddenly his feet were pulled from beneath him.

"Owe!"

His face scraped against the streets, causing it to burn tremendously. He looked back at his feet and found them wrapped in chains that continued to wrap higher around his legs. He quickly tried to free himself but soon found himself being dragged along the rough surface beneath him. When the dragging ceased, Mik found himself completely wrapped in chains all the way up to his shoulders. A foot kicked him over forcing him to stare back up into the eyes of the man that had grabbed him. Mik found himself screaming continuously while the stranger bent down closer to meet his gaze.

"Please let me go, I just want to find my big sister— please," said Mik feeling a tear forming in his eye.

A sinister smile appeared upon the stranger's face, which scared Mik into more tears. He tried to scream, but the chains that ensnared him slithered around the back of his head, and soon covered his mouth. Mik stared helplessly up into his captive's eyes, jerking his head back and forth trying to resist the binds that held him. The stranger raised his hand above his head, and soon Mik found himself tumbling into a world of darkness and shadow. His body felt light as if he could fly. He eventually surrendered to the comfort of the darkness that surrounded him. The shadows soon subsided, and all that was left was the warm amethyst gaze of his big sister, as she wrapped her arms around him.

$$A \Omega$$

The story continues in
**Mission: 2**
of

# The Bloodline Revelations

ΑΩ